HARSHEST DAWN

BEYOND CASCADIA
BOOK 4

S. KIRK PIERZCHALA

HERON'S
GATE
PRESS

Copyright © 2023 by S. Kirk Pierzchala
All rights reserved.

Cover art and design, © 2023 Wryson Creative

No part of this book may be reproduced in any form or by any electronic or mechanical means, including information storage and retrieval systems, without written permission from the author, except for the use of brief quotations in a book review.

This is entirely a work of fiction. Any resemblance to real persons or events, living or dead, is purely coincidental.

❀ Created with Vellum

For my Husband

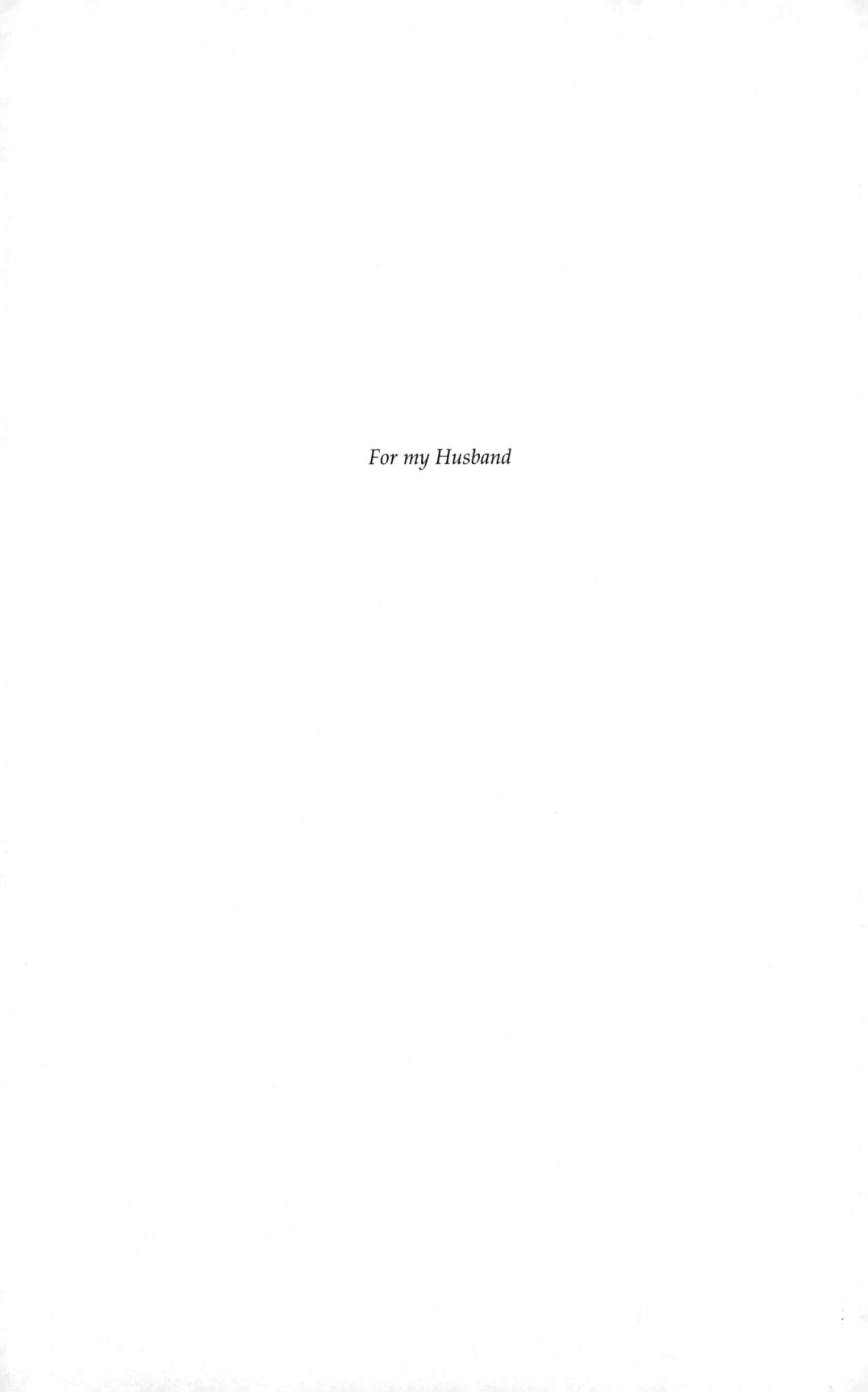

PROLOGUE

WITH NUMBED, robotic persistence, the man's gaze remained fused to the black asphalt ribbon unwinding before his vehicle's headlights.

"*Almost there, almost there,*" he murmured under his breath, sucking all the marrow of comfort he could from the lie.

This mantra had circled through his head for hours, existing just under his sense of outright panic, matching his frightened heartbeat.

Less than an hour to go...I think I'm going to make it...almost there.

Reaching for the thermos beside him, he fumbled it open with one hand. Clumsily, he drained the last of the stale truck stop coffee, black and urgent as the deep July night through which he hurtled. Coffee spilled down his chin, he wiped his mouth with his sleeve. The car veered towards the center lane; he dropped the empty thermos to the floor, grabbing the wheel in both hands to jerk the vehicle back on course.

His heart thudded even faster. His dark eyes, normally bright with good humor, were painful, red-rimmed and weary from hours of scanning the route for any patrol cars or local police. Stress had carved lines of care into a youthful face now taut with uncertainty. As he entered the final stretch of his dash for the border, it seemed miraculous he'd come this far without attracting the authorities' notice.

Or without running out of fuel; sporadic rationing of some resources had already commenced throughout the region. Shoppers were being issued "commerce authorization" passes—paper substitutes for the traditional CitizenTrust digital passes. Due to the current widespread disruption in both the power grid and the official internet, previous methods of information, surveillance, and control were in flux.

The man had grown up in an atmosphere of stagnation and decay. Yet over the last nine months or so, circumstances within this region had deteriorated more rapidly. Then without warning, two weeks previously, a massive power outage had plunged vast swathes of the West Coast into darkness. Citing the threat of impending chaos, Oregon Governor Cassian Gray had deployed the National Guard with harsh alacrity. The move was coordinated with similar actions in Washington and California. During the general confusion, it was unclear whether martial law was officially in effect or not, but most people were too fearful to ask what was really happening. And any answers from official sources wouldn't have been trustworthy.

What was now clear to the fugitive, or as clear as could be pieced together from the scraps of rumor swirling about the region, was that he was behind enemy lines in a new country. A coup had been in the works for many months, and the former American states of Washington, Oregon and California were now decisively under the control of a political faction calling themselves the 'Successors'. The state legislatures had been dissolved and were being combined into one entity, represented by a mysterious Central Committee. It was unclear what sort of country these new leaders ultimately meant to establish, but from the fugitive's perspective, the early signs weren't encouraging.

He offered heartfelt thanks to Allah he was still free, and thanks that his wife had gotten herself and the kids out of the state the previous week. At least, he assumed she had: it was impossible for them to communicate with each other under the circumstances.

When I'm over the border, I'll rest for an hour or two, he promised himself. *And maybe I'll be back in satellite range, so I'll try and connect with Connie then.*

The antiquated Quasar satellite network was an alternative to the state-run communications, but with so many satellites disabled or killed by hostile governments over the decades, there were many gaps in coverage for both phone and internet service. Conversing with his loved ones at a distance was now a hit-or-miss proposition, made even more hazardous by the fact he was a fugitive.

In any case, I'll be ready for another four hours' solid driving before I need another break. I'll sleep in the car. Calculating he'd be at his final destination in under ten hours, he forced himself to not think of his goal, or his family, any more than he had to. From moment to moment, he existed in a state of blind trust.

Up ahead, brake lights now winked in the gloom like the eyes of predators, growing more insistent until the man was forced to slow down at the end of a crawling train of traffic. He spotted a couple of patrol vehicles parked alongside the highway. Troopers were directing traffic.

Probably just a wreck, he assured himself, even as he started trembling, stomach churning, perspiration trickling down his brow. *Nothing to do with the border. It's normal for the flow to bunch up like this when anything happens on the highway. The border is still open, that's what the last intel told me. It's got to be open—.*

His encouraging self-talk did nothing to relax his tightening jaw and shoulders, or to loosen his tense, sweaty grip on the wheel as he inched the car forward. There were no signs of a collision that he could see. The confusion he now witnessed could only mean that, like himself, many others were attempting to flee.

His heart quailed when he noticed the menacing shapes of armored troop carriers positioned along the route, as well as many fatigue-clad men, heavily-armed. The faceless anonymity of the menacing, mask-like helmets granted the soldiers a different sort of power than what lurked in their weapons. *The rumors are true,* he realized with a clutch of sober fear.

The National Guard command had openly switched sides and turned against the populace. As far as he could tell, U.S. forces had also withdrawn from the region as, desperate to avoid a full-scale civil war, President Vanessa Chakrabarti took a wait-and-see approach to the turmoil. Meeting no resistance, the secessionists were inexorably taking advantage of her lack of action to secure their position.

Insulated in his own car, the man still felt the mounting panic poisoning the night. The impatient blaring of horns, the anxious revving of older, internal combustion engines, the silent, entitled pressing forward of the electric or hydrogen cell vehicles—all betrayed their drivers' desire to be elsewhere.

Through lowered windows, people shouted angrily at those cutting in line. A few more vehicles peeled away and lumbered off the road, into the dark. Clouds of dust drifted everywhere, throwing back a dazzling, disorienting glare from the bouncing headlights.

Stay calm, he told himself. *Don't attract attention. This old heap won't make it over open terrain this rough—I've got to stay in line and pass through the official checkpoint.*

As his car crept forward, the man did not allow himself to be rattled by the angry honking of horns, the glimpses of faces distorted by fear on all sides. He thought fleetingly how disappointing it was that, in times of danger, fear so easily led to a selfishness that could turn deadly in an instant.

Ahead, he discerned more armed shapes, illuminated by the baleful, harsh beams of portable security lights. Beyond these, a wall rose out of the darkness, where no wall had been before.

Composed of portable blocks of concrete and topped with sections of chain-link and razor wire, it threw its forbidding wings out for several hundred yards to either side of the road, far into the night. More and more traffic piled up at this barrier.

Mind racing, the man sat alert behind the wheel. In the dust-choked gloom, it was impossible to see how far for certain the concrete and wire barrier stretched into the desert. A desperate few drivers now left the asphalt, charging frantically over a terrain strewn with rocks and low, dry shrubbery, searching for a gap in the wall. For a moment, he pondered joining them as they bolted into the darkness.

Stick to the plan, my false ID is solid. He was certain that after a quick pass over a trooper's work tablet, he'd be waved safely through the checkpoint. There was no need to panic—not when he could virtually taste his goal.

Troops rushed forward to confront the rebellious drivers and force them back into line. Churning tires threw more dust clouds into the air, which then drifted lazily past the blazing security lights.

Loud shouts exploded into the night from further up the queue of traffic, followed by squealing tires and the unmistakable *whomp* of vehicles colliding at a low speed. A pickup truck with a camper top broke out of line, ramming its way through the clot of other cars to its right. As it left the highway and tore into the wasteland, soldiers raced after it, opening fire with both traditional ballistic and newer energy weapons.

Shattered glass answered their hail of bullets, sparkling like a shower of diamonds under the pitiless lights. The acrid smell of melting rubber reached the man, announcing that energy beams had found their targets. The crippled truck veered into the concrete barricade. Enforcers rushed the vehicle, continuing to fire into the driver's compartment. Screams rang from the camper shell as a woman and two small children clambered from the back. Both children fell beneath the enforcer's weapons. The woman was dragged away into the dark.

Eyes following this scene in shocked, impotent horror, the man thought again of his own wife and two small kids. What if something like this had already happened to them, yet he would never know for sure?

A sharp rap sounded on the window to his left; a trooper was glowering down at him. The man lowered the glass with haste and offered his ID disc. The trooper waved it over the sensor on his tablet, then frowned at the results.

"José Mendez, you from Nampa?"

"Yes, sir, I was on a business trip to Portland for my company—we distribute parts for agricultural equipment…I got stuck when all…all this happened. I can show you the order…,"

The trooper offered him an impatient grimace. "Well, that's too bad. Lots of folks' plans disrupted, everyone gonna have to put up with some inconvenience until things settle down and we get back to normal."

"Yes, sir. I understand. But technically, I'm not a citizen here, I need to be in Idaho—,"

"Well, it might take a long time to get that all sorted out. So relax and sit tight." Straightening, the trooper pulled a flashlight from his belt and played the beam through the window, into the back seat. "Mind if I check in there—and the trunk?"

"Of course, go ahead. Sir." The driver's sickly, deferential smile congealed into a mask as he popped the trunk, then continued to wait with his hands visible on the controls while the trooper went to the back of the car.

The enforcer's manner and movements remained polite and calm, impressive in light of how much noise and chaos continued to roil out of the night following the shootings.

After a few moments, he returned to the driver's side and presented the ID disc. "Okay, Mendez, everything looks in order, but you're going to have to turn around and go back," he began, but paused as another man rushed up to join him.

The newcomer snapped, "Hey—Cox! You get the bulletin that came through this afternoon?"

The first trooper scowled in annoyance. "No, I came on duty fifteen minutes ago, and it's been an apeshit circus out here. What bulletin?"

"We're to double-check all Hispanic males, anyone who looks forty years or under. Don't just wave his disc—give him the full face scan."

"Shit. Okay." The first trooper turned back to the driver and motioned him out of the car.

Oh, hell, the man thought as he climbed from his seat. He recognized the second trooper from having trained with him a few years earlier at the Northwest Regional Law and Safety Agency, but the man didn't seem to remember him.

Bathed in the cold perspiration of fear, the man calling himself José Mendez stood mutely with his back against his battered old car, his hands kept in plain sight. The outline of his short, dark hair gleamed with sweat; he knew his own bland face was stiff with anxiety, but he was powerless to appear normal.

A work tablet's camera was thrust at him and the chime of the program sounded as the face-recog function offered its expert opinion.

Reading the results, Trooper Cox uttered a low grunt. "This checks out—you can go, but you gotta turn around and head back to Portland or somewhere away from this mess."

"Sure, thanks." Struggling to hide his relief that the false data he'd implanted in the Agency's system was accepted, the man smiled as he took his disc back and opened his car door.

"Hey, just a minute! I've seen him somewhere before, his name isn't Mendez." The second trooper stared at the man intently before breaking into a grin. "Oh yeah—I know who you are!"

Detaching a set of heavy zip-ties off his belt, he advanced with smug, triumphant motions. "Officer Enrique Rodriguez—seems you're headed the wrong direction! They're looking for you back at Headquarters, so why don't we get going?"

As his heart dissolved with resigned terror, the fugitive stood, stupefied, distantly noting the sensation of the ties being pulled snugly about his wrists. He watched as his vehicle was searched again and everything in it seized before he was pulled to a temporary processing van parked near the checkpoint.

He had almost made it. The comparable freedom and safety of the United States were a mere two hundred yards away. But in the chaos of a sudden and violent political rupture, 'almost' might as well have been a million miles beyond his reach.

PART ONE

CHAPTER ONE

SPIKES OF WANING daylight pierced the surface of the water, wavering on the sides and bottom of the pool as the man glided to the far end. Twisting swiftly and pushing upwards, he shattered the liquid's surface and floated beneath a cloudless dome rich with the turquoise of the advancing July evening.

For a time, he dwelt suspended in an embrace between limitless sky and water. Awareness of his own body, and his swarm of incessant thoughts, faded to insignificance when measured against the immensity of that sensation. His blissful connection with untroubled vastness only lasted a few moments.

When the curtain of full evening fell swiftly and a single star appeared above him, Owen MacIntyre decided with reluctance it was time to quit the pool. Yet he drifted a little longer, consulting the data displayed inside his awareness, fed to his mind by his vision implant. This unit, slimmer than a pair of sunglasses, was a surgically embedded neuroprosthetic, a somewhat cumbersome but effective apparatus that replaced his missing eyes.

Years earlier, he had awakened in the hospital following a violent assault from emissaries of a disgruntled narco-terrorist. Alive but blinded, he found himself outfitted with this old yet serviceable Vision Implant Augmentation unit. As he adjusted to the VIA device, and to life as a cyborg, he had suffered a period of serious resentment and frustration, but was now generally at ease with his technological enhancement. Sometimes he even joked that he preferred the term 'neuroaugmented' over 'cyborg'.

Across his field of vision, a message now appeared in small, glowing letters: *"Congratulations on meeting another week's health targets. All parameters normal, heart rate particularly improved."*

"They damn well better be," he muttered aloud to the device. There was no one else around, he was alone at the back of the property, a sprawling, exclusive residence nestled in the foothills near the southern end of Colombia's Cordillera Central mountains.

The home was encircled by a semi-formal tropical garden that included an expansive patio containing the pool, while on the far side of the patio, the outline of the hacienda rose against the starlit sky. The luxurious estate was lush with all kinds of life, the air typically full of birdsong and the chattering of small monkeys, the buzzing of insects.

As he climbed from the basin, Owen pushed his streaming dark hair back over his skull, while water sheeted off his broad shoulders and gleamed on his lean form. Still considering the visor's update, he thought, *after almost three years of no smoking, and working out every chance I get, there's bound to be some good effects.*

It was a relief to get confirmation there was still no evidence of damage from the massive influx of stimuli the device threw at his brain every waking moment. Even at an energetic thirty-two years, he felt he needed all the strength he could muster to deal with his new circumstances. He was still adapting to being thrust into a new life through a drastic turn of events in his homeland.

Crossing the patio to a chaise lounge and tile-topped table, MacIntyre picked up a chilled bottle of *cerveza*, removed the cap and took a drink of the pale gold beer. Using the thought-directed controls in his visor, he accessed the home's universal entertainment system, turning up the volume of the current playlist. Speakers, concealed in the plantings, and under the eaves of the residence, responded with a powerful beat, providing an invigorating counterpoint to the restful scene.

As if in response, across the patio, the hacienda's French doors opened and a young woman with dark brown hair stepped into the evening. She advanced towards MacIntyre, her flowing, sleeveless dress revealing much of the warm tints of her healthy, sun-kissed skin, her lissome feminine curves.

Hands on her hips, she planted herself before him with a smile in her light gray eyes.

"You're back earlier than I expected," she remarked in a low tone, her voice both husky and musical.

"But still—later than I hoped." He gave her full, expectant lips a quick kiss, followed by an encore that lingered over the intoxicating taste of her mouth. He murmured, "Teresa and Isabella left a little while ago, but where's Diego?"

She said softly, "Diego just dropped me off, then turned around to go spend time in town with his mom."

"So it's just you and me. Perfect."

With the guard, the housekeeper and the housekeeper's granddaughter gone for the weekend, the two of them were alone, as under the canopy of burgeoning stars, a cool breeze blew away much of the day's sultry heat.

Owen set the bottle down on the table, freeing his long, muscular hands to stroke the woman's shoulders as he pulled her closer. The remaining pool water on his chest seeped into the fabric covering her breasts, where they were pressed against him, below his quickening heart. His thoughts selected a different song from his playlist; the music surrounding them shifted in key and tone while growing slower. Also growing more familiar, personal. Seductive.

"Remember this song?" His touch slid down her back and came to rest on her waist; he began gently but possessively guiding her body in time to the beat.

Pulling back slightly, her brow arched, a shadow whispered over her face. "Of course I remember—it got us into a lot of trouble, once upon a time. Which reminds me...," Drawing a finger along the edge of his visor, then down his angular nose, her voice dropped to a low purr. "Are you *sure* we're alone? What about your wife, isn't she around somewhere?"

His lips brushed her ear. "Yeah, somewhere—,"

With a sudden giggle, the woman struggled free of his arms. "But she *hates* being pawed by a human sponge—you're *soaking!*" Taking a few steps back toward the French doors, she added over her shoulder, "Aren't you hungry? Teresa left us supper—I'll bring it out before it gets cold."

"Geez, woman—talk about sending mixed signals!" Grinning, he grabbed a towel off a nearby chair, throwing it over his shoulders as his appreciative gaze followed her.

Sometimes, it was hard to believe his luck that the sweet-tempered, patient and demurely beautiful Sofia Volkova had agreed to marry him. At others, he couldn't believe a self-centered cynic like himself had taken a chance on the whole outdated, unpopular institution in the first place. Yet here they were, over two years in, still happy and comfortable in each other's company.

She soon re-emerged from the kitchen and set a tray laden with fried *arepas* and fresh fruit on the table. "Here—they're still warm."

He selected the largest *arepa* and bit into it, enjoying the fact that Señora Ortega prepared her small cornmeal fritters with enough cheese that one or two were a substantial supper.

Sofia also took one and nibbled. "Isn't she an amazing cook? I feel so spoiled! And she's such a lovely, kind woman."

Owen grunted in agreement.

Settling beside him on the lounge, Sofia's open, heart-shaped face grew more thoughtful. "I guess I have to admit, I'm adjusting to the energy-sapping humidity of this place more easily than I thought I would. At least it's a fun change from the bone-chilling damp we left behind."

Throwing his head back, Owen uttered a relaxed laugh. It was a relief to hear her make a joke, a sure sign she was getting back to normal after the stresses of the last few months.

She soon grew pensive. "I'm really grateful to Don Tomás for getting us out of Oregon so quickly. I'll never forget the relief I felt when I saw his private jet waiting for us at the airport! But still, this arrangement seems so…weird, I guess. I mean, to be staying here in his hacienda, while he's in that little apartment in Palmira. Are you sure we should have agreed to move in?"

"Yeah, I know it's weird, but he insisted. He meets with the archbishop frequently, so it's more convenient for him to be located in the city."

"Well, he's been very generous to us. Do you think he'll change his mind?"

"About the living arrangements, or about his plans to become a priest?"

"Either, I guess. You know him better."

Owen thought over his complicated history with the impulsive and zealous Chinese-Colombian billionaire, Tomás Chen-Diaz. "I can't say, really—he's kind of random. And complex. But I think he's serious about this religion thing. Something happened to him, he had some kind of profound inner experience, I guess. But it wouldn't hurt to be prepared for anything."

"Oh, thanks, that narrows it down," she laughed dryly. Then she quietly repeated, "'*This religion thing*'? Don't be so dismissive about his choices."

"Sorry, I didn't mean it to sound that way. You know how much I respect him."

She fixed him with a concerned look in her soft, intelligent eyes. "I know it's hard for you, having to take his hospitality like this. Have you...well, have you really...you know...?"

Lifting his hand and tapping the edge of his implant, he said, "Have I forgiven him for this? Sure, but sometimes on a bad day, I have to remind myself he was a different person that night, totally under the thumb of his brother Francisco and his clone."

Nearly three years earlier, Francisco Chen-Diaz, an influential executive on the boards of two international corporations, had been involved in a narco-terror plot against the United States. The fallout from that debacle was that Francisco was disinherited, his illicit clone was dead, and under protest, his younger brother Tomás inherited his brother's position in the family business. But now Tomás wanted to move on, and had recently turned some of his responsibilities over to Owen.

Sofia remarked, "After all you went through, I guess it's something of a miracle you're both friends now."

"Yeah, life sometimes takes you down some really unexpected paths." Determined to move on from an uncomfortable subject, he asked, "How was your first class with the kids at Nido de Paloma?"

"I think it went well, they seemed to really like me. But I hope I didn't take on too much by promising the project director in Medellín that I'd head the music program for the little ones. I don't have much experience teaching such young kids."

Owen grinned at her with affectionate pride. "They're going to love you, how can they not? And I'm really happy you've jumped back into teaching so soon, considering how sudden this change has been."

Nodding, she finished another bite of her *arepas*, then reached for a slice of mango. "So—now tell me about *your* week. It seemed like you were gone forever. This was a big deal, right? Your first in-person meeting with the other members of the board? Could you tell if they resent the fact you're replacing Tomás?"

He'd had less than a month to adjust to his new role of Acting Director of the Paloma Foundation charities, headquartered in Calí. Owen didn't feel qualified to be overseeing it, but Chen had faith in him and was insistent he give it a try. And when Tomás got an idea in his head, it was hard to talk him out of it.

Owen took a long drink before answering with a nonchalant wave of the bottle, "As deals go, it was pretty modest. I don't think they resent me, but it's also clear they don't know what to make of *el Americano*, 'Evan Lazarus'. But at least they were polite."

"That's good, I guess."

"And frankly, there's not much for me to do. Tomás' executive assistant, Raul Peréz, runs the day-to-day operations. But I have to face the very real possibility I may never fit in. This is a very traditional culture and I'll always be regarded as an outsider. No matter how enthusiastically Tomás vouches for me," he concluded with a faint smile.

"Vouches for your made-up persona, you mean." Sofia gave a slight, reluctant sigh before continuing, "One thing I hate about this situation is having to use an alias. I feel so dishonest and, well…*sneaky*."

He brushed some crumbs from his bare chest, took another drink, then tapped the end of her nose with his finger.

"I'm sorry 'Mrs. Lazarus', that's how things are now, at least for the foreseeable future. It's a small price to pay for security, like being in a witness protection program. Besides, secret identities are a staple of romantic adventures. Try to see the fun in all this."

"Are *you* having fun?"

"Sure, don't I look it? At least I'm adjusting to reality."

His casual tone hid that inside, it was painful to accept the cold, hard fact that California, Oregon and Washington, honoring the legacy of their former Tri-State pact, were now officially a separate entity from the United States, styling themselves the 'People's Democratic Republic of Pacifica'.

Like pressure on a major fault line, political stresses had been building in the region for years, before recently erupting into a full-blown and decisive secession. In the months prior to the rupture, Owen, like many others, had been in denial about the seriousness of the situation, being focused on retaining his position at the Northwest Regional Law and Safety Agency.

While not deeply wedded to his status as an accredited cyber defender at that problematic institution, he had wanted to depart gracefully in order to not attract attention to his clandestine work for the Restoration movement. This secretive organization, sometimes privately referred to as '*novus ignis*', was a loosely connected network of ideologues committed to combatting government overreach and cultural decay.

Owen had been drawn into their orbit about a year prior, when he'd discovered he had some very close connections all along; his deceased grandfather, Evan, had been a key player in the organization. Thus it was an easy choice for him to put his valuable skills, honed by training at the Agency, at the service of the movement's goals. These goals included subverting existing institutions and systems, and setting the U.S. back on a path to greatness. Or at least to adequacy.

Regarding recent events, perhaps it was foolish of him to have counted on having more time than he did to plan his departure. Despite growing up listening to his grandfather's rants about history and politics, he had never internalized the fact that political structures tended to fall apart slowly at first, then gather speed until their inevitable collapse. Even those aware of rot and dysfunction could be fooled by an exterior semblance of normalcy, telling themselves things weren't quite as bad as all that, as they clung to the dissolving status quo.

So he had gambled on having a little more time, but his gamble didn't pay off. Fleeing charges of treason, he and Sofia had barely made it out of the country before the borders closed.

Sofia repeated, " *'The foreseeable future.'*" She lifted his right hand, meditatively running her slim fingers along the tendons and muscles of his forearm, then twisting the gold Paloma Foundation signet ring about on his finger. The minuscule carving of a dove nesting in a lotus blossom glinted in the golden patio lights.

Frowning, she said, "How long *do* you think we'll have to live like this?"

"Homesick for Oregon?"

Both her hands tightened over his as she raised her eyes to his blank visor. He was surprised at the hardness of her expression.

"Lord, no! I shook the dust from my feet, believe me. Of course, I'm worried about some of my friends, and Fr. Cosimo…but in the end, most of the region deserves what they've brought down on themselves. It's just…well, do you have any idea how long we'll end up staying here?"

He shook his head. "I'm taking it one day at a time."

Lowering her eyes, she bit the corner of her lip in a way he found irresistible. "So, you can't say yet if you're going to switch careers? Work exclusively for Paloma and disengage from everything you were doing before? I mean, obviously, you'll never be able to go back to the Agency."

He snorted. "Obviously."

"What about the work you were doing with Greg Park? Do you think he's involved in anything to do with…uh, pushing back against this 'People's Democratic Republic of Pacifica?'"

Owen thought over how his relationship with his former captain at the Agency had changed so radically over the past weeks. Like himself, Park was something of a disgraced fugitive at the moment.

"I've heard they're calling themselves 'Pacifica' for short," he observed. "In any case, Greg and I have touched bases, but we haven't discussed anything like that. I doubt the situation is anything he or his people can deal with right away."

He continued to mull her question. It seemed to him the Restoration was out of its depth in these serious geopolitical waters. If they were working on a plan to confront Pacifica, he had not been informed. Thus, his own work for them was on hold, and he couldn't say how or when it would be reactivated. Maybe they didn't need him anymore, and it was time for him to focus on building a new life here.

Uttering a sigh, Sofia raised her face to the dome of star-pricked, deep indigo overhead. "In any case, I'd like to talk more openly with my family. Have you contacted either of your parents yet?"

"Just my mom," he admitted with reluctance. "I don't dare try to contact Dad in Seattle. He's literally behind enemy lines." It was a few moments before he added soberly, "I know this uncertainty isn't pleasant, but it's still too early to say when it will be safe for you and me to go back to America, even the more stable regions."

A shiver passed through Sofia's frame. "I'm not sure I ever want to go back. I suppose I will some day…but now…,"

Setting his empty bottle aside, he put his arms around her. "Do me a favor, will you?"

"Depends," she whispered.

"Don't worry about the future." He pressed his face against her glossy hair, inhaling the faint, spicy scent of her shampoo. "Let me take care of everything. In the long run, it's all going to be fine. Just forget about everything except us, here and now."

He felt the tension fade from her body. As she melted into him, he savored the privacy granted by the lush plantings and showy blooms nodding all about them in the shadows. The raucous birdcall that seasoned the air during the day was giving way to a chorus of noisy insects. A new song on the playlist started, adding a slower, introspective tempo to the peaceful scene.

At the moment, he believed his own words. At the moment, it seemed impossible that any danger could touch them, that there was any such thing as danger anywhere in the world, or that it was seeking them.

After several minutes, she pulled back and regarded him; placing her hand protectively on her belly, she said in a tone both grave and beguiling, "It's hard not to think about the future, to worry about…what kind of life *he's* going to have."

If possible, she looked more beautiful than ever as she said that. He grinned. "He's going to have a great life. Trust me."

Caressing her jaw, he slid his fingertips along the dimple that hid near the corner of her mouth, even as he studied the light in her eyes.

She breathed, "Whatever happens, there's no one I'd rather be exiled with."

He was both humbled and aroused by her intense, trusting gaze. It penetrated his expressionless visor without effort, as if she was convinced his eyes were still there, just hidden from everyone but her.

Without another word, he drew her chin up and kissed her with slow, possessive assurance.

CHAPTER
TWO

THE REINFORCED TRAILER, serving as a field office, shuddered in the heavy concussion wave and subsequent rolling blast of noise. Walls shivered, paper documents slid off the small work table.

"What the *hell*—?"

Instantly awake, Hayden Singer lurched from his cot and wrenched open the trailer door. Singer's German Shepherd dog scrambled to attention and stood at his side, whining and stifling a slight bark.

"Greta—stay!"

The last thing he needed was her following him into the pre-dawn summer morning to investigate an explosion, likely a hostile attack. She was more of a family pet than a professionally-trained K9, and he didn't want her underfoot at the moment.

Urgently tugging on trousers and boots, Pacifica's Chief Security Enforcer then caught up his heavy khaki shirt, thrusting his arms into the sleeves. He fastened and tucked the shirt tail in his waistband with swift, sure movements as he descended the trailer steps.

As he smoothed back his dome of silvery-gray hair, Singer's muscular, dominating form charged into the morning chill. He was greeted by chaotic shouts, the sight of shadowy figures running back and forth in confusion. Several yards to the east throbbed the glow from a burning troop carrier.

The east—where the outlines of heavy construction vehicles reared against the impending dawn, racing against time to set more pre-fab concrete modules along the Oregon/Idaho border.

The east—where loose bands of Idahoan vigilantes and unsupervised militias, unhappy at both the new country of Pacifica on their doorstep, and resentful of the trickle of refugees spilling into their territory, had taken it upon themselves to cause trouble and make a tense situation even worse.

Singer hailed a passing officer, demanding, "Walker—what happened?"

Breathless and wide-eyed with agitation, the young woman barked, "Javelin into the construction site, sir!"

"Casualties?"

"Don't know yet, but it looks likely."

Medics, clad in outdated Oregon National Guard uniforms, rushed to the flaming vehicle. Singer strode after them at a more sedate but still urgent pace.

Damn, I do not need this now, he thought grimly. But in such fluid circumstances, he had to be prepared for anything.

He arrived at the wreckage moments before Captain Oscar Ruiz did; the short, paunchy man was still fastening his camo uniform. The bewildered expression in his bleary eyes was hardening into a look of angry fear.

Without acknowledging Singer, Ruiz started shouting at the nearby soldiers, "I want a report on where that Javelin launched from! Then take out their position ASAP!"

Turning, he pretended to have noticed Singer for the first time. "Sneak attack, Chief, but we're going to retaliate like a ton of bricks."

"No, we're not," Singer retorted in a cool and commanding manner. "I'm sure whoever launched is on the move, and not waiting for a response. But more importantly, Pacifica is now attempting to engage in talks with the U.S. authorities to re-survey and establish this new border zone. This may be the work of local agitators, but anything *we* do will be seen as an official response. You seem to forget we're a separate country now, and not in any position to be attacking the United States."

Ruiz drew himself up. "We need to show them they can't attack us without paying a heavy price."

"Captain, I appreciate your sentiment, but our job here is to secure our side of the border and prevent citizen flight." Hayden Singer's peculiar, light eyes caught the man's gaze and held it. "We must enforce that mandate in a calm and professional manner, not allowing ourselves to be distracted by a few hot-headed malcontents. That will send a stronger signal than lobbing rockets back and risking an international incident. I think President Gray would agree."

"Who's in charge here?" Ruiz sputtered.

Good question, thought Singer.

Lifting one broad shoulder, he said, "Quite possibly, the man President Gray hand-picked to both head the new Internal Security Agency, and to oversee consolidation of various emergency response agencies. Me, in other words."

Confusion still reigned over who was responsible for what and where respecting the jurisdiction of the Guard, and the quasi-military enforcers of the Northwest Regional Law and Safety Agency. The latter had been re-designated as the Internal Security Agency, or ISA. Singer had held the position of Superintendent in the Agency's previous incarnation, and was still adjusting to his new title of Chief Security Enforcer. He was determined to navigate this treacherous no-man's-land and remind everyone of his established authority on no uncertain terms.

Turning his back on the captain, Singer strode to the smoldering carrier. He walked purposefully, and with enough self-possession, to hide the slight limp that sometimes plagued him. Two charred bodies had been dragged clear of the wreckage and set to one side. The agonized groans of the sole survivor stained the morning, as did the low, encouraging murmurs of the medics tending to the man's extensive wounds.

Singer watched for several moments, unmoved by the sight of the hunks of seared flesh and exposed intestine. He walked on to survey the activity at the wall. Crews were fitting concrete sections into place and stretching coils of razor wire beneath the glare from the towers of portable work lights. Engines and generators rumbled in the crisp desert air.

This particular site was located on I-84, but the plan called for reinforcement of all border crossings, then extension of the wall out from each of these until everything eventually linked up.

More than one thousand miles' worth of border separated the former states of Washington, Oregon, and California from Idaho and Nevada, and needed to be secured as soon as possible. Reports from the Canadian border confirmed that that northern nation, sympathetic to Pacifica's progressive philosophy, was helpfully apprehending fugitives and sending them directly back. Thus there was less pressure to establish a physical barrier there.

Far fewer refugees sought to flee at the southern border. There, it seemed those inclined to escape California were reluctant to risk the hazardous regions influenced by the warlords and cartels of northern Mexico.

Walking along the barricade, Singer reflected that it was along the eastern border that previous generations had attempted their own secession via the ballot box. Portions of some Oregon counties had even voted to leave and join Idaho in a legal but doomed bid to establish the super-state of "Greater Idaho". That failed attempt was regarded as an historical oddity, reflecting the discontent endemic in the least populated, most reactionary parts of the region.

But the charred corpses behind Singer made it clear a few modern locals were carrying on the tradition of restiveness.

Signaling for the operator to quiet his engine, Singer drew near the cab of one of the big cranes. The driver's eyes held a fearful, almost cringing look.

Singer said crisply, "I want to commend you and your crew for working through this disturbance. And for sticking to such a grueling schedule, and producing results despite an unreliable supply chain. Good work."

Relief spread over the driver's face. "Okay, yeah…thanks, sir."

With a smile and a nod, Hayden made his way back to the trailer. Ahead of him in the burgeoning morning light, the dominating slash of his own attenuated shadow stretched for many yards across the scrubby land.

Inside the shelter, he started the coffee machine, then fed Greta. The dry kibble rattled into her dish, competing with the hissing sounds of the machine. Accustomed to fresh meat, she gave the bowl's contents a disappointed stare before crunching the kibble with an air of resignation.

While Hayden waited for the brew to finish, he retrieved some fallen papers from the floor and slid them back into their folder, the one with the newly-designed flag imprinted on the front.

Pacifica's flag was based on an old emblem of an evergreen tree, towering proudly against a backdrop of three horizontal bands of blue, white and green. The updated design added mountains, and blocks of browns that nodded to the California deserts, as well as a more traditional-style federal seal in the center.

He thought of how the bursting forth of this autonomous country, this expression of truly progressive ideals, inspired by the region's exceptional and acclaimed ecology, was long in coming. In the decades following the crisis of the Cascadia earthquake, the culture on the West Coast had grown further isolated and independent, becoming something of a de facto nation, permanently dyed the deepest shade of political 'blue' in all of America.

Thus it seemed inevitable that the political philosophy of Interim President Cassian Gray and his compatriots would find its ultimate expression in a real country, not just a state of mind, a mere kingdom of lofty dreams. After this recent and clear split, Pacifica represented a fresh start, one free from the stifling layers of oligarchy and cronyism that had brought the United States to the brink of ruin.

While Pacifica was certainly much smaller in geography and population, the founders were pragmatic and had a specific vision for success. Hayden had been granted glimpses of the future roadmap, and told to prepare for pushback and unrest, especially when the supplies of State-sponsored recreational drugs and electronic entertainment dried up. For the time being, most urban citizens were confused, but still looking to the authorities for guidance.

It was the rural-dwellers who were more likely to resist the new regime. Some of these were successfully crossing the border; those remaining would need to be closely monitored. But in the end, troublemaking would be futile. With true believers at the helm, progress was unstoppable.

The coffee machine signaled it was ready. Singer poured himself a scalding cup and returned to stand at the small table, regarding the piles of documents before him. They were various reports, and his personal notes, electronic and hard copies, from the previous week's meeting at the capitol with the fledgling Central Committee.

The terrible state of communications in the new country had been at the top of that meeting's agenda. Landlines had been non-existent for at least twenty years. Cell service was still unreliable where it was most needed—out in the remote areas of the region.

For now, the new regime relied on a network of couriers to shuttle info between agencies via memory sticks, paper or even verbal messages. This was a slow, awkward but common protocol employed by elite corporations and black market operations alike, and Singer hated it. But he could not deny that it was reasonably secure, plus it gave him an excuse to establish a clandestine network of operatives who answered to him personally.

It was whispered among Committee members that the People's Democratic Republic of Pacifica might be loaned an older but still serviceable quantum satellite from sympathetic Chinese authorities, but such an agreement was not finalized.

In matters beyond their borders, President Gray had confirmed to the Committee that Washington, D.C. was still reeling from Pacifica's surprise birth. Furthermore, he was confident a sizable number of U.S. congressmen and senators were themselves sympathetic to Pacifica's goals. The media at large was also opposed to military response. Consequently, the U.S. citizenry was being bombarded with Pacifica-favorable propaganda from news outlets and entertainment channels alike.

"Thus far," Gray had reminded them all with an air of triumph, "Vanessa Chakrabarti isn't proving to be the second coming of Abraham Lincoln. If she follows historical trends, nothing will be done about Pacifica except talk, and a bunch of window-dressing in the form of toothless sanctions."

Gray had also pointed out how previous administrations' failures to push back against foreign interests' violation of national sovereignty had established a precedent of weakness. These violations included Russia's usurpation of Alaskan fishing territory, and China's economic annexation of Hawaii, as well as the Luna City moon base. To say nothing of the various Mexican paramilitary criminal cartels operating for decades with impunity on U.S. soil.

Stepping from the table to the window, Hayden stood enjoying the heat of the coffee cup in his hands while observing the construction of the wall, feeling a thrill of excitement about the future.

As swallow of warm liquid slid down his throat, he made note of patterns and universal truths, the most important being: while the new country continued to take shape, it was exceedingly vulnerable. It existed in a state between success and failure that was far more precarious than anyone dared admit publicly. Singer hoped President Gray's clandestine outreach to China, Russia and the southern warlords would help tip the balance in Pacifica's favor.

Such diplomatic maneuvers were outside Singer's scope of duties. His focus was to strengthen security inside the new country, and he was excited about the challenge.

He left the window and sat at the table. Greta grunted in pleasure and settled near her master's shiny boots. From time to time, Hayden fondly stroked the dog's head. He methodically sorted through his notes and notifications, pausing when he came to an update on a prisoner named Enrique Rodriguez.

There was no evidence the rogue officer had any useful intel, but on the other hand, it would be a serious lapse in security to not squeeze everything possible out of him. Singer's brow furrowed as he asked himself if it was worth traveling back to ISA Headquarters on the coast, in the city of New Astoria. He was tempted to conduct the interrogation of this man in person.

Picking up and activating his videoskin, Singer swiped to some department personnel files and reviewed the details of yet another ex-agent of the former NRLSA. He studied the photos with mixed feelings. Beneath the Chief Enforcer's veneer of icy professionalism, a corrosive drop of rancor towards the fugitive, Owen MacIntyre, continually gnawed.

With a sigh, he set down the videoskin. "Looks like I'll have to drive back to the coast and have a chat with Rodriguez," he said aloud in a low, threatening tone. "If nothing else, he might have some insights as to where his buddy, that smug 'neuroeaugmented' prick, is hiding out."

Greta lifted her head and flicked her ears towards his voice. A slow, cruel smile meandered over Singer's face as he fondled the dog's ruff. "And if Rodriguez doesn't come clean, I know some other arms I can twist."

He rose and carried his empty cup to the minuscule sink in the corner kitchenette. He rinsed it and set it aside to dry. "Okay, girl are you ready to come with me while I make some important visits?"

With an eager whine, Greta leaped to her feet and wagged her tail.

CHAPTER
THREE

UNDER THE HARSH light of the early August dawn, violet hatch-work shadows streamed from wire fencing crowned with curls of vicious razor wire. Thick shadows also painted the enclosed exercise yard, where the crowd of men were arranged in precise rows, their shaved heads sunk in numbed apathy.

That morning, the detainees had awakened in silence, climbed from bunks and shambled down corridors without whispers or muttering. Each wore a slim neurocontroller headset which monitored electrical activity in the brain and heart, reporting any signs of agitation. While these were not the most advanced of devices, they fulfilled their purpose of keeping each prisoner's mind in a mildly befuddled, tractable state.

To Enrique Rodriguez, when he first wore the device, it felt like a blanket rested over his thoughts and emotions. The circlets could also deliver appropriate stimulation to key areas, providing either a reproachful jolt of pain or a rewarding trickle of dopamine.

Beyond the fence, empty grassland stretched for miles in all directions, relieved here and there by a few trees or low hills near the horizon. A cloudless sky arched above, the pristine air not yet contaminated with the stench from the crude privies at the far end of the yard. Those noxious fumes would ripen over the coming hours in the warmth of the sun.

Stealing a glance upwards, Enrique noticed the patient silhouette of a turkey vulture drifting lazily, high above the compound. *It's early in the day to be expecting a meal,* he thought with a burst of defiance. *None of us are dead yet.*

An eerie, sullen quiet prevailed before commencement of the Power Cult ritual. The ritual was simple: slogans, represented by basic pictoglyphs, appeared on large video screens erected at the front and sides of the yard. Reciting these slogans aloud, the assembly honored the many aspects of Power residing in the balance of unity and diversity, Power manifesting in waterways and deserts, rock and leaf, cloud and wave, heat and cold.

Head hanging listlessly, Rodriguez mouthed a semblance of agreement. All around him, he heard the words chanted or sung in stumbling, imperfect unison. Obeisance was paid to the bland symbols on the huge banners stretched throughout the compound, the fabric fluttering intermittently in the freshening morning breeze.

Afterwards, the men filed into the dining hall for breakfast. Rodriguez took his tray, with its insultingly skimpy portions of food, then walked to his assigned seat without looking to the right or left. He seated himself gingerly, thankful his bruises were healing.

However, deep breaths or sudden movement were met with a sharp pain in what he assumed was a cracked rib. He never once looked at where a new biotracker had been injected into his left forearm. He feared if he betrayed any interest or acknowledgement of what they had done or were doing to him, he risked more punishment.

The walls were hung with sheets of more pictoglyphs, listing rules and admonishing the residents to think of the ways in which they could contribute to Pacifica's greatness. Each man consumed his meal without removing his eyes from one of the large screens positioned about the chamber. These continually streamed messages from President Gray, extolling Pacifica's ideals of citizenship and duty.

Enrique chewed with caution, avoiding the painful gap in his sore jaw where a tooth had been knocked out.

Two impressions remained of the hours immediately following his capture; the memory of how skillfully his former superior, Hayden Singer, had inflicted pain, and of how he himself had successfully resisted revealing anything useful.

Enrique supposed he should be grateful that Singer had shown enough restraint that a lost tooth and cracked rib were his worst injuries. He also supposed he should be thankful that Greg Park had insisted on compartmentalizing information, so that no one operative within the Restoration was entrusted with very much intel.

Despite the chaos and pain of his hours with Singer, Enrique had held fast and was adamant that he did not know anything about Greg Park or Owen MacIntyre beyond their previous professional interactions at the Agency. Whether or not Singer truly believed him, Enrique had soon found himself remanded from the Agency's interrogation suite, to this re-education camp in northeastern Oregon, to reconsider his obstinance.

He was unsure where this facility was located; the windows of the bus had been blacked out, in addition to having metal screens welded over the glass, but he guessed it was south of Pilot Rock.

Jolting along in an overheated, crowded bus which stank of the sweat of anxiety, Enrique had managed to engage in a few muttered conversations with his fellow prisoners. He hadn't learned anything helpful; apparently, he knew more about the camps than any of the others did. After all, while working at the Agency, he had remotely surveilled their construction process via satellite.

On his arrival, he had been assigned a number and issued a neurocontroller. While he knew remaining in a docile, receptive state made him safer, his instinct clamored that he not go along with this. After several days of mindless toiling in a work shed, he pilfered a couple of lengths of wire which he secretly fashioned into a small tool.

Late one night, hidden in the blackness of the barracks, he had gone to work. Without making the slightest noise, he pried his circlet open and painstakingly manipulated the settings. He lowered the device's sensitivity across all functions, rendering it little more than decorative headgear.

Spoofing biotrackers was his forte, so he was confident his tampering would not be detected. And while he'd miss the occasional trickles of reward-hormones, he did not need to have his traumatized wits further dulled. His waking existence would become less bearable, but he wanted his mind to be his own.

He regretted that he couldn't also dig the tracker from his arm, but without access to that device's remote monitoring equipment, the tampering would have been immediately noticed.

Even while wearing the altered circlet, during waking hours he continued to perfect a technique of keeping the surface level of his thoughts engaged with shallow, transitory observations. He worked to induce in himself a state of placid contentment, even while beneath those sensations lurked more dangerous and weightier concepts and considerations.

As he observed the actions and demeanor of the other inmates, he was confident he had a greater command of his thoughts than they did. It occurred to him that, even if he hadn't tampered with his own device, he had lived a different enough sort of life than the others, that he had stronger immunity to the effects. He was grateful to his parents and grandparents for forbidding the use of such casual but intrusive tech when he was younger—he'd been kept from games and communications systems that linked straight to the brain of the user.

Furthermore, his years of training in the Information Tech Oversight Department at the Agency had made him conversant with many modern mind-control and propaganda techniques. Knowing they were in use was a big step towards subverting them, and helped him resist the mantras of the daily Power Cult devotions.

Recalling his time at the Agency, he wondered what Captain Park and Owen were doing, and where they were. He guessed Owen had escaped a week or two before himself, before the border was closed, before the coup was public. He was unsure about Park's status or location. He had no way of knowing if either of them knew he was in this camp. If they did know, what could they possibly do to help him?

Consuming the last few bites on his plate, he fought a strong gag reflex. The food was abominable; the taste of the plant and insect-based meal lingered in his mouth long after he finished it. He wondered if it contained sedatives, but decided he didn't feel any different after eating it. It was merely a foul-tasting, quivering glop, and not very filling.

Thus far, there wasn't much indication that any kind of hard, sustained labor was going to be required of the detainees. In fact, it was difficult to tell what purpose these facilities served, and he was beginning to believe they existed primarily to send a rumor of fear through the general populace. Such an effect would be well worth the inconvenience of constructing and operating them.

In addition to the general uncertainty and sense of danger that oppressed him every waking moment, Enrique found the hardest thing to bear was being forbidden to pray. Following his submission to Islam nearly two years earlier, he had embraced the rhythm of the daily *salah* routine, and now to have it denied with such targeted cruelty, left him feeling lost and resentful.

So his prayers and petitions to Allah were offered, silently and secretly, from the depths of his heart. This secret routine was the rock on which his personality struggled to preserve itself day to day, hour to hour, moment to moment.

Following breakfast, the inmates were led across the exercise yard to an imposing, dreary-looking shed. Newly-constructed, it still smelled of raw lumber and clean concrete. Recalling floor plans of the facility that he had seen back at the Agency, Enrique was pretty certain there was at least one other, similar workshop on the far side of the camp, in the women's section. He had no clue how many female prisoners were there; so far, he had only caught one or two glimpses through small gaps in the heavy fence that bisected the compound.

Now, the cowed men shuffled to their places at their assigned stations. The bare-bones workshop was uninsulated. The morning's chill soon dissipated; as the sun beat on a metal roof laden with solar panels, the space became stifling. The previous scents of fresh lumber and construction dust that had greeted Enrique when he first arrived at the facility faded, replaced by the smell of unwashed bodies, an occasional whiff of cleaning fluid, and through the open windows high in the wall, the latrines at the far end of the exercise yard.

As Enrique began assembling the components from the overflowing buckets and bins adjacent to the workbench, he reviewed his mental notes about the security systems and the guard's routines. It was his duty to avoid trouble and stay alive, but it was also his duty to escape this place if the opportunity arose. Realistically, he knew there was little to no chance of this happening, but tepid dreams of freedom helped sustain him.

That afternoon, as his ordeal dragged on, his hope became conflated and entwined with his prayers; prayers that this nightmare would somehow end soon, prayers that he would someday see Connie and the kids again. He had forbidden them to seek shelter with out-of-state relations, insisting they make their way to someplace rumored to be remote and difficult to access, someplace Greg had mentioned to him in secret.

He also prayed that if the worst happened and he never reunited with them, they would at least be safe and well-cared for, wherever they wound up living. Although it was almost more than he could bear to think of, he trusted that they would carry on and build a new life without him.

Part of his mind re-addressed the task before him, and he wondered whether he should slow his work down, in order to interfere with whatever the overall plan was for these items. He remembered reading or hearing about prisoners in Nazi camps who had intentionally sabotaged the radio units they were forced to assemble for German troops. Would it be worthwhile to try something like that here? Or would it only attract unwanted notice and put himself at risk?

It's my duty to survive, he reminded himself again. Not to unnecessarily risk punishment or death. He could defy the guards by keeping his head down, becoming as unremarkable as possible. His family was owed his best efforts at survival.

Later that afternoon, an officer entered the workroom; Enrique looked away, lowering his head further as he concentrated on his task. It made no difference; the guard crossed the room and stood near him.

"AB zero nine—time to take a break. We've got another job for you."

Rodriguez set down the pieces of the implement he had been assembling. Although he offered no resistance, the guard still made a point of grasping him by the arm and marching him out. Enrique submerged his fury at the man's touch, focusing instead on his curiosity about where he was being taken—a curiosity heavy with dread.

The corridors were plain, drafty and lit with the bare minimum of light fixtures. The facility seemed to be powered only by a combination of solar panels and diesel generators.

The tight-lipped guard escorted him across the exercise yard to the single-story building containing control rooms and officers' quarters. Inside, they entered a chamber filled with several desks laden with monitor screens. A uniformed man, seated in an office chair before one screen, turned towards them.

The man was large, overly-fleshed, with sandy hair and prominent, watery blue eyes. He wore a dark jacket with an insignia proclaiming him Camp Commander. With a jolt of apprehension, Enrique recognized Stan Bauer.

Back at the Agency, Sergeant Bauer's bullying tendencies were well-known. Consequently, Enrique had avoided him, and took particular care to take little part in the bad-blood between Bauer and MacIntyre. But there was no escaping him now; Enrique's shocked look elicited a nasty grin from his former colleague.

"Don't *you* look delighted to see me," he drawled. "I arrived late last night to take over command here. Singer has a lot of faith in me."

Enrique forced an inarticulate, noncommittal sound from his dry throat.

Bauer said, "So, Enrique Rodriguez—or do you prefer your new code, 'AB zero nine'?"

Rodriguez grunted.

"You're right—it's not a very friendly name. Well, Enrique, it's great to get a chance to have a little heart-to-heart. Sit down and make yourself comfortable. Here—let me take that for now." Without warning, Bauer rose and pulled the controller off Enrique's brow. He tossed it aside and it clattered on the desk top. "It's best if your reactions are one hundred-percent natural."

Warily, Enrique lowered himself into the proffered seat, not taking his eyes off the commander. Bauer remained standing, leaning over the prisoner with an air of casual dominance.

He said, "The good news is—I've been reviewing all the surv footage we have of you since your arrival, and I'm impressed with how well you've been behaving. Not a moment of trouble, not a single complaint. No smart-ass comments or dirty looks. To be honest—I never would have thought you'd make it this long without some corrective therapy."

Enrique tightened his jaw but remained stonily silent.

Bauer seemed happy to fill the quiet with the sound of his own voice. "But there's bad news. There's always bad news, isn't there? In this case, it's that Singer is impatient. He thinks it might be a mistake remanding you here, instead of holding you in the interrogation suites back at HQ. Seems you're getting too comfortable. You're treating this place like some kind of summer camp or rest home, and settling right in. So prove him wrong—tell me where we can find Park and MacIntyre."

Enrique's voice was scratchy and dry—dry from lack of water, dry from fear, from exhaustion, from disuse. He rasped, "I'm telling you what I told him—I have no idea."

"I was afraid you'd say that."

Enrique wondered if the man was knowingly aping Hayden Singer's tone and manner, or if the echoes were due to the fact both men were swaggering thugs.

The commander added, "I've spent some time studying your old personnel files. You were raised Christian, weren't you?"

Enrique mumbled in the affirmative. Bauer shook his head in disappointment. "Yet, you had no problem turning your back on your family traditions and joining the Franklin Street Mosque back in New Astoria. Did you do that out of personal conviction, or just to fit in with a particular crowd and reap the cultural perks some of you backward, religious types enjoyed from the State?"

The line formed from Enrique's lips remained a dry, stubborn crack. Whatever trap the other was setting, he had no intention of falling in it.

Bauer went on, "*'What's his fucking point?'*, you're probably wondering. Well, to my way of thinking, since you're the kind of man who can betray your whole traditional heritage, turn your back on your family's religion, send your wife and kids away without any protection, you won't have any qualms letting us know where that bastard cyborg is hiding out. Oh, excuse me—he prefers the term *'neuroaugmented'*, doesn't he?"

Rodriguez said nothing, even as his heart grew icy and dropped through his core at the mention of Connie and the kids. Yet he betrayed no agitation, clinging to the hope that Bauer was just messing with him, that they had not been caught yet.

After studying his captive's resolute visage a moment longer, Bauer emitted a regretful sigh. He activated the nearest monitor, then made a selection from the onscreen menu.

"I know you told Singer you have no intel for us, but we can't bring ourselves to accept that. So let's see if we can find something that might make you more willing to talk."

The screen now displayed a view of a cramped, dingy chamber containing only a narrow bed, on which sat a young woman. Her head was shaved close to the scalp and she huddled at one end of the bare mattress, clutching a short hospital-style garment about herself. The view was foreshortened, the camera being located in the upper corner of the room.

As Rodriguez and Bauer watched, a man entered the room. He wore the uniform of a camp guard, but his face was concealed behind a black cloth mask. It was clear from the look on the woman's face, from the way she shrank back against the wall, that she suspected what was coming next.

Just as it was clear from the way the man advanced, unfastening his belt, that her fears were correct.

"Keep watching," commanded Bauer in a guttural rumble. He drew his side arm and rested the weapon's muzzle against Enrique's temple. "Don't worry—he won't get violent. We have the highest respect for the female reproductive system around here."

The hard tip of the pistol dug more insistently into Rodriguez's flesh, but he did not dare wince or give the faintest sign of revulsion as the act proceeded—in real time and unstoppable.

After several moments, his resolve failed, and his eyelids fluttered as he glanced away from the screen. Bauer caught this and tapped his temple with the gun. "No—get your eyes up here."

Bringing his face close, Bauer hissed through his too-wide grin, "It's hard for you isn't it? That whole loving husband and father routine, the upright religious persona—you always thought of yourself as some kind of do-gooder hero, didn't you? And yet here you sit, a damned useless, pathetic excuse for a man. Unable to help her."

Enrique's nostrils flared and sweat poured down his face. His hands balled, then unclenched. He felt close to vomiting. Could he grab Bauer's gun and use it against him? If he somehow managed to wrest it from the bigger, well-fed, energetic man, he knew it was impossible to get down the corridor without being caught. He chewed his lip until it bled, but still said nothing.

On top of the limp girl, the guard on the screen seemed to be taking an eternity.

Bauer said, "That's right—when you keep looking, it becomes easier to watch. That's the secret—watch until the part of you deep down inside that wants to be there, in his place, comes up to the surface and takes over. Perhaps that's not as deep as you've been telling yourself."

After an excruciatingly long time, the guard finished with the girl, pulled on his pants and departed.

Enrique choked, "Why did I have to see that? What did it have to do with me?"

Bauer drew back but did not re-holster his weapon. "Well, I'd like to keep you guessing about what we have planned for you down the road. But ask yourself: *'What's happening to Connie right now, if she's in another facility? Or even little Antonia? And am I going to be required to participate in these acts myself?'*"

Enrique's face blenched, and Bauer laughed. "And here's another big question: what have Park and MacIntyre done for you that's worth your loyalty? They set you up, then abandoned you. They escaped and left you behind."

Enrique felt Bauer's eyes boring into him, bulging with anticipation, waiting for his mouth to open again.

He said, "I...don't know...where...they...are."

Bauer spat. "I'm not buying that. I'm sure you'll remember if you think hard enough."

Enrique's head twitched in defiance.

Bauer persisted, "And what about this question: what are the *ideals* behind this 'Restoration' shit? It's so vague and high-minded, but has anyone explained to you what it actually means? Is it worth this, when you could just give us a few names and be free, maybe even be allowed in on the ground floor of establishing a new country? Think about it. That's a big fucking deal, isn't it?"

"Yeah...I'll...think about it," whispered Enrique.

Shaking, his eyes slid back to the young woman on the screen; she was on the edge of the bed, hugging herself into a tight ball.

A part of him knew Bauer was right. He didn't really know what the Restoration stood for; he'd blundered into his involvement with Greg's secret group, and was now trapped.

His head throbbed as he wondered how much longer he could hold out, before he'd start searching for some fabricated but convincing scrap he could give his captors. How long would it be before his own humanity crumbled, and he ceased to care about protecting his colleagues?

Moving behind the chair, Bauer gave his captive's shoulder a hearty shove. "Good, but don't think too long. And for now, get back to work."

CHAPTER
FOUR

OUT OF BREATH from his thirty-minute jog, the dark-haired man's formerly eager steps slowed to a trudge. He was grateful for the pleasant breeze, off Lake Washington, that cooled the sweat on his brow as he made his way up the tree-lined street. The residential road wound through the hilly neighborhood in the historic, elegant West Bellevue enclave outside Seattle.

Genetic conditioning had granted Slate Singer a willowy, muscular frame and slowed his aging process, so he appeared to be thirty, rather than his true age of almost forty. On a good day, he felt no older than twenty-three. He was proud of that, less so of the fact his mentality was often comparably lagging. Whenever his conscience pricked, telling him that perhaps he was behaving immaturely, he blew it off by assuring himself that a youthful, energetic outlook made up for any other flaws he might have.

This evening, his pleasing blue eyes were fatigued from another day of staring at his computer screen, but becoming soothed by the comforting scene around him. He regarded the neighbors' rooftops below him, peeking decorously between the branches of the ancient, overgrown plantings of pines, the scattered rhododendrons that towered almost as tall as trees. Beyond these homes, he glimpsed the shoreline, where beneath the setting sun, the gray-blue waves of the lake lapped rhythmically against the beach.

A generation or two earlier, this had been an affluent and desirable neighborhood. Even now, in its state of genteel decay, it retained the wistful beauty of an aging film star. On picture-perfect evenings like this, Slate admitted he was madly fond of it, that he was lucky to have grown up here, and that he intended to live here the rest of his life.

Slate's progress slowed further as he neared his childhood home, familiar to him as his own face in the mirror. The modest split-level was the site of some of his most treasured memories, and impressions of past birthday parties and neighborhood barbecues were made even happier through the blur of time. He saw the branches of the tall cedar where his unauthorized treehouse had been briefly located; construction of that modest, clumsy structure had consumed most of his eighth summer. His fathers had attempted to screen it from the neighbors, but in the end, had cheerfully paid the fines to the city when it was reported.

Slate thought how his dads had given him an ideal childhood, taking lead roles in a neighborhood education pod that ensured Slate had plenty of play and exploration time in the company of a circle of approved peers.

While Noah and Alan Brooks hadn't concealed his origins from him, they hadn't harped on it either, instead waiting until he was old enough to understand before explaining about the surrogacy and the genetic conditioning. No one in the education pod or the neighborhood in general mentioned it, either. Family arrangements such as the Brooks' were not usually discussed openly in their social caste, but were smiled at with an unspoken approval.

Slate resumed walking and noticed the sense of watchful, wary quiet that gripped the neighborhood. The violent demonstrations triggered by pockets of resistance to the new regime had by and large been confined to the rougher sectors of the city, and were mostly mopped up, but despite the appearance of returning normalcy, it felt like people were still on edge.

As Slate approached his house, he noticed a glow in the front windows. It seemed his partner had returned days earlier than normal. With a sigh, he forced down a faint lurch of guilty disappointment. Relations were very strained between the both of them lately, he was tired of the sniping and arguing.

Gathering courage, he climbed the front stairs and let himself in. Making his way with quiet steps to the kitchen, the first thing he saw was an open wine bottle sitting on the island. His mouth twitched in annoyance; that particular vintage wasn't meant to be gulped down like tap water on an average weekday.

A businesslike clicking of claws on tile sounded behind him, and a magnificent German Shepherd entered the kitchen. She quivered with excitement at the sight of him, and Slate crouched to ruffle her fur and let her lick his face.

"Hey, girl—welcome back. You need your nails trimmed, don't you?" He straightened and poured himself a glass of wine; might as well, since it was open.

Shoulders back, abdomen pulled in tighter, a resolute expression on his refined, boyish features, he then went down the corridor to the front room.

A tall, well-built man stood at the large picture window, silvery head bowed as he contemplated the view.

Slate said heartily, "Hey—! You're back early this week, that's so great." He crossed the room and touched Hayden with hesitant affection on the shoulder, receiving a fleeting smile in return. Slate then sank onto one of the contemporary sectionals sofas of buttery-soft vinyl that bordered half the room. He toyed with his wine glass.

Hayden Singer remained standing. "Yes, I was able to get up here sooner than I expected."

There was something about the way the older man paused that warned Slate to brace for another sales pitch about why they needed to move. About why Hayden's responsibilities at the newly-designated Internal Security Agency, headquartered in New Astoria, took precedence over Slate's software development job.

At the moment, Slate was unsure he'd be able to resist the onslaught. He swirled the light golden wine in his glass, frowning distantly as he thought about the awkward reality of offering criticism about anything Hayden was involved with. Even after more than seven years together, Slate sometimes felt he knew virtually nothing about the other man.

When they'd first met during a hiking trip in Yosemite, Slate had been at an especially naive, vulnerable point in his life. Hayden was fifteen years older, and projected a charismatic self-possession that Slate found comforting and irresistible. But over the past year or two, Hayden had grown more overbearing and short-tempered. Many times Slate found himself on the point of asking the other about his dissatisfaction, but often found it easier, in the end, to hide in the safety of a less controversial topic.

With his own fragile glass cradled lightly in his large hand, Hayden at last turned from the window and joined Slate on the sofa. Although he sat with his body brushing against Slate's, he seemed removed, and kept his gaze lowered. When he spoke, there was a stiff, rehearsed quality to his manner.

"I was at a special meeting in Salem this morning. Conditions are stable at the moment throughout the country, but the latest intel indicates we're in for some trouble over the next three to six months."

"Why?" asked Slate innocently.

Hayden shook his head. "Never mind, I'm not at liberty to say. Just trust me. But my own duties at ISA are going to get more time-consuming. So I feel it's time to discuss our personal situation."

Slate gave a delicate shrug, both resigned and inviting, then sipped his wine. He was aware of Hayden's muscles tensing further as the older man drew in a portentous breath and prepared to make his case.

"I guess what I want to say is, that in order for me to concentrate on these new duties, I can't have so much of my time taken up with travel."

Slate's dark, manicured brows furrowed. "I know what else you're going to say. And I'm still not ready to move."

"Well, I am. In fact, I just bought a home in New Astoria, in a planned development." Hayden's voice grew more animated, allowing Slate an unexpected glimpse deeper within the other. "It's beautiful—hell, it's like a palace! There's an amazing view over the city, you can see all the way to the mouth of the Columbia. Reminds me of my old neighborhood in San Francisco. You'll love it."

"Sure, sounds great, I'd love to see some pics. There's nothing wrong with owning more property."

"That's not all." Draining his glass, Hayden paused. Shifting his body away so he could meet Slate's eyes, he announced, "I found a buyer for this place."

Slate went rigid with dismay. "You did *what*? Without even consulting me? You can't just sell my home without my permission!"

"My name's on the deed, so I can if I pressure the right people at the bank. But I'd prefer to not have to do that."

The bluntness of this assertion hung between them like a bad smell.

Tugging his lip, Slate thought a moment before answering, "Look—I know this arrangement isn't perfect, but it's not the end of the world to have to travel between cities like this, is it? We've done it most of our time together. And lots of professionals do it, and politicians, celebrities. It's our lifestyle now."

Hayden appeared to consider this observation. Then he rejected it. "Those days are over. I can't be seen wasting so much time and fuel to maintain a second home."

Slate set aside his wine glass with a theatrical flair, then crossed his arms, muttering with a spurt of petulance, "I really wish you had talked with me first."

Hayden's nostrils flared, but his voice remained level. "I'm sorry, you're right. It's just that—,"

Relieved that an argument had been averted, Slate was eager to appear open-minded. "Just what? What can we do to make this arrangement work better for the both of us?"

Placing his own glass on the coffee table beside Slate's, Hayden wrestled off his gleaming leather boots and pushed them aside. Stretching out his long legs, he relaxed even further into the cushions and clamped his hand possessively over Slate's knee.

He said, "I suppose because I've been so busy these last few months, it feels like we're strangers. I really want you to come down and stay with me more often."

"Really? Is that all?"

Hayden uttered a low laugh. "Isn't that enough?"

Slate could not remember the last time he'd heard him laugh like that, sounding both at ease and hopeful. He studied the other's face, the unnerving, piercing light eyes beneath heavy brows, the strong, straight nose and well-formed mouth.

With a rush of emotion, Slate found himself agreeing. "Heck, yeah. I'm open to doing that."

"Good. But I want you to promise you'll reconsider moving down there permanently if the situation requires it."

"Sure, I'll...consider it."

"And once we're settled, we can revisit some of the other plans we've discussed."

Slate's heart jolted with hope. "You mean—a baby? Is that what you're going to say?"

Hayden frowned as he loosened his stiff new uniform shirt of deep gray. "I know you're still disappointed about that debacle with TotalityCare, when the egg donor and surrogate backed out of the deal. I'm disappointed too, more than I let on. But conditions are far from ideal at the moment—the whole healthcare system is in flux."

"Yeah, yeah, I understand that. But still—do you think there's a chance?"

Angling his body down to a more comfortable slouch, Hayden pressed his head back into the sofa and closed his eyes. A knowing smile played at one corner of his mouth as he answered, "There's *always* a chance. But why don't we set our sights on something more manageable?"

"Like what?"

Hayden gestured to the coffee table. "Hand me my videoskin."

Slate passed the device over and waited with growing interest as Hayden activated it and held it up. "Check out this guy."

Slate looked at a screen filled with images of a champion GSD stud and is record of awards. "You're *finally* going to breed Greta?"

"Well, I'm seriously thinking about it." Singer set the device back down and regarded Slate's happy reaction. "I haven't decided for sure if this is the stud I want, but he's the best I've found so far. So, if you still think that's something you want to add into our already hectic lifestyle—,"

Slate crowed with delight. "Hectic for you maybe—*I* think puppies would be relaxing."

Hayden chuckled. "You're crazy, but whatever makes you happy. Is there anything ready for dinner, or should we go out?"

Slate jumped up. "There's plenty here. I'll heat something up."

In the kitchen, he smiled to himself and shook his head in wonder. He wasn't thrilled about Hayden's threat to sell this house, but at least the older man was coming around to Slate's desire for breeding Greta. The idea of a litter of puppies tumbling about the house—whichever house the couple ended up settling in—made any circumstance bearable.

CHAPTER
FIVE

THE AUGUST MORNING light streamed through the window, caressing the prayer book in Fr. Cosimo Nicholl's hands. It touched his lean, sparsely bearded face, lined with care despite his relative youth. When he completed the first set of prayers, the priest left the sacristy and entered St. Columban's church, commencing the Sunday Liturgy with a sense of dread.

As the ritual progressed, he pretended to not notice the unfamiliar visitor standing in the back of the church. The stocky older woman in a dark uniform, with her light-brown hair scraped into a severe knot, sported an official Internal Security Agency patch on her jacket. She also gave off an unpleasant, supercilious aura, as she stood with arms folded throughout the entire proceedings. Her small, sharp eyes remained fastened on the priest's every movement.

Her presence stirred memories that were never far from Cosimo's awareness. Dark impressions from his youth, during the most frenzied wave of religious persecutions that had briefly gripped the nation. While the violence hadn't lasted long, and was confined to a few specific regions, it had still left deep scars throughout the national consciousness.

Before that era of violence, most established churches had already caved to state authorities in matters of health and contentious gender issues, proving their loyalty to the secular sphere over the Divine. The hold-out minorities were then subjected to years of sustained harassment via a smothering web of local, state and federal regulations, meant to suffocate growth and strangle their dwindling influence on the culture.

In this hostile atmosphere, the young Cosimo's own faith had paradoxically been rekindled as he discovered his vocation. Eschewing politics, he had committed himself to a life of prayer, service and gardening. It was admittedly a solitary life; in the years prior to his ordination, he'd not met any woman in his slim circle of acquaintances willing to share such a poor and ascetic existence. After his ordination, if a candidate had come along, it would have been too late. Nonetheless, he was comfortable with his life and rarely looked back with regret.

That morning, the priest conducted the ritual with practiced, assured motions; he delivered his homily with a clear, steady voice. Afterwards, the tiny band of worshippers gathered in the parish center. Soon the ISA representative entered the hall: Cosimo noticed hostile, anxious glances darting towards her. The sharpest came from Joe Murchison, one of the parishioners most resentful of the authorities. Despite his lumbering, gentle appearance, Murchison was something of a hot-head, and he made it clear he disagreed with Fr. Cosimo's sermons about forgiveness and patience in the face of adversity.

With a binder tucked under her arm, the visiting agent crossed the room and approached the priest. "Excuse me, *Father* Nicholl…can you spare me a few minutes?"

"Yes, good morning. How may I help you?"

The woman flashed him a taut grin. It may have been meant for a warm smile, but came off as sinister. Waggling the fingers of her free hand at him in a nervous twitch, she said, "Hi, I'm Denise Bolling, Acceptance Compliance Enforcer with ISA."

"Ms. Bolling, pleased to meet you." He gestured towards a meager display of pastries on a platter near a coffee urn. "May I get you something? I'm sorry we don't have much…it's becoming more challenging to scare up the staples week after week. But you're more than welcome to what we have."

She was thrown off-stride by his cordial offer. "Oh…yes, coffee. Thanks."

He filled a cup and carried it for her as they took seats in a secluded corner. Fr. Cosimo watched with guarded interest as Bolling drew several sheets of printed paper from her binder.

She said, "These are a few of the new regulations that are going into effect immediately. With the outages in the grid and the internet, we're making a point of hand-delivering these to each of the faith communities. So no one is left out," she concluded with an effort at magnanimity.

"Thank you, that's very considerate."

Nicholl accepted the papers. A frown shadowed his face as he read; his lips compressed with skepticism. He thought, *They'll sure have the devil of a time enforcing some of these regs in the Muslim community, the one religion they've always coddled. Don't they realize there might be a backlash?*

His gaze strayed to a print of the Virgin Mary posted on the far wall. Over the years, Cosimo had been horrified to see various practices of sharia law become protected, even administered by, the local secular authorities here in New Astoria. He thought of how many local women and girls—Christian, Muslim or even 'nones'—that had suffered under an inequitable system. A system that, in the name of tolerance, turned a blind eye to the activities of predatory *taharrush* gangs, the groups of young males that roamed some neighborhoods and targeted unaccompanied women.

Indiscreet lovers caught within sharia-compliant zones risked punishment at the hands of the Public Virtue Division—regardless of whether or not the offenders were Muslim. In spite of some disaffected mumbling in private about the activities of these intrusive PVD patrols, most people had been trained to accept without judgement many obnoxious behaviors, and a two-tiered justice system, for the sake of cultural diversity.

Reeking with irritation, the woman's rote, brittle words shattered his musings, as if she'd read his mind. "The Acceptance Compliance Division has taken great care to create guidelines acceptable to all faith traditions. These are relatively minor adjustments that can be worked into any style of ceremony or belief system."

He sighed. "I'm afraid that reflects an utter lack of understanding of the subject. Do you really think myself, or any of the other local imams or pastors, are going to implement these guidelines?"

The enforcer repeated slowly and distinctly, "They are minor adjustments."

"Minor to you, perhaps. But to me, they are insulting. And unacceptable." Lowering the papers, Fr. Cosimo stared at her over the tendril of steam lifting from her forgotten coffee cup. He said, "Tell me what you thought of our liturgy."

Bolling reached for her cup and fiddled with it. "So, well…it was colorful, I guess. Lots of historical and cultural significance."

"'Colorful'? I appreciate your phrasing. An outside perspective can be…amusing."

She snapped, "I'm not here to amuse you. Don't forget that."

"I won't. But can you tell me, was it at all interesting? Did it…stir anything in you?"

Her face stiffened with the unease of one rarely asked to deviate or consider anything beyond a few blind but firmly rooted concepts. Or perhaps her fear was related to the presence of a comms unit implanted behind her left ear. Cosimo had no idea if the unit was capable of recording or transmitting their conversation, given the current internet and phone issues. Perhaps it somehow issued punishments. Yet even if it wasn't functional, he guessed she was trained to assume it was.

She protested, "I'm only concerned with threats to security or with violations of public health standards, or equity and inclusion regulations. I don't need to know the differences between these rituals."

"Was there anything at all unexpected?"

With a roll of her eyes, Bolling snorted. "It was a hell of a lot longer than I thought it would be, that's for sure."

"I'm sorry about that. We're used to the length. You see—we get lost in the beauty."

Bolling stared at him a moment before leaning over the table and dropping her voice to a hiss. "I don't care about 'beauty'. You people are worshipping pieces of bread—do realize how crazy that is? Very soon, all of this—," her stubby hand waved contemptuously towards the chamber, "—and all these people and their obsolete, inconvenient, hate-filled ways—and you in particular—will be gone, once and for all. We've put up with you for far too long."

She shoved her chair away from the table, rose, and strode from the hall.

Cosimo looked after her, reflecting, *Methinks she doth protest too much—they're acting scared and uncertain.* But that meant they were also dangerous. At the moment, he felt a little dangerous himself. Picking up the printed directives, he tore the sheets in half, then quarters.

Rising, he turned to face the anxious congregation, who greeted the sight of the paper shreds with fleeting grins and scattered applause. He hoped these frightened people would absorb some of his own serenity; at the moment, he felt this was what he was born to be. He was ready to accept, to endure, whatever the coming days demanded of him.

CHAPTER
SIX

"*MIRA, SEÑORA! MIRA, MIRA!*"

A small stuffed jaguar toy waved insistently before Sofia MacIntyre's face. Gently pushing it aside, she offered a kind smile to the proud child holding it. She said in halting Spanish, "Oh, that's beautiful dear, but let's talk about our toys *after* we're finished with the lesson."

Sitting up tall and squaring her slim shoulders, she clapped her hands for attention. The restless children, arranged in a semi-circle on the rug before her, awaited her next instructions. She was delighted to have so many bright eyes fixed on her; the energy she felt from this small group was invigorating.

She said, "Well done, everyone! You were all excellent listeners today. Now, please take your instruments back and place them where you found them—no shoving and don't run. *Gracias.*"

She watched with satisfaction as the class of pre-school-aged children scrambled to their feet and scampered off to place their simple instruments in the designated baskets, which waited in the corner of the large, welcoming classroom space. Sofia then rose from the rug and brushed the wrinkles from her long skirt, fondly observing the students as they departed. As she also left the classroom, she was joined by the facility's director, Señora Gomez.

"They haven't stopped talking about you since your last visit! You have such a lovely, natural way with children," commented the older woman, as they both walked to the atrium at the center of the facility's common space.

"Thank you," said Sofia. "I'm so happy to be teaching again, it's a lot of fun."

"And I'm so impressed with how well they behave for you! I must confess, when we first began this project, I wanted to use the 'peaceful scholar' headset technology to maintain quiet and discipline, but Don Tomás talked me out of it. He was adamant the children be allowed to be themselves."

Eyes widening with sincerity, Sofia said, "Oh, I totally agree with him! They have to learn self-discipline as naturally as possible, especially while their brains are still maturing. Those headsets can cause long-term damage in so many areas of human development."

The señora nodded. "I appreciate your perspective. Thanks so much for volunteering your skills here."

Reassured by the woman's friendly, gushing tone, Sofia added happily, "This is much more enjoyable than virtual classes. I want to keep visiting these kids in person at least once every couple of weeks!" In truth, she was still a little anxious about the logistics of traveling between Palmira and Medellín on a regular basis, but for now was committed to making the arrangement work.

"Even after the baby arrives?" The señora's smile deepened as she gestured politely towards Sofia's abdomen.

"I haven't decided yet, but I think it won't be too difficult to work the baby into my schedule somehow." Sofia placed her hands on her front. "Maybe I'm being unrealistic, maybe I'll have to go back to doing a bit more online. But for now, I'm up for anything." It was true she felt energetic, and her February due date seemed an eternity from this sultry afternoon in late August.

"That's the spirit," said Señora Gomez, white teeth flashing in her glossy ebony face. Bright glints of light came from the green and red gems in the minuscule parrot earrings at the older woman's lobes. Sofia wondered if her own personal style would ever evolve to the point where she'd be comfortable wearing something so flamboyant. She had trouble imagining that it would.

In the atrium, the women stood beneath a huge, hand-crafted sculpture formed of mixed-media resin and glass flowers and vines. These were studded with LED lights, and the whole creation was wired for sound, emitting soft nature noises and musical phrases. Sofia thought it was a beautiful, fun piece that captured the sense of optimism that permeated the entire building. She loved this bright, cheerful space, and was growing to think of the facility as symbolic of her feelings of comfort and confidence in her new life here. This life wasn't what she had expected; when she had visited before with Owen, circumstances had been artificial and restrained, as they'd mostly been confined to the Chen-Diaz hacienda during a large house party, hosted by Tomás and his then-girlfriend, Selena Vasquez-Medina.

Señora Gomez, following her gaze about the atrium, commented, "I gave your husband a grand tour when he was here before. I could not tell what he thought of the artwork, he seemed reserved."

"Oh, he's just very thoughtful. He has a lot on his mind lately, but trust me, he's excited to be involved with this."

The Nido de Paloma community for at-risk women and children represented a deep aspect of Tomás Chen's personality, it was close to his heart. Consequently, both she and Owen were honored to help out. She did not know much about Tomás' background, but was aware that he was deeply ashamed to be heir to a legacy that had arisen from the infamous Colombian illegal drug industry. What had been born in lawless violence had morphed into a series of legitimate pharmaceutical companies, which had then become socially acceptable as more world governments partnered with these to placate their restive, dispirited populations. That the authorities could further profit through licensing, taxation, and cronyism, also helped build the industry.

This type of partnership was wide-spread throughout most western cultures, and few who benefitted from the arrangement at the level that Tomás enjoyed shared his scruples. Thus, after inheriting his disgraced brother's responsibilities, he had gradually separated himself from Vibora, the family company, and put his own resources into the Paloma Foundation. Sofia was happy to help carry on Tomás' vision, even in such a small thing as teaching these toddlers a few songs and showing them how to play simple instruments.

With an inviting smile, Señora Gomez asked, "Do you have time to join us for dinner today?"

"I would love to, but I should go home soon." Sofia glanced across the atrium to where the patient, muscular form of the bodyguard stood. The overhead lights glinted on his shaved head and the frames of his sleek, Augmented Reality security glasses.

Sofia had no idea what the phlegmatic Diego Rojas thought of this situation, but he was receiving considerable recompense for these trips. At first, she had been uncomfortable having a personal guard, but was now used to his taciturn but reliable presence.

She embraced Señora Gomez, who, clearly delighted the American was falling in so easily with local customs, hugged her back tightly. Sofia said, "Adios—see you in two weeks!"

During the drive to the airport, Sofia's mind was busy with a tangle of thoughts and emotions. She was genuinely excited for the opportunity to put her professional training into practice—her chances of imparting her love of music to others had been largely curtailed back home in Oregon, after she lost her teaching job due to her CitizenTrust ranking being illicitly downgraded by a vengeful neighbor.

She also basked, with a warm, inner delight, in a recent revelation from Owen: he was now seriously considering putting his Restoration involvement on the back-burner, while making Paloma a priority. This news, together with the fact that she'd had some conversations with her parents about conditions back in the U.S., made her feel more confident about the future than she had for many months.

The jet scarcely reached cruising altitude before they began the descent to the Palmira airport. After an uneventful drive into the foothills, it was late evening when Rojas guided the family vehicle through the automatic gates of the heavily fenced estate.

Sofia took a few bites of the supper that was left in the kitchen, then covered the dishes and put them away. Looking for Owen, she climbed the stairs and went to the master bedroom, to find him leaning over an open suitcase on the bed. He was dropping a few items into the pack, but turned toward her with a happy grin.

"Hey, great, you're back. How was it?"

"It was wonderful, the kids are doing surprisingly well." Her air was distracted, she remained in the doorway, glaring at the travel pack. "What's going on? I thought you weren't scheduled to be back in Calí until next week?"

He paused for a fraction of a second. "I was, but something's come up."

Her heart sank. "You're not going to Calí, are you? This is for Greg Park, isn't it?"

"Not exactly." His back was now to her as he pulled some undershirts from the chest of drawers. But she knew he was aware of her disappointment.

He admitted, "Well, yeah, it is."

"I can't believe you're doing anything with him now! I thought we decided you're going to focus on Paloma, that we're well out of all of that."

"I never ruled out continued involvement with Park. I just said cutting back was a possibility."

The blood drained from her face and her heart surged to her throat as a possibility occurred to her. She asked, "You're not...I mean, this has nothing to do with...*him*, with Hayden Singer, does it?" Just saying that name aloud made her skin crawl.

"Of course not," he scoffed. Yet he remained almost motionless for a long, strained moment. Then a ripple of bravado thrummed through him as he said, "Listen, he's not worth my time."

She crossed the room and seated herself on the bed, face still pale as she focused on him. "Can you promise me you're not going to do anything...risky?"

An air of annoyance tensed his body as he returned to the closet and began pulling aside the garments. He said, "Do you know where my gray-blue, long-sleeved shirt is?"

"The silky one I got you for Christmas? That was left behind."

She tried not to think of all the other things they had been forced to abandon, her own favorite clothes, the icon that was a wedding gift from her parents. At least Owen had salvaged files of some of her favorite out-of-print books and was having them re-printed and bound for her.

She added, "Don't change the subject. Are you promising me or not? Nothing risky?"

"We have different definitions of 'risky', don't we? Sort of a man-versus-woman thing."

One of her brows tilted in irritation. "Don't give me that—!"

"Okay, well, bottom line is: no—I can't promise that."

Her agitated fingers tugged at and then stroked the hem of her top. "Please be honest—you're absolutely sure this has nothing to do with Singer?"

Owen straightened and said adamantly, "I have no intention of allowing that piece of shit to dictate how or where we're going to live the rest of our lives. Besides, I'm sure his hands are full, trying to help run the precious little Utopia he and his cronies have birthed. But for the time being, we need to be a little cautious until things die down a bit. Later, though...we'll see."

He tossed some socks atop the shirts in the suitcase. After a long exhalation, he added, "Generally, the political situation has stabilized. I've been monitoring everything pretty closely, and I think it's safe enough for me to pay a visit. Besides, I'm going nowhere near Pacifica, and I'll be traveling under a different ID, I'll be fine. Anyway, this trip is—," he paused, waving a hand expansively. "It's a trip…for intel gathering, it's not an assignment, there's something Greg wants to show me. I'll only be gone over the weekend."

"Can't he just send you some video files?"

"It's not the same." A smug expression slid over his face as he asked, "Why aren't you doing your classes remotely?"

He stepped over to her, reaching to possessively stroke the top of her head. Flushed and irritated, she pushed him away.

"That's not the same." Even as she tried to not sound disappointed, she failed miserably.

"Hey, you know I'm doing the best I can to keep things normal." Anxiety darkened his tone as he asked, "Don't you trust me?"

I have trust issues with everyone lately, she wanted to snarl back. *From the trauma of the last couple of years, remember?*

Recalling how his every waking moment seemed spent protecting her or helping others, she swallowed her complaint. The last thing he needed was for her to undermine his confidence, especially since she had no information about where he was going or what he was doing.

She said, "Yes, of course I trust you. So…have a great trip. Say hi to Greg for me."

"Will do." He bent closer, lifting her chin and dropping a quick kiss on her doubtful lips. "Like I said, I won't be gone long. Greg's hinting at some interesting developments. Might be important, or it might only be a fun diversion."

He returned to his task and she watched him continue to pack, thinking over how some people, like Señora Gomez, might regard him as reserved or even aloof. Of course, they didn't know him well yet, hadn't seen the relaxed side he shared in private.

Following his quick yet sure movements, she was pleased by the boyish, conspiratorial half-grin he intermittently flashed her in response to the intensity of her gaze.

She had other questions, such as: *If you ever meet Singer again face to face, what will you do? Would you kill him for what he tried to do to me?*

Unready to voice this aloud, she smothered the words behind a forced smile. While she wasn't ready to forgive or forget, she also knew revenge fantasies were pointless and unhealthy.

Without warning, from deep inside herself came a slight fluttering sensation, followed by a faint tap. Her face lit up as she placed her hands on her belly. "He kicked!"

Owen halted. "Really? Are you sure?"

"Yes—put your hand here!"

Eagerly, Owen sat beside her, pushing up her shirt and placing his hands on the firm flesh of her bare belly.

After waiting a few moments, he announced, "I can't feel anything. He's avoiding me!"

She laughed. Owen took his videoskin from the bedside table and powered it up. Then he selected one of his visor implant's scanning features, linking it through the videoskin while announcing, "He can't hide for long."

"Can you record some of this for my mom?"

"Sure."

Delighted, they viewed the indistinct human form that squirmed energetically within the soft confines of an obscure inner world.

Sofia said, "I think he's going to have your nose."

"How on earth can you tell? He's so blurry."

"Can't you see it? It's obvious!"

Her voice thrilled with affection; Owen replied with a smirk, but looked uncharacteristically self-conscious. She noticed his cheekbones reddened somewhat as he bent over her.

After a few minutes more watching the small form, Owen switched off the device. "I feel bad, spying on him." He set the videoskin aside and rested his open palms on her stomach.

Placing her hands over his, she said, "You can press harder. You won't hurt us."

They both held their breath; after a moment, she thought she felt another slight sensation. She said, "It's too faint for you, I guess. Give him a month or two to get bigger."

"Sure."

Eyes locked on their intertwined fingers, Sofia added, "Please don't be gone too long."

Fingers tightening over hers, he said, "You can bet I'm coming back to you two as soon as I can."

CHAPTER
SEVEN

SLIDING open the glass patio door, Richard MacIntyre stepped into the rooftop garden of his high-rise condominium. The older man's spare, gently stooped form passed along the manicured paths of the minimalist, Asian-inspired garden. At the safety rail, he paused to look over the city.

His dark eyes squinted toward Puget Sound, and the Space Needle, renamed Hope Spire. The landmark pierced the lowering veil of clouds, lit with evening gold while above drifted layers of gray-violet.

The late summer evening was quiet; traffic was muted, and the celebratory riots that had rocked the downtown over the past weeks were now subsided to a mere smolder.

Shadows deeper than the oncoming night wound through large swathes of the cityscape. Electricity had been unreliable during the past month or so, and there was no discernible pattern as to why some locations had service while others didn't. These blackouts were growing more frequent and widespread, even for a region that still doggedly attempted to derive most of its electricity from wind, solar and biomass.

Throughout the neighborhoods, ads for the new government communications carrier, FreeVox, heralded the imminent return of wireless voice and internet service within the region—at least in most urban areas.

MacIntyre had also noticed a few campaign banners cropping up about the city, for candidates from new political parties with exciting names such as the

Successors, Rise Up, or Forward Now. There was increased talk of special elections being scheduled soon, to replace the current interim governing body, the Central Committee.

MacIntyre was still dazedly coming to grips with the uncertainty and inconvenience into which his life had been plunged without warning. Or if there were advance warnings about the formation of the People's Democratic Republic of Pacifica, he had been too caught up in his daily work to notice. Now it was here, all about him; without lifting a finger, he found himself living in a 'new' country. He had no clear opinion on the matter, but generally felt uneasy.

Turning his attention back to his garden, he inspected some of the potted bamboo and ornamental Japanese maples rising demurely from huge concrete planters punctuating the space. As the light continued to fade, more solar garden lamps came to life, illuminating the paths and a few meticulously planned points of interest about him.

The finished product was just as simple and restful as he had originally conceived it, but since his exhaustively detailed, computer-generated plans had been so life-like, he felt little pleasure in the experience of the real thing. Reality wasn't markedly different than the simulations had been. He already felt inclined to rip it all out and start a different project, just to feel again the interest and excitement of a new beginning.

A new beginning, he observed moodily, thinking over the disruptions to the internet, and the enthusiastic public rallies that had spilled into violence on several occasions. Thinking of his last glimpse of his stock portfolio, and its precipitous downward trajectory following the PDRP's emergence.

He thought also of the agitated phone call he had received two days earlier from his ex-wife, Jocelyn.

He had not been surprised by her peremptory tone, her insistence that he help her locate Owen. She claimed their son and his wife had disappeared from New Astoria weeks earlier, and that while Owen had communicated to her that the couple was safe, he refused to reveal their current location.

Richard was unsure what she expected him to do about this situation. He reminded Jocelyn that Owen and Sofia were adults, and that the former had a track record of entertaining dangerous ideas and associates. If that habit had blown up in his face, it wasn't his parents' responsibility to rescue him. Jocelyn had ended the conversation in the familiar state of displeasure which typically marked their infrequent interactions, and Richard proceeded to dismiss the exchange from his mind.

He was not entirely successful. Shivering as the evening wind mounted, he returned to his condo. Wandering into the kitchen, he supposed it was time to eat. He placed a container of leftover *pad thai* in the microwave, detachedly observing as it revolved beneath a bombardment of invisible waves.

He was resigned to meals consumed in the company of silent memories: memories of his failed marriage, of his young daughter, killed in an accident on an icy winter road many years before. Memories of his own outspoken, abrasive father who, during an atypical bout of depression, had agreed to a state-authorized 'Passing' ceremony. Memories of a son who turned against him after that, and who rarely reached out.

Richard was twitched out of this doleful reverie by his front door's chime. The survcam revealed two men in dark uniforms. He opened the door and regarded them with vague apprehension.

The taller, broader of the two immediately flashed an official ID. "Richard MacIntyre? I'm Lt. Easton Foster from the Internal Security Agency, Northern Command. This is my colleague, Sgt. Matteo Torres."

"Good evening," MacIntyre said guardedly. "What can I do for you two gentlemen?"

"We need you to come with us to the offices of the Northern Command." The lieutenant made a jerking motion towards the corridor. His manner made it clear he was not to be questioned.

"Yes, of course." MacIntyre obediently collected his jacket. He pulled it it on as he accompanied the men from the condominium, approaching an unmarked law enforcement vehicle at the curb. Richard was ushered into the cramped back seat, with Foster settling himself solidly beside him, Torres supervising the controls. Neither officer spoke to their passenger during the tense drive across the city.

They arrived at last in the subterranean parking structure of a huge, menacing concrete edifice. They took an elevator up several floors, then went quickly along a maze of crowded corridors. On a subconscious level, Richard took a professional architect's interest in the building and pronounced it efficient but needlessly dreary.

"In here," announced Foster without warning, as they stopped outside a glass corner office with sliding doors. Its venetian blinds were lowered for privacy. Torres slid the door aside and motioned MacIntyre over the threshold without another word.

From behind the desk, a broad-shouldered man in dark-gray shirtsleeves, with a mane of silvery hair and cold, light eyes shadowed by heavy brows, looked up with an impassive expression. A large German Shepherd reclined on the floor near the desk; the dog cocked its head and watched as Richard crossed the room. The man behind the desk rose, showing himself to be even taller and more imposing than Richard had initially guessed.

The man extended his hand. "Richard MacIntyre?" His cordiality put MacIntyre more at ease.

"Yes, hello."

"Pleased to meet you—take a seat."

"And you are—?"

The man's smile stiffened. "Take a seat."

Richard did so, avoiding eye contact with the German Shepherd, lying only three or four feet away. He'd always been uncomfortable around dogs.

He refrained from staring about the room, but couldn't help notice there was no name plate on the desk, no identifying certificates or awards on the walls. The man opposite him wore no badge or ID tag.

MacIntyre asked, "Excuse me, but who are you and why do you wish to see me?"

The man regarded him a moment before saying, "My identity isn't important at the moment. Mr. MacIntyre, I'm sorry to inconvenience you, but I need to ask a few questions. And I need your replies to be honest."

The man's air of authority was undeniable. Richard said, "Well, yes. Of course."

"Excellent! May I get you a coffee or tea?"

"No, thanks."

His mysterious host was quiet for several moments, adjusting some of the folders on his desk. Then he said in a pedantic, stiff manner, "Mr. MacIntyre, you and I are fortunate to be living through exciting times. Unprecedented times. We are privileged to be witnesses to the birth of a new era. The previous order was weak and aimless in its vision, its lack of resolve. It was corrupt and ineffectual. But even as a new day dawns in this region, the emerging country of Pacifica is at a vulnerable point in its history."

Bewildered, Richard nonetheless nodded sagely at this speech.

The man went on. "Due to this vulnerability, we must be extra vigilant to do all we can to protect our new nation."

"Erm…yes, certainly."

Picking up a work tablet from the desk, the man made a selection and angled the screen towards Richard. "Tell me—can you identify this person?"

The screen displayed two separate images that looked like personnel files from a law enforcement agency. They also looked like before and after photos: before, a young man regarded the camera with the same deceptively vacant but also arrogant expression that had been so exasperating to his parents during his teen years. The 'after' showed the same man, but older and wearing the black visor-like vision implant he had earned through his dangerous duties as a cyber defender at the Northwest Regional Law and Safety Agency down in Oregon.

Studying the photos, it struck Richard that perhaps what he had always interpreted as arrogance, was in reality thoughtful reticence. He himself knew what it was to be judged aloof and prideful by jealous colleagues.

"Yes, of course I can identify him," said Richard in a low voice. "That's my son, Owen MacIntyre."

Nodding, the nameless man set the tablet down. "Would you say you have a close relationship with your son?"

Richard frowned and lifted his long hand in a vague gesture. "Close? We don't visit often, but we speak once in a while."

"Excellent. When was the last time you heard from him?"

Jocelyn's nagging alert replayed in Richard's mind. He knew he must answer with caution, but also truthfully. He said, "I think we last spoke about four or five months ago."

"What about?"

"I don't recall it clearly, but I guess we probably talked about when he'd be able to come up to Seattle for his next visit."

At the time of that conversation, he'd sensed neither Owen or Sofia were exactly spoiling for a chance to see him again. Their visit of the December before last had been strained and awkward; that trip had ended with unspoken relief on all sides, and the parties had gone their own ways.

"Did he say when that might be?"

"No, we didn't pick a date."

"And you're certain this was before the recent disruptions in travel?"

"Oh, yes. Definitely before."

"Have you had any communications with him since the restrictions went into effect?"

"No, connections have been too unreliable."

"Yes, it's been challenging for all of us. But tell me, when you last spoke with him, did he mention whether or not he was planning to go on a trip outside the West Coast? Or even outside the United States?"

MacIntyre's heavy brows contracted. "No, we didn't discuss anything like that at all. In fact, he mentioned he was so busy at the Agency, he had no idea when he'd be able to go anywhere."

The man made a low, considering noise in his throat as he processed this answer.

Eager to appear helpful, Richard added, "I guess you'd probably get more information from his Agency. I know nothing about his schedule, certainly not since all this Pacifica business began."

Leaning back in his chair, the man stroked his chin as his eyes narrowed. "Thank you for that excellent advice. But if we knew where he was, we wouldn't be bothering you."

Still pretending to be ignorant of Jocelyn's information, Richard sat up straighter. The dog reacted to his sudden movement with a low growl.

He asked cautiously, "You mean—he's missing?"

"Yes, that's the general gist of this interview."

It was impossible for MacIntyre to ignore how intently the nameless man scrutinized his reaction to this news. Mind casting about for the least incriminating response, Richard hazarded, "Don't the officers all have trackers?"

"Ideally, yes, but it seems Greg Park allowed your son to opt out of that requirement."

"Gregory Park—wasn't he a captain at the Agency?"

"Yes. He was also a close associate of your father, Evan MacIntyre, and a frequent guest at your home many years ago. I'm sure you haven't forgotten that?"

"No, of course not. But we haven't spoken for quite some time." MacIntyre hoped he didn't look as pale and sweaty as he suddenly felt.

He had purposely buried the history of Park's visits and that man's obvious fascination—and agreement—with Evan on politics and culture. "Probably twelve or thirteen years, at least."

The man behind the desk bunched, then smoothed his lips. When he spoke, his tone was still easy. "Your son was in professional contact with Captain Park for at least thirty-six months, from the time he started employment at the Agency, and was presumably on cordial terms with him until his disappearance. And you yourself had no interactions with Park during that time?"

"No, not since I moved to Seattle. As you pointed out, he was my father's friend, not mine."

"And yet, entertaining the both of them in your home on a regular basis, I'm sure you heard some intriguing conversations. Did you know Evan was on a watchlist of associates of domestic terror suspects?"

"I knew he was...outspoken. But that was years ago."

"It's all on the family's permanent record."

Richard could not tell if the man was joking or not, and swallowed hard.

The man continued. "In any case, I'm sure you remember some things. I imagine there's nothing more stimulating than when bright and opinionated personalities gather around the family dinner table. The critical mass of ideas can be very influential on impressionable young minds, such as your son's."

Suppressing his mounting annoyance, Richard asked, "I'm sorry, but where is this going? I'm really confused."

His faraway tone tinged with a slight mockery, the man said, "It must have been very difficult for you to stand by, helpless, as your sole surviving child was courted, then corrupted by those men. To witness his affections being turned from you, taken over by them and their ideology. I imagine it was painful for you to basically...*lose* him like that. Especially so soon after losing your daughter."

MacIntyre's nails dug into the sweaty palms of his tightly clenched hands, as he fought the sudden stirring of his own hurt feelings, the sense of betrayal he'd endured during those years.

His interrogator added, "I'd very much appreciate it if you could recall any connections between those days, and anyone Park or your son might be in contact with now. Any name, any mention of any location—however distant— would be helpful."

"Believe me, if I could remember anything at all, I'd tell you."

"Would you tell me that Jocelyn Griffiths placed a call to you two nights ago, and you spoke with her for almost fifteen minutes? Or did that incident slip your mind?"

Richard jerked his head to one side in a negative motion.

The man insisted, "Did the two of you discuss the whereabouts of your son?"

"Yes, of course. She has no idea where he is, either."

"Where *they* are, actually. His wife is also missing."

Concealed in his lap, Richard's hands convulsed again. He said, "Don't you have a transcript of the call? I'm not hiding anything."

The man leaned back in his seat with a slight, luxurious stretch of his shoulders. "I'm sure you've noticed the utilities have been unreliable in the recent weeks."

Confused by this sudden shift in the topic, Richard said nothing.

His host went on, "It's difficult to say when they'll be completely restored. In fact, between you and me, there is the possibility that the region's food supplies may also be impacted over the coming months. I don't say any of this to alarm you, it's just that these types of privations are to be expected in a period of flux."

Richard made a noise of wordless agreement.

"But I can assure you—resources are always more readily available to some groups than others. For instance, individuals who commit to full cooperation will have uninterrupted access to all the basics. In addition to not having their financial accounts seized."

The shade of a response struggled, then died, in Richard's throat.

The man said: "So, if anything at all pops up in your memory, if you hear from your son, even the slightest, most trivial communication—please let us know at once. I don't work out of this office very often, but Lt. Foster will provide you with my private contact protocols when he takes you home."

Abruptly, the man leaned forward. "Because in addition to possessing information helpful to the PDRP, I believe your son has absconded with regime property. I can't stress enough how eager I am to locate him."

Feeling his gut loop into icy knots, Richard nodded. Through his memory, Jocelyn's voice insisted, *"They are so secretive, but I suspect Sofia is pregnant! You'd think they'd at least want to share that news with us, wouldn't you? Why hide it? What are they afraid of?"*

CHAPTER
EIGHT

OWEN MACINTYRE SURRENDERED the car and left the rental office, relishing how good it felt to stretch his legs after the drive from the airfield serving Rapid City, South Dakota. Before that, he'd endured a lengthy commercial flight from Calí, traveling under yet another false name.

Across the cracked, weed-dotted parking lot of the rental business, a man waited near a beat-up brown sedan. The first thing Owen noticed about his former supervisor, Greg Park, was how healthy and energetic he appeared. Over the last months, the sixty-something, Korean-American widower had recently lost enough weight, and radiated enough confidence, to seem almost twenty years younger. An impressive feat, considering the stress he'd been dealing with the last eighteen months or so.

The next thing Owen noticed was his sense of deep fondness towards the older man, who'd been a part of his life since childhood. Memories flooded him as he caught Greg in a brief, spontaneous embrace. "Wow, it's really, really great to see you again!"

Greg responded with a vigorous clap on the younger man's back. "It's crazy how it feels like it's been years, not just a couple of months."

As they drew apart and stood regarding each other, MacIntyre felt a pang of regret for all they had lost, as well as bittersweet happiness for shared times. Owen felt a profound gratitude that, whatever might come, at least they had this opportunity to see each other in person again.

"Well, let's hit the road—there's a lot of ground to cover. Literally and figuratively," said Park, wiping the lenses of his eyeglasses on his shirttail. The men slid inside the automobile and fastened their seatbelts. The interior was cramped, flimsy and dirty, typical of the poor-quality, aged vehicles most of the population made do with.

As they left the parking lot, Greg said, "I'm glad you took the time to meet with me. And don't worry—I'm not going to wheedle out where you've been hiding."

Owen offered an easy grin. "Not hiding. Just catching my breath and… recalibrating. What about you? Any sign you're being watched?"

"No, and don't worry, I'm taking every precaution. Say, how are you fixed for resources?" Greg's manner was earnest, fatherly. "Remember, if you need anything, the network takes care of its own."

"Good to know. But I'm fine for now. I made sure my accounts were out of reach of the chaos." Relaxing into his seat, Owen added, "Fill me in—what's the latest? Heard from Enrique?"

Greg frowned. "Not directly. But it's rumored there's a chance he might meet up with us soon, maybe even during your visit."

"Great, I've been fighting a bad feeling about him."

"Everyone has bad feelings these days." With a short, bitter laugh, Greg steered the sedan down the freeway ramp and forced the aged contraption to pick up speed. "Pacifica is hanging over us all like a toxic cloud."

"What's your take on whether or not they'll be successful, or will they crash and burn?"

Greg pondered this question. "It's still too early to say. As you can imagine, D.C. is an enflamed termite's nest of insanity at the moment—there hasn't been a situation remotely like this since the eighteen-sixties. It seems three of the senators from the rogue states are repudiating the coup, but three others are taking their chances with the new regime and have been stripped of their seats in the Senate."

"What about the Representatives?"

"At last count, about two thirds have self-exiled from Pacifica and are loyal to the U.S. But of course, under the circumstances, they're completely unable to represent their constituents."

"Yeah, I imagine that would be tricky. Any other inside dope?"

Greg exhaled a dissatisfied breath. "No. But broadly speaking, the secession has thrown a huge monkey wrench in our other plans."

"I assumed that. I'm bracing for the details."

"Well, under the radar, President Chakrabarti had made a lot of headway, cleaning entrenched progressive 'Successor' sympathizers or actual operatives out of the Government on all levels. And she was getting ready to issue several important Executive Orders, including one that rescinds many of the old restrictions against the rogue churches. Even though most of them aren't enforced anymore, it could be a huge, positive public relations jackpot."

"Okay, what else?"

"In academia and industry, some of the old-guard are retiring from their influential spots, and we've been able to move some allies into many important positions."

"What about the mindshaping campaigns running over the last two years? Any signs those are still impacting the general populace?"

"Somewhat, but remember—those are only a small part of our overall plan, our 'long game'."

"Well, sure."

While not involved in any of these efforts, Owen was still familiar with the ways in which public opinion could be shaped, how behaviors could be nudged and guided into specific tracks. Past regimes had built an impressive system that used education, entertainment and state-sanctioned drugs to craft a docile, if unproductive, society. The *novus ignis* initiative was learning to overcome moral squeamishness and implement some of these methods in their own cause.

He asked, "Okay, so tell me how Pacifica changes things."

Park sighed. "It's like this: our side is tempted to downplay this coup as a pathetic gesture, but for many folks, it represents a tangible Utopia. The sudden success of this endeavor—even if it's only an illusion—has injected a lot of life into a political philosophy that was almost dead."

One hand lifting from the wheel in a frustrated gesture, Greg said, "We've made significant advances against the decay, the apathy, and were getting closer to erecting a replacement structure over its corpse, but now—many of the 'old guard' progressives are rallying to this new symbol. So they're scrambling to turn popular opinion in favor of the new country, using all the public and private tricks in their arsenal."

Shifting, Owen distantly considered the passing landscape without really seeing it. Low, shrub-dotted hills undulated to their right, rolling brown grasslands spread on their left. He said quietly, "Then Chakrabarti had better get on the ball and ramp up a counter-propaganda campaign, hadn't she?"

"Believe me, we've got people working on that, too. But what we really need is some specific, actionable intel about what's going on within their borders."

"Well, I've got nothing. I doubt appearing in front of Congress to testify that Hayden Singer fired me and then menaced my wife will rally folks to military action."

Park shot him a concerned look, "What do you mean—how did he menace Sofia?"

Not replying, Owen deliberated over the events of the last year. It didn't take much for him to relive the sense of foreboding he'd felt when then-Governor Gray had summarily removed Superintendent Campbell and replaced him with the unknown Singer. Looking back, it was obvious the move had been one of the key plays in the build-up to the eventual coup.

At the time of Campbell's dismissal, Owen's foreboding had not been mitigated when he'd gotten to know Singer better, and even now, he still grappled with the deep loathing he harbored toward his former Superintendent. He would never forget Singer's expression, icy yet perversely delighted, as he'd forced Owen to watch Agency surveillance footage of the lashings Sofia had received from the Public Virtue Division. And that was only one foul thing among many he'd done.

Subdued, MacIntyre answered at last, "I'd rather not say. Long story, over and done with."

"Then, no, you're right—that wouldn't help turn the tide of public opinion," murmured Park doubtfully. His manner became more businesslike, yet also brighter. "But none of this is why I asked you to visit."

"Yeah, I didn't think so. Where are we going?"

"Someplace...very intriguing." The man pushed his old-style eyeglasses up to the bridge of his nose while keeping his gaze on the road. "What if I told you we're about to enter a whole new world?"

Since Park was typically pretty cut-and-dried in his opinions, not given to hyperbole, Owen wasn't sure what to make of this. He said, "Guess I'd say it was mysterious hints like that that brought me here."

"Okay, now, I don't want to get too excited about this, because nothing is perfect," Greg said guardedly. "But I've spent the last few weeks in one of those alternative communities we've heard rumors about, and if the stats the Aeon Institute and others have been compiling about these strongholds are true, we've got a much bigger pool of allies in the age-old 'culture wars' to draw on than we realized."

Elbow resting on the edge of the car window beside him, Owen dubiously rubbed his long, lean jaw. "I know there's rumors of parallel communities scattered about, but aren't they exaggerated? Are any of them more significant than small enclaves of religious communities, like the Nightcrawler nomad clans? Or the—I don't know…gangs of off-gridding Libertarian Gnostics?"

He pointed to the flat grasslands streaming past his window. "The population of these groups can't be very significant. There's practically no one *out* here. When I was on assignment, traveling with Tomás Chen, we didn't even see any signs of Nightcrawler caravans."

"That doesn't mean they weren't there. That's how it seems to anyone who isn't looking—these groups are masters of concealment. Plus, they're content to capitalize on the rumors they prey on unsuspecting urbanites. Of course," added Greg, with a pragmatic shrug, "Many of them actually *are* a threat to unsuspecting travelers."

"Tell me about it."

"Hey, those paramilitary raiders were a breed apart," protested Greg. "Plus Chen was a magnet for kidnappers."

"That he was," Owen grunted in agreement. As he watched the landscape, he recalled the intense, stress-saturated hours he'd spent in the California wastelands, in the clutches of opportunistic thugs who hoped to collect a hefty ransom for Tomás. Unwilling to hand over payment, Tomás' brother, Francisco, had resorted to violence to free them both.

That escapade had taken place almost three years before, when Park had tasked MacIntyre with investigating a plot to import Thorn, an unlicensed and dangerous hallucinogen. Forced out of his office, from behind his computer screen, MacIntyre entered a larger world that in many ways, he was still coming to terms with.

At the time, both Chen-Diaz brothers were targets in the investigation, and after befriending the unsuspecting Tomás in Chicago, Owen had spent nearly a week in his company, taking an unhurried trek across the country to San Francisco. Once they were beyond the vast suburban zones sprawling out from the cities, Owen saw firsthand how desolate, how abandoned much of the nation was.

Although America had not suffered as devastating a 'demographic winter' as that which depopulated most Western countries, the effects of the previous decades' global depression were still very much in evidence everywhere they went. Owen and Tomás had driven through many hundreds of miles of bleak emptiness without seeing another human soul. Occasionally, the wastelands were punctuated by the upright, decaying skeletons of small ghost towns, which soon became mere flickers in the rearview mirror of Tomás' little sports car.

In some ways, that road trip had been an excursion to an ancient, long-abandoned empire, an empire ravaged by economic decline, conflict between cultural factions, conflict between a directionless, unhealthy populace and its own semi-functional government.

Park's voice cut into Owen's reverie. "Yeah, all our lives we've been told there's nothing out here worth experiencing. Or else that it's flat-out dangerous, that no one but backward hicks or vicious bandits live in the countryside."

Grinning, Park shook his blocky head with its grizzled hair, cut in a close, no-nonsense buzz. "So, most urban dwellers go about their business with heads down, just trying to survive, confident in their assumptions that they're safer where they are. The territories between cities are considered worthless."

Owen nodded.

Park continued, "But those assumptions are part of the long-term propaganda war the older regimes pushed. Even the Aeon Institute dismissed these alternative enclaves for years. But at last they've sent some observers into the field and now we know the real numbers are far, far different. The Feds have *no clue* about the reality out here."

He jabbed his finger toward the driver side window, indicating the empty grasslands and occasional trees whipping by. "And if they do, they have no plans to deal with it—because they can't comprehend the import. They don't want to believe it."

As they traveled in a southeasterly direction, Park revealed his theory that, over the decades, the authorities had dealt with the rise of sophisticated, extensive parallel cultures by developing an intentional blindspot regarding them. Like a dog that had sustained significant injuries while driving a badger to its earth, they had learned after a few tussles that it was not worth the effort to pursue them.

Furthermore, he reasoned the civil authorities were too busy propping up their bloated bureaucratic infrastructure, while looting the last dregs from the once-robust economy, to devote dwindling resources to investigation or harassment of these alternate communities.

"So it turns out, it's been this way for years," Park concluded, voice resonant with enthusiasm. "But it's not just the authorities censoring or manipulating the data—these communities have intentionally kept very low profiles."

"Yeah, they sure have." MacIntyre countered, "But so much former farmland—even national parkland—was sold to foreign corporations decades ago. Doesn't that severely limit where these types of enclaves can be located?"

Park chortled. "Oh, come on—don't you have any idea how big this continent really is? There are hundreds of thousands of acres no one wants, and where no one is looking, no matter who owns it. Think of the mushroom cultists in our own state and national forests back in the Coast Range. Well, in Pacifica, now. In any case, we never had accurate figures for how many groups were hiding out in our own backyard."

Recalling how well these cultists, and extensive illicit businesses such as gun smithing operations, had concealed themselves, MacIntyre had to concede Greg's point.

Park continued, "Plus, real estate regularly exchanges hands and some CEOs are more sympathetic to *novus ignis* than the government realizes."

"Interesting," murmured Owen. He considered his next comments with care before admitting, "I need to be honest, though—I'm not sure how much more time I can devote to Restoration work."

Park shot him a frown. "What are you saying? Have you started a new career already?"

"Sort of. Look, it's just that, under the circumstances, I need to re-evaluate what I want to be doing, for the good of my family."

"Family? You mean—?"

"Yes."

"That's wonderful, congratulations!"

"Thanks." Owen's brief smile faded almost at once. "So, I guess I want to know: do you really need me? Don't you have others who can breach systems and monitor campaigns and so forth?"

"Of course we do. But it's not just a matter of skills. It's a matter of loyalty, of commitment."

Frustrated, Owen absently rubbed his temple. He hadn't planned on voicing his doubts so suddenly, and under these circumstances, but he didn't like keeping Greg in the dark.

Calmly and firmly, he said, "Greg, you know I'm loyal. I'm just saying I need to restructure what my commitment will look like going forward. I might need to cut back and become more of an…occasional consultant."

His former captain exuded a disappointed silence. Then Park said crisply, "We can discuss this later. Let's focus on where we're going today."

"Okay, fair enough. I assume we're headed to one of those enclaves now?"

"Yes. But for obvious reasons, they have strict security," cautioned Park. "And although I'm staying with them, and I've vouched for you and really laid it on thick, let me do most of the talking. You're not armed, are you?"

Thankful he had decided against bringing his small beam pistol, MacIntyre answered easily, "Of course not."

"And they have strict rules regarding tech use within their boundaries. They won't be happy to see that VIA unit, but I think I can convince them you're trustworthy."

"And if you can't?"

"Prepare to disappear into a shallow grave, I guess. Or at least be prepared to be scanned thoroughly when you leave, to confirm you haven't recorded anything."

MacIntyre answered with a sarcastic snort, "Great, you're really selling it. I can't wait to meet these guys."

"Trust me, it'll be worth it."

They continued through a veritable wasteland for another hour or so. By late afternoon, they entered a small hamlet, little more than a handful of ramshackle dwellings lining a gravel road.

Waiting at the far end of the street, the double-wide manufactured home of faded blue had a battered contractor's trailer parked in the drive, and was surrounded by a minimalist yard strewn with a few simple toys. A child's bicycle lay abandoned on the small patch of threadbare grass.

After parking the car, Greg and Owen approached the front door of the home. The door soon opened and a man stepped onto the porch. He raised then dropped his hand in a tepid greeting, then made a slight gesture that indicated he wanted them to meet him at the back of the house.

There, an expansive deck dominated the space. The man descended the deck steps and stood impassively before the newcomers. He was in his late thirties, clad in mud-spattered work clothes and heavy, worn, leather boots. His black hair fell to his shoulders, his dark eyes were set in skin of deep brown, and expressed reserved alertness.

He said, "Sorry, but the baby's asleep, so my sister doesn't want anyone coming through the house."

"No problem," Greg grinned. "Steve, this is the guest I told you about." He turned to Owen. "This is Steve Two Buffaloes."

The man nodded politely towards Macintyre. "Hello."

Owen returned the slight nod. "Pleased to meet you. I'm Griffin Lewis," he said without missing a beat.

Park addressed their guide, "This visit was pretty damn hard to set up."

With a laconic shrug, the man said, "Yes, but that's how things need to be. Which reminds me—," From his back pants pocket, he drew an older model, enforcer-grade scanner. "Sorry about this."

"No problem," said Park. He and MacIntyre remained motionless as Two Buffaloes passed the device over them both in a desultory manner, then studied the results on the screen. He did not strike Owen as hostile or suspicious, just doing his duty.

"Okay, let's go." Two Buffaloes indicated the end of the dusty lawn dotted with more abandoned toys. Where the mangy grass ended, a small dirt trail whispered into the golden-brown grassland stretching to a distant stand of trees growing near low hills.

Along the trail, the three of them walked single-file, an air of anticipation growing as they passed through the dry grasses and dying wildflowers of late summer. The tranquil scene was intermittently ruffled by the melodious warbling of Red-winged Blackbirds, glimpsed among the waving golden tops of the grass. An occasional grasshopper flitted by drunkenly with a clacking sound, to land briefly on the packed dirt trail in front of them before careening off again.

MacIntyre began to sense that Two Buffaloes, in addition to not being prone to small talk, was also building drama through his intentional silence as he led them a quarter mile through the fields.

Then, without warning, the man stopped.

Trying to locate what their guide was looking at, MacIntyre scanned what appeared at first glance to be an empty, slightly hilly meadow that sprawled about them to all horizons. After a moment, his visor picked up a few anomalous distortions in the view, and then he knew where to focus his attention.

He caught his breath, a disbelieving grin dawning across his face as he gasped, "What the hell is this—!?"

Park turned to him, beaming with delighted pride. "Impressive, isn't it? Welcome to Underhill."

CHAPTER
NINE

AS HE PREPARED to step from the small side chamber and commence that weekday's Liturgy, Fr. Nicholl sought to keep his mind locked squarely on each moment as it came, to not look too far ahead. To trust and be at peace.

It was a struggle. He was still disturbed by Enforcer Bolling's unannounced visit to the rectory the night before, following on her warning of the previous Sunday. Accompanied by an armed escort, she had brusquely entered the residence and ransacked Fr. Nicholl's bookshelves, seizing a couple bins' worth of incriminating titles and catechetical handouts. The priest was issued a fine on the spot for not having a copy of the Power Cult's "Book of Guidance" displayed in a prominent location.

When both officials departed, Cosimo had stood a moment reading another copy of the 'suggestions', the ones he had torn up before. These included the relevant passages from the Book of Guidance on which he was required to preach over the next weeks, as well as the specifications, down to the quarter inch, of where the propaganda placards and photos of the President and the Secretary of Cooperation were to hang in the main body of the church.

While he had no intention of complying with any of this, he also felt no sustaining rush of defiant strength at his resolution. Rather, his mind and emotions were worn down, he was coming to the humbling realization that he was not one of those strong, confident, merry leaders to whom his dwindling congregation could look with hope during times of turmoil and danger. Instead, he felt a strong temptation to give up and comply.

Dredging up some strength, he had at last resolved to not enact the demands on this list. In any case, it was a waste of time to work with these officials, most of whom had the intellectual depth and subtlety of pit bull dogs. They would never be satisfied, would merely see his compliance as a weakness to be further pushed and exploited.

As a not-so-subtle taste of things to come, soon after Bolling's departure, the parish buildings were plunged into darkness when the electricity was cut. The fuel for the emergency generator being long spent, Cosimo was grateful it was still summertime. The darkness of that night made him feel like a child again, reminding him of the years following the disastrous attempts by global climate engineers to adjust Earth's mean temperature by spewing sun-screening particles into the atmosphere.

With a wry smile, he recalled his mother's comments on how the arrogance of experts often led to inconvenience or outright suffering for the common man. She had been a spare, gray-faced but gentle woman, not given to complaining. But as she watched the anemic stalks of the vegetables struggling in her garden, starved of natural light and CO_2, she had more than a few acid words for those who believed they knew better than the average person how the world worked in reality.

Cosimo believed the current campaign of harassment was a similar bid by the regime to establish control over that which they had no business controlling, a bid which the priest knew in his bones was doomed to fail. Whether or not he lived to witness that failure seemed irrelevant at the moment.

He made no effort to sleep that night, but instead went to the church and prayed for hours, kept company by the light of a single candle and the warmth of his own faith. He did not pray so much for guidance, as for continued strength to go forward one hour at a time. Little comfort came to him and in the morning, his head felt heavy, his thoughts were slow and scattered.

Now as he left the side altar and entered a church illuminated chiefly by sunlight, his heart sank when he saw how few people were present. Agnes Okamoto, who for years had overseen distribution of food to the families living in camps on the city's edge, was missing. He hoped that Agnes, as well as the MacIntyres, were among those who had successfully fled before the borders were sealed.

He was fairly certain the curvaceous and ebullient young Jen Connor was still in the city, but likely hiding out at home. Praying in secret, perhaps hating herself for her cowardice, yet desperate to survive. He dared not risk attracting attention to her by visiting or even sending someone to check on her.

Among those who still dared come, he guessed some attended out of defiance, some from inertia, others were motivated by a placid, trusting love. Determined to be a beacon for these few, he had kept the parish schedule as normal as possible.

Looking over the handful of worshippers, he sighed and blinked back unexpected tears. These few were so loyal, so obviously filled with trust in and love for the Lord. He felt unworthy to be their shepherd.

Clearing his throat, he began his sermon. "Why do we ever act surprised at man's inhumanity to man? Each generation believes it should be spared inconvenience, persecution, atrocities. But why? Why should those of us who know how Christ was treated expect to be spared any of this? When were we ever? We know history. And those who live without Christ—whether they are existing in ignorance or else seeking Him out to destroy all traces of Him in their own hearts, in the culture—they are indeed a fierce, determined adversary. They wield the weapons of the world. We have only gentleness and love, which is why it feels we are always losing."

As he preached, he noticed various sensations passing over the faces fixed on him, like clouds and sunlight chasing each other over the waters of a lake on a wild spring morning. He saw concern, he saw wearied resignation. He saw peaceful acceptance. But on Joe Murchison, he saw stone-faced resentment.

Nicholl had engaged in enough private conversations with Joe to understand the burden of frustration and hate for the authorities under which the man was struggling, and Cosimo feared the consequences should he succumb completely. From some of the man's rhetoric, he suspected Joe had connections with shadowy locals, the types to run guns or set up some kind of resistance movement. But Nicholl felt it wise to keep these suspicions to himself.

Voice stumbling as he re-focused his thoughts, the priest continued. "In the face of this great wave of dread that now hangs over us, we must remember that all things will come to an end in God's own time. Whether it is all at once, or bit by bit, ultimately makes no difference. What matters is how we meet that end. Will you meet it with trust, or anger?"

The silence that fell after he ended his remarks was more ominous than he could bear. With difficulty, he picked up the threads of the ceremony, tongue clumsily reciting prayers that were typically closer to him than the beating of his own heart. In his distress, his mind seemed to play tricks on him. Faint strains of music came and went from outside the church walls.

Once, he paused his prayers to listen more closely—was it his imagination? But no: a tune, both lively and haunting, interweaving melodies and beats enticing and degenerate, was sounding louder and louder. It was also faintly familiar, like the eerie, elusive melody from a dissolving dream that lingered but could never be captured entirely.

A few worshippers grew restless, glancing with troubled expressions back to the main doors.

Perhaps someone is driving by the building with their car radio on full blast, Cosimo told himself.

But he knew this was not what was happening. His hands shook as he redoubled his efforts to pray. Even with his back to the main doors, there was no mistaking the sound of these opening; the music grew much louder.

Heavy footsteps marched down the center aisle. Acceptance Compliance Enforcer Bolling's voice rang out: "Everyone, may I have your attention, please? Forgive the interruption, but all are invited to join us outside for a brief intermission! Please, it will only take a few minutes—!"

At the sound of this announcement, Cosimo lowered his head and closed his eyes for a moment. The time for worrying about what he might do in this situation was past. It was time to act—by not acting.

Raising his head and turning, he looked out the open church doors. He caught a glimpse of colorful flashing lights, pulsating in time to the music. Bolling carried a sheaf of posters under her arm, cheerful images printed on thin, rigid plaques. Three other officers accompanied her.

Gripped by confused indecision, the worshippers watched her quickly advance to the front of the church, where she began affixing the rigid posters over the sacred paintings on the iconostasis. She moved with bold, theatrical motions that belied the slight trembling of her hands. Soon lively graphics and simple slogans, together with the larger-than-life portraits of the new government officials, beamed at the assemblage.

Swallowing, Cosimo found his voice and said, "I'm going to have to ask you to take those back down and leave the building while we finish the Liturgy. Whatever circus you've set up out there can wait."

Bolling's bright smile congealed. Then, at her signal, the armed officers began to stride down the aisles, making demanding flicks towards the congregants with the ends of their weapons.

Ignoring Cosimo, Bolling faced the congregation with raised hands. "If you will all just step outside for a few minutes, I think you'll be pleasantly surprised by what you'll find. There's nothing to be frightened of, if you just come with us."

The small crowd exchanged bewildered, distrustful glances. Whispering among themselves, a few looked to the priest for guidance. He could only twitch his shoulder, encased in the brocade of his heavy vestments, in a helpless shrug.

Beneath the threatening gaze of the armed officers, the group trickled dutifully out of the building. The AC Enforcer caught Cosimo's eye and jerked her head meaningfully towards the end of the receding crowd. "You, too."

Suppressing a sigh, he stepped down from before the altar and walked along the center aisle towards the oblong of daylight and fresh air. Lowering her voice, still smiling stiffly, the woman turned to Cosimo. "After our presentation, you'll be given an opportunity to tell them you made a mistake, that you meant to deliver the sermon as outlined in the notes I gave you."

Cosimo's gaze remained straight ahead, his head erect as he answered, "How do you know I didn't? You cut the power, so the survcams were offline."

This time, her laugh was sincere. That made it seem even more dangerous. "I don't need to see an active stream of your ceremony to know you didn't follow the guidelines. I only have to look at your face. Am I right?"

He answered with raised brows and a thin, gray smile.

Outside, the music became more obnoxious; it rolled in waves from a large, customized van waiting in the church's parking lot. Fin-like panels of videoskin deployed from the van's side, while from the roof was unfurled a large, umbrella-like dome. Chairs, tables, and trays of enticing food were set up. An enforcer's patrol car was also parked nearby.

The scene was dappled with a pattern of colored lights, winking in time to the music, which slowly became less brash, more soothing. Most of the congregation milled anxiously on the perimeter of the gathering space before the bus, but a few began to take seats and look towards the screens.

There's a subliminal tone in that music, Cosimo thought glumly. This would confirm the rumor that the regime was ramping up its own targeted mind-shaping techniques on the populace. He guessed the settings on the devices worn by Bolling and her accomplices cancelled out the subliminal tones and allowed them to focus on following orders.

But he himself felt the vibrations emanating from the vehicle, was aware of the intangible, unearthly tingle seductively passing through his awareness. As the sensation increased to a blend of complacency and mild, trustful curiosity, he worked to thrust those feelings aside.

The videoskins and the dome now shimmered to life, bursting with inviting imagery of blissful citizenry gamboling among nature scenes, too perfect and too beautiful to be real people or places. They were mythic, fairytale dells and meadows. The guards stood by to ensure no one left their seats. A few of the younger children tried to get closer to the food, but were restrained by their parents. Most sat perched on chairs in attitudes of unease, but those expressions were gradually softening.

Except for Joe Murchison's. Nicholl noticed the man seemed more agitated than usual; his deep brown face was a mask of suspicion, he appeared to be restraining himself with great effort. Sweat trickled down the sides of his skull to grow lost in the tight curls of his grizzled black beard.

Mindshaping tones don't calm everyone, thought the priest dimly. Sometimes they triggered the opposite of the desired effect.

The presentation contained faint themes of praise, in a weak parody of a more traditional service. When it ended, Bolling put her hand on Cosimo's arm and drew him forward.

Under her breath, she said, "Explain to them how what you do for them is similar to what we are offering. We have the same goals, too. And we have as much music and pretty pictures as you do, but we are so much happier and united. Can't you feel it yourself?"

Cosimo shook his head. He was surprised to hear how calm yet loudly his own voice sounded. "You won't convince anyone by just aping a few outward trappings. You know your Book of Guidance is a joke. Everyone despises it."

Bolling tipped her head back and flared her nostrils, taking her time to look each one of the group in the eye. Her voice rang through the parking lot: "Is that true? Do you all despise the wisdom in the Book of Guidance?"

No one spoke. Feet shuffled, shoulders shrugged.

Then Joe shouted, "Yes! Damn right we do!"

With a disdainful glare, the woman announced, "That's really too bad, because it means I'm going to have to shut down your gathering for today and take Mr. Nicholl to Headquarters, where someone will talk sense into him."

She made a quick gesture to the nearest officer, then readdressed the assembly. "Let's hope I won't have to come back for the rest of you."

Pulling a set of heavy plastic zip restraints from his belt, the officer stepped up to Cosimo, then fumbled under the latter's vestments as he sought the priest's wrists.

There was a tide of shocked and confused mutterings from the congregation, but no one moved to aid Cosimo. AC Enforcer's voice, sounding exasperated, announced, "Please—everyone remain calm. A new presider will be assigned to this community within a day or so, and you will then have the freedom to resume your worship services, with only a few modifications—,"

Joe called out, "*Stop right there!* Hands off him—let him go!" Joe stood rigidly, a small gray pistol gripped in his large hands. "I said—let him *go!*"

"Joe—this is not what I need you to do," began the priest. The arresting officer wrenched the ties shut on him, while the other two instantly covered Joe with their own weapons.

"Drop that—*now!*" commanded the one closest to him.

Ignoring this, Joe's eyes locked on Cosimo as he pleaded, "What else can I do?" The small pistol trembled in his hand. "If they take you in now, who knows where you'll end up—at what point are you going to put your foot down and tell them *no*, you're not going along with all this?"

"I think the chance for doing that is long past," Cosimo turned to him with a rueful smile. "It's time I stretch out my hands and be led where I don't want to go. But we've known this hour would come sooner or later—haven't you heard anything I've preached all these months? These years? We were always living on borrowed time."

Lifting his head, he addressed his flock, "All of you—please—don't make it any harder for me or for yourselves—,"

He looked back at Joe, while pouring as much firm gentleness into his gaze as he could. Murchison lowered his hands.

One of the other officers drew closer, reaching out to snatch the pistol.

Joe jerked his hand away; startled screams erupted as a bright energy bolt seared into the pavement near Bolling's feet.

Another bright bolt answered from the farthest officer's weapon.

Murchison uttered a sharp cry, face twisting in pained shock. He crumpled and collapsed, knocking aside several folding chairs. Noxious smells from the burnt cloth and seared flesh over his heart drifted in the morning air.

"I said remain *calm!*" shrieked Bolling. It was difficult to tell if she was more frightened or angry. "Everyone—out of here, now! For your own good, go home!"

With a dreamlike sense of unreality, Cosimo found his arm grasped firmly as he was shoved toward the patrol car.

He managed one glance over his shoulder at the frightened group standing over Joe's body. From that moment, their looks of stunned, helpless horror were seared into his spirit.

CHAPTER
TEN

OWEN QUICKLY LEARNED that the village of Underhill existed partially at the surface, but mostly just beneath, what appeared to be hundreds of acres of undeveloped grasslands and gentle man-made mounds. Its engineers had pushed the art of camouflage to the point of practical invisibility. When Owen observed the surroundings more closely, he spotted a few entrances in the hillsides, but if he hadn't been shown where to look, he'd have missed them.

Steve Two Buffaloes led the visitors through one of these portals, then instructed them to wait as he went ahead and consulted with two young men who, despite their lack of uniforms or obvious armaments, gave off unmistakable sentinel vibes. After passing through this checkpoint, their guide left them and Park was free to take Owen on a tour.

Traveling further into structures carved from living rock, they explored a network of corridors, passed private living quarters, and admired public meeting spaces. Obedient to the injunction against recording what he saw, MacIntyre nonetheless remained alert and made mental notes about every detail.

Despite extensive use of concrete and molded fiberglass to reinforce the layers of local shale and chalk, the overall result of the construction was surprisingly light and airy. There was an organic aesthetic in the softened angles and rounded corners that reminded MacIntyre of a virtual reality tour of ancient Cappadocia and Derinkuyu, in Turkey, he had taken in grade school. As well as of the Australian town of Coober Pedy.

After exploring several levels, Greg took him back up to the surface and they strolled among the low-profile roof gardens. As Owen critically reviewed the entire complex from that perspective, he was again amazed at the simple but effective optical diffuser features that concealed the open-air structures from prying patrol drones and satellites. This effect was made more impressive given the geography.

It was one thing to conceal unlawful, off-grid encampments throughout the forbidding wilderness of the Pacific Northwest's impenetrable forests; it took a different level of tech, and a very bold mindset, to pull it off on the open, exposed prairie.

A distant flutter of camo netting caught his attention and he zeroed in on a group of large, inorganic shapes clustered on the far side of the network of crops. As his VIA unit implant brought the shapes into focus, he quickly dismissed his earlier guess that they related to agriculture.

Turning to Park, he said in a low, excited tone, "Hey, that's a microreactor, isn't it?"

Park nodded. "Bingo. Powers this whole complex, plus a few more settlements to the east."

"Wow, that's fantastic. Wish we had been allowed more of those back in Oregon, we'd have had fewer blackouts."

"Yeah, well you know that control of power is itself a form of power."

"No doubt." As Owen continued to evaluate both the immediate surroundings and the far landscape, he was struck by a sudden thought. "Is this settlement part of the Oglala reservation?"

Park laughed. "No, we're outside their borders here. But there's some overlap in the communities, intermarried families and such. It helps that they share some basic philosophies."

The scene was bathed in the rose-gold light of the setting sun. With his visor set to maximum field of vision, Owen drank in the panorama, aware of a timeless, placid and inexorable sense of strength and optimism that seemed to quiver in the air, the very ground. A few yards away, a large crowd of young children ran about in the fields beyond the extensive garden plots. Puffs of dust and happy shouts drifted through the peaceful evening.

He commented wonderingly, "I've never seen so many kids in one place."

"Me, neither," Greg confided cheerily. He added, "Did you know your granddad wanted to start his own education pod for you and some of the neighbor kids when you were six or seven years old? But there weren't enough kids in the neighborhood. Plus, your parents were horrified at the idea, of course."

"Yeah, I can imagine. But at least Evan got back by underwriting my training for the Agency later." Owen's attention again focused on the kids. He murmured, " 'Peach Blossom Spring' isn't just a Chinese legend."

Greg chuckled. "Well, this is as close to that as you can get in the real world."

Once the sun sank below the horizon, the visitors left the deepening evening behind and descended again into the colony, finding it now lit with lanterns, as well as ribbons of more efficient illuminated cables. Although the lanterns weren't strictly needed, Owen guessed they were an aesthetic choice and appreciated the cheery, homey glow cast throughout the corridors.

As they entered a communal dining hall, Park said, "Help yourself to anything—I'm treating tonight. They have their own unique credit system."

Taking up plates and utensils, they passed along the abundant buffet running the length of one wall. MacIntyre hadn't realized how hungry he was, and was heartened by the amount of fresh beef and the variety of vegetables dishes on offer.

As they took seats at a small, more private table in a corner, Greg said, "I've been working since I arrived about three weeks ago, and have earned a good bit of credit."

A bottle of deep-amber beer stood beside Owen's plate. Contemplating the label's old-fashioned woodcut of a bison, he asked, "They have their own currency system? I'm surprised that hasn't brought the Feds bursting through their doors."

"Well, they deflect that kind of scrutiny by still officially accepting all forms of U.S. currency, even digital. But they prefer not to."

"Okay, I see. What have you been doing for them? Fishing is your only survival skill."

Greg looked hesitant. "Actually, I've been working in one of their mushroom farms. I'll take you on a tour after dinner."

Owen's jaw dropped as his brows rose over the top of his visor. "Wow, like one of those species of ants that grows fungi underground?"

Corners of his eyes wrinkling with good humor, Greg stabbed a forkful of tender, smoked brisket. "Yeah, exactly like that."

The surreptitious glances from a few of the other diners didn't bother Owen. He was used to the fact that his VIA unit was the first thing people noticed about him, and as both an outsider and a cyborg, he knew he stood out in what was presumably a very close-knit community.

After the meal, Greg was eager to show him some more interesting features of the colony, such as the extensive work and store rooms, the brewery and a distillery. At last, Greg ushered him into a large chamber in the industrial zone, part of the gourmet mushroom operations that formed a key component of the local economy.

"Here, let me show you what I've been doing—," Greg indicated a rack full of pendulous, compost-filled grow bags parked along one side of the room. At first, Owen was attentive to the other's eager summary of the workings of the crop, but soon his mind wandered away from the flood of biological minutiae to more practical details.

He regarded the cavernous, well-lit workspace. "Do they get a lot for this variety?"

Park nodded. "Sure do. It's a breakthrough in genetic modification and it's a damn impressive meat substitute. In fact, all the crops from the hydroponics rooms are quite profitable. The local cities seem to run on vegetables."

"Helps keep them tractable, I guess. Along with the other mushroom crops —the 'medicinal' ones."

With a laugh, Park glanced back at the other workers and said under his breath, "They don't approve of growing those here. But some of the Libertarian settlements don't have an issue."

"Yeah, I'll bet not," agreed Owen, his mouth twisting in lopsided amusement. "But there's got to be more to this economy than mushrooms and beer."

"Of course." Greg dropped his voice further and asked with a carelessness that did not conceal an underlying excitement, "Do you know anything about the honey mushroom?"

Resting his hips against a nearby metal cabinet, Owen folded his arms across his chest. "Let's say I did, but forgot it all. Refresh my memory."

"It's possibly the largest living thing on Earth, and it's been spreading through the Malheur National Forest for thousands of years. Seasonally, a few mushrooms can be observed growing on the trees, but most of the organism is unseen, underground."

"Tentacles in all sorts of industries, in other words?"

Greg ran his stubby, muscular hand over the heavy plastic sheeting of a large grow bag. "Precisely. It turns out many of these communities have connections to high tech businesses that fled Silicon Valley and the Seattle area a couple of decades ago." He added under his breath, "And not just industry—even without participating in person, their influence throughout other sectors of society rivals what the Aeon Institute, and the Restoration, have been working for decades to achieve."

Owen exhaled a silent whistle. "That's exceedingly...reassuring."

"Exactly."

After the tour, Park took him to his private quarters. Gesturing to the mini fridge in the kitchenette, he asked, "Another beer? Or something else?"

"Thanks, but you know, I'm good with just water at the moment."

"Visor still giving you trouble in that area?"

Owen was momentarily taken aback by the question, then remembered he had confided that the implant's connections interfered with his hormone balance, sometimes amplifying the effects of alcohol. "Yeah, I need to cut back in general."

"Good for you."

Greg pulled a chilled glass bottle of water from the small refrigerator and passed it to Owen as the younger man settled on the couch.

Taking a beer for himself and then sitting in a shabby overstuffed chair, Park kicked off his shoes. Then he settled back and fixed his guest with an earnest gaze. "So—tell me your honest impressions of Underhill."

Absently stroking his chin, Owen said, "I think it may be too good to be true."

Greg looked disappointed. "What's that supposed to mean?"

Owen thought about what he had witnessed over the last few hours. He shook his head. "I mean...it's stunning. I'm glad you wanted me to see it for myself. It's great there's more to some parallel societies than one guy, ten women and a couple of goats insisting they're a sovereign nation."

Park guffawed. "Well, I wouldn't discount those people, either. From what I've learned, anything's possible."

Owen said, "I think the fact they developed organically, that they aren't a planned, top-down community, is a good thing for their chances of long-term survival."

Greg's eyes brightened. "Yes, I agree."

Owen took a drink, feeling his typical cynicism reasserting itself. Raising one shoulder, he added, "What they've built is impressive, very attractive, but I'm curious—how does it fit into the big picture?"

"That's exactly what we need to determine. We have to face the possibility the goals—or at least the methods—of *novus ignis* might need to be re-evaluated."

"Can you explain what you mean?"

Park sighed. "I mean—this entire subculture has become its very own thing, and only one of many 'things'. Social identities throughout the country have been fragmenting into smaller and smaller micro societies for generations. Pacifica is just the most recent, most extreme example. I guess the best term is 'Balkanized'."

"Yeah, that's a good take. But your colleagues realize we aren't going to restore an idealized United States, don't they?" Leaning forward with his forearms resting on his knees as the bottle dangled from his fingers, Owen hazarded, "You know I'm not a monomaniac on the subject…maybe I know more history than most of my generation, but I sure don't have the nostalgia that you and your colleagues do. I can't feel fired up about a place that ceased to exist decades before I was born. We're not going back to baseball and apple pie, to the…fantasyland from classic films or tv."

Greg regarded him with a long, perceptive look. "Of course not. Maybe I was too eager to think you'd be fired up about the idea of reclaiming something from the past, I thought you'd be like an adventurer hot to mount an expedition based on the directions from an old treasure map. But maybe you're too cynical."

Owen didn't reply. He lowered his head, uneasy at the other's gentle displeasure.

Greg took a drink of his beer and stared into the distance. "You know, when I was younger, I was more like you than you realize. I was pragmatic and frankly, a bit of a political agnostic. But over the years, I've seen too many coincidences, too many small events that can't be discounted, that all add up."

Raising his head, Owen cocked a brow. "What do they add up to?"

"I believe that overall, we're being guided towards something good. Maybe the 'map' is a fake, or it's saying something we haven't figured out yet. Maybe we'll never reach our destination, but on the other hand, we might find something completely unexpected along the way. We might have the chance to build something new on the foundations of a lost empire."

A portentous lull settled over the chamber. Park set his own bottle aside and interwove his fingers as he leaned forward. He said, "I've almost talked Anne into coming out for a visit. I think she'll like it."

"Professor Riordan? From the Aeon Institute?"

"Yep, that same Anne." There was no mistaking the fond respect in the older man's voice as he spoke her name. It sounded deeper than mere professional esteem.

Owen concealed his knowing smile behind another drink of water.

Greg asked, "Is there a chance Sofia would be interested in migrating?"

With a hearty laugh, Owen gestured around their surroundings. "Are you selling condos here, or what?"

Greg's scowl was tempered with a wistful chuckle. "It's just that…well, this place gives me hope. It embodies what I always imagined the original American spirit must have been like. The ingenuity, the determination." He picked up his bottle. "Come on, Mac, isn't that appealing?"

Owen grew more serious. The idea of settling someplace like this, was undeniably intriguing. Underhill was substantially unlike the decayed Texas suburbs where Sofia's parents were settled, a remnant of America's supposed heyday. Underhill was also a very different environment from what he and Sofia were experiencing in Colombia.

He wondered if they would ever be at home there, in an unfamiliar culture where he had to keep his head down and get by at the whim of the entrenched oligarchy. While he wasn't ambitious, he knew it might be hard to really advance under the circumstances.

"It is appealing, and I'm grateful you convinced me to visit. But I have a lot to consider."

Later, after Greg had retired to the small bedroom, Owen tugged a blanket over his shoulder while trying to find a comfortable way to fold his tall frame on the short couch. The chamber was surprisingly chilly. He was resigned to a restless night, his mind filled with impressions from the long and eventful day, with the import of everything he'd witnessed. Even the sleep-stimulating Theta waves the implant generated weren't helping him relax.

Peach Blossom Spring, he thought. *Shangri-la. Rivendell. Galt's Gulch.*

Out of legend, the names of these fanciful, hidden kingdoms dazzled his imagination, provoking hazy but comforting impressions of Sofia sitting in a field of yellow grass, laughing, as she held a sturdy infant boy in her arms. Both were carefree and looking ahead to a future of dazzling promise.

CHAPTER
ELEVEN

SEATED behind the controls of his vehicle, parked in a steep, narrow driveway, Hayden Singer contemplated the dead windows of the small home nearby. Its coat of federal blue paint, with cream trim, was degraded by the merciless salt air. Its minuscule front yard had been mowed with a cursory, uncaring hand that hadn't bothered to trim the overgrown shrubs on the margins.

The neighborhood was thick with similar unassuming houses; weather-beaten, cheaply constructed structures that had sprung up as part of the massive post-earthquake rebuild decades earlier. This particular home was one of the modest, single-family dwellings the old Agency had provided its more elite agents. It was currently unoccupied.

From the rear seat, Greta emitted a slight whine, as if asking Hayden to explain why they were here. She had been patiently at his side all day while he worked in his office at Headquarters, and could not understand why they'd taken a detour here instead of going straight home for the evening.

He roused himself and opened the car door. "Hey, pup, ready to get digging for evidence? Let's go, girl."

He led the way up the front stairs, Greta pattering after him. After entering, Hayden secured the door behind himself, then stood a moment in the entryway. Despite the fact he'd ordered the electricity restored a few weeks before, the surroundings had the clammy, un-lived-in feeling of an abandoned dwelling. The sliding glass door off the kitchen was open a crack; a few dead leaves had drifted in and collected near the empty pet dishes in the corner.

Greta uttered a rumbling growl and cocked her head towards the door. Outside, a gray-striped cat sat on the rail of the tiny deck, looking into the kitchen. Hayden pulled the door shut; Greta barked and the cat blinked at them both. Then it rose, stretching with slow, seductive carelessness as the dog's growls increased. It jumped from the railing and disappeared into the neighboring yard.

Singer began examining the possessions in the house. Untidiness sprawled throughout the rooms, silent beneath the dust, but it was not the mess left by residents who had fled in haste. It was the disorder of rooms that had already been ransacked by the authorities. By men acting on Singer's orders.

Following the MacIntyres' flight, he'd had the home sealed. Owen's computer had been sent to the Agency tech lab for analysis, and unsurprisingly, was found to be wiped clean of anything related to suspected Restoration activity.

Now Hayden was conducting a private inspection of all the items still on-site. He'd already scoured the home office in person, removed desk drawers and examined the frame for secreted flash drives, notes or discs. Thus far he had found nothing useful.

This afternoon, he walked the rooms with slow, meditative steps, retrieving items from the floor, handling them with his bare hands, replacing each one where he reasoned it had been located originally.

On the main bookcase in the front room were a handful of framed photos, which he approached and studied. Singer had already compiled extensive dossiers on the missing couple's respective families, and could easily put names to all the frozen faces smiling or squinting back at him.

He regarded the Volkov family as less interesting than the MacIntyres, but didn't rule them out as being potentially useful. He never abandoned any scrap that might come in handy, even if he didn't immediately see how it fit in the overall picture.

Picking up a photo of the youthful Owen with his parents and sister, Singer's lip curled in mild contempt for what looked like a last-ditch attempt to present a happy, united family to the world. He knew the whole arrangement had flown apart less than two years after the picture was recorded.

Setting all the photos in the bottom of a nearby cardboard carton, he returned to the shelves to peruse the book titles. It gave him a perverse thrill to touch these items, as if he was gaining a secret power over his adversary. Especially through touching the books.

A commentary on the French Revolution caught his eye and he selected it, turning the pages with delicate, considering motions. On some level, he was both jealous and threatened by the knowledge contained in these books.

The volumes of philosophy in particular represented a vast intellectual kingdom, far beyond anything he or his colleagues had access to during their perfunctory State-approved education, where their learning was little more than rote memorization of State-approved slogans. To Singer's eyes, most of what was printed in these old books might as well have been written in a foreign language. His own interest in military history was usually explored through virtual reality or video files, not text.

"Very impressive library," he muttered aloud to the absent owner. "The books you left behind in your Agency office were decoys, weren't they? Nothing too controversial or incriminating there. The real library was here at the house all along. Dear old grandpa's legacy, isn't it?"

With such a high sentimental value, Hayden assumed it was painful for the younger man to leave this collection behind. It was also valuable, and potentially dangerous. Singer believed the library might tell him many useful secrets. He meant to search each page of each book in the entire house, alert for any sign of the old-school, but still useful, cryptography techniques he suspected would appeal to the traditionalist members of the Restoration.

Thus far, he had discovered no pinpricks below words or single letters, but continued to look for any seemingly innocent marks, underlining or smudges, that might form a pattern, the hint of a code, any code.

There was nothing out of the ordinary; as far as he could tell, any underlined passages, dog-eared pages and highlighting, all related to the ideas themselves in the particular paragraphs, rather than their usefulness in passing secret messages.

"I'll bet anything you didn't read most of these," he addressed his adversary, in a spiteful hiss. Replacing the book on the shelf, his fingers lingered for a moment on its shabby spine. The thought that anyone would willingly consume so much printed material made his head feel thick and stupid.

"You couldn't have, not at your age. You didn't have time."

MacIntyre had always given off a quiet vibe of being superior, of having secrets, that Singer found both maddening and alluring. He assumed much of this was a façade, a persona worn like a stylish jacket. But some part of him wanted it to be true, wanted to be further challenged by the other's mysterious, sophisticated depths. On another level, he caught a glimpse of how he also wanted MacIntyre to be equally impressed with him, but realized he had nothing to offer but threats.

Hayden went down the corridor to the stairs, climbed to the master bedroom. As Greta waited beside him, he stood in the doorway, regarding the rumpled bedclothes, the garments tumbling from the bureau drawers and laundry hamper.

At the closet, he ran his hands languidly over the remaining shirts and jackets. He took a well-worn plaid shirt off its hanger and methodically examined the pockets and seams. Finding nothing, he tossed it on the bed and selected another. He repeated this ritual for many minutes, the pile of clothes steadily grew.

Greta's whines penetrated Hayden's awareness, and he gave an encouraging wave of his hand. "Go ahead. Make yourself at home."

She sprang on the bed, turned around several times, then settled with a blissful grunt in the midst of the garments and disturbed sheets.

"Good girl," he murmured, seating himself on the edge of the mattress. For several moments, he absorbed the colors, the shapes of all the objects filling the room, the styles of the clothing, the titles of the books.

Then his body sank backward on the bed beside Greta. Closing his eyes, he put everything out of his mind except what he could smell, hear or feel around him. There were dim traffic sounds from the street outside, a lingering whiff of mildew, and very faint, fruity shampoo from the pillows near his head.

Greta sighed, and he reached for her, running his palm over her silky ruff. As he sprawled across the absent couple's rumpled sheets, he thought of the private lives lived within these walls, the acts enjoyed on the surface beneath him.

As memories of other beds and other humiliations prodded him from his subconscious, his clutching fingers tightened into the dog's fur. He lived with a visceral discomfort around the mundane horror of a simple bedroom door, fueled by his early years with his mother and her two partners. His most primal memories were of sensing how the adults regarded him as being in the way, that he was unwelcome. At least at first.

His mother had cast off her legal name of 'Dorothy' and remade herself as 'Morrigan' prior to joining the faculty of the Social Studies department at UC Berkeley, where she also attained a position at that school's Center for the Study of Sexual Culture. By age five, Hayden had internalized the fact he was something of a prop to appear in publicity videos, to be lavished with affection in front of news crews whenever the press was covering his mother's latest academic publication or political opinion.

In later years, Hayden speculated if he himself hadn't actually been the subject of an ongoing academic project; perhaps Morrigan had been making extensive but secret notes about him. If so, she never published the results. And he did not dig deep in that area, as there were other events in his childhood that he did not want to be reminded of any more than he could help.

Despite the social status afforded by Morrigan's position at the university, the Singer family hadn't qualified for a superior housing allotment. Dysfunctional economic conditions had put even the most humble of historical bungalows beyond the pooled resources of the three adults. From their neighborhood, the well-preserved mansions overlooking the Bay were as distant as Olympus, the occupants unchallenged and unquestioned as they carried on the customs of their oligarch predecessors.

Thus Hayden's earliest memories were of cramped, chaotic, narrow rooms filled with indolence and mental illness. He was trapped like a small ghost in a filthy, crowded anthill of an old apartment, where a child could scarcely find the exit to fresh air and sunlight.

When he did manage to slip out unsupervised once or twice, it was to explore what passed for a neighborhood in the surrounding acres of graffiti-covered concrete, government social service buildings, low-caste street camps and burnt-out vehicles. While this wasteland was in some ways intriguing, it was also overwhelming for such a young child, so he invariably, if with reluctance, went back home.

There, he spent much of his time hiding in his room, emotions numbed, immersed in his virtual reality equipment, set at maximum volume. The digital experiences offered an illusion of freedom, they helped shout down the awareness of what he'd once glimpsed through the partially ajar door to his parents' room. For an interminable moment, he'd been transfixed with revulsion at the sight of the doughy rolls of fat hanging off his mother's body, of the clamor of animalistic groans and cries as Layton and Cade took turns with her, then with each other.

Escaping from that reality into the world of VR, he returned repeatedly over the months and years to exciting battlefields, in any place or time. He learned strategy at the sides of wise emperors and legendary generals. Their stiff but otherwise life-like visages became something of a family to him. He was especially fascinated by and drawn to the culture of Sparta.

Overall, the technology helped his unformed and vulnerable ego secrete a protective nacre about the ever-present horror of his untenable situation. His mind survived by building up an image of himself as a genius, talented and indomitable. The examples in the games gave him more strength to plan, to hack out the kind of life that would at last make him comfortable and respected. Someday, perhaps even feared.

His thoughts returned to the present. In a moment of honesty, he wondered if he wasn't spending too much time focusing on MacIntyre—did the fugitive cyber defender possess any information that would be helpful to Pacifica, or had that been a projection, was Singer deluding himself?

But even the slightest lead was better than nothing, so he once again fell to contemplating the pieces he had to work with. He was haunted by the feeling he was overlooking very important, very obvious clues, but was frustrated by not knowing where to begin.

I don't have time to read all these damn books for signs of codes, he told himself with a flash of anger. *But the fact he kept them must mean something.*

Abruptly, he recalled the existence of Sofia's InNova game account, which he'd learned about in the hours before the couple escaped. Was it possible that important files had been concealed inside the game library?

Jumping up, Hayden returned to the home office where the VR helmet and sensor gloves were stored. He looked up the account's password in the case notes stored on his videoskin, then powered up the illicit Quasar satellite link he had previously brought here, waiting for a connection with one of the few functioning satellites still serving the region.

When he at last succeeded in accessing the game, he found himself entering an elegantly-appointed formal drawing room, a setting from Jane Austen's novel, "Persuasion". He suppressed a condescending chuckle at this glimpse into Sofia MacIntyre's psyche. When Sofia's friend, Jen Connor, had been questioned, she indicated that the couple had spent considerable time in this game, which in itself raised red flags in Singer's mind—he didn't think MacIntyre was the type to play video games, certainly not one as dull as this.

So what had he been up to in here? Simply humoring Sofia as part of a tame, vanilla-flavored heterosexual fantasy? Or had he found another use for the tech?

Hayden stood in the illusion of the sumptuously appointed room, surrounded by settees upholstered in rich silk, illuminated by the soft light from a multitude of slim beeswax tapers. He regarded the stiff, false figures that peopled the set, accurately costumed in the attire worn by the British upperclass in the early 19th century.

One of the characters resembled MacIntyre from his old personnel files, before his implant was installed. It was an impressive digital recreation, clad in a British Naval officer's uniform that more than hinted at the athletic physique beneath. Hayden caught his breath, then strode up to the apparition and ran his gaze over it lingeringly.

"Good afternoon," he said with uncharacteristic levity. "We've got a lot of catching up to do, don't we? You can start by telling me what hole you're lurking in, out in the real world. Then you can tell me where you've concealed your files. Anything you took from the Agency system, anything related to the Restoration network. Trivial things like that."

It couldn't hurt to be direct, and he felt the confines of the false world to be liberating.

The digital construct turned towards him, disconcerting in its smoothness and lack of expression. It was also startling in its resemblance to Slate at the time they first met. But of course, this *inkarn*, this digital shell or mask, was dead and empty. It did not speak. Whatever mode this game was supposed to be played in, Singer hadn't found the right setting.

Still, he was determined to try. "If there's any extra files in this game, direct me to their location. Please."

There was no response from the digital MacIntyre. Singer thought of all the resources the Agency had put into the original's training, only to have him betray the authorities' trust. Drawing closer to the form, he studied the slight shimmer formed of countless points of light, simulating the glow of living human skin. A pulse appeared to throb in the curve of the throat muscles.

The expectant lull of the illusory venue was broken by Hayden's husky murmur. "I wanted you to be a lieutenant…*my* lieutenant. Maybe even something more…your skills would have been so valuable to ISA, valuable to *me*."

It seemed the closer he looked, the more shrewd and disdainful the copy's eyes grew. A knowing, sarcastic shadow crept into the corner of the apparition's well-formed mouth. The collection of ones and zeros was mocking him.

"Damn it all, would it have really been so hard to play nice? Some day you'll regret having such high *standards*—," Cocking his elbow, Hayden drove his fist full-force into the figure's gut. His sensor gloves recorded a ghostly, unsatisfying sensation of impact. The inkarn doubled over as expected, but momentum carried Singer drunkenly forward, careening into a real-world office chair.

"Fucking *hell*—!" he snarled through his clenched teeth.

Wordless, the inkarn straightened, smoothed its costume with cool, self-assured motions, then strode sedately to the other side of the drawing room.

Fuming, Singer left the false MacIntyre and perused the bookcases lining the chamber. There were some suspicious gaps that made him suspect specialized files had, in fact, been placed in this setting and later retrieved. This was impossible to prove, and he was growing frustrated.

"This is a dead end," he remarked aloud in disgust.

Ending gameplay, he tugged off the helmet and gloves, flinging them back into their case. He stood with folded arms, head sunk in thought. What did he hope to accomplish by picking through the abandoned bones of his prey's past life? Was he trying to build a case from non-existent clues?

He rebelled against this idea. *It's much too early to give up! There's still a lot of work to do—I'll ask someone who has more technical skill—.*

Consoled by this plan, he carried the case with the helmet and gloves downstairs and added it to a box of clothing and assorted items. Greta shadowed his steps.

He left the house and dropped the box in the back seat of his car. As he slid behind his vehicle's controls, the videoskin in his breast pocket trembled with a notification. Pulling it out, he read a private update from AC Enforcer Bolling; Hayden's brows lifted and his mouth twitched with satisfaction.

Then he engaged the motor, backed out of the driveway and sped up the hill, heading to the oppressive ISA building that overlooked the city.

There was no guarantee the priest from St. Columban's could shed light on MacIntyre's whereabouts, but Singer was eager to see what he could do to make him talk.

If nothing else, it might prove a pleasurable diversion.

CHAPTER
TWELVE

NEITHER SUNRISE NOR SUNSET, the golden light thrummed with more life than could be contained in the normal course of things. The light was everywhere and nowhere at once.

Just as the man walking before Owen was not there, yet was more real than could be comprehended. When the man stopped and turned to face him, Owen's heart leaped at the familiar smile, the wrinkles of good humor at the corners of the sharp but kind eyes.

Had they been conversing and were interrupted? Concepts and images, like webs, drifted between them on the balmy air. Or perhaps Owen had reentered a familiar stream as it ever flowed, yet also remained motionless and unchanged. He stood beneath a wave forever on the point of crashing over an eternal shore. Questions cascaded through in his mind and he was bursting with joy.

His grandfather's smile broadened in response to this joy. They stood regarding each other in the midst of a vivid, wild-flower spangled field, their minds trading images and ideas.

Evan MacIntyre replied to Owen's sense of puzzlement: *Of course, folks only get glimpses once in a while, if it's deemed necessary, or if they are in the right frame of mind, but yes—this is the end goal.*

Ideas, not words, unfolded in Owen's mind like lotus petals reaching for the sun. Still, cynicism battled elation as he objected, *Nothing we build on Earth can ever come close to this!*

A sense of merriment, sparkling like the foaming waters of a young waterfall tumbling over mossy rocks, greeted this assertion.

Of course not, only fools believe that's possible! But you're not off the hook, you must still try to improve anything you touch. Start inside and build outward! I watch you struggle, you carry so many unnecessary burdens. You need to ground yourself, your whole being in the present, then what's meant to happen will unfold more easily.

How do I build for the future without thinking about it?

Relax your grasp and admit how much is beyond your control—and be prepared for the results to not look like what you expect. Or they might be temporary. And beware of safe havens along the way—just when you think you've found what you were looking for down there, you may get kicked out and have to start all over again.

I don't understand any of this...

You're not expected to understand. And you're not expected to fix everything where you are, just do what you can. That's why you must trust and let go.

I don't like letting go. I'm afraid of what will happen when I do.

I know. That's your biggest burden. And as you learn to trust, be wary of false visions.

Are you kidding me? What kind of advice is that?

The light began to dim, the shining plain on which they stood tilted, shuddered and started to dissolve. Owen fought it, desperate to remain, even as an inexorable force pushed him away.

He shouted the next thought entering his mind: *How are we even speaking?*

Simple—.

With a serene, knowing tilt of his head, his grandfather stretched out his hand and tapped Owen's right temple with his forefinger. An exquisite pang resonated at the site, then disappeared. Then the old man was gone, fading into the dull black of nothingness.

Choking back a groan, Owen awoke suddenly and lay disoriented for several seconds. The sensation that his deceased grandfather had just been with him was acute, but he argued it was only a dream. Just as he frequently told himself that his last encounter with Evan, during his own nine minutes of clinical death years earlier, had also likely been a dream.

This latest interaction *had* to be an illusion, his subconscious working to process the significant events of the last few hours by serving up this imaginary meeting.

As his surroundings solidified, Owen realized he was alone in the underground chamber. He threw off his blanket and rose, stretching out the kinks his muscles had acquired while sleeping on the sofa. He dressed, shaking off the lingering sensation of emerging from a bizarre, yet comforting dream.

But he wasn't dreaming the sophisticated, subterranean village of Underhill; he was still very much here. Leaving the chamber, he saw a message from Greg scrawled on a slate board on the wall near the bookcase: *Went to church for the 6:00 a.m. service.*

By Owen's calculations, the service was likely ending by now. He soon found the church, a large chamber carved in living rock several streets away from their quarters. Mass was concluding; he entered and stood respectfully in the back of the dim chamber, studying the pillars and wall niches which artisans had embellished with either abstract or nature-inspired designs and representational art. The overall effect was part catacomb, part Romanesque architecture.

"Many of these alternative settlements are Christian," explained Greg as he joined him. "Folks aren't forced to believe anything, of course, but citizens are expected to follow, or at least respect, local rules and customs. This village happens to be Roman Catholic."

Owen nodded. Park added, "Anne's a Catholic. Did I mention that?"

"Maybe," MacIntyre smiled. It was impossible to not notice the other's boyishly self-conscious, smitten tone. He wondered if the mysterious Professor Riordan, whom Owen was yet to meet, returned Greg's obviously warm feelings. He asked, "Roman or Global?"

Greg was aghast. "Roman, of course. Anne would never have anything to do with a philosophy that's so close to the Power Cult. She considers Global to be heretical traitors."

Owen gestured toward the altar, asking, "What about you? I know you read the Bible from time to time, but are you ready to sign up for all this extra stuff?"

Appearing both defensive and defiant, Greg jounced his shoulder. "Hey, maybe I'm gathering more data, so I can have some deeper conversations with her."

Owen grinned. "Good idea."

They were interrupted by the arrival of a small, dark-haired boy with solemn eyes who came up to the men and stood at attention.

Park smiled down at him. "You're Chaska, right?"

"Yessir, Mr. Park. You are wanted in the smaller conference room down on Fourteenth Street. There's some visitors."

"Visitors? Who else knows I'm here?" Park looked puzzled, then his face lit up. "Enrique!"

The boy twitched one shoulder but remained regarding him with an expectant air.

Greg said, "Thanks for letting me know. Here—," he fished in his pocket for some small coins and handed them to the young messenger. "Tell them I'm on my way."

The boy trotted out of the chamber and the two men followed. They passed through corridors and across the grand courtyard that formed one of the main gathering spaces of this village. From here, they entered a series of well-lit passageways that were large enough to evoke the feeling of traditional city streets.

At the entrance to the conference chamber, they were met by the sight of a group of men and women gathered around a family huddled at the far end of the room. MacIntyre recognized the woman as Connie Rodriquez, Enrique's wife. A dark head scarf loosely framed a face markedly thinner than he recalled. She had an exhausted, harried look.

Bewildered and on the point of tears, young Antonia and Luis stood by their mother, clinging to her long, loose trousers and rumpled coat.

Greg stepped forward and firmly grasped the young woman's hands. "Connie—great to see you! How are you holding up?"

"Greg, how do you think I'm holding up? For almost a month, me and the kids have been living on peanut butter and crackers out of the back of a rental car the size of a shoebox. Do you know how hard this place is to find, with the weird directions Enrique gave me? Where is he?" Anxiously, she looked past him, towards the doorway. "Is he here?"

Greg grew concerned. "No, not yet."

An expression of frantic terror leapt to her eyes. "He arranged to meet us here! I thought you knew that—where is he? What happened? Did they get him? Oh, God, they got him, didn't they?"

"We don't know that…when was the last time you spoke with him?" asked Park in a low, urgent tone.

Connie groaned, wildly shaking her head. "I don't know, I don't remember! Over three weeks, probably…he told me to not call him once I was on the road, that he would call me. But he hasn't!"

"Okay, okay, I understand."

Connie's eyes locked on his. "Have *you* heard from him recently?"

"No," admitted Park. "Not since the night he told me he'd sent the three of you on ahead of him, and that he planned on leaving a few days after that, by a different route, but before he thought the border would be shut."

"He was too late—!" Her breath came in shaky gasps. "He was too late, wasn't he?"

Leaning over her, Park said firmly, "I'll do everything I can to find out what happened. The problem is, that under the current circumstances, reliable intel is almost impossible to get. So we don't have a clear idea of the conditions inside Pacifica—you understand that, don't you?"

Connie stared at him. Then, drained and hopeless, she nodded dully and sank onto a nearby bench. Beside her, her young daughter began a high-pitched, sustained sniveling; Connie lifted her to her lap and rocked her.

"Yes, yes. I understand." Her face seemed to age another decade.

An older woman with a long, white-streaked braid of glossy black hair, who had been watching from behind Two Buffaloes, now stepped forward and touched Mrs. Rodriguez's arm. "You need to come with me now. Let's get some food in these kids, then you can all rest."

Dazedly, Connie climbed to her feet and allowed the woman to guide her from the room, the children still clinging to her coat.

When they were gone, Owen joined Park near the doorway. He growled, "This could be really bad. And not just for him. Do you think he's told them anything yet?"

"No way of knowing for sure, but it doesn't seem like it. A good sign is that there's been no action against any of our operatives."

"That you know of."

Park groaned and pushed up his glasses, passing a hand over his eyes.

Owen said, "What are we going to do about getting him out?"

"Out of where? We have no idea where he is."

"Then what were you just telling Connie?"

Park fixed a grim, hunted gaze on a random spot on the far wall. "I don't know. I had to say something."

Voice rising, Owen demanded, "There has to be a way of getting better intel out of Pacifica and learning if he's being held at HQ, or if he's been moved to a camp. Or if he had an accident and is in a clinic, or else he's lost in the desert or something."

"Maybe." Park sounded doubtful.

Urgently, MacIntyre went on, "But if they did get him, what if they break him? I know he doesn't have access to much data, but everything your colleagues have built could be seriously compromised if they get *any* key intel."

Park made no answer. Without thinking, Owen said, "Well, at least you don't play favorites. You're willing to abandon him as quickly as you did me to those raiders out in the California desert."

His thick spectacles unable to obscure his hurt look, Greg protested, "I had no choice."

Owen felt his lurking resentment against the other continue to lurch to life when he recalled being abandoned to the raiders. Then soon after, following his assault by the Chen brothers, he'd been equipped with this older model VIA unit rather than the latest in augmented artificial vision, or even basic, normal biological eyes. He'd discovered this was because the older tech was sturdier and easier to customize without going through official channels.

Even though he could never entirely accept Greg's questionable judgement in those incidents, he knew it was pointless to hang onto his resentment. But sometimes it flared and he had to beat it down.

MacIntyre's face hardened as he interrupted, "Yeah, I know. I understood why you couldn't do anything for me under those circumstances, but this is different. This is worse. Because he's way more valuable than I was. We've got to do something."

After a leaden pause, Park's face clouded as he snapped, "Lord, I know that —! Did you think I don't? We'll have to reorganize and secure all our data, right away—!"

"Of course, if he's already talked, it might be too late. But if he hasn't, surely the network will want to try to extract him?"

With a distracted air, Park ran his hands over his gray-flecked hair as he exhaled. "If Singer's holding him at HQ, it will be next to impossible to break him out of there. Plus, it could even be a trap. We'd better hope he's been moved to a camp—might actually be easier to extract him from one."

"Do you know anyone who can help soon?"

"Yes, maybe," said Greg, a spark of hope animating his features. "I've got some contacts with resources we might need. But we have to leave here and set up a meeting at once."

During their exchange, the men at the far end of the chamber, including Two Buffaloes, were throwing them anxious glances, while whispering among themselves. Finally, Two Buffaloes approached Owen and Greg.

"What's up? Anything more we need to know about?" There was an unmistakable edge of wary displeasure beneath his diffident manner.

Glancing at the other men behind Two Buffaloes, Park answered, "We thank you all for your hospitality, but it's time we were moving on."

Two Buffaloes tipped his head toward where Connie had last been seen. "Was she followed?"

Greg made an effort to sound confident. "Pretty sure she wasn't. But it's not a bad idea to increase your security for a few days. Look, I'm really sorry about this."

A moment of strained quiet enveloped the chamber. Then Owen turned to Two Buffaloes. "Will she be allowed to stay here?"

"Yeah, sure. No problem." With reluctance, the man raised his dark eyes to Owen's visor, then looked away even as he tugged his scanner from his pocket. "Well, if you two are moving along now, I need to check that contraption for any unauthorized recordings."

Owen endured the security scan as Park waited impatiently to one side.

When it was done, Greg said shortly, "Let's pack up and get out of here."

A steely determination flooded Owen as he fell into step alongside his former captain. He said dryly, "Yeah, looks like we've been cast out of Eden and it's time to get back to work in the cold, hard world where guys like you and me belong."

Greg threw him a sharp, grim look and uttered a humorless grunt.

CHAPTER
THIRTEEN

LORD JESUS CHRIST, *Son of God, have mercy on me, a sinner.*

Like tendrils of aromatic incense, the words wove in and out of Cosimo's mind. In the hours following his arrest, they became incoherently jumbled with other memories, expanding and contracting out of sequence.

Son of God, have mercy on me…son…sun…will anyone water the sunflowers while I'm gone? The vegetables?

A vision of the wilted leaves and parched dirt in his carefully tended patch behind the rectory drifted past his mind's eye. The leaves became the torn pages of Bolling's directive, burning up in the flame from a church candle.

Sometimes, it seemed he had been taken only a few minutes before. At others, he'd been trapped in this windowless chamber, under these merciless fluorescent lights, for a hundred years.

His vestments had been stripped off him shortly after his arrival, and since the room was cold, he shivered in his simple black cassock. The hard metal chair and the blaring illumination couldn't keep him awake much longer. His left eye was already swollen shut from a severe punch; his good one burned with fatigue. It closed, his head nodded, and for several blissful moments, he drifted towards sleep.

Outside his study window, a crow landed on the sill and looked at him, its beady eyes filled with poisonous contempt. A dagger-like beak rapped against the window glass, shattering it.

"Wake up," said a voice.

A hand was shaking his shoulder. Cosimo's head jerked up and he regarded the blurry image of Hayden Singer, clad in his dark-gray uniform, spotless leather boots, and supple, black leather gloves. One hand clutched a water bottle. Cosimo had not heard the door open; to his sleep-starved brain, the Chief Enforcer seemed to appear and disappear at will, without warning.

Cosimo struggled to appear alert, but his head felt like it was stuffed with lead weights wrapped in cotton. Random, surreal thoughts and fragments of impressions continued to parade through his awareness.

Son of God, have mercy on me…the valley of the shadow of death…who else has a key to the church? Do they dare go and tend to it? The Sacrament?

He thought of the small pieces of holy bread, concealed in the ornate tabernacle. He knew well enough the lock would not keep out determined enemies, and that truth added to his sense of helpless failure.

Have mercy on me, a sinner.

Other familiar words of favorite prayers and comforting psalms jumbled with the impressions from his arrest, with the images that had flashed on the van's videoskins. His brain was tossed on a flood of hallucinations, but he was too exhausted to even be disturbed.

The basement interrogation room at the Internal Security Agency Headquarters had no clock or calendar. Nor were there any obvious instruments of torture. There was a hard metal chair and a stainless steel toilet, all enclosed by walls dingy with fingerprints and stains, lit by ceaseless lights. Forced to make do with obsolete equipment, the institution enjoyed a reputation for having personnel expert at wielding what they did have, making great use of psychological techniques rather than the latest high-tech devices.

The chief's level, controlled voice asked the same questions over and over again. Only once had he raised his hand to plant a blow; afterwards, he'd seemed to think better of this approach, and softened his tone.

The priest hadn't been officially charged with anything yet, but Singer punctuated his questions with references to the last Liturgy's numerous infractions. 'Inciting violence' seemed to be the most serious issue. With no survcam recording to confirm his side of the story, to prove he'd tried to diffuse the situation and calm Murchison down, Cosimo knew it was his word against Bolling's. Any attempt to defend himself would be futile.

So instead, he braced for another round of mind-numbing questions. Questions he could not answer because he did not *have* the answers. Since Cosimo had not the slightest idea where Murchison had obtained his pistol, or where Owen MacIntyre might be hiding, the questions and answers always followed the same general pattern.

Singer gave the appearance of believing these denials, but always circled back to ask the same things, over and over. With altered wording, yet the same content and thrust. But Cosimo sensed this arrangement could not last long. Even now, he groggily detected an edge of boredom in the other man's manner. A remote part of Cosimo's mind wondered if a bored Singer was less, or more, dangerous than the version that had been harassing him for hours.

"So, Mr. Nicholl—it would seem your congregation is a hotbed of dissenters. Lots of troublemakers there for such a small group. Do you think anyone else has access to more firearms?"

"No idea," said Cosimo for what felt like the thousandth time, his voice a croaking whisper in his parched throat.

"Oh, I'm sorry—are you thirsty?" Singer uncapped the water bottle and offered it to Cosimo, whose hands had been freed hours earlier when it was clear he had no fight in him.

When he'd finished drinking, Cosimo wheezed, "Never heard about any weapons. Always preached peace. You have access to years' worth of recordings to review."

"Yes—I've watched many of those and I noticed a subtle undercurrent of rebellion in your style. But nothing...actionable." Singer took the bottle back and capped it. "We've had the rest of your congregation in here over the last hours, and they haven't been helpful, either. Maybe I need to apply more pressure."

"Please...let them go."

"Oh, we did. For now."

Boots squeaking as he paced back and forth, Singer said nothing for a few moments. Then he asked in a calm, conversational manner, "Tell me—did you form any deep friendships with any members of your little flock? Those older survcam records show that MacIntyre was absent from time to time, and I'm trying to determine where he was going. Did he ever mention to you that he traveled on business?"

"Never."

The water only partly revived Cosimo, exhaustion made it hard to drag each word past his numb lips. He remembered a private meeting one afternoon in his study, a young man bewildered and struggling to express himself. The priest thought: *But he did travel...thought he'd once traveled through death and back...a severe reaction to a drug...he left a cup of tea on my desk. It must be ice-cold by now.*

"From death to life," he said, voice ringing loudly in the small room. "Resurrection."

Pausing, Singer glared at him, then stepped nearer. He made a fist and cocked his arm. "If this is about that Jesus fraud, drop it."

Cosimo shook his head. "No...'*Lazarus, come forth*'. Yet not from darkness... from the light."

Was it light, after all? The blinding energy of the Cosmos, or the light of one small candle? Glowing flames spread, leaping higher and devouring wood and cloth, dancing on gleaming candlesticks and vessels.

For a moment, keen interest sharpened the chief's pale gaze. "What did he tell you about himself?"

"He's not sure he's a...believer...even after all that. Too many questions, afraid to let go."

"Afraid to let go of what? What did he share with you?"

"Only came sometimes because his wife wanted him to. I assumed he was...sleeping in on the other mornings."

Singer surprised his captive by uttering a sardonic laugh. His arm lowered, glove creaking as he relaxed his fist. "You may be onto something. Sometimes the simplest answer is the right one."

After another thoughtful moment, the chief demanded, "Did Ms. Sofia ever confide in you whether or not she suspected her husband was involved with illicit activity? Did she mention whether he traveled around the country? Or out of it?"

"Never."

"What about in confession?"

The priest gave a helpless shrug. "If she had, I would not be free to tell you."

His interrogator's face grew stormy. "Don't you understand that things would be much more pleasant for yourself and your followers if you'd agree to make a few trivial modifications to your ceremonies and customs? Most other churches don't have a problem with this, they've been compliant for years. The

Global Catholic Church in Portland has no issue with passing along intel to us from their private 'reconciliation sessions'."

"I don't doubt that. We're separate from them...entirely different."

"Why are you so stubborn?"

The priest's wearied mouth twitched upwards. "I'm afraid it's impossible to explain...to someone...someone like you."

"Maybe you underestimate me." Singer's hand shot out and grasped the other's hair. He wrenched Cosimo's skull back and watched him blink in the bright light. The priest said nothing.

Singer growled, "Fine, don't talk. You're past making much sense, anyway. But I guess you'd say you're the last of a dying breed, one of the few still clinging to your 'principles'. "

Releasing him with an irritable shove, Singer stepped back, face receding to an indistinct, dead mask. "Or maybe you're just fucking stupid."

Cosimo's head sank again and his eyes closed against his will.

Faintly, like words coming to him from the length of a long tunnel, he heard Singer add, "At any rate, there's no point attempting to preserve any kind of working relationship, it's impossible."

"Yes," whispered Nicholl.

"Yeah, it's a relief to admit that and get it out in the open, isn't it? Anyway, since there's nothing more to be achieved here, I might as well send you to the next phase of your journey."

Cosimo squinted at him with puzzled trepidation.

Squaring his shoulders, the man loomed with even more menace before he nonchalantly paced to the door. "Once you get settled in your new location, you'll probably regard our time together here with fond nostalgia."

With a curt laugh and a shake of his head, Singer left. The electric lock engaged behind him with an ominous *clank*.

It was perhaps forty minutes later that a guard arrived to take him away, but when Cosimo later looked back on that moment, it seemed no time at all had passed between the door shutting and opening again.

CHAPTER
FOURTEEN

"OKAY—EBERSOL'S running a little late, but he's definitely eager to meet us," said Greg with a note of relief. He placed his phone back in his pocket as he shifted in the passenger seat of yet another rental car. He added, "Not sure how much he'll be able to accomplish on such short notice, but he's always been ready to step up in the past."

After their hasty departure from Underhill that morning, Owen and Greg had scrounged a last-minute flight to San Antonio. Now they raced across Texas, northward on Interstate 10. A blanket of flat, greenish-brown terrain, enlivened by a few meager trees, stretched to the horizon on all sides. The road surface beneath their tires was cracked and unevenly patched, the concrete barriers on either side crumbling and blackened with scrape marks. The road was virtually empty.

Greg had spent much of the trip on either his old phone or newer videoskin, contacting key Restoration players to advise them of the situation with Enrique. Owen could imagine each person on the other end of these conversations, dropping their current activity, scrambling to check security protocols and upgrade passwords.

It was his turn at the vehicle controls; he was tense with the uncertainty of the situation, with his own sense of helplessness. Being behind the wheel gave him something concrete to do, at least gave him the illusion of control.

He asked, "Who is this Ebersol guy? Do you trust him? You're certain he has the resources we need? Because we need access to some military-grade pieces. Drones and experienced operators, maybe some discreet, independent agents who can advise us for a price."

"I know what we need," said Park. "Don't worry—Charles Ebersol's at the top of my list of folks who can help with all that."

Still skeptical, MacIntyre pressed, "So he knows how to get his hands dirty?"

"Exactly. And he knows folks who are known to get their hands downright bloody when they need to. Or where to find specialized tech." Park suddenly seemed ill-at-ease as a thought occurred to him.

After a moment, he confessed, "In fact, Ebersol's the one who got your VIA unit, and the medical team to install it, to you as soon as I asked him."

There was no immediate answer from Owen. Then he said, "I thought that was through official Agency channels."

"Well, no. It wasn't."

Owen shrugged. "Okay, thanks for telling me. So I can assume he'll know who I really am, and I can ditch this 'Griffin Lewis' persona when we meet? 'Cause he's kind of a drag."

Greg laughed. "I hadn't noticed he's any worse than your real self."

Owen chuckled, then grew serious as he thought over that morning's events. "Our hosts back at Underhill were damn quick to show us the door when they sensed there was trouble. Doesn't bode well for them becoming reliable allies."

"They aren't fans of undue hostile attention."

"But weren't they expecting the Rodriguez family?"

"Accepting refugees isn't the same thing as leaving your citadel to throw rocks at a bear." Park explained, "Listen, at least we are all on the same page when it comes to the big-picture. We may be on different paths, and we may not use the same methods, but we all agree on some kind of mutual end goal. A healthy, prosperous nation that isn't pushed around and spat on by the rest of the world."

"Okay, sure." Owen was surprised by the other's sudden vehemence. "It's just I'm not so sure those are their goals. Seems more like they are content for the rest of the world to keep going to hell as long as they're left alone."

"I think you're wrong. And besides, Underhill is only one community."

"So, then, convince me: you say these enclaves have solid economic connections to the outside, and even wield influence in key institutions, but what other connections have they got to the broader society? I assume they have nothing to do with the StarTraxx tracking implants or the CitizenTrust social cred program, but do they even vote in their local elections? National? If they aren't in the system—,"

"That's an excellent point," said Park. "Some communities do, some don't."

"Any idea on the numbers of those who *don't* participate? How hard would it be to convince them to take an interest?"

Park laughed sardonically. "Pretty hard, I'm afraid. It's not that they aren't interested—it's that they're openly hostile to the concept. And of course, since their members are 'unplugged' from popular devices and networks, they aren't susceptible to tech influences."

There was a pregnant pause, and Owen sensed Park had something important on his mind.

Eventually, Greg cleared his throat. "You know, President Chakrabarti would be able to mount a much more formidable response to Pacifica if she had more support in the House and Senate. But if there was a broader consensus among the people themselves, that would help, too."

"Well, sure. I assume you have Dustin Khatri and his mindshapers working on that, like you did before her election," said Owen tautly, not pleased with where this conversation was trending, but ready to face facts from his past.

His previous clandestine assignments from Park included hacking the StarTraxx tracking system and the CitizenTrust database, in order to subvert those programs and re-enfranchise some of the population who'd been shut out of the voting process. He'd also taken a few other, entirely unauthorized, steps to facilitate that last item.

"Yes, of course. Khatri's methods are very effective." Looking away from Owen, Greg added, "But as thorough as his operation was, it couldn't have accounted for such spectacular results. He tells me there's evidence of tampering with election numbers in specific races."

An accusatory stillness filled the car. Owen's hands tightened on the controls; there was a harshness beneath his soft tone when he finally broke the tension.

"I distinctly recall you authorizing me to get results favorable for Chakrabarti, by whatever means necessary. You should have known how I'd see that."

"You were never authorized to rig the election," Park pointed out.

"Hell—! Do you people want to win or not?"

Park did not answer.

Owen added, "Anyway, how is that any less ethical than manipulating the populace through dopamine levels triggered by online gaming?"

"Propaganda campaigns based on brain chemistry are fair game," countered Park. "Direct election interference is treasonous."

MacIntyre sliced the air with a quick, impatient jab of his hand. " '*Treasonous*'? What does that even mean these days? I'm being *treasonous* to a regime that sold out our Constitution before I was born?"

Greg attempted to interject, but Owen spoke over him. "If this *novus ignis* movement is just a collection of disconnected ideals and a few timid publicity campaigns, I don't see how there will be any long-term victory. As long as operatives like myself, like Enrique, are putting ourselves at risk, you shouldn't be so squeamish. You guys should be willing to use *every* tool necessary to win."

He set his jaw and focused on the silvery heat inversion shimmering on the road ahead of them. Despite the vehicle's AC working full blast, the temperature inside was barely tolerable; his sweat-soaked shirt and the seat of his jeans were sealed to the slick upholstery.

Another thought occurred to him, and he added with exasperation, "If you're still hiding behind loyalty to the shreds of the Constitution, stop it. I shouldn't have to tell you that no one else does, it's not worth it. We've all known that since our training days back at the Agency."

After a thick pause, Greg said, "Yeah, thanks for reminding me. But maybe I should have been more clear when we discussed which methods were sanctioned and which weren't."

MacIntyre replied with a disgusted snort.

Greg said, "In any case, you've proven it can be done effectively, and without immediate detection. Which brings me back to what I was saying about Chakrabarti needing more allies."

Incredulous, Owen uttered a bitter laugh. "Oh, I see! You *do* want me to work my magic again in the off-year election."

"Yes, that's exactly what I want." Park looked queasy as he added, "I know you said you wanted to distance yourself from *novus ignis*, but this is an area where you can have a significant impact. We may never know what happened to Enrique, but you can help bring down Pacifica this way."

"And that means bringing down Singer, doesn't it?"

Greg threw him a perceptive look. "You want to finish what you started to tell me about him and Sofia?"

Owen's hands tightened on the wheel. "No."

"Listen, this doesn't need to get personal. When things get emotional, that's when mistakes happen."

"Emotional? We're pretty sure the guy organized a false-flag bombing against our own Agency! That explosion killed Ted Petrenko, remember? He died right in front of me!"

"Of course I remember! We can all agree Singer's a bastard who's guilty of a hell of a lot. But you need to set that aside and keep your focus on the final objective."

Owen's frown continued to deepen, but he knew Greg was right, he risked making mistakes by clinging to personal animosity. On the other hand, animosity sure helped to keep the fires of determination burning.

As he pressed his shoulders back, his foot nudged the accelerator forward. "Okay, I'm committed to this."

"Great. I'll get you the list of the key races. It won't be nearly as much work as last time, and you've got over a year to put everything in place."

"I'll do my best."

Park said, "As long as we're on the subject of things I wasn't supposed to know about, what can you tell me about a gunsmith back in Oregon named Woods or something? No, wait—Reed? Weren't you assigned to look into his operation?"

"Perhaps."

"Make any worthwhile connections?"

"If you mean connections that might be of use to help run a resistance movement within Pacifica—perhaps."

"Good. Not saying we'll ever need them, but it's a good idea to start an inventory of all possible assets. 'Every tool', as it were."

Owen grinned approvingly.

It was early afternoon when they pulled into a rest stop on Interstate 10. Park made a beeline for a battered table shaded by the dark-green metal roof of a picnic pavilion. He set down the chilled bottles of water they had purchased earlier. Owen collected the wrappers from their recent fast-food meal and crammed them into the overflowing trash receptacle at the poorly maintained rest stop, before entering the facility.

When he returned, he didn't seat himself, but paced on the patch of grass beneath the scant shade of the nearby trees. The faint breeze on his damp shirt felt wonderful and helped him relax somewhat.

The sun blazed down on the small strip of dry grass between the parking lot and the worn asphalt of the highway. Cicadas buzzed ominously in the trees overhead.

Soon the stillness was ruffled by the mumble of a dusty old pickup truck approaching from off the freeway. It pulled into the lot and parked nearby. A burly, prosperous-looking man exited. He had thinning hair and a placid expression behind his thick mustache, and he headed straight for them.

Greg rose to greet the newcomer and made the introductions. Charles Ebersol's sharp glance at Owen's visor contained a trace of startled recognition, but he didn't comment on the device.

Instead, he remarked apologetically, "Sorry to make you two wait. Took me longer than I thought to finish up a couple of things. Oh, thanks." He accepted a bottled water from Park.

"No problem," Park assured him. "I appreciate you coming on such short notice."

The men seated themselves at the picnic table. Park gave a brief outline of the situation, then paused and waited for Ebersol's evaluation.

Interlacing his fingers as he rested his elbows on the table, Ebersol said, "Well, Greg, it's interesting that you should come to me about this. A few in my inner circle have been watching the situation in Pacifica with keen interest, and we're concerned about the rumors concerning these camps. You say you've got some schematics of these facilities?"

Greg pointed to Owen. "He's your man on that subject."

MacIntyre shook his head. "I don't have much, I'm afraid. Just some still satellite images and a few other files from the construction phase, likely nothing you can't get yourself. But I'll share everything I have."

"Hmm…," Ebersol's pouchy, nondescript eyes grew more thoughtful. "Sure, we'll add it to what we're going to collect from drone passes."

Owen asked, "Can you tell us what's being rumored?"

Ebersol shook his head. "Not without endangering our contacts. And they are just rumors. But if Rodriguez is as high-value an asset as you claim, extracting him will give us a reason to collect even more data. This operation could also be a test run for any future actions."

Park shot Owen a glance of suppressed excitement, then addressed Ebersol. "He's high-value, alright. If he breaks, a lot of people could be in danger."

"Okay. Does he have a working StarTraxx implant?"

"No," said Park. "We never used the StarTraxx system at the Agency, we had our own. And I'm ninety-nine percent sure he took his out before he left, and put a false loop in the system."

Ebersol frowned, twisting his bottle in his squat fingers. "Understandable. But that makes it a hell of a challenge to ID him among the other detainees in those facilities."

MacIntyre interrupted, "I'm sure all the inmates who arrived without a chip have one by now. Send me all the signals your drones pick up from every prisoner, and I'll sort through and match them to Enrique's biometrics."

Ebersol looked skeptical. "You'd have to get into the old Agency personnel records—,"

"No, I took all those relevant files with me when I left."

Ebersol was impressed. "Excellent," he said with gruff heartiness. "But that only helps us locate him. Getting him out is another matter entirely—assuming he's even in a camp."

As Park and MacIntyre fell into a tense silence, the noise from the cicadas became more abrasive and taunting.

The businessman reiterated, "I make no guarantees on whether we'll be successful."

Greg nodded. "Of course not. And reimbursement…?"

Ebersol's placid expression was lightened by the flicker of a smile. "Don't worry about cost. I'm pretty sure the expenses for this will be covered by the usual Restoration funding network."

"Even mercenaries?"

The Texan smirked, his brows lowering in a knowing tilt. "Especially mercenaries. Lately, we've all been setting aside quite a bit for that item on the budget." He took a long pull of water, then waved the bottle.

"If the administration isn't willing to take direct action against the People's Democratic Republic of Pacifica, there are a few powerful players elsewhere who are."

Park looked disconcerted, but answered pragmatically, "I hope this doesn't lead to a bunch of loose cannons working at cross purposes."

"Why not?" The man's shoulders hitched up as a laconic grin spread below his mustache. "Sounds pretty exciting to me."

"I want to be included in the rescue op," announced MacIntyre.

Park and Ebersol exchanged uncomfortable glances. Ebersol said, "I appreciate the sentiment, but I don't think that'll be necessary."

"No, I don't mean on the ground—I'm not trained for that. But as a consultant at your command center."

Ebersol chewed his mustache a moment, then looked at Park, who gave a curt, affirmative tilt of his head.

The stocky businessman gave Owen a smile. "Sure, why not. But I'll be leaving in a few minutes, so grab your gear."

Greg turned to Owen and raised his hands in a blessing-like salute. "Do whatever you can. I'll catch a flight back to Boston. Keep me posted on everything."

With a sense of accomplishment, Owen wiped some perspiration from his brow and drank the rest of his water. He'd have to update Sofia that he was being delayed indefinitely. She wouldn't be happy, but he strongly felt he had to do everything in his power to help his colleague.

CHAPTER
FIFTEEN

DESPITE THE INTENSE discomfort of the journey on the crowded bus, Cosimo, in his abject weariness, had caught a few hours' shallow, unpleasant sleep. That little amount was enough to revive him, so he was reasonably alert by the end of the trip.

Eventually, the prisoners had arrived late in the evening at a stark camp in the middle of nowhere. As the priest stumbled off the vehicle and was urged into a barracks, he barely had time to make note of the clear desert sky arching over a mostly flat landscape containing a few rocky hills towards the northeast. A coyote yipped nearby, another replied, unseen in the deep, ominous night.

Inside, Cosimo stood obediently with the other new arrivals as his head and beard were shaved. His skull and whole body were scanned. When it was discovered he had no biotracker capsule, one was injected without ceremony into his arm. He was issued a neurocontroller, and a thin, shapeless overall garment of drab gray-brown.

Over the course of the following hours, Nicholl adapted to the routine. He did not make a pretense of participating in the morning Power Cult ritual, nor did he speak out against it. He was not penalized for this, and dimly supposed that might come later. He did not recognize any of his parishioners among the other inmates, but he didn't know the situation in the women's section.

The blanketing effect of the controlling circlet soon became a comfort to him. He knew he should be fighting against it, but was losing strength. It was remarkably easy to retreat to his inner core of trust, where he rested completely in God's will. *Lord Jesus Christ, Son of God, have mercy on me, a sinner,* were the only words sounding clear and sharp in his mind.

Martyrdom, whispered a voice deep down in his heart. The prospect stared him in the face every waking moment, and he stared back complacently. A small part of him wondered if such an end would, after all, be the most preferable. He did not think for a moment he was worthy or prepared, but at least it would be an end.

Whether or not he had the strength to bear up under any of this no longer mattered. He was here, it was happening, and he was, in fact, bearing it. So he continued to endure the sleep deprivation, the poor food and the hours of mindless activity without a single inner complaint.

As Chief Enforcer Singer had observed, there was something liberating in finally having the uncertainty come to an end, to be living in reality.

A few days after his arrival, his sleep was rudely shattered when a guard roused him. Shoved from the barracks into the dim, poorly-lit corridor, he found the Camp Commander, a thuggish man named Stan Bauer, waiting for him personally.

"So, *Father,* I hope you slept well." Bauer's eyes gleamed with a predatory glint. "Have you thought more about where the cyborg might be hiding out? Or where your idiot thug of a parishioner got his hands on a Scorpio pistol?"

"No," mumbled Nicholl through his haze of exhaustion. "As I told your chief before, I know nothing about any of that. Told him several times, in fact. I'm sure he heard me."

"Yeah, he heard you, but had his doubts. Now, I think we're starting to believe you. But you should be happy—seems there's another way for you to be useful. We have a special assignment for you today, so let's get an early start."

For a moment, Cosimo's heart quailed, and his knees weakened, but he managed to walk as Bauer led him to the same clinic-like room where his head had been shaved; before he could react, a stone-faced medic stepped up and savagely deployed a syringe against his upper arm.

"Energy booster," explained Bauer with a disconcerting chuckle.

Lips sealed in a tight line, Nicholl didn't consider asking for an explanation. It would make no difference, and there was no point in drawing the commander into a conversation. It was clear the man was little more than an upright animal, there was no humane center in him worth searching for.

Leaving the clinic, they approached the center of the building, where a series of rooms abutted what Cosimo had deduced was the women's half of the camp.

Bauer unlocked one of these doors, announcing, "You'll never guess who's waiting in here for you! An old friend of yours—no, I mean a young friend!"

Bauer pulled Cosimo over the threshold, adding: "I'm sure you remember her from your congregation, I'll bet she's unburdened her heart to you in private lots of times. Maybe you even dreamed of doing something more than just listening to her problems…so now's your big chance."

Releasing Cosimo's arm, Bauer snatched the neurocontroller off the priest's brow and twirled it flippantly on his thick fingers. "You'll both perform better without these."

Before them, a girl crouched on the edge of the bare cot. She glanced up, her white face sick with fear.

Even as she looked away, Cosimo recognized Jen Connor. Her dark auburn hair was shorn to a velvety stubble, she also wore no subduing circlet. She had lost weight, but her face was still youthful. Yet it was also haggard, with deep brown-violet circles below her downcast eyes. Too mortified to face him, she struggled to pull her inadequate hospital gown more snugly about herself.

Bauer noticed this and said loudly, "Oh no, none of that—!"

He crossed the room and wrestled the garment clear from her body, chortling derisively as he watched her bend forward, huddling her arms across her round breasts, leaning forward to hide her hips.

"Well, you can both guess what's expected of you," said the commander briskly, balling up the garment and tucking it into the circlet. Turning to Cosimo, he lowered his voice. "Her fate depends on your compliance. Understand?"

Paling, the priest gave a curt nod that was little more than an involuntary shudder.

Bauer's nostrils flared as he leered, "And don't think we won't know if it doesn't happen."

The door clanged shut behind him. Cosimo remained standing, swaying in a sudden wave of dizziness. The moment was too unreal to be humiliating; he felt detached, but also full of compassion for this poor girl he'd known for perhaps five years.

She had shown courage in choosing to join the congregation of Saint Columban's, drawn to the community and the holiness of the ancient Liturgy. She was popular and made friends there. She was naturally energetic and full of high spirits; he knew from her private confessions that those high spirits often brought her to the brink of serious trouble, but he had counseled her through these episodes. He had at one time thought she would go on to become a saintly woman.

Now she wept with her head lowered, refusing to look at him. She was shivering; there was no blanket on the mattress with which to cover herself.

Cosmo turned his back, unfastened his loose overalls and stepped out of the crude garment. He held it out behind himself.

"Jen, here—,"

He felt the proffered clothing, still warm with his body heat, taken from his hand, heard rustling as she drew it on.

She whispered, "Thank you, Father."

Glancing back, he saw she had reseated herself. Arms and legs lost in the folds of the dirty fabric, she still shuddered uncontrollably; he couldn't tell if that was due to cold or shock.

He moved to the corner of the room behind her, asking tentatively, "Have they…done anything to you since you were brought here?"

She shook her head. "Just some injections, before bringing me to this room."

Cosmo looked about the small cell. While it was plain, it was not uncomfortable. In fact, compared to the harsh barracks, it was a den of luxury. He noticed the cold air from the overhead vent had ceased, replaced by a steady, reassuring warm breath. But Jen continued to quake.

Still facing away from him, she gasped, "What will they do if we don't…?"

Bauer's parting threat resounded in Cosmo's mind. He answered evasively, "I'm not sure."

Jen's cracked voice stumbled on, "I don't think I can face anything more, I'm so tired of being scared. It's wearing me down…down to nothing."

"That's the point, they want that."

"What if we…just for the cameras…made it seem we were…?"

With the ghost of a wry smile, he stepped closer. "Jen, they wouldn't be fooled for a moment. And afterwards—do you really think they'd let us go?"

She sighed. "No...no, I suppose not. But what do we do now?"

Without the controller, Cosimo's thoughts were sharper. But even if he were still suffering its enervating and thought-clouding effects, he couldn't mistake Bauer's meaning.

Her fate depends on my compliance, he reminded himself grimly.

Was that true, or was it a lie to force them into what they abhorred, and would both look back on with agonized regret? Yet if he did submit, and complied for her sake, how culpable would he be under such duress?

If he resisted, he'd likely be rewarded with his own swift execution. He'd never actively sought martyrdom, had been exceedingly prudent in his dealings with the state until lately. Now the threat seemed more like a tantalizing promise.

He picked his next words with caution. "For now, we keep doing what we're doing—nothing. Don't give them what they want."

"But—,"

"It won't be pleasant, but this is how we defeat them. So just be strong."

When she looked up at him, a bleak smile tugged the edges of her pale mouth. He sensed she hadn't smiled for many days, and the sight of that tiny action lightened his own heart.

Then her smile died. "I can't be strong...I...I just can't. I told you before, months ago, about that time when they first took me to the camp at the high school and questioned me. I told them everything I knew about Sofia and Owen, about that stupid VR game Sofia and I were playing. I don't know why they kept asking about the both of them, but I told them everything I could think of, just so they'd let me go!"

He remembered her distraught confession in the days following that event, not long after the MacIntyres had disappeared from the city. He said quietly, "Yes, I know."

"But I wish I hadn't. I'm so, so sorry."

"Yes, of course."

She continued to shiver and jerk. Unmindful of his own nakedness, he approached the bed and sat beside her. He covered her hand in his, attempting to still her trembling with the calm pressure of his own fingers. Despite the increasing warmth of the air in the room, it felt like the wings of death were brushing his exposed, wiry shoulders.

Pulling one hand free, she smeared her tears away. "It's not fair…all I want is to be left alone, to live my life. I wasn't hurting anyone! They just came to my apartment and took me away…I had no time to pack anything! What gives them the right?"

"The world gives them the right…they are the world, we are not."

"But why is this happening at all?" She began sobbing again, harder than before. Placing his arm about her, he held her close. She felt like a baby or a frightened animal as he bequeathed as much of his own strength and peace to her as he could. After several moments, her trembling lessened.

He said, "Whatever happens, as bad as it gets, it will be over soon. And you're never truly alone—He is with you. Think of that, and you can bear anything."

"But I don't want to die."

His eyes crinkled as he smiled warmly. "To be honest, neither do I. But God will give us strength."

"He hasn't yet, not for me."

"Don't say that."

Putting her head back further, she met his eyes, and as he studied her face, the lines of her mouth, he imagined what it would be like to run his fingertips along those seductive curves.

With dismay, he felt an unmistakable rush of warmth spreading throughout his body. A tingle that echoed desires long denied.

It's the injection…! he realized with horror.

Struggling against his rising discomfort, he pulled away from her. "If there's anything else you need to tell me, this might be your last chance."

Her face shadowed. "Oh, yes…but you know it all! I'm weak, I'm terrified! I've betrayed my friends, I'm afraid I'll do anything to get out of this place…,"

He cut her off gently. "Keep praying for strength. Let's do that now."

They closed their eyes and bowed their heads. He uttered low words of encouragement and trust, growing more aware of how she moved closer, her shoulder pressed against his. He enclosed the softness and warmth of her slim young fingers within the gristly shell of his hands.

As he prayed, low and under his breath, his words grew more disjointed and random. He ceased speaking. Opening his eyes, he studied the light gleaming on the short ends of her hair.

He reached for her jaw, tilting her head back and falling into her wide eyes. Heat was growing in her expression, calling to the heat now radiating through himself. Unaware of where he was or what he'd been thinking mere seconds earlier, he clasped the sides of her skull and brought her lips to his.

Arms encircling him, her hands stroked his back. Tenderly at first, then with a wild desperation. Her touch made him feel he was no longer a skinny, useless, lonely old man. He saw himself through her impressions at that moment; he was heat and power personified, reciprocating her hungry kisses and overtaking her with his unstoppable passion.

For a fraction of a moment, he observed his own actions, as if from an incalculable distance, with a disbelief blended with pity. If he could stop then, what would the consequences be?

He thought of her words, *"I don't want to die."*

Then he was engulfed in his awareness of Jen's scent, of her moaning in his ear, her form yielding beneath his grasping hands as he pulled the overalls off her. He was aware of nothing but the unstoppable weight of his body as he pushed her down on the bed. His identity dissolved in the achingly crazed clamor of his own lust, as it sought, found and devoured.

A wall of fire swiftly consumed them, then just as swiftly, was gone. As his blood became ice, he was rudely reminded of the pathetic reality of their naked, shivering bodies, of the harsh angles of his bony knees against her legs. He was immobile, fighting the urge to vomit, his desolate tears dripping onto Jen's neck.

He was dully aware of her voice, stuttering, "It's…it's okay, it's okay. It's not your fault…it's not our fault…,"

Loud, purposeful footsteps approached in the corridor outside and the door opened.

Cosimo sat up and blearily regarded the unfamiliar guard, heavy-set and sullen-faced. Beckoning to the priest, the man said harshly, "Commander wants you in the courtyard now."

Behind them, Jen uttered a strangled wail and began weeping again. "It's not fair! We did what you wanted, now leave him alone!"

"Shut up, bitch," the man snapped.

Sobbing, Jen extended the discarded overalls. Without meeting her eyes, Cosimo accepted the garment and pulled it on.

As the guard led him down the hall, a wave of tranquility such as Cosimo had never before known enfolded him without warning. It was piercing, yet infinitely consoling. For a fleeting moment, the darkness of what he'd just experienced was obliterated by a light that exuded love and compassion.

Cosimo left the building and emerged blinking into the morning sun, noting that each dust mote dancing in the beams was inexpressibly precious, that every breath he took was more real, more sweet than any he had drawn before. His serenity blossomed into exhilaration, into a joy fit to burst his heart. Each beat within his ribs became the song of a bird about to be released from its cage, ready to fly home.

Then his dazzled eyes registered the crowd waiting in the courtyard, the triumphant look on Commander Bauer's slab of a face. Like the sun fading behind a bank of black storm clouds, darkness again overtook Cosimo.

Yet he walked forward, mounting the steps of the dais until ordered to stop. Cosimo's vision of the commander was fractured, blurry through a sheet of his own tears.

He heard the man's whispered taunt, "So much for your vows of chastity, you dried-up old sinner—you fell sooner than any of the others."

CHAPTER
SIXTEEN

THE MAN in the cave decided that a heavy chunk of rough basalt stone made an acceptable ersatz dumb bell. Taking a break from his surveillance work, he hefted the rock in his hand and did a few repetitions. On the bare brown skin of his left arm, a coiled serpent tattoo rose and fell with each rep; when he switched to his right arm, it was a colorful image of the Sacred Heart that swelled and stretched on his biceps, as his muscles flexed and then loosened, over and over again.

He had a lot of free time on this hot afternoon in late August, and this was as good a way as any to kill it. Plus, it was enjoyable to give his mind a break from his monotonous watch duties.

When his muscles began to burn, he set the rock down, rose, picked up his shirt and drew it back down over his sweaty torso. He moved to the front of the cave where he lurked during the bright daylight hours. Dark eyes squinting in the harsh sun, he surveyed the neighboring rocky slopes and the surrounding terrain of dead, yellow grass.

He looked down at the rock-simulating camo tarp that concealed his powerful hovercycle. Even this close, and knowing where it was parked, the cycle was hard to detect. One edge of the tarp was pulled back to expose the small solar panels on the back of the craft, which were making the best use of the blazing sunlight.

He wanted to take a closer look at the electricals on one of the rear motors, but decided to wait until twilight threw a more protective shade over the location. Despite the remoteness of this hideout, he knew the guards at the nearby facility sometimes flew their own security drones in the area, and he could take no chances.

Taut and wary, his well-knit form retreated into the shadows of the cramped, dusty space. He rooted through his pack for an energy bar. Unwrapping it and chewing the inoffensive hunk without noting the taste, his mind focused on his small computer as he flipped it open, again studying the data he'd gathered that morning.

Most of the cave's floor was taken up with his vulture-shaped reconnaissance drone. A thing of beauty when drifting through the sky, earthbound, it was an awkward hassle to work around in such close quarters.

Over the last day or so, the man had downloaded considerable amounts of data regarding the nearby camp. It had taken him two days to locate the target. When Rodriguez's biometric signal—weak, but unmistakable—had been confirmed at this location, the man in the cave had traveled in person back to the dangerous eastern border to pass the news to a courier. Then he returned to this observation post and gathered more details about the camp's physical set-up, security measures and daily routine.

Resting beside his computer, a compact Quasar internet device hadn't been much use on this mission. The old Quasar satellites in orbit in this hemisphere were often targeted for destruction, and things had only gotten worse since China was allying with Pacifica.

The vulture-shaped drone did have microwave-internet capabilities, but there weren't any other similarly-equipped drones in the vicinity to relay the signal.

So, for the time being, the man waited for an alternate satellite connection to come online before he could easily pass his data along. If it took too long to establish a connection, he was prepared to deliver data—again by a flash drive—to the next trustworthy member of the network he might encounter.

The footage he collected this morning would be of particular interest to his employer. Dispassionately, he re-wound and augmented the critical sequence. It seemed all the male detainees had been gathered on short notice to watch an execution. The man in the cave compared the footage with the target's biometrics, watching as Rodriguez's heart rate staggered and soared while being forced to witness the quick, brutal event.

When the footage ended, the man in the cave transferred this data to several flash drives and concealed them in different pockets throughout his bag and his jacket. Then he pulled from his equipment case a small rigid, oblong container; from this he took a dark object which he carried to the computer and connected via cable.

It wouldn't take him too long to download and then program the camp's schematics into the new device. And it would be backed up with live remote control as well. Once he was done here, he'd patch up the cycle's troublesome motor and wait for nightfall.

After days of concealment and spying, it was time for bolder, but still stealthy, action.

CHAPTER
SEVENTEEN

OWEN MACINTYRE PUSHED AWAY from the computer workstation, massaging his stiff neck while fighting a yawn. A notice in red text flashed across his field of vision: *"You have been sitting for much too long. Your resting heart rate and blood oxygen levels are unsatisfactory. Recommend you get up and move."*

Yeah, genius, tell me something I don't know, he retorted inwardly as he shut off the alert. He couldn't shut off the fact he knew the monitor was correct. No longer having eyes to grow strained and fatigued meant he tended to remain staring at a computer screen, lost in a project, for far too long at a time.

Unclenching his tense jaw muscles, he said aloud to his companion, "I'm going out to get some fresh air, maybe go over to the diner. Let me know if there's news."

"Sure, no problem." Carson Ross, the shadowy figure hunched at another screen across the chamber, grunted his response without looking up.

The cave-like space, filled with computers and satellite-monitoring equipment, was where Ross kept tabs on Charles Ebersol's inventory of illicit military resources, both tech and human. It was also where Enrique's rescue op was being supervised.

After he'd parted company with Greg, Owen had accompanied Ebersol to this intel den, concealed in the labyrinthine recesses of a mattress factory, and had gotten right to work. The operation was small but efficient. As far as Owen could tell without asking too many questions, Ross' responsibilities were chiefly concerned with facilitating the logistics of key operators and equipment. He monitored when and where they were needed, and coordinated responses.

Executing these duties was a tall order, given the spotty state of comms in wide swathes of the country, but he seemed to be good at his job. Whether or not Ebersol and his men were ideologues also, sincerely committed to Restoration goals, was difficult to determine. Park trusted him, so that had to be good enough for now.

Shortly after his arrival, Owen had established a VPN and accessed his files back home, allowing him to share his data on Enrique's biometrics and the physical plans of the camps. Following that, there wasn't much more he could do for the rescue op, but he insisted on remaining. If Enrique was rescued, Owen wanted to be the first to interview him about his experiences, and even if that happened via computer, he'd still be physically closer to Enrique from here than back in Colombia.

For the time being, MacIntyre existed in a no-man's land, unready to return home, unwelcome at Underhill, yet reluctant to set up operations anywhere else. Ross had assigned him a workstation, and he was able to fill the time by beginning the election-related task Greg had assigned him. But so far in advance of the actual event, there hadn't been much for him to do. He decided his time was better spent researching Cassian Gray and his cronies in Pacifica's government.

Accessing the Aeon Institute's databases, he commenced compiling his own dossier on the key figures in the region. He was curious about whether Gray, in particular, was a true believer, an opportunist, or a figurehead providing cover for players who remained in the shadows. MacIntyre's own sense was that, if nothing else, the man was a naturally shrewd politician, well-marketed by his handlers. Yet after several hours' worth of study, Owen was no closer to a clear answer. Perhaps Gray's motives were a blend of all three theories.

Thus, as Owen shut down the work station, he felt irked by a lack of real progress on nearly every front, and was ready to clear his mind.

"You need to take a break, too," he commented to the tech as he rose and crossed the room. "Sure you don't want to join me?"

"Maybe in a bit. Got to finish up one more thing," murmured Ross. The sickly light from the screen illuminated the strands of long, gray-streaked hair framing his wan face, glinting in eyes that were locked on multiple channels of data continuously refreshing before him. Still not looking at Owen, he said, "Hey—you got a gate key?"

"Yeah, I do. See you later."

MacIntyre crossed the chamber, slid open the concealed door and passed through a dummy storeroom. During his sojourn in this dilapidated building, he had become familiar with the maze of towering racks, laden with supplies of wood strips, heavy springs, bolts of padding and fabric. Hidden in plain sight, cases of valuable, illicit resources shared the space with the prosaic mattress supplies. There were also concealed corridors, presumably leading to other hidden computer dens. The canyons of dusty racks soared upward into the shadows lurking beneath the distant ceiling. Below, rows of finished mattresses, sheeted in plastic wrap, extended throughout the cavernous halls.

MacIntyre hadn't explored any of this, and wasn't about to presume on his host's trust by starting now. The facility was empty of workers at that late hour, but survcams were always on duty. He passed down a brief corridor to the rear exit, where he heaved open the heavy security door and stepped into the night.

The factory behind him was surrounded by a deteriorated asphalt parking lot. The building bore a faded sign reading 'Crusader Enterprises', with a hackneyed logo of a medieval knight brandishing a broadsword. A smaller version of the logo appeared on the dusty sides of an old but serviceable delivery truck parked nearby. Everything still radiated warmth from the previous Texas day.

Spoiling for exercise, Owen began a brisk walk about the perimeter of the mostly abandoned industrial park, shaking the cramps from his muscles while taking in deep breaths of the sweet night air. It was all very refreshing after the stressful hours spent in the stagnant den. He unfastened the gate in the chain-link fence about the property, then relocked it behind himself. He strode toward the nearest intersection, beyond which beckoned an all-night diner, situated close enough to the highway to be convenient for truckers.

Although he tried to keep a professional attitude, he couldn't help speculating what Enrique's last weeks might have been like. How badly damaged was he by what he'd endured? If he was rescued, how long would it take for him to recover?

The tired phrase, *'Our thoughts and prayers are with you,'* drifted through Owen's mind. That sentiment was something he'd never been comfortable expressing himself, at least not aloud, not to people who were actively suffering. But where else had a portion of his thoughts been the last days, if not with his former colleague?

Regarding prayers, he wasn't sure how or if they worked. The idea of petitioning an entity that was all-powerful and omniscient seemed like a waste of time. But if it was a requirement for a relationship with God, he wasn't sure he liked that arrangement, either. It seemed arbitrary and imperious.

Yet his own limited experiences in that area indicated that yes, the Cosmos was undeniably run along lines of mutual cooperation, and certain responsibilities were expected of its citizens. In the end, as the mechanism of reality was out of his hands, he preferred to not think about the finer details.

And while he was no therapist, he was at least a sympathetic friend. The truth of their past friendship could provide a safer space in which the captive could unburden himself. Whether or not Owen would get the chance to speak with him, however, was still very much unknown. Thus far, this op was a waiting game. A waiting game playing out in the dark of ignorance.

He considered the possibilities, as he'd mentioned to Greg, that Enrique had met with some disaster unrelated to the new regime, or perhaps he would turn up any day now, alive and well. Or maybe the truth of his fate would never be known. The thought of that last option was what haunted Owen the most, and was the main thing he tried to escape by immersing himself in research over the last twenty-four hours or so.

Tugging open the old, stiff glass door of the restaurant, habit pulled him to the same booth where he'd dined last time. It offered a view of a parking lot and the weak trickle of traffic coming off the freeway ramp.

Waiting for his order, he contemplated the humble scene outside the window. Signage from a fuel station and a few small markets blinked halfheartedly, striving to attract the attention of the scarce customers, while rows of sentinel streetlights marched into the bleak distance. The highway seemed virtually abandoned.

He knew Sofia's parents lived in a small city not far to the north; this was a comparatively stable, secure part of the country. Stable or not, he wasn't convinced it was the sort of place he'd want to settle with Sofia later. Not anymore than Underhill, in fact.

Taking a sip of coffee from the cup just filled by the server, he suppressed a grimace at the taste of the bitter, diesel-grade brew. He'd been spoiled by the quality of the coffee back in Colombia.

Contrasting his past home with the shelter he and Sofia now enjoyed, he wondered: where was the best place for them to settle long-term? If he had free choice of any location in the world to raise his family, where would he go?

That exact question had never before occurred to him, in that exact light, and he spent some time analyzing it. As he did so, he experienced a keen and poignant impression, a vision of ancient evergreens looming in a wall of mist, the haze beyond their guardian shapes clearing to reveal wild surf crashing onto a narrow beach.

The coast of the Pacific Northwest was where he had always felt most at home, even if he hadn't appreciated it at the time. He'd taken the vistas, the weather, the trails, the untold shades of green, for granted. And now he was shut out from it all. For a moment, he felt a hot, righteous anger against those who had upended his unassuming life and forced him into exile.

Maybe I'll never be able to go back, he thought. *But I'll sure as hell do what I can to try.*

"Here ya go." The scrawny, older waitress clattered a plate, heaped with a savory omelette, on the table before him. Despite her clipped tone, friendliness was behind her tired gray eyes. "Need more coffee?"

He regarded the half-empty cup, debating. At least with his visor's medical updates muted, he couldn't be nagged about having too much coffee, even a brew as bad as this. There was no arguing against the fact that any caffeine was still caffeine.

"Sure, thanks."

The gurgling sound of the hot beverage streaming from her carafe was comforting. The prices here were high, but the food was fresh and the portions generous, belying what he knew about the region's decayed supply chain. The mushrooms in the omelette were rich and meaty, and he thought again of Underhill and what it would be like to live long-term in such a secretive, insular environment.

As he watched the server attend to another customer, he considered striking up a conversation and asking about the restaurant's suppliers, the conditions in the local economy. But he was pretty certain such probing questions wouldn't be appreciated. Plus it was unwise to draw too much attention to himself.

Chewing a mouthful of eggs and mushrooms, he returned to his immediate problems and took a cold, hard look at his own emotion-fueled impatience regarding Enrique, comparing it to Ross' detached professionalism. He also compared it to his own training—he well knew how technical challenges impacted this type of operation, knew how to set aside larger concerns and focus like a laser on the task at hand—why now did he find the lack of intel to be so aggravating?

Why didn't someone as well-connected as Ebersol have access to anything better than a decaying satellite system at the mercy of hostile powers, or an unreliable cell network? And a cadre of astute but fallible couriers?

What was needed, he mused idly, was an entirely different type of communication device. Something immune to the weather or geographical limitations. A technology that did not rely on antiquated cell towers, or decaying internet infrastructure, or outdated satellites. Something undetectable, a device impervious to enemies and hackers.

Something beyond known scientific boundaries—sure, no problem, he thought, sarcasm tingeing his exasperation. *Something magical.*

Abruptly, he arrested another forkful of omelette halfway to his mouth, heart lurching with excitement.

Beyond all known scientific boundaries. *Magical.* His mind raced again over his wish-list of ideal attributes.

Safe, accessible in all conditions. Impervious.

Instantaneous.

How could he have forgotten that such a device already existed, although in prototype form, and that he was one of the few people on Earth who had access to the research? Admittedly, it would require massive funding to develop the concept further, but perhaps Ebersol would be interested in the idea.

And if not Ebersol, Owen had other, powerful connections he could approach.

How to pitch this? he thought with mounting excitement. *As a commercial device or a military one?*

Through the plate-glass window, he saw a familiar lean, stooped form approaching. In another moment, Carson Ross entered the diner and slid into the ratty, torn vinyl seat across from him.

"Hey, that looks good," he said, regarding Owen's plate with the dazed air of someone waking from a long, deep slumber. He looked about hungrily and caught the server's notice. "Although I'd prefer hash browns, myself."

After she left with his order, Ross looked at Owen with a knowing smile, the dim light from the low-hanging lamp carving dark shadows beneath the man's red-rimmed, saggy eyes.

"You could use some coffee, too," said Owen.

Ross' mouth tugged wryly as he gestured for the waitress to come back and bring him a cup. When she was done and had left again, he leaned forward. "Just got some news."

Owen tensed. "Good or bad?"

"Courier got word from our operative in the field, just over the border in Pacifica. The target's biometrics were picked up about a day ago, in a detainment facility near Pilot Rock."

"Fantastic," exhaled Owen in relief. Enrique being alive and located was fantastic; surrounded by guards, not so much. "What's next?"

The tech made a vague motion with one hand. "Couldn't say. Up to the field agent to throw a plan together on the fly."

"'On the fly?'" MacIntyre echoed with displeasure. "That doesn't inspire confidence."

Ross' attention focused on the plate of steaming food set before him. Around a mouthful of fried potatoes, he said, "'S professional. Well-equipped. Can adapt to just about any circumstance. Relax."

"Yeah, sure." Owen fought a disappointed sigh. "You're right. I just really hate not knowing more."

"You get used to it, when you have no choice," said Ross. He downed some coffee. "Just do what you can. Trust and let go."

Startled, Owen commented, "You're not the first person to tell me that. But I'm not sure I agree."

Ross lifted his cup again, smiling over the rim. "Then brace for an unpleasant life."

With a noncommittal grunt, Owen scooped another forkful of egg and mushrooms.

As his initial relief regarding Enrique faded, his thoughts returned to the idea that had just occurred to him.

A new way of gathering and sharing intel, a new way of communicating. He was determined to follow up on it when he returned home; it just might lead to some exceedingly remarkable places.

CHAPTER
EIGHTEEN

THE ASSEMBLAGE of living corpses had been interrupted not long after commencing the early shift in the camp's work shed. An announcement over the PA system ordered everyone to cease their activity and report to the exercise yard. The detainees left the workbenches and filed outside, where the clear air still retained the mindless insult of hope that reminded Enrique of his past life. High overhead, the familiar, ominous outline of yet another vulture, alert for the promise of death, drifted over the compound.

The ragged prisoners lined up and stood blinking as the large screens on the sides of the area switched to life. Commander Bauer stood alone on the dais.

The men watched as another guard appeared, escorting a prisoner, his overalls unfastened and hanging off his thin frame. It was a moment before Rodriguez recognized the man as the priest from the small Orthodox church in New Astoria. Cosimo Nicholl, he thought his name was.

The PA system played the official State anthem; the video screens reran the Power Cult slideshow the crowd had already seen at dawn. The gathered men, whether through an instinct for self-preservation, or manipulation from their circlets, responded with more enthusiasm than usual.

When the images faded, Bauer's voice rang out: "Did everyone notice how this guy up here with us, this *priest*, did not join our inspirational song? He refused to sing our majestic, noble anthem? He doesn't bow his head or raise his hands like the rest of us? Does he even know how to smile?"

It was clear Bauer did not expect an answer, so no one spoke. The commander went on: "Does anyone here get the sense that he thinks he's better than us? That he's too good to participate in helping build up this new endeavor of Pacifica? He thinks his backward superstitions, his imaginary friends, are more important than being part of a real community!"

All around Enrique, men shifted from foot to foot, not daring to steal glances at their neighbors, heads doggedly lowered. There was a subtle air of relief that what was transpiring on the platform was happening to Nicholl instead of themselves.

Bauer turned to Nicholl and shouted, "But you're just a fucking hypocrite! Everybody, look at the holy hero!" His out-flung arm swept towards the nearest view screen. On the surfaces of all these, larger-than-life scenes of Nicholl and a red-headed girl now dominated the exercise yard.

Enrique fought to keep his attention away from the activity on the screen, instead focusing on the priest. The man looked gray and numbed, head lowered, unable to escape the images and sounds of his recent actions.

Bauer thundered at the defeated man, "You've spent your whole life pretending to be better than the rest of us, telling everybody in your church how to live their lives, but look how fast you took her! Everybody can see you for what you really are—untrustworthy, a hypocrite. A filthy parasite!"

The priest's head sank lower but he said nothing.

Bauer's face reddened. "There's no place here for parasites, for those unwilling to build up the community, those opposed to the virtues of our new nation. We have no use for those who are stuck in the dark ages!" As his voice reached a fever-pitch of rage, he pulled a small blade from his belt.

Stepping close to Nicholl, Bauer stooped and struck at the priest's groin with a savage, slashing motion. Blood, vibrant and glistening, sheeted down the man's inner thigh. He remained upright for what seemed an eternity. Enrique winced yet could not look away; for a split-second, the priest's face seem to flicker and resemble someone else.

Nicholl finally bled out and slumped, dropping to the platform with a *thud* that echoed leadenly through the plaza. The yard was silent for only a second or so before Bauer made a curt gesture towards the crowd. "Break's over—everybody back to work."

With a low, scraping mumble of feet shuffling over gravel, they complied.

Now, as Enrique worked, he kept his head down and robotically reached for the components and constructed one apparatus after another. The shock and horror of what he had witnessed was only one facet in the continuous agony of his existence.

During the previous week, he had been taken to Bauer's office twice more and questioned. He was also shown footage of Connie and Antonia being abused by guards at another facility. As much as he told himself they were computer-generated fakes, he could feel the taunting memory of those images slowly annihilating his sanity.

He experienced waking nightmares, hyper-real visions in which he helplessly witnessed the abuse over and over again. Because he'd tampered with his neurocontroller, there was no dampening effect on his thoughts, so he existed in a heightened state of fear for his family. Only a desperate hope that the scenes were false helped him fight the powerful urge to go to Bauer, to beg the commander to take any scrap of info he could conjure up concerning Owen or Park.

To tame this fear, to blunt the horror of the images, he drew on other memories. He focused on the sweetly private moments spent watching Connie hold Toni as the girl slept, or the times his own strong hands had fed Luis or changed his diaper. He clung to the recollection of both kids' soft breath against his cheek when they snuggled close to watch a movie with him, the bright chirping of their excited whispers and giggles, the happiness in their eyes.

Yet this particular day passed in a cloud of visceral dread and helplessness worse than usual. Fumbling with exhaustion and struggling to distract himself by focusing on the task of building the nameless devices, he continued to puzzle over these items for the next three hours or so of his shift.

At last, it dawned on him these units served no purpose other than to rob him of his time, of any dignity the concept of *work* itself ever had. He realized this when he recognized a small, but distinctive and familiar dent on one of the pieces he was plugging into the main housing. He had seen this blemish the week before, and was now surprised when he saw the exact same piece tumble out of his supply bin. After that, he paid close attention and became convinced the workers were, in fact, re-using the same parts over and over again.

It appeared the items were assembled in this room, collected, then distributed to the women on the far side of the camp, who presumably stood in long lines at similar work benches, undoing the results the men had spent days preparing.

What's the fucking point? A dying remnant of outrage grumbled low beneath Enrique's surface placidity as he shoved the latest completed apparatus into the collection bin.

An abrupt flick of movement on the floor behind him caught his attention, and from the corner of his eye, he watched a light brown rat dash along the floor, following the perimeter of the room. The construction of the building was rough and unfinished; the creature soon located and ducked into the large crack running between the concrete floor and bottom of the heavy plywood walls, which had no baseboards.

This was the third rat Enrique had seen in as many days. Or perhaps he had only seen the same one three times. With numbed, detached curiosity, he wondered how it managed to survive here in such a clean environment, where every crumb of food at every meal was accounted for and consumed by the inmates. In a way, he envied the little creature. Envied vermin, free to pass between walls and fences, with no thoughts or concerns other than where to find a few scraps. He was also surprised to recognize he had a gleam of happiness for it, in its lowly innocence.

For hours, Enrique's shaking hands continued to collect pieces and screw, clamp and flip them into place before sweeping the finished items into the main receptacle.

At night, in the darkness of the barracks, Enrique's inner visions of his family's torment alternated with an incessant stream of components and useless parts. He felt the smooth tubes and bundles of wires beneath his fingers. He saw them covered with a shiny curtain of blood. He saw Bauer's face, contorted with contempt.

In contrast, he saw Nicholl's resigned expression. Enrique thought how he might have glimpsed another face within the priest's. Moment by moment, that unforgettable face, fused with Nicholl's serene expression, replaced the blood and the hate of the other impressions. Enrique almost had the sense of an actual, distinct presence joining him as he relived the scene.

Gradually, Enrique grew peaceful, his anxiety for the future lessened. For a few minutes, at least, the surrounding darkness seemed safe and welcoming. He began to relax. The night was well advanced when he heard a faint scrabbling on the supports of his metal bunk. Then came a rustling over the thin mattress near his head and he realized a rat had climbed up beside him. Without thinking, he reacted and caught it, smashing it into the mattress. Instead of squirming and writhing under his grasp, it vibrated.

It vibrated with an unmistakable, machine-like quality. Its eyes gleamed bright blue, and as he brought his other hand up to it, he saw a tiny stream of words projected over his palm. Disbelieving but mesmerized, he stared at the message until the basic meaning sank into his brain.

Incredulous hope stirred in him, then a thrust of excitement. Following the instructions written in light on his skin, his trembling fingers felt for a small button under the fake fur, and he pressed it. The eyes grew dim and the robot, life-like, struggled to move again under his hand. He let it go and in the gloom, strained to watch as it climbed down the edge of the bunk. It zipped across the floor, squeezing itself under the locked door of the barracks.

Long after it disappeared, his gaze remained fixed on the thin crack of dim light beneath the door, uncertain the incident had actually happened. There was a real chance he had completely lost his mind and was hallucinating. In case he wasn't, he began reciting the message over and over to himself, imprinting it in his consciousness.

Because he didn't dare forget a single word.

CHAPTER
NINETEEN

THE OBSERVER in the cave had packed most of his equipment. Each step of his proposed plan replayed in his head, as with a strong sense of accomplishment, he neared the end of this phase of his operation. Everything was on schedule for extracting the target at 0400 the next morning.

At the moment, it was time to review the last batch of data he'd just downloaded from the condor drone, lately returned. The man unhooked the slender cable and began winding it even as his eyes remained on his computer screen. As the program searched for Rodriguez's vitals, a heavy frown crept across the man's face. In growing alarm, he scanned all data the robot bird had captured that day. Something was very wrong.

"Oh, *shit*," he spat aloud into the watchful hush of the cramped cave. There was no trace of Rodriquez anywhere in the facility. But nor was there any sign that another public execution had taken place. Could the target have jumped the gun and escaped on his own during the night?

No, the man thought. *Surely he wouldn't run off like a fucking idiot, not when he knew to wait for me…but if he did, the drone would still have picked up his signal…he wouldn't get far on foot and would still be in range. And if he were missing, the camp would be in an uproar.*

Rising, he took a few steps about in the tight space, mind working furiously. *They must have moved him during the time when the drone wasn't surveilling*, he realized. Returning to his computer, he began reviewing the aerial footage, zooming in now that he knew which clues to look for: tire tracks from the busses and supply trucks.

Most tracks seemed to come from routes that ran east-west, which made sense; prisoners and food were coming from the west. But there were one or two trails that ran north-south. Could they have transported him to a different facility? If so, which one, and why?

If they suspected the observer's presence here in the rocky hills, they'd simply have confronted and apprehended him. Why bother to move the target?

Unless they needed him for something.

The man pulled up a detailed map of the region and traced a route from the Pilot Rock facility southwards. It was possible they had taken the target down to the old lithium mine on the Nevada border, the one that the former state authorities had retained the rights to, back when a portion of Malheur county had joined Idaho. Quickly, he accessed his extensive database about the region and began scanning more maps.

After a while, the man sat back on his heels and rubbed a hand over his tired face as he swore under his breath. Assuming that removal to the lithium plant was the most likely explanation, this development shoved his plans back at least a day. And it was going to be the devil to get word to the contacts that were expecting them to meet up in Idaho.

Despite this setback, he was determined to succeed. Priding himself in his adaptability and resourcefulness, the man folded the wings of the condor drone with care and eased it into its case. He soon completed the rest of his packing, and loaded all his equipment on his hovercycle. He was ready to commence his unplanned trip southwards.

CHAPTER
TWENTY

DISORIENTED WITH FATIGUE AND ANXIETY, Enrique struggled to comprehend the brief safety lecture the foreman presented to the newcomers at the lithium processing plant. Hours before, he'd been shouted out of his bunk during a bleak stretch of night, and hustled, with six other men, onto a small shuttle bus. The glimpse he caught of the sky told him it was approximately two o'clock in the morning. There had followed a four-hour journey through the dark, during which Rodriquez grappled with his sense of despairing disappointment that he would not be meeting with his mysterious rescuer.

Still, he clung to hope that all was not lost, thinking, *Maybe he'll figure out what happened and adjust his plans. Maybe he'll track this bus.*

A harsh dawn was breaking over the distant, low hills and plains dotted with sagebrush when they arrived at their destination. Armed guards dragged aside razor-wire topped gates of chainlink, then shoved these shut behind the bus after it entered. Shuffling down the vehicle steps and stealing a glance about his surroundings, Enrique was surprised to discover the place was a mineral processing plant. After a cursory tour of the small operation, he and the other prisoners had been broken into smaller groups and assigned to different tasks, under the supervision of a foreman and a brace of armed guards.

The facility was small, its diesel-powered generators were old, and not up to the task of powering all the equipment. As he mindlessly applied himself to hand-shoveling ore from the pad to the first conveyor belt, Enrique blinked back the sweat that was soon streaming into his eyes. His healing rib protested with each dip and turn of his torso.

The sun crept inevitably to its zenith. Beneath a cloudless sky, remorseless rays baked the metal structures, scaffoldings, pipework and tanks of the utilitarian compound. The entire operation loomed like a nightmarish parody of a children's play structure in a public park.

As he worked, Enrique wondered why he had been sent here. Had Bauer gotten wind of the planned rescue? But if that was the case, why not just ambush the operative when he arrived? If this was a punishment, why not gloat over him a bit before sending him here? Maybe the explanation was as simple as the fact that he was still stronger and more agile than many of his fellow prisoners.

Enrique felt a nebulous optimism that morphed over time into something more concrete, when he realized this place offered more opportunities for escape than the camp had, whether or not there was anyone on the outside still trying to help him.

The security set up is bare-bones, he noted. *There's only one flimsy course of chainlink and wire, and the double gate at the single entrance. And only three guards. But the foreman and the supervisors are armed, so that's another three weapons.*

Three was also the number of double-wide trailers at one end of the property; one for the prisoners' sleeping quarters, one containing provisions and a large break room, while the last housed the operation's offices and overseer's quarters. Two small hovercycles were parked near the offices, likely used for an occasional patrol or courier duties. Over the chemical thickening vat stretched a covered platform and narrow walkway that doubled as a guard tower.

As Enrique worked, he stole intermittent glances at the form lurking in the shade of that small structure, catching a menacing outline of the man's rifle against the sky.

"Hey, you!"

Enrique jumped at the sharp snarl, uttered by yet another guard who had approached without a sound and stood a couple of feet behind him. "What are you looking at?"

Straightening somewhat, Enrique answered with effort, voice coming weakly through his cracked lips. "What?"

The man took one slow, menacing step closer. "I said, '*What are you looking at?'* I seen you been distracted, looking around."

Hands tightening on the shovel handle, Rodriguez answered with caution, "Looking at? Nothing…there's nothing to look at."

"You being a smart ass?" The man hefted his rifle. "You thinking of making a run for it after dark?"

The man was tall and wiry, his stance taut with a serpent's readiness to strike. His uniform was caked with dust, his battered sunglasses could not contain the casual malevolence of his gaze.

Enrique's mind lit with a lightning flash of an idea; of smiting him with the shovel and grabbing the rifle, perhaps commandeering a hovercycle and getting over the fence.

In an instant, the vision was gone. There was no way he'd make it past the other sentries. And he felt certain he was much too weak to swing the shovel with enough force to catch the man off-guard.

He answered tepidly, "Just trying to get my work done."

"Oh, and I'm interrupting you? So sorry—!" The rifle's muzzle darted upward; a sharp, vicious blow connected with Enrique's cheekbone. The thug raised the weapon again to bring it down on his prey's neck, but Rodriguez's reflexes kicked in. He brought the shovel up, instantly blocking the rifle's swift descent.

For an interminable moment, each man's force cancelled out the other's.

Feeling the sting from his own sweat dribbling into his split cheek, Enrique knew what little strength he had was ebbing, was aware the full brunt of the guard's malice was about to burst past his own feeble resistance and engulf him. His feet were already slipping a little on the gravel, he could feel his balance shifting.

"Hey—what the hell's going on here?"

The foreman ran to join them, face flushed with heat and outrage. "Mulroney, what's the meaning of this?"

"This shit attacked me." With a slight shove, the guard pushed the shovel handle away from himself, causing Enrique to stagger back and almost fall.

Squinting in the unremitting glare of the day, the foreman fastened his skeptical gaze on the uniformed man. "Really? Should I review the surv records to confirm that?"

With a snort, the guard nonchalantly brushed grit from the creases of his jacket.

The foreman added, "You know we're short able-bodied workers, that's why we had this lot brought down here. The last thing we need is pricks like you roughing them up. This operation is vital to the national economy, unlike your cesspit camps. Get back to your post."

In answer, the man clenched his rifle defiantly as he strolled back across the compound.

"Sorry about that, let's get your face cleaned up," mumbled the foreman, taking Enrique by the arm and leading him to the central trailer to see the wound was cleaned and dressed. Enrique noticed the man avoided making eye contact with him throughout the entire process.

As he returned to his shift, Enrique wondered who the man was, what his life had been like before Pacifica, if he was a true believer in the cause and wanted to be here, or if he, too, was trapped behind the enemy lines of his own home.

When the workers were allowed a brief lunch in the dusty and stifling break room, Rodriguez ate his food as slowly as he dared, shifting the morsel to the right side of his mouth, as his left cheek was now aching and swollen beneath its bandage. He was thankful the wound was the same side as the missing tooth.

The routine here was more relaxed than at the camp, and there was only one guard outside the main door. The men ate wherever they felt like, but no one spoke or made any attempt to interact with anyone else. No one stopped Enrique from pacing the edge of the room and studying the faded, forgotten posters and out-of-date notices on the message boards.

As he read, snippets of history and miscellaneous facts emerged from his own memory. He vaguely recalled there had been some dispute over lithium mining in past decades. The contention had primarily involved environmental concerns about the older, inefficient processing methods used by the Australian company awarded the original contract. It seemed the current plant now incorporated some updated methods, but it was obvious the place had only recently been reactivated as a State-owned enterprise. There was a sense of urgency and tension in the air, the sort of atmosphere where dangerous mistakes could be made, someone could be shot by a jittery boss or untrained, unprofessional guard, at any moment.

With an air of feigned disinterest, Enrique continued his circuit about the room. He wondered if the plant was at risk from troublemakers on either the

Nevada or Idaho sides of the border. But it was such a remote, sparsely populated location, he doubted there was a significant anti-Pacifica presence. On the other hand, there was also a chance that the border here was less secure than up in the northeast corner of the region.

Which means, that if I do get out of here, there's a real chance I can make it to safety, Allah willing, he thought solemnly. *Even if I'm on my own.*

A few surreptitious glances at his fellow inmates reminded him there were no promising candidates to invite along with him, should he find an opportunity to make a break. It was impossible to get close to any of the other detainees and sound them out about their trustworthiness. In any case, he assumed interference from the neurocontrollers would make any positive responses unreliable. In order to survive, he was forced to regard them all as enemies, even as they suffered alongside him.

Nonetheless, when he was herded back to his work station, he felt more confident and alert. And as the day waned, he noticed the distinctive outline of a turkey vulture laconically passing over the area. Smiling inside, he pretended to not notice it. *Looks like he figured it out after all,* he thought with relief. *I won't be going it alone.*

That night, on his creaky cot, he lay awake and alert, ears strained for the familiar scrabbling sound of the mechanical rodent. There was a small gap between the bottom of the main door and the cracked, dirty vinyl flooring, so he expected the mechanism wouldn't have too much trouble forcing its way in.

It was perhaps three o'clock in the morning when he became aware of the little machine hauling itself up the metal tubes of his cot and approaching his head. He caught its message in his hand: *Be near gate in fifteen.* His heart lurched in excitement. He hit the return button, holding his breath as he listened to the device whisk back down and across the floor.

He counted the seconds until he heard a faint sound near the bottom of the wall, and saw the nightlight shining on the floor near the toilets wink out, as the rat cut the power to that section of the trailer.

Holding his breath, Enrique rose from the cot, casting a brief look of loathing at his neurocontroller circlet where it lay discarded on his thin, filthy pillow. He lifted his shoes from the floor and crossed the room, praying the surface beneath him wouldn't creak.

All about him, the gray gloom was filled with indistinct, lumpy shapes and the sounds of exhausted, hopeless breathing. Enrique arrived at the main door and touched it. There was no answering alarm; he pushed it further, confirming the rat had also successfully deactivated the lock.

Outside, he saw the lights in the guard tower above the evaporation tank were still on, but no one seemed to have noticed several of the smaller security lights were out. But he couldn't count on that continuing.

Enrique turned around the corner of the trailer and passed along the shadow of the wall. The entire facility was painted with ominous, complicated shades cast by the networks of scaffolding, conveyer belts, and tanks. The shadows formed patterns of even deeper darkness through the dim night. He moved across the facility, flitting from dark stripe to dark stripe. The harsh gravel hurt his feet, but he did not utter the slightest gasp.

At last, he stood hidden behind the metal supports that held up the roof over the ore receiving pad, a few yards from the gate. Motionless, he strained his ears for any warning sounds.

With no security lights near him, and a fine cloud cover rolling from the west to conceal the stars, the night was almost impenetrable. All he could do was keep listening, ignoring his own heartbeat as it hammered in his head. He kept a crude count of how many minutes had passed since the nightlight was extinguished. More than five, less than eight. At least, he was pretty sure.

Without noise, he put on his shoes. Then waiting in a tense, wary half-crouch, Rodriguez focused on the guard tower. The lone occupant was still unaware of anything amiss in the scene below him.

It's so quiet out here, he'll hear the slightest noise, Enrique groaned to himself. *Any second—.*

From far out in the blackness, he heard a faint, fluttering drone, like an advancing army of mechanical moths. Still no reaction from the guard; even at that distance, he could tell by the man's sloppy posture he had not heard anything to arouse suspicion.

Hurry up, hurry up, hurry up! Allah please—get them here before the sentry looks around. Strike the guards blind and deaf!

The droning sound grew more insistent, it seemed impossible the guard would not hear it at any moment. After several nerve-racking seconds, Rodriguez saw a heavy shape sail over the nasty arcs of razor wire atop the fence. The stone-gray hovercycle, buoyed aloft on an air cushion produced by four large rotors, lowered and lingered effortlessly, less than two yards distant.

The black-clad, helmeted operator pointed directly at him and beckoned with a commanding air. Enrique broke from the shadows and clambered aboard, seating himself behind his faceless deliverer and clasping his arms about the other's waist. The next instant, he felt the solid upward push of the craft beneath him, as they ascended and sailed over the fence.

As the cycle banked to the left, Enrique looked back at the security tower and thought he glimpsed the sentinel was wearing VR glasses; he guessed the man was too immersed in some mindless game to hear the cycle.

Behind them, the lights of the processing plant soon fell away and dwindled to pinpricks, then to nothing. When Enrique glanced back every few moments, he saw no sign of pursuit. Then, without warning, the cycle began to sink. The operator landed it skillfully, then twisted in his seat and addressed Enrique.

"Quick—your tracker—!"

Rodriguez extended his left arm. The man grasped it, and passed a small, pistol-like implement over the skin. A signal beeped; Enrique flinched as the tiny capsule was located and sucked from his flesh. Holding his sleeve over the wound to stop the bleeding, Enrique then watched as the man jerked a mech rat from his jacket, inserted the tracker deep into a compartment on the false rodent. This he activated and tossed to the ground; the item sprang to a semblance of life and dashed away into the gloom, racing away from their position.

"Might buy us a couple of hours," pronounced the operator, as he switched the cycle back on and they began to gain altitude.

As they flew through the night, the roar of the rotors seemed deafening to Enrique. They were not loud, but compared to the stillness of their empty surroundings, the noise was a prolonged, outrageous scream. After about ten minutes, an irregularity disrupted the sustained hum. Almost undetectable at first, an occasional hiccup grew more insistent, and the craft began to sink lower.

The operator said nothing, but gestured towards a rapidly approaching rock formation, looming out of the black night. The hovercycle gave a straining moan and lurched to one side; the operator struggled to keep it level as it plunged earthwards. It tilted acutely, nearly throwing them.

The operator wrenched control back long enough to manage a gentle collision with the ground, then the man switched the craft off. They both disembarked; the operator pulled off his helmet, revealing himself to be an earnest-looking man in his late thirties with short black hair and friendly eyes. He regarded the cycle critically.

"It's rated for two riders, but it's been giving me some trouble lately," he grumbled apologetically. "Thought I'd fixed it, but I'm going to have to work on it again before we can make it to the rendezvous." He looked up from the craft towards Enrique.

Extending his gloved hand, he added warmly, "Hey—I'm Miguel Campos. Pleased to be able to help you out, Mr. Rodriguez. How are you feeling?"

In answer, Enrique's legs turned to water and he collapsed. Campos dropped his helmet and clutched at him, lowering him gently to the dusty earth. Beneath the sheltering outcropping of black volcanic rock that reared into the featureless night, Enrique began to sob. He hugged his knees to his chest, hiding his face.

Nonplussed, Campos regarded him a moment, then brought him some food and a water bottle from the cycle's saddle compartments.

"Here, I guess you need this. While I'm working on the cycle, can you keep an eye peeled and let me know if you spot any sign we're being followed?"

Enrique nodded, still unable to speak. He pulled the top off the bottle and gulped down several mouthfuls of water. Still trembling, he then tore open the food package and devoured the contents. He kept glancing back the way they had come, dreading at any moment to see advancing lights from either a truck or pursuing hovercycles.

There was an unreality about his current freedom; not only was it difficult to believe in, it was very much uncertain, not guaranteed. It could vanish in a moment. Wiping his eyes on his grimy sleeve, he forced himself to chew more slowly and be more alert. A few yards to his left, Campos was muttering over the control panel on the front of the cycle.

"Diagnostic's reporting an intermittent short in the electrics on the left rear rotor," he announced. He didn't sound too concerned. "I can patch that right up and we'll be out of here soon."

He replaced his helmet and activated a built-in headlight, which he kept trained on the open panel to the craft's rear. He also kept up a cheerful stream of commentary as he worked, but Enrique was too numb and on edge to pay much attention.

Eyes straining into the vast open darkness behind them, he felt a cool breeze and shivered. The water bottle was almost to his mouth, when he froze and squinted more alertly into the void. Had he seen a wavering spark of light, or was that his imagination?

An inarticulate grunt of distress burst from him as he scrambled to his feet, clutching at Campos' sleeve.

"Coming," he croaked. "Back there! Lights coming—!"

With a grim expression, Campos lowered the visor on his helmet and activated a scanning feature. Then he turned to Enrique.

"Yeah, there's two cycles incoming—," he unholstered a beam pistol, then snatched a second one from inside his jacket. Pointing to the rock formation behind them, he urged, "We need to get up there!"

They scrambled up the black, broken rocks for about thirty feet, then Campos signaled for Enrique to join him behind a formation that provided partial cover. Without speaking, he accepted the pistol Campos handed him and kneeled, unmindful of the inhospitable rocks digging into his skin. As he peered over the edge of the rough surface at the approaching lights, Enrique prayed the operators would miss Campos' cycle in the poor visibility and speed on past.

It seemed their pursuers had their own scanning equipment. Almost instantly, the glowing red of the crafts' running lights swerved and described a smooth arc, as the riders circled back to where Campos' machine was parked.

Campos breathed, "We'll pick them off as soon as they stop."

Rodriguez replied with an almost imperceptible nod. He eased the muzzle of the pistol up and secured it against a blister of rock before his face. The ready light on the back of the weapon assured him the device was at full power, and the security chip was disabled. He was free to fire at any time, and noted with grim satisfaction that, when it mattered, his hands were almost steady.

The first cycle slowed to hover not far from the disabled craft, Campos squeezed his trigger. A narrow flash knocked the rider off his machine, which drifted to one side before dropping with a thud. Enrique fired at the second man, missing his target. That rider urged his machine up, coming around and behind them both in an instant.

As they were buffeted by the stiff breeze from the rotors, the operator fired, and Enrique felt a point of hot pain searing into his upper arm. Without thinking, blinded with pain and animal-like terror at the risk of being re-captured, he lunged upwards toward his attacker.

He caught and held onto the front end of the cycle, pulling it off-balance. The nose plunged downwards as the rear shot up; instantly, the entire craft flipped over, narrowly clearing Enrique's head.

With a strangled shout of dismay, the rider lurched and slid over the front of the craft. As he flailed and tumbled, Campos fired, hitting him square in the neck.

The riderless cycle then veered and impacted against the rocks, crumpling like paper.

Campos jammed his weapon back into his holster as he drew near Enrique. "We should be left alone for a bit. Show me your arm."

Dazed, Enrique was hardly aware that the man was pulling his overall aside to examine the burning hole in his lower left biceps.

"Just a pin-prick," Campos announced. "Damn, you're tough, though. Took some strength to pull that cycle right out of the air like that! But let's get some meds and a dressing on it anyway."

The men picked their way back down the slope. Campos removed his helmet, then rummaged through his supplies for pain-numbing antibiotic ointment and a bandage. After seeing to the wound, he returned to his cycle to continue repairs.

Now the immediate danger had passed, Enrique began quivering. He reseated himself near the craft and watched as the man worked. After a few minutes, he asked huskily, "Where do we go from here?"

Campos glanced over and offered him a dusty grin. "I'm taking you to meet a caravan of Nightcrawlers on their way from Utah. We'll link up just over the border."

"Which…border?"

"Nevada."

Enrique coughed. "Have you heard…is there any news about…about…?"

"Your wife?"

Enrique nodded.

Campos said, "Yeah, she and the kids are all safe. You'll be together again in less than two days."

As the reality of this assurance sank in, Enrique's body let go of the unbearable burden of stress under which he had struggled for months.

With a deep sigh, he relaxed, tilting his head back and gazing up at the blanket of darkness, too moved with gratitude to utter another word.

CHAPTER
TWENTY-ONE

THE SOFT COMFORT of the blanket was very different from the thin, scratchy coverings beneath which Enrique had shivered the last few weeks. The mattress cradling his weary body was like a blissful cloud. Why had they given him such luxury? Was it a trick to confuse him, to lull him into gratitude?

Warily, his lids cracked open and he took in the disorienting jumble of his unfamiliar surroundings. He was lying in a cramped camper, parked and motionless, while the pale evening light slipped through the cracks of the curtains. Relief seeped through him when he remembered he was safe in a Nightcrawler caravan.

Impressions from the past hours flooded back to him: how he and Campos had ridden the hovercycle through the desert and finally through the incomplete border wall, how they barely caught up with the caravan as the latter was heading towards Paradise Valley to make camp before dawn. Before Enrique collapsed from nervous exhaustion, he'd been told there were no signs anyone had traced them this far, but they assured him security would be high.

Stiff and weak, he sat up. He could not remember the last time he'd slept so soundly, and without a single nightmare. But while not strictly ill, the shock of the whole experience left him weak and achy, with flu-like symptoms, and he could recall only disjointed fragments of the last several hours.

The important thing was that it was over.

It's over, he told himself again. *I'm free. I'm free, they can't touch me. Bauer can't touch me. I'll never have to see his ugly face ever again or hear his voice. I'll never have to—.*

A wave of nausea gripped him. He also realized he was hungry, but dismissed that. It wasn't important now. Suddenly, from somewhere outside the camper, he heard a loud, familiar chant. It called him outside.

Throwing aside the blankets, he staggered upright and looked around the cluttered space, spying a large jug of water near the little sink. He washed his face and his feet, then, catching up a dish towel that didn't appear too dirty, he opened the trailer door and stepped into the growing chill of the desert sunset. Overhead, on a network of slender poles, stretched yards of the camouflage netting favored by the Nightcrawler community.

He crunched several paces away from the door and turned to see the sun's upper rim just disappearing below the western horizon. Spreading the towel on the lumpy ground, he remained standing with upraised arms for several moments as his tongue, drunken with joy, stumbled over the familiar prayers. Then he kneeled and continued the ritual, tears streaming down his face.

Never before had he felt so much gratitude, so much peace. It felt as though a hand were stroking his head, comforting him, telling him everything was fine, everything was going to be good. The nightmare was truly over.

Nor was he alone in offering his prayers; scattered about the desert were several other kneeling forms, and his voice joined theirs. The Nightcrawler culture was notoriously secretive, so he didn't know many details about his hosts, but it seemed true that many of their numbers were Muslim. Either converts or descendants of immigrants, they had over the decades avoided the larger culture as they created their own unique take on a traditional nomadic lifestyle.

When the *maghrib* prayers finished tumbling from his lips, he rose, picked up the towel and walked back to the trailer. He heard voices coming from the other families in the surrounding vehicles, and saw some older teens engaged with dismantling and packing up the protective netting. But none came to check up on him, and he was too self-conscious to approach anyone.

Inside the ramshackle camper vehicle, he noticed a set of clothes, neatly folded, on the countertop in the kitchenette. He was too filthy to put these on, so he stepped into the tiny bathroom and took a minimalist shower. He longed to stand in the warm, cleansing stream forever, but assumed resources were scarce in the Nightcrawler community and wanted to be a thoughtful guest.

Emerging from the bathroom, he kicked aside the discarded prison uniform, and dressed himself in the new clothes. The jeans, shirt and fleece jacket were loose on him, but were clean and soft. Afterwards, he scoured the cabinets for something to eat. He found some fresh fruit and crackers. There was a little cheese and some fruit juice in the tiny refrigerator. He was ravenous, and began devouring the simple meal, his stomach growling and contracting in anticipation.

For several minutes, the only sounds were of his own chewing and swallowing. This pleased him; he enjoyed the sensation of being alone, but safe. Unwatched, free, with no constraints to his own thoughts and most basic actions.

Looking for more to drink, he wistfully contemplated a jar of instant coffee in the cabinet, but was pretty sure it would be too rich for his guts at the moment. Instead, he poured himself a little more juice, watered it down, then seated himself on the rumpled bedclothes.

Footsteps sounded outside the trailer, followed by a knock at the door.

Enrique froze in dread, a habit he knew might take time to discard. Steeling himself, he rose and opened the door to see Miguel Campos' friendly visage.

"Hey—mind if I come in?"

"Of course not."

Enrique stepped back and Campos entered, flashing an easy grin. "Hey, it's good to see you're awake. We let you sleep all day, thought you needed it. How are you feeling?"

Enrique looked down at his juice glass and realized it was trembling in his loose grip. "Okay...I guess."

Campos shut the door. "Well, you look great considering what you've been through."

Enrique nodded. Voice still weak, he managed to say, "Thanks. Thanks...for everything."

"Sure, glad to help."

"These people...they're okay with me being here?"

"Don't worry, they're experts at looking the other way and asking no questions...for a fee. And as long as the disinterest is mutual."

Campos parked his seat against the small counter, while putting his hands on his hips. He was not tall, but his fit and well-muscled shape was obvious beneath his jeans and leather jacket. There was an air of energetic eagerness about him; he seemed to be the kind of man who was more comfortable doing things instead of talking about them.

He said, "Now that you're up and about, I need to fill you in on some stuff. We'll be on the road again about twenty minutes. I'll be driving this rig until the next rendezvous point, where we'll switch to a smaller train heading northeast. There's a van embedded there just for us, which I'll drive the rest of the way, while you kick back and continue to rest."

Enrique nodded. "Yeah, sure. Any sign yet we're being followed?"

Campos shook his head. "Nada. But that doesn't mean we aren't looking over our shoulders every step of the way. Just because we're out here in the middle of nowhere doesn't mean we can't still be spotted, which is why the protocol requires us to do most traveling at night."

"Right."

Campos straightened. "The plan is to be at the rendezvous by nine p.m. At some point, when we get a good satellite connection, one of your colleagues is going to check in with you."

"Any idea who? Is it Greg Park?"

"No clue. Anyway, after we switch vehicles, we'll be at our final destination about ten hours after that. There's some important folks waiting to see you at the end of the trail."

Enrique regarded him with an eager, wordless look. Campos laughed. "Yep—that's where your wife and the kids have been waiting the last few days."

Even though he'd already been told they were safe, Enrique couldn't stop a trickle of more tears. Campos gave him an encouraging punch on the shoulder and then departed. Minutes later, the desert was filled with the sounds of a few antique combustion engines rumbling and belching to life, as well as the faint hum of electric or fuel-cell vehicles.

After opening all the curtains, Enrique stretched on the bed and continued to calm himself as he felt the conveyance lurch and rumble from the campsite, then crawl onto the cracked asphalt of the old road. He watched glimpses of the darkening sky roll past the windows as the camper gained a little speed, but they never went particularly fast.

He began counting the hours until he'd be with Connie again, would put his arms around Toni. Did Luis even remember him? How much had both children grown? It had only been about three months since he'd last seen them, but it felt like a lifetime.

As he struggled to even recall Connie's face, horrific scenes from the past weeks surged forward in his mind and obscured her image. Feelings of hopelessness, of being out of control, of being victimized, of the continual terror, engulfed him again.

Groaning, he clutched weakly at his temples. Part of him wanted to talk with someone about all of this, but most of him wanted to bury it all and never look back.

CHAPTER
TWENTY-TWO

HAYDEN SINGER'S office at the Internal Security Agency overlooked a courtyard. It was a bleak space formed of cracked concrete, with a set of small bleachers at one end. The bleachers faced a metal post rising squatly in the center. As Hayden stood at the window, hands clasped behind his back, he mused over the significance of the yard and the pillar.

From this height and angle, the rusty streaks befouling the column couldn't be observed, but he knew well enough they were there. It was in this yard, at this pillar, that the secular authorities had for years administered sharia-based punishments on behalf of the Muslim community.

Although he'd ordered all such activities to cease, he was in no hurry to have the courtyard decommissioned. The tradition of fear the pillar represented was too useful to dismiss, thus he was prepared to reinstate similar punishments, under different codes, should the ISA need an extra tool in its arsenal of public relations controls.

Previously, in addition to enforcing some sharia codes, the Equity and Inclusion Office in the old Agency had sought—and prosecuted—cases of discrimination or blasphemy against the Prophet. At the same time, the authorities turned a blind eye to instances of harassment against Christians. The few churches that promoted idealized, desert-scripture-based sexual morality and gender roles, risked extra scrutiny and even fines.

Yet if a young gay or lesbian was found dead under circumstances that hinted at Muslim involvement, the death was not to be investigated. Nor were certain instances of domestic violence, child marriages, or rumors of honor killings.

On both a personal and strategic level, he was beyond glad the era of catering to the Muslim community was at an end. Now that the sword of cultural Islam had outlived its usefulness as a weapon to sow mistrust and division throughout the population, it was time for the regime to rescind its privileged status.

Already, reports confirmed the general populace was delighted with the authorities for disbanding the Public Virtue Division, and both Singer and the Comms Secretary agreed that that goodwill should be fostered, especially in light of ongoing martial-adjacent law and looming shortages.

The Central Committee had approved plans to more actively promote the Power Cult among the populace. To that end, the ISA had already mandated daily gatherings for all officers and civilian employees, and now the Comms Department's plans called for a slow build-up of interest via a new wave of positive propaganda. As shortages increased, participation would improve when linked to direct food rewards. It was hoped punishment for the hold-outs would not be needed.

Balancing punishment and reward, testing how far a community could be pushed towards a desired goal without triggering a backlash, was both an art and a science. The mere threat of pain and suffering was often as effective a tool as actual physical harm. Yet even such subtle tools were best used judiciously, and attuned to the subject.

Singer turned from the gray morning view and reseated himself at his desk. Swiping his computer screen, he resumed scowling at the survcam footage from Pilot Rock, recently delivered by a security courier. The flash drive had contained the usual reports from Commander Bauer, including dull but important columns of current stats about the facility's operations. Plus footage from the latest interrogation sessions.

As he reviewed the videos in Cosimo Nicholl's file, he was conflicted. While it was clear the priest had no useful information, this ending seemed needlessly harsh and wasteful. Plus, if word ever got out, the local Christian community now had a genuine martyr to inspire them.

Closing Nicholl's file, he then switched to the latest info on Enrique

Rodriguez: still alive, integrating into camp life. Yet no sign he possessed any actionable intel regarding MacIntyre, Park or the Restoration.

With a drawn-out, dissatisfied exhalation, Hayden pushed back in his seat, drumming his fingers on the edge of the desk as his mind wrestled with his options. Was it possible he was wrong about Rodriguez' depth of involvement? Were Park's associates compartmentalized into such isolated cells that their operatives truly had no idea who else was on their team? Perhaps it was time to pay another personal visit to Rodriguez and find out once and for all. Hayden checked his schedule for the next few days and began calculating where he could carve out the hours required for such a trip. A knock on the door interrupted him, and he looked up as Officer Holmes entered.

Presenting a small slip of plastic and metal, the man announced, "Chief, a courier from Pilot Rock just delivered this."

Sensing bad news, Singer accepted the flash drive. "Did he say what's on it?"

Holmes said, "Trouble with one of the prisoners." He gave off a strong whiff of anxiety, which Singer put down to his own cultivated reputation for not suffering fools gladly.

"Which one?"

"Guy by the name of Enrique Rodriguez. I think he used to be with the Information Tech Oversight Division."

"I know who he is!" snapped the chief. "What do you mean—'trouble'?"

"Sir, it seems he escaped."

Singer regarded him in disbelief. "Did they send a party after him?"

"Yes, sir. Of course. But those officers were killed."

"Killed?"

"Yes, the rescuers were better prepared than the lithium facility guards expected."

Singer snarled, "What was he doing at the lithium plant?"

"Sir, I don't—,"

"Never mind—when did this happen?"

"Day before yesterday, sir."

Infuriated, but working to maintain an air of self-control, Singer jammed the drive into the side of his computer and called up the data.

There was a slight tremor in Holmes' voice. "Sir, will the courier be needed to take a reply back?"

Singer waved his hand in a short, impatient chop. "Yes, but I need to review this report for myself first." He rapidly scoured the new data, trembling with suppressed fury when he read the description of the event.

As far as he could tell, none of the other Pilot Rock prisoners knew what had happened. He shot a glance at Holmes. "Does anyone outside the processing facility know about this?"

"Not that I know of, sir."

"Excellent. Please keep word of this incident to yourself." Rising abruptly, he added, "I need you to cancel my meetings for today. Dismiss the courier—I'm driving over to the eastern sector in person to follow up on this."

"Yes, sir."

As he made his way to his vehicle in the facility's parking garage, Singer's mind throbbed with outrage. *I'm going to have a few words with that incompetent jackass, Bauer. And I'll bet anything that somehow, on some level, MacIntyre or his associates were involved with this.*

It was unlikely he'd be able to keep a lid on this event, but he was desperate to try.

PART TWO

CHAPTER
TWENTY-THREE

"SO, you said Connie's doing good, right? Does she look happy? How are the kids? You saw them all in person, right? Did you…did you…did you talk to them?"

Standing to one side of the concrete and tiled deck encircling the hacienda's swimming pool, Owen MacIntyre reviewed for the third time his recent conversation with Enrique, recorded through a computer embedded in one of the Nightcrawler vans.

His own videoskin displayed a foreshortened view of a passenger cabin, with Enrique occupying a black upholstered seat. The former captive's fingers clutched with febrile motions at the arms of the fleece shirt hanging off his wasted frame. The camera relayed how his eyes burned like intense coals in his battered face as he eagerly awaited Owen's answer.

MacIntyre heard his own recorded voice say reassuringly, "They're a bit worried about you, but they're in good hands. Connie's waiting to speak with you as soon as you and I are done here."

"Why not now?"

"It will take a few more minutes to set up a link to their location," Owen said. "But while we're waiting, I need to discuss some things. When you get to the village, expect that Greg will arrange a full official debriefing. Be prepared for extensive interviews. So it might be a good idea if you tell me everything you can while it's fresh in your mind, just you and me. Not so much pressure."

Enrique's haunted look intensified as his mouth drooped into a reluctant line. He slumped back in his seat, empty eyes focused on a point on the floor near his boots. He seemed frozen and unaware when MacIntyre's voice continued:

"Take your time, whenever you're ready."

After a prolonged silence, Enrique lifted his head and met the camera. "I want to help…it's just…,"

"Yeah, it's hard. You've been through hell. I understand—." Realizing even his most compassionate tone was inadequate, even intrusive, Owen had shut his mouth and waited.

Rodriguez choked, "They have the women separated from the men. Except they take the younger ones and…mostly it's the guards who…the guards who…," He passed a shaking hand over his eyes, then continued brokenly, "They wanted me to participate…in what they were doing to the women. To break me down, I guess. And they had footage of Connie at another camp, said it would only stop if I gave in and told them where I thought you and Park were,"

"Fake," said Owen with firm assurance.

"Deep down, I knew it was, but still….they kept trying to force me. And the priest from Sofia's church…,"

"Cosimo Nicholl?"

"Yeah."

"Oh, damn, damn!" Owen had forced himself to ask, "How do you know they were forcing him to participate?"

Rodriguez took a long breath and steadied himself. "They ran a video of it, on the stage…and accused him of being a hypocrite. Ridiculed him before… before Bauer did it, with a knife…made us all watch the execution."

"Ah, geez, no—," Now Owen turned the recording's volume down a few ticks; even on the third viewing, the news didn't get easier to hear. He heard his voice ask, "And what did you tell them? About me and Park?"

Enrique didn't seem to hear his tentative words. A glassy, distant look was creeping over his face. Gently, Owen insisted, "Did you tell them anything about the Restoration?"

Enrique's answer was a long time in coming, but it was what Owen wanted to hear, and it seemed heartfelt: "No."

"You understand why I had to ask, right?"

"Yeah, yeah, Mac. Of course."

Silencing that footage, Owen then flipped to the recording of the full testimony prepared for Park and some members of President Chakrabarti's cabinet, pausing at the most damning passages.

He felt his blood pressure surge dangerously as he did so. It was painful to watch his friend, traumatized and prematurely aged, drag forth his halting, detailed account of the atrocities he'd witnessed. It was infuriating to listen to the actual words, to see the drone footage Miguel Campos had provided of Cosimo Nicholl's murder. That event was so shocking, Owen had not shared the news with Sofia. He wasn't sure when or how he could.

The horror of these revelations seemed unreal on that warm afternoon beneath careless clear skies. And he was still grappling with what Greg had shared with him following release of the testimony: in Park's opinion, the evidence of atrocities might eventually bolster President Chakrabarti's case for taking action against Pacifica, but for now, that hard-won evidence wasn't convincing either the public or key lawmakers.

"The Defense Department isn't impressed with Enrique's testimony about the abuses in the camps," Park, exasperated, had updated Owen earlier that day. "And, sure, the footage of Nicholl's murder is troubling, but it's just one death."

MacIntyre had struggled to hold back his anger at this news. It triggered flashbacks to when, after having caught Francisco Chen dead to rights in the middle of a narco-terror plot, he was unable to bring charges against him and Tomás. The were too privileged. Plus, certain vested interests had wanted them dropped.

"What more do they want?" he'd snapped at Park. "Footage of the rapes in the camps? Would that be enough evidence?"

"I don't know, Mac. But be patient, we've got top people working on a response."

"'Top people'? That's hardly reassuring. Well, what about the lithium angle? If they're exporting, can we at least bring more sanctions?" Even as he spoke, Owen knew this suggestion was useless.

"There's no evidence they're doing anything other than trying to ramp-up their own domestic battery production. There seems to be an uptick in timber and grain exports, but needless to say, they're selling to folks who don't honor sanctions."

With a sigh, Greg shoved his glasses up and pinched the bridge of his nose. He went on, "I know it's damn frustrating, but remember—there's a few powerful senators who don't want to hear anything bad about Pacifica. They're pushing for it to succeed, to prove the old 'American Experiment' a failure once and for all."

"Maybe they're right. Why are we even bothering to fight this war?" Owen's bitterness had surprised even himself.

Park replied, "Don't let a set-back dishearten you so much. Remember, we're in this for the long haul."

"Yeah, sure." MacIntyre steadied his breathing before asking, "But do you know if there's any move to provide covert support to any budding resistance movements?"

"There may very well be something in the works, but I'm not privy to it. We need to be focusing on our long-term projects."

Switching off the recording of this conversation, Owen lowered himself into one of the patio's chaise lounges. He found it almost impossible to let go of his frustration, now containing hefty doses of disgust and disillusionment. He was approaching a fork in the road of his life's journey, and the sensation was not pleasant.

If Restoration operatives could not convince lawmakers to take immediate, forceful, diplomatic or military action against Pacifica, what good were they? Would they merely supplement any electoral successes by mounting yet another high-tech mindshaping campaign? Did they believe they could turn the population against the new country by directly altering brain chemistry, instead of presenting a clear case for the threat and taking needed action?

He asked himself again if it was a waste of his time and talents to continue his involvement with *novus ignis*. Or was the problem that he was focusing his efforts in the wrong areas? He thought of the idea he'd had while working in Ebersol's intel lab, but where to begin? He'd need access to massive amounts of funding, preferably funding unrelated to Paloma Foundation or anything to do with the Chen-Diaz family.

Without warning, a voice shattered his intense rumination: *"Buenas tardes!* May I join you?"

Owen regarded the tall, dark-haired man stepping from the kitchen. Framed by the colorful, traditional tile work decorating the patio's stucco arches, Tomás Chen stood a moment, looking a little lost in his own home.

Rising eagerly to meet his benefactor, Owen said, "Hey—Tomás! I was just thinking about you!"

The visitor moved with an easy, loose-limbed grace that complemented his height; his strong-featured, open face was alight with amiability.

"I hope you don't mind my stopping by without notice," he said, grasping Owen's hand while massaging his shoulder with his free hand.

"Good Lord, no! I wish you'd visit more often. And this will always be your home, not mine." Owen waved him to a seat and poured him a drink.

Accepting the glass, Tomás contradicted him. "No, it won't. I have to stop thinking I can always come back here, anytime I feel like it. My life is going to be different soon, but some old habits keep pulling me back."

With an understanding shrug, Owen sipped his own drink.

Growing more animated, Tomás announced, "But I've made time to get away for some camping before I leave for the seminary. I'm going to visit the *Parque natural Las Hermosas* one last time. Do you want to join me?"

After the stress of the last few weeks, the idea of a few days spent in the heart of nature, away from any political concerns, had undeniable appeal. Owen answered readily, "Oh, sure! I'd love to do some more exploring around there."

"Wonderful! Oh, and I'm giving away more of my things, and I wanted you to have these."

Tomás fished a flat, black case from his pocket, which Owen mutely accepted and opened. It was a set of ornately illustrated, animated tarot cards made from sheets of thin, durable videoskin.

With a far-away, wistful tone, Tomás said, "They were very important to me at one time in my life. They're so beautiful…it was the beauty in them that helped me through some very difficult experiences…it led me into a different world and helped me keep my sanity." He smiled sheepishly. "Or at least, what little I've got."

"You're doing great." Grinning, Owen shuffled through the images, impressed with the mesmerizing quality of the ever-shifting, fractal-inspired artwork. His gut responded with a faint lurch to the illusion of depth and motion created by the infinite regressions.

Abruptly, he slid the cards into the case and snapped it shut. "They'll still belong to you—I'll just safeguard them for awhile."

Tomás nodded. Growing more serious, he said, "And speaking of leftover belongings, I suppose something should be done with all of Selena's things. They're still in her studio?"

"Yes, I believe so."

Owen had not given much thought to the collection of unfinished fashion projects languishing in the private quarters over the garage. Tomás' mistress had left them behind, following her severe nervous breakdown and hospitalization.

He asked, "Do you want me to donate them somewhere?"

Tomás lifted a shoulder. "I'll ask her mother if she wants any of it first."

"Good idea. Well, otherwise—how has life been for you lately?"

"Very quiet and orderly. I like living in a much smaller place."

"Sounds like ideal practice for being a monk."

"Priest," corrected the other.

"Right. Well, isn't that what you wanted?"

"Yes, well—," Tomás toyed with his glass, then set it aside without taking a drink. He uttered a diffident laugh. "Sometimes it's *too* quiet. I just need to hear voices other than my own, what's in my own head."

"So you weren't kidding about your sanity?" Owen spoke lightly, but he regarded the other with concern.

Slumped in his seat, Tomás' large hands trailed over the armrests. A forlorn look shadowed his expressive, long-tailed hazel eyes. After several wordless minutes, he sighed. "No, I only want someone to talk with."

"Even if it's me?"

Tomás smiled. "Especially if it's you…despite everything, you always stuck with me and told me the truth, even when I didn't want to hear it."

"Sure." Owen sat forward in his seat. Without thinking, he said, "It's not too late."

"Not too late for what?"

"Well, I mean—," Owen lifted his hand. Now that he was committed to continue, he had to answer with diplomacy. "You aren't ordained yet. You can still come back, we can work together on Paloma business and accomplish a lot. You know I'd sign my duties back over to you in a heartbeat."

Tomás' wandering glance became more earnest and returned to Owen. "My new life means a lot to me."

"Yes, of course, but—,"

Tomás spoke over him, "Once, I asked you to commit to working exclusively with me as a business partner, but you weren't interested. What changed?"

"I know I said that then, and I'm sorry. But it turns out, it's more of a challenge to balance all my obligations than I thought it would be."

"Your obligations?" Tomás regarded him with a somewhat fierce tilt of his heavy brow. "Other than Paloma, what are you *obligated* to be doing?"

Owen's teeth worried his lower lip and his fingers absently twisted the gold signet ring of the Paloma foundation on his right hand. It felt unusually cumbersome that evening. He had no intention of going into detail about how his entanglement with the Restoration was fragmenting his attention while dissipating his energy.

Provoked by the prolonged quiet, Tomás insisted, "The turmoil back in your home state—are you still involved with that?"

"Not much. It's more of a huge…distraction."

"Yes, I imagine it would be. Well, officially, I have no influence on the situation, but I need to ask you something: if you're ever tempted to use Paloma resources for any political activities in your home country, please don't."

Owen's brows rose. "Can you be more specific? By 'resources', do you mean assets other than 'funds' or do you mean *everything?*"

Tomás shook his head. "I suppose I just mean 'funds'. Anything else—like aircraft or business connections—I won't ask. Just be cautious, and don't lose sight of what I trust you to do here."

"Of course I won't." Owen saluted him with a slight wave.

So much for enlisting his help on my grand idea, he thought wryly. *Looks like I'll have to reach out to the next billionaire on my really short list.*

Tomás continued, "I think it would be terrible for you to get caught up in trying to direct the course of something as huge as a country, and lose sight of the good you can accomplish here. Just because Paloma operates on a much smaller scale, that doesn't mean the work isn't important." With a warm but self-conscious upturn of his lips, he concluded, "I'm sorry—please forgive the sermon."

"Aren't you supposed to be practicing sermons?" Owen laughed. "But hey, I understand what you're saying, and I appreciate your insight. Thank you."

At that moment, voices reached them from inside the hacienda; Sofia and Isabella had returned from a shopping trip. They walked out onto the patio, trailed by Diego Rojas and the housekeeper, Teresa Ortega.

"*Don Tomás!*" squealed Isabella. The girl rushed forward, her thin, plain face made beautiful with joy.

Tomás rose and greeted her with a warm hug, then grinned at Diego. The taciturn guard ducked his shaved head and smiled in return. Owen noticed the man seemed happy to quietly bask in the presence of his former employer, that he responded to him in a way he never did to Owen. Which was understandable; Rojas had served the Chen family for years, and the MacIntyres were outsiders.

Sofia said, "What a pleasant surprise! Can you stay to supper?"

"I probably shouldn't. I have a schedule to follow—,"

Sofia's musical laugh was low and sincere. "Oh, that's nonsense! You're still free for weeks and weeks yet!"

"Yes—but I'm borrowing your husband for a camping trip soon."

A shadow passed over Sofia's face as she shot a sharp glance at Owen. "You're leaving again?"

"Purely recreational this time—trust me."

She looked partly doubtful, partly relieved. "Well, in that case, I'm sure you'll both have fun."

His arm encircled her waist and he grinned at her. "That's the plan!"

Late that night, after Tomás' departure and while the home was quiet with sleep, Owen's mind was too alert and restless for him to relax. He made his way to the hacienda's book-lined study, where antique bronze statues rested in niches, the light stucco walls were adorned with sleepy oil paintings in heavy gold frames.

Unlocking one of the drawers of the heavy old desk, he reached under some random papers and withdrew a small, clear casket. In the soft lamplight, he studied the broken fragments of a miniature electronic device, spattered with specks of dried blood. A single strand of dark hair was embedded in the blood.

The sight of the broken device brought back many memories. Reflexively, he ran a finger along the seal between his VIA implant and his skull, thinking how strange it was to now be residing on the property where Francisco Chen had presumably first hatched his dark schemes.

Focusing again on the pieces in his hand, Owen's heart rate quickened, his palms grew damp. He forced himself to briefly relive the frightening impressions of events from three years ago, when he first encountered the man, a clone, who had worn the twin of this broken device, a mysterious hypertransmitting unit. After the assault, Owen's fragmented account of the incident hadn't exactly convinced the authorities that Francisco and Tomás Chen were even involved.

The fact Francisco, following the seizure of his weaponized drug, Thorn, was behind bars and isolated from all comms tech was a hard fact to overlook. Furthermore, there was no proof he had cloned himself. But convinced otherwise, Owen's determination to uncover the truth of the matter had driven him to track Tomás and the clone, Alejandro, to China, Japan and at last, back to Colombia.

In the end, Alejandro was dead, and Francisco was stripped of all money and social status. His hypertransmission device was forcibly removed from his brain, and the shards now rested in Owen's palm. By the end of the Thorn adventure, Owen's instincts had been proven correct. Were they correct now, regarding the path ahead for his involvement in the Restoration? He was gripped by his earlier, bitter frustration at the lack of a clear plan regarding Pacifica.

He paced the study and stopped before a window, regarding the shapes of the plantings outside the building. At that hour, their dark silhouettes seemed unfathomable and menacing. Filled with dangerous unknowns.

The Restoration's long game makes sense strategically, he admitted. *And their experts are far more experienced than I am. But so much of what they are doing is theoretical—just because they're experts doesn't mean they have all the answers, that their long-term plans are fool-proof.*

He couldn't shake his thoughts about what life in Pacifica must now be like for his former neighbors and co-workers. When humans had no alternative, they could acclimate to just about any circumstance, but it was never pleasant living under brutal authority in a precarious economy. Just getting along, existing from day to day in a climate of fear, was hardly living.

Snippets of the recording of Cosimo's murder played again in his mind's eye, and suddenly, his resolve hardened.

It's taking too damn long for the 'experts' to really achieve anything. I'll start work on my idea tomorrow. It might come to nothing, but it might also be exactly what's needed to help.

With a sense of release and a resolute smile, he turned the casket over again in his fingers. Then he went to the desk, replaced the container and locked the drawer.

CHAPTER
TWENTY-FOUR

OUTSIDE THE OFFICE of President Cassian Gray, the security guard stood at attention, erect as a suit of armor in a museum. Unlike a museum display, a strong sense of alertness lurked behind the deceptive impassivity of the man's Augmented Reality glasses.

Hayden Singer approached the guard, saying crisply, "Tell the president I'm here."

"Yes, Chief Enforcer," the man replied with a nod, then disappeared through the door. After several moments, the door reopened and the man beckoned Singer over the threshold. "He'll see you now."

President Gray's office in the former Oregon State Capitol building was unadorned and business-like. Gray traveled to Olympia and Sacramento as infrequently as possible, making it clear by his actions that Salem was to be regarded as the seat of power for the new regime.

At the moment, the president stood to one side of the antique desk, perusing some documents. Singer approached and stood at attention. "Good afternoon, Mr. President. I understand you wish to discuss a few things with me in private."

Gray looked up with the hint of a smile. The president was medium-height, well-proportioned and fit. His sandy hair was full, the creases on his face gave him, if not a look of wisdom, at least a venerable, trustworthy air. He was talented at projecting a sense of self-possession that helped put his audience at ease—that was undoubtedly a factor in his original election to the governorship, which seemed decades ago, not just a few years. Today, his nondescript yet classic, balanced face was more serious than usual.

Setting the papers down on the desk, he took Singer's hand in a firm shake. "Good to see you, Chief Enforcer Singer."

He motioned him towards a nearby overstuffed chair. "I know you're busy these days, and it can be hard for you to make time to drive down here. Take a seat, make yourself comfortable. Coffee?"

"No, thank you." Singer remained standing for a fraction of a second; his instinct was to dominate from his impressive height. But after months of working for this man, he knew Gray was immune to such subtle mind games, might even resent them. So he relented and took the proffered chair, regarding the now-seated president with a guarded but attentive countenance.

With an arm flung casually over one of the armrests of his own leather office chair, Gray began to rock the slightly seat from side-to-side as he spoke. "Well, Hayden—do you mind if we dispense with the formalities here? 'Chief Security Enforcer' sounds impressive in public, but it's a bit of a mouthful in private."

"Whatever you prefer, Mr. President."

Gray laughed. "Very good. *That's* a title that gets easier each time you say it, isn't it?"

"No doubt, sir."

After smoothing a wrinkle in the front of his cream-colored dress shirt, Gray said, "In any case, Hayden, I want to say how impressed I am with the job you've been doing over the last months. These conditions are pretty challenging—no, frankly, they're hellish in some spots—but I admire your ingenuity, your creativity, your dedication. You've become invaluable to my administration, and I wanted to thank you for that personally."

"Thank you, sir. I really appreciate that."

Weaving his fingers, the President sat forward and rested his elbows near the center of the desk. "Unfortunately, things are going to get rougher. The fact we had to postpone our own elections here in Pacifica means people might get confused, maybe dissatisfied."

"Yes sir. It's extremely unfortunate that key parts of the infrastructure are still not up and running."

"Indeed." Gray's mouth quivered with a smile. "But we have to work within our current limitations until our allies come through with their promised aid."

Hayden perked up at this hint. "Do you mean the Mozi quantum satellite, Mr. President? Is there an updated timeline for that, sir?"

The President jerked both his thumbs in a noncommittal twitch. "China keeps changing their story, and we aren't in a position to complain. But I don't think it will be in place before December. Of course, you will get updates as soon as possible."

"Very good."

"In the meantime, the Communications Secretary is ramping up a PR campaign to assure folks new elections will be held sometime next year. Spring, we hope. It will take a few months to acclimate everyone to the idea of starting over on an entirely new electoral schedule."

"Yes, Mr. President."

"But of course, that's more of a propaganda issue. There's a few more pressing concerns that are more in your line." Falling silent, his meaningful glance strayed to the piles of documents on his desk.

Singer waited, the lines of his body tightening as he appeared more alert and professional.

Gray looked up and met his eyes. "The data from the Budget Committee just arrived, and as expected, the economic situation in Pacifica is…shaky."

"Growing pains, Mr. President."

Gray uttered a laugh, unexpected and dry. "Oh, indeed! But that doesn't absolve us from taking steps to ease those pains."

He lowered his gaze to the desk while a troubled expression crept over his face. The bags under his eyes made him appear more stern than usual. At last, he said, "The layers of cultural and administrative rot in this region go much deeper than I anticipated when I first decided to run for the Governorship. Now that I'm regularly getting classified reports from our different departments, I can see the road to a strong, independent country is going to be much more difficult, especially with the quality of the average citizen we have to work with."

Hayden inclined his head in agreement, even as he shifted in his chair, wondering where Gray was headed with these observations.

Sighing, the president went on, "It won't be easy, but after much soul-searching, I've decided to accept the recommendations offered by numerous agencies for an extensive cost-reduction initiative. To that end, I'm enlisting your expertise to help implement some of these recommendations."

"With all due respect, what does the ISA have to do with economic policies? We can't cut more from our own budget."

Gray's glance flicked towards Singer. "Oh, I don't expect you to. We'll be cutting costs elsewhere. For example, our new version of the TotalityCare health program will need to be severely streamlined—we can't provide the same level of benefits."

Singer frowned. He was unsure where the President was going with this, but took a stab at an intelligent answer. "If the health program needs to cut its membership, can't they mount a voluntary 'Passing' campaign?"

Gray nodded. "Yes, that's on the Health Department's list of possible solutions. But a voluntary program will take too long, and that's where I'll need you to pick up the slack. Discreetly."

Singer did not answer for a moment. Then realization dawned and he tilted his chin up. "Yes, Mr. President."

"Good. Along the same lines, since Pacifica no longer participates in the Federal Haven Shelter Network, we don't have the resources to provide free chemical compounds and housing for the addict community. Consequently, there's a real danger they might get restive and cause issues. It would be best if their numbers were reduced. Soon, but also with… discretion."

"Understood, Mr. President."

All trace of his previous discomfort gone, Gray became more bright and brisk as he warmed to his next topic. "And of course, all of this is in addition to continued monitoring of the remnant religious communities. Keep an ear to the ground for unrest, any signs of growing civil disobedience."

"That's been my primary focus the last few weeks."

"Excellent." Gray leaned back in his chair, his penetrating gaze still holding Singer. "As long as you're here, there's one other thing we need to discuss."

His elegant fingers plucked a file folder from the documents. He passed it to Singer, eyes narrowing as he watched the chief open it. Singer began reading a dossier he himself had compiled and submitted weeks earlier. It was a dossier on Owen MacIntyre.

The president said, "It seems in addition to your other duties, you're devoting an inordinate amount of time towards locating the whereabouts of this man. I'm doubtful this so-called 'Restoration' you describe is a real movement, and if so, that such a loose collection of malcontents is in any way a threat. So I don't see what his value is to us."

Face flushing, Hayden said, "Mr. President, the Restoration movement isn't merely a 'loose network of malcontents'. There's considerable, mounting evidence that they do pose a threat to the stability of the remaining United States, as well as to Pacifica."

Singer grew uneasy as he observed a warning frown further crease Gray's face. The president took the file back and flipped through the pages with nonchalant but portentous motions. "I'm not convinced. There is zero concrete evidence tying this man to any larger, outside group. And even if such a group existed, I don't see how they could seriously threaten us."

Singer said, "With all due respect, sir, you don't have the background in security that I do. The Restoration may be a loose network, but I suspect they're very committed ideologues with long-term goals, and I firmly believe they're working to undermine our efforts here. MacIntyre has many connections—within our borders and within the network at large. I refuse to believe he's dropped everything to do with matters on the West Coast, that he's just getting on with his life."

For several tense moments, Gray observed him with a calculating expression. "It's true I don't have the experience in security matters you do, but I can recognize techniques of data manipulation. And when I look at the evidence included here, it looks to me like you're *wishcasting* rather than working with hard facts. Hayden, do you think it's possible you're spinning an entire thesis out of nothing?"

Singer's jaw tightened as he swallowed an irritated reply.

Gray continued: "In my view, whatever this group is, they aren't an immediate threat, and they certainly aren't on our doorstep. For the time being, as we continue to build our strengths here with our limited resources—very limited resources of assets, time, and energy—we must focus inward. The Communications Secretary will need your full attention to help monitor any grumbling about the cancelled elections and the next round of shortages."

Singer nodded. "Understood, sir."

At least he could be thankful Gray gave no indication he'd heard about the illicit Scorpio pistol units, like the one that had shown up during Nicholl's arrest. And while Singer could have offered Enrique's escape as evidence of the work of a larger network of enemies, he had decided against it. Instead, his official report on the event exonerated Bauer, and put the blame for the escape on the foreman of the lithium plant.

Leaning forward, Gray continued to press his point. "What may or may not be happening beyond our borders isn't as important as what's happening within, right in front of us. So you need to put this other issue on the back burner. Root out any trace of personal interest that might be clouding your judgement."

Singer felt a prick of outrage at the insinuation his preoccupation with MacIntyre was personal. His hands clenched in his lap, even as he answered in a chastened manner, "Mr. President, my every waking thought is dedicated to ensuring the success of Pacifica. If, at times, I am a bit…over-zealous, then forgive me. I certainly don't want to become myopic where genuine security issues are concerned."

Slapping the cover of the dossier shut, Gray extended his hand once more. "Glad to hear it, and I'm glad we've had this talk."

"Yes, Mr. President. Thank you for taking the time to advise me personally." Hayden shook the other's hand with a semblance of vigor and soon departed the office.

As he left the capitol, his pale eyes and impassive visage barely concealed his inner rage and humiliation. While his mind acknowledged the truth in Gray's concerns, he was heartsick with anger at being corrected.

On the drive north, he forced himself to shrug these feelings off; they deserved no attention. He was a professional, and was committed to maintaining the emotional detachment needed to discharge his duties as efficiently as possible.

Adjusting the night vision settings of his headset, Singer peered closer at the shadowy, indistinct shapes moving inside the run-down house at the end of the short, unpaved driveway. Even with digital enhancement, it was difficult to make out what was happening. But he knew the rest of his team was close by, concealed in the shadows alongside the ramshackle building.

The comfort of the unmarked vehicle where he had been working the last hour or so was beginning to wear off, although there was no place he'd rather be at the moment. While it wasn't his job to do stakeouts, being involved onsite in this operation helped him recapture some of the thrill of the gritty, hands-on work he had done during his years in California.

His overseeing of the take-down of a nest of religious freedom agitators at a San Francisco mosque years earlier had been seen by some as excessive, but given that it took place during an uprising, he felt it was justified to send a strong signal to troublemakers. Still, the bad publicity had led to him being demoted shortly after. He had languished for a few years as a sergeant at a maximum security facility in the southern portion of the state.

At least that job had given him the opportunity to study certain types of psychology up close, while refining various interrogation and punishment techniques. Ironically enough, his record at that facility was what brought him to the attention of those seeking a replacement to head up the Northwest Regional Law and Safety Agency.

Since his recent private talk with President Gray, Singer had spent two weeks monitoring the congregation of the tiny Franklin Street Mosque. The group under surveillance was deemed most likely to be angered by the suspension of the Public Virtue Division and the banning of the public call to prayers.

Since the small congregation was obviously on guard, it had been impossible to introduce a spy. Furthermore, putting out feelers or befriending informants was likely to rebound badly on the ISA at this point, in the deteriorating relationship between the mosque and the authorities.

So it came down to a matter of intense surveillance. Even though this group was not known to have engaged in any subversive activities, Singer felt they would make a good public example. Tonight, the net was drawing close about them.

Beneath the cloudy night sky of late October, frost was forming on the unkempt lawn and plantings bordering the edge of the suspects' property. Through his headset, Hayden watched the puffs of breath steaming from the hidden forms in the bushes surrounding the nasty little shed of a house.

Sergeant Holmes was in charge on the ground during this operation; he was doing an excellent job and seemed to have organized everything just right. There was no sign the inhabitants of the house had a clue about what lurked mere yards outside their walls.

Soon, Holmes' command to *'move in!'* crackled in Hayden's earpiece. Singer opened the door of his vehicle and slid out, struck by the chill night air, feeling his heart thud with excitement. He watched the nearest officer, huddled behind one of the cars parked on the side of the road, spring into action and lurch stealthily forward in a low crouch.

Singer observed with grim enjoyment as the other armored men guided a remote-controlled battering ram up the shallow front steps and against the door. Perhaps the ram was overkill, but it was impressive and known to evoke fear in those who found themselves cowering on the other side of whatever barrier it was sent to breach. For Singer, it was well worth the wear on the equipment to make a show of their technology; the malcontents didn't need to know just how close to the edge ISA was operating, with its dwindling resources and out-of-date tech.

The door buckled like wet cardboard. In the front room, forms scattered, diving for the rear entrance, where more officers awaited them. As he remained outside, Singer saw the glowing green outline of one small shape slip past the men at the rear of the building; it was now making its way along the structure.

Singer bolted from behind the shelter of the car door and, weapon in hand, rushed to intercept the figure. In the confusing shadows thrown by the overgrown shrubs, the hooded form appeared small and lithe, perhaps a young teen. Less than a yard from Singer, it froze, seemingly paralyzed with indecision.

Singer lunged, ready to pounce like a dog on a kitten; the youth raised its hand. An unexpected, intense glow glanced off Singer's stomach; he felt only a momentary, dazzling spray of warmth as his thin sheet of body armor diffused the pistol's energy beam. He felt no physical danger, did not even consider firing back. Blind anger drove him to snatch at his assailant, grasping its shoulder and whirling it around forcefully.

His prey felt like a doll beneath his powerful, leather-encased grip; the youth struggled and squeaked, kicking ferociously at Singer's shins. Sheathing his own weapon, he then effortlessly wrestled the small pistol from the youth's weak grasp. The teen sank fierce teeth into the unprotected gap on Singer's wrist, between his glove and shirt cuff.

The chief caught his breath at the sudden pain, but his grip tightened further into the youth's hoodie, even as the wearer squirmed and slid free of the garment. Singer caught a glimpse of a pale, curvy torso intersected by a black brassiere. He clutched harder, his gloved left hand grasping the girl's long, soft hair.

"Hold still, you stinking cunt," he hissed, drawing his right arm back and striking her across the jaw. She fought to not cry out, but whimpered as she hung by her hair from his other hand. He dragged her to the front of the property, thrusting her towards one of the other officers.

"Take this bitch—when you get what we need from her interrogation, send her to Pilot Rock," he sneered. "They'll have some important work for her there."

All occupants registered at that address was soon accounted for. In addition to the girl, there were two older women and six men of varying ages. Their processing commenced swiftly at the fleet of ISA vehicles now clogging the driveway.

Holmes left the house and approached Singer, announcing, "We've finished securing the crime scene, sir. Scanned it, no booby traps. Do you want to come in now and supervise the wrap-up?"

"Yes. Good work, Sergeant," said Singer, striding towards the house. With Holmes tagging along behind him like a proud kid, the chief strode from room to room, glancing about with a keen, practiced eye. All devices had been seized and would be analyzed, but for now, there were no obvious sheets of plans, no bomb-making equipment. Just many dishes of food, specialty items likely prepared for some private celebration.

The lack of evidence of a major crime wasn't an issue for Singer; the girl's weapon was sufficient seed from which to grow whatever case against them was required. He began making mental notes about what other details would need to come out during the interrogation of the suspects.

Whatever he wanted to be discovered, would be. After all, it had been easy enough for him to orchestrate the false-flag riots and bombings that had rocked the region prior to Pacifica's birth.

In this specific case, the seizure of a cell of terror suspects, real or manufactured, and a public execution or two, would go a long way to prove to President Gray that Singer knew what he was doing and had Pacifica's security well in hand.

CHAPTER
TWENTY-FIVE

SOFIA STOOD to one side in the abandoned studio, feeling drab and mousy in her simple linen skirt and top. She watched her guest, Señora Lupe Medina, flip through a few of the sketchbooks spread on the work table in the center of the chamber. The older woman's body was clad in a leopard-print sheath dress that revealed every one of her ample curves.

"*Oh, mira estos hermosos colores!*" The rich Spanish phrases rolled so quickly from the woman's mouth that Sofia had trouble following. "These sketches—she has so much talent! Such an eye for beauty!"

"*Sí,*" said Sofia, smiling despite her inner disquiet. "Your daughter is a wonderful artist."

Sofia didn't feel up to being a gracious hostess that morning, but nonetheless put on a welcoming smile and waited patiently as Lupe sorted through her unfortunate daughter's belongings. The studio/living quarters, located in the remodeled garage of the Chen-Diaz estate, overflowed with a bewildering profusion of fabrics and art supplies. Despite all the bright colors and sumptuous textures, Selena Vasquez' unfinished fashion projects retained a forlorn, tragic air.

As she turned the pages of a sketch portfolio, Señora Medina asked coquettishly, "And do you know where Don Tomás is this afternoon?"

Sofia said, "He sends his regrets, but he had to meet with my husband in the city, to go over some legal matters for the Foundation. It seems there's lots of little things to take care of before he leaves in November—do you know he's going to a seminary in Russia?"

Lupe shook her masses of luxurious, raven curls as her boldly outlined eyes grew soulful. "Sí! It's a story for the ages, isn't it? He can't live without her, and no woman can ever replace her in his heart, so he's going to shut himself off from the world."

"Yes, I suppose so," Sofia agreed, revealing no more of her own opinion about Tomás' and Selena's relationship.

She had only interacted with Selena briefly, and other than the latter's abundant physical charms, wasn't sure what Tomás had ever seen in her. To Sofia, it seemed his goals and ideals were very different than the aspiring fashion designer's had been. She wondered if, on some level, he had come to regret the relationship even before the young woman's mental breakdown.

It was tiring for Sofia to watch Lupe exclaim in delight over her daughter's works. The woman seemed oblivious to the pall of failure and decay that pervaded the space. Sofia guessed this was how Lupe dealt with the heartbreak of her only child being so emotionally damaged by her experiences as a trafficked comfort worker, in a high-end American brothel, before Tomás had secured her release.

When Señora Medina decided which clothing items and sketchbooks she wanted to keep, Sofia invited her to the hacienda for refreshments. Lupe was thrilled to see inside the legendary Chen-Diaz residence. After the tour, the women adjourned to the patio and sat in the shade as Teresa Ortega brought a tray of food and drinks.

With a flutter of her thick lashes and a meaningful flick of her long, iridescent purple nails towards Sofia's modestly swelling stomach, Lupe said, "So, how far along?"

"I'm due late February."

"Oh, dear! And you haven't transferred yet?" asked the older woman with authoritative concern.

Sofia frowned. "Excuse me?"

"My sweet, you should have had a surrogate carrier from the beginning! But it's not too late to get the pregnancy transferred— in fact, I know one or two young girls who'd be glad of the job. I insist you let me set you up with one of them—believe me, you'll feel so much freer. No sickness, no pain or mess at the end, either."

Unsure how to reply to Lupe's unexpected suggestion, Sofia focused for a moment on the light glancing off the ice cubes in her drink. "No, thank you. I appreciate the thought, but we don't feel that would be right for us."

"Are you sure? There are so many advantages!" Lupe proceeded to rhapsodize about the benefits of such a move, and also branched out into a report of how her own daughter's extensive prenatal genetic conditioning had made her such a lovely specimen.

Sofia's mind drifted away from the woman's words, instead recalling the lectures she'd grown up hearing from her parents, who were staunch defenders of traditional Christian teachings in matters of human biology.

John and Maggie Volkov made certain their children knew the arguments for and against various genetic manipulation techniques. Sofia's stomach still writhed when she recalled her father's dark tales of abuses in research facilities, notably Chinese, in the race to boost population and mass-produce made-to-order humans customized for different applications. There had been much experimentation, and colossal failures of the artificial wombs, untold losses of tiny lives.

Cultural backlash against some of these practices had led to the half-hearted creation of global guidelines and ethical standards for human reproduction technologies, but these weren't universally enforced. After the promise of artificial womb technology hadn't panned out, there was a massive rise in the use of surrogates—some more willing than others, depending on which culture the women had the misfortune to be born into.

Yet, steady advances in CRISPER gene-engineering technology made the fine-tuning of embryos for wealthy parents a lucrative industry, and thus laws were always being bent, re-written or ignored.

Sofia and Owen had no objection to heading off the risks of inherited diseases; her own parents had done as much for her and her brother, and Owen wished his had chosen that option for him. There was also the chance their son would want to go into some profession that required proof of minimum genetic health, so they had agreed to give him a better chance in life by starting some basic conditioning in the first trimester.

But an embryonic transference wasn't on the table. Since this wasn't a high-risk pregnancy, mere convenience was not a good excuse for the expense and unnatural trouble. Sofia could almost hear her dad, sounding like a fiery Old

Testament prophet, expounding about how little good ever came from interfering with Nature's original biological blueprints.

Most important to her, however, beyond all the debate for or against such a move, Sofia could not forget how long she had waited for this experience. She had been thankful, even in the midst of her months of morning sickness, and could not imagine forgoing a single, blessed second of knowing her little son was nestled, secure and oblivious, directly below her heart.

With a smile, Sofia said, "Thanks for the advice, but it wouldn't feel right to have someone else take on the pain and the...uh, *mess* that's mine by right."

"But that's what *they're* paid for! *You* don't have to live like a peasant from two hundred years ago! And you should think about all the damage you're doing to your figure," Lupe observed airily, punctuating her warning by waving a mango slice. "Of course, this is just general advice, but I should think that, *in private*, your man would prefer it if you get that tight little belly back as soon as possible." The fruit quickly disappeared between her generous, violet-red lips, then she reached for her drink.

Sofia's cheeks flamed and she tossed her head, brushing her hair back from where it draped over her collarbone. She managed an awkward laugh. "Um, *in private*, that's...um...not an issue for him."

Yet even as she spoke, her hands lowered and she massaged the tight surface of her stomach. She could not help wondering what Owen really thought of her changing shape; he almost seemed to be making excuses to be gone most days of each week, and when he was home, he was busy late into the night, coming to bed hours after she had fallen asleep. She couldn't remember the last time they'd indulged in one of their other favorite activities —reading aloud to one another from a relaxing book.

Of course he was consumed by important projects, but he made time for Tomás. Was Owen making excuses to avoid spending more time with her, was he avoiding touching her? Could he possibly find her changing shape off-putting?

Don't be ridiculous, she admonished herself, gripped in a wave of melancholy. *I'm being so selfish and trivial. How can I think like this, after the horrible news I've just had?*

Pushing this heavy thought away, she struggled to refocus on her guest.

Lupe was saying, "My dear, if you have anything at all on your mind, just think of me as your substitute mama."

Sofia laughed brightly. "That's so sweet, thank you. But we are doing great."

Señora Medina's eyes twinkled as she regarded her over her the edge of her glass. "Ah, that's so inspirational to hear! Bless you both!"

It was late afternoon when the woman departed. Fighting a headache, Sofia's defenses crumbled against the emotions and thoughts she'd had kept at bay during Lupe's visit. Agitated, she drifted from the entertainment room and into the larger, more formal sitting area where a small grand piano held court. Seating herself, she played nothing in particular but let her fingers explore the keys on their own.

After a few minutes, she combined a simple melody and chords, all in a minor key, inspired by the tones she had been accustomed to sing at Liturgy. The beauty of the tune brought her no solace, just another wave of tormenting memories. Faltering, she lifted her hands from the keyboard and wiped away the tears leaking down her cheeks.

"Señora?" Teresa stood in the doorway, observing her with concern. "Señora Sofia, what's troubling you? Can I help you with anything?"

"No, I'm fine." Sofia left the piano and sank onto the couch at the far end of the room. "It's only...the tune was sad."

An understanding look deepened the woman's kind expression. "You are homesick," she said. "And far from your family, with a baby on the way. That is a hard thing for a woman."

"It's not just that...I've had bad news this morning. I learned my parish priest back home was...murdered."

Murmuring a prayer, Teresa crossed herself, then her sturdy, work-roughed hand lingered at her throat as she touched her tiny silver crucifix. "Who murdered him? Is it known?"

"The new regime," Sofia admitted. Even though it was the harsh reality of life, everywhere and in all times, it still felt shocking to admit that men walked the earth who treated their fellows like animals.

"Then señora, he is a martyr," said Teresa with simple conviction.

Sofia lowered her head. Engulfed by the sobs she'd fought for hours, she hid her face in her hands and rocked slightly, not caring what the woman thought of her, yet grateful she wasn't alone.

"*He's a martyr.*"

Those were the very words she'd moaned when Owen at last shared the news. He had been reluctant to inform her, holding the news back for several weeks before deciding she needed to know. There was no easy way to express it, and in his own way, he'd been as distraught as she was.

"Martyr," he'd repeated after a lengthy pause. "Yeah, that's a serious word, isn't it? But I don't know what else you'd call him. He was…a remarkable man."

Part of her wanted to ask more details about what he knew, but most of her recoiled. She wasn't ready to hear, and doubted she ever would be. The important fact was this: while living in New Astoria, she had conversed weekly with a man who was now a legitimate martyr. A patient, good-humored man who had heard her secrets, had offered counsel and wisdom during some of her darkest moments.

Resting in Owen's tight embrace, it had been several agonizing moments before her sobs waned and she asked, "What about…anyone else from St. Columban's? Agnes, Joe…is there any news at all?"

"No, honey, I'm sorry. I'm so, so sorry."

The painful ache of that conversation still hung heavy on her, as she now lowered her hands to her lap and sat wrapped in her sad thoughts.

Tilting her head and studying Sofia with a knowing gleam in her eyes, Teresa asked, "Señora, do you think it is time to come with me to Mass again?"

Sofia did not answer. She had gone with Señora Ortega to the local Catholic church once or twice, but had felt out of place. She told herself she would keep looking for a suitable Orthodox congregation—surely there were some in Colombia? Once she located the right place, it would be easy enough to get back into the habit of regular attendance.

It was strange how, when she had been living in Oregon under threat of actual persecution, she had doubled down on her commitment to attending church in person. Now, relatively safe in a country that—for the time being, at least—didn't much care what she did, she felt confused in her thoughts and motives.

She coped by doubling down on praying, telling herself that reading a few more pages of scripture in the morning, a few more in the evening, engaging in a few more moments of quiet meditation, would surely make up for the fact she wasn't attending Liturgy. These Catholic churches were nice, but not good enough.

But isn't that just pride? she thought. She should be humble and take what was available in the circumstances where God placed her, instead of holding out for what she thought was best. *What would Fr. Cosimo tell me to do?*

She squirmed at the thought of his mild yet piercing eyes. She didn't have to guess what he'd tell her, he told her with the manner of his death.

Not meeting Teresa's gaze, she said, "Thank you, I'll think about it."

With an understanding, diplomatic smile, Señora Ortega said, "Did you wish supper at the same time today?"

"Yes, thank you."

Señora Ortega made no move towards the door, but remained observing her employer. "Forgive me, Señora, if I may say it—you are also restless. You have a sharp mind and are very creative, so you are frustrated because your body is now in charge of growing your son without your conscious involvement. You are, as they say, just 'along for the ride' at this point."

Intrigued by this observation, Sofia's large eyes softened. "I hadn't thought of that, but you may be right."

After Teresa left, the older woman's words lingered in Sofia's mind but didn't impart much consolation. She still felt trapped. *There's nothing I can do about the situation back home,* she lectured herself. *I shouldn't feel guilty we escaped, I should be thankful. This is what happens in war, and there's nothing I can do about it.*

As she sank further into the welcoming softness of the couch cushions, she was flooded with an onslaught of memories. Memories of singing in St. Columban's little choir, of the bright icons and gilt lamps shining beyond drifting veils of incense. Of Fr. Cosimo's low but clear voice as he preached and prayed.

The physical safety she'd been relishing now seemed like a mockery of the suffering she had left behind; the happiness she was enjoying felt unearned, somehow defiling. And yet she too, had known hours of uncertainty and terror. A darkness that lurked on the edge of her awareness these past weeks now drew nearer, and she forced herself to confront more memories, impressions of her time in the neighborhood re-education camp. She recalled her dawning horror when Sergeant Stan Bauer had laughed at her distress, her helplessness. Her stomach churned at the memory.

She kept from Owen the fact she still suffered nightmares about those last few hours. That she still raced through a distorted dreamscape, fleeing the building with Owen as they raced to the airfield. Their escape still seemed like a miracle to her, and below her gratitude was a sense of guilt, and the question of why they had made it out while others hadn't.

Even though it was Fr. Cosimo's decision to remain with his parish, why wasn't he protected? Why hadn't a hero intervened to save him? Why did God sometimes intervene and produce miracles, while at others He let horror unfold without lifting a finger to stop it?

More tears coursed down her face, she was wracked with sobs. Her spirit cried out in primal, bewildered agony: *why did You let this happen, Lord? Why aren't You doing more to help Your people?*

She was answered with an impenetrable wall of silence. When she grew exhausted from weeping, she was faced with the immutable reality of circumstances: action against evil must always be undertaken by flawed but well-meaning people working behind the scenes, people like Owen and Greg, or Tomás. Herself, even. Every small choice each of them made in their lives was meant to add up to something bigger, something worthwhile in this fight.

Yet as much as she admired and supported them, she knew they were only men. Awareness of her own weakness told her they could never accomplish much in the larger scheme of life, against the evil that seemed to always be winning.

CHAPTER
TWENTY-SIX

SLATE SINGER PAUSED his compact car at the housing development's gates. The forbidding aspect of the black metal was only somewhat softened by a layer of elaborate scrollwork, through which could be glimpsed the exquisitely maintained, secluded neighborhood beyond.

Lowering the car window, he passed his keycard over the sensor. The barrier slid aside and he drove through, his little car passing along the aggressively charming, winding streets of the planned community. The exclusive development meandered for acres at the top of the hill, and was overseen by well-preserved historic trees, chiefly lofty Doug Firs, as well as a few venerable oaks and maples. The latter were showing larger swathes of autumnal gold and orange among their clouds of green.

Slate still hadn't fully adjusted to the move to New Astoria. He also fought lingering resentment against Hayden for pressuring him to sell their property back in Bellevue. Slate recognized he tended to give in too readily to the other's plans, but wasn't sure how to push back.

For better or worse, this was their new home, and he knew he must grow to love it as he had the old one. The development reminded him of a self-contained, picturesque village, walled off from the rest of the world, protected from the dreary, crowded neighborhoods that tumbled below. The artificiality also reminded him of an amusement park or VR game environment; part of

Slate mourned the fact this settlement did not have the genuine vintage, organic character of his childhood surroundings.

Yet he had to admit it was beautiful, and that Hayden had chosen one of the best floor plans in the entire development. It was an imposing, Frank Lloyd Wright-inspired creation, painted a rich sage, with ebony wood accents. It was perfect for entertaining. However, it was unclear when or if they'd start throwing any parties. They had discussed hosting an open house to introduce themselves to the neighbors, but that plan had stalled when they picked up on the general wariness—or perhaps outright fear—their neighbors seemed to exhibit when being introduced to Hayden. Maybe Slate was being overly-sensitive, maybe there was a chance they'd forge new friendships in time. For now, however, he felt like a rootless stranger.

Inside the garage, Slate parked alongside Hayden's heavy, dark-gray car, switched off the motor and collected his shopping bags. The atmosphere inside the house was still chaotic from the move; boxes of random items were shoved in corners of most of the spacious rooms. Hayden had added to the congestion by bringing more crates of books and men's clothing home a few weeks before.

When Slate complained and asked where they came from, Hayden mentioned there might be shortages, and these items might become scarce. "They're your size, and clean, so don't bother laundering them," he'd said dismissively.

At the time, Slate thought he detected a faint trace of aftershave lingering on the fabric. Some of the items matched his style, and were good quality, so he overcame his repugnance at wearing what might have belonged to a rival, and dutifully hung them in his closet. He did not usually allow himself to look too closely at some of the troubling aspects of his relationship with Hayden. For the moment, he was committed to believing the advantages outweighed the disappointment.

Slate set his purchases in the kitchen and began to put the items away. The combined kitchen and dining space was huge, state-of-the-art and beautifully appointed. It was also somewhat intimidating, and Slate was continually re-arranging his favorite mugs, platters and wall art, attempting to create a more comforting environment.

Loud, theatrical sounds came from the front room, signaling that Hayden was in one of his tired moods that evening, and intended to de-stress from work by spending the rest of the evening on the sofa before a screenful of violent images. He owned an extensive collection of documentaries and award-winning films, biographies of famous generals and their most important battles.

Entering the main room, Slate paused and stood a moment, trying to catch Hayden's eye with a meaningful glance.

When the other didn't respond, Slate spread his arms with a flourish. "Look, I'm wearing one of those shirts you salvaged. Like it?"

Hayden picked up the remote and paused the feature. He regarded Slate with a blank expression, free from either lust or even simple affection. "It's good, I guess. Fits better than I thought. Guess you finally lost those last three pounds."

Slate rolled his eyes, but was still pleased. "Yeah, I did. Thanks for noticing."

"Why are you so late this evening?"

"I was shopping. I'll start dinner in a minute." Slate joined him on the sofa, eager to unload about how stressful the last few hours had been. "I'm sorry I was late, but it was fucking chaos at the open Market—the lines are *insane*, and I had to go to a bunch of stalls to find what I wanted. People were squabbling over the dregs."

Hayden did not look at him directly. "I'm afraid it might get worse before it gets better." On the coffee table before them was a cut-crystal, square-bottomed glass, a quarter-full of rich amber bourbon. Hayden picked this up, sipped it. "Probably best to avoid the Market from now on. They'll likely be raided soon, there's too much potential for subversive activity in that environment."

"Oh, okay. Well, thanks for the head's up." Slate was disappointed at the other's lack of sympathy. "But shopping in the regular stores isn't much easier—the shortages are hitting them harder. It took me forever to get some beef for Greta."

Hayden scowled, "Did you lose the special pass I issued you?" He tilted the glass from side to side, studying the liquor. "It will put you at the head of any line, and you'll get whatever is on your list. At a discount, too. Many of these businesses are hiding their best merchandise in the back rooms. Plus they're price-gouging."

"I know, but I'm uncomfortable using it. I don't like being stared at. And I don't want to use our relationship to get an unfair advantage over people."

Slate also did not want to talk about how he had witnessed officers hauling away an old woman trying to buy food without her resource card. He knew she should have complied and gone away, but he still wished they hadn't been so rough with her.

Hayden raised a shoulder in mild annoyance. "Fine, if that's what you want. But I'd prefer you either capitalize on your status, or else stay home and order everything via courier."

"I can't exactly do that, either," protested Slate. "The internet still doesn't work here ninety percent of the time."

"I know, damn it," said Hayden. "So use your account at ISA."

"Okay, I guess I will. At least there's a seventy percent reliability rate there."

"But you're doing an amazing job with that seventy percent," said Hayden with a sudden, less-than-convincing attempt at jollity. "How was the rest of your day?"

Slate rubbed the bridge of his nose as he closed his tired eyes for a moment. "So yeah, I've plugged a few more security holes, and the next thing we're going to do is look at connecting up the communications lines between different outposts throughout the region."

"Good. You make it sound like a pretty easy task."

"Yeah, maybe. But it's not great working with all these limitations. Like power outages, and supplies not where we need them, or perhaps not even existing at all."

Hayden drained off the remaining bourbon and set the glass down with a harsh *clink*. "I never promised this situation would be easy. But like I said, you're doing an excellent job."

"Thanks."

After a weighty pause, Hayden asked, "Have you made any progress on that other matter I asked you to look into?"

"Do you mean the private user account on the InNova corporation's gaming platform?"

"What else have I asked you to look into?" said Hayden, voice dripping with impatience. "Have you found any evidence the account was used to conceal or transfer illicit files?"

Eyes falling to the bourbon glass, Slate thought over his recent experience of investigating someone else's private game account at Hayden's behest. This particular game was staged in a 19th-century drawing room, and one of the characters bore a superficial resemblance to himself.

On closer inspection, Slate had noticed that the false creation had a far more potent and sardonic air about it than he himself had. And the shape of its mouth, its way of carrying itself, was far different. Nonetheless, it was a weird sensation for him to interact with the digital doppelgänger.

Slate said, "Well, I did poke around in the account, but I didn't find anything out of the ordinary. In fact, it's been sealed off on the other side, so for all intents and purposes, the account's inactive. There's no point in messing with it."

Hayden gave a disappointed rumble. Voice thick and words blurred a shade, he insisted, "But you saved the account for me, so I can keep checking it on my own?"

"Yeah, of course." Recalling the boxes of clothes and the attractive digital male apparition, Slate tugged at his shirt cuff, wondering again about its previous owner. He'd been fighting a nagging feeling that Hayden's claims regarding illicit files were phony, but now felt the urge to speak up.

Clearing his throat, he said, "Um, hey, I guess if you need some kind of diversion, if there's something in that game you want to…explore, I'll join in."

Hayden tilted his head and fixed him with a stare.

Clumsily, Slate rushed on, "But don't we need to get some, uh, specialized equipment? They sell…stuff for in-game, use, right?"

Body jerking with a curt laugh, Hayden said, "Fuck it, you're actually blushing."

Slate shrugged and looked away.

Hayden's laugh faded, he passed a hand over eyes. Then he answered with a shade of defensiveness, "Trust me, kid, this is business, not entertainment."

"Oh, sure." Feeling more relieved than he wanted to admit, Slate settled back into the cushions. On impulse, he said in a light and pleasant tone, "Say, I've been thinking. Now we're more settled here, is it time to revisit a certain—,"

Hayden cut him off, "I know what you're going to say: '*what about a baby?*'"

In the tense lull that followed, Slate realized too late that he had picked the wrong time to bring up this subject. Waiting for Hayden to continue, he tried to ignore the sense of foreboding seeping through the evening, the sense of strained emotion.

Hayden growled, "I've been thinking about it too, and this is what I've realized: if we continue to pursue surrogacy, it'll be nine-plus months at the very least, because we don't know how long it's going to take to find a suitable candidate in the first place."

Slate's heart continued to sink. Once again, Hayden was gearing up with a list of carefully prepared objections. Timidly, he persisted, "Is it possible to contact the previous candidate and offer her a better compensation package?"

Hayden's visage wrinkled in anger. "No, she skipped town, and under the circumstances, it's almost impossible to get a hold of her." Relaxing somewhat, he forced a smile. "Anyway, newborns are a lot of work. Are you sure you want to add that much stress and hassle to what we've got going here? I think we should consider an older baby, perhaps one from foster care."

Fingers drumming his knee, Slate thought a moment. Then he said with a laugh, "You know, *I* was a surrogacy."

"Yeah, yeah, of course I know that."

"And I had a full course of genetic conditioning. It worked great. Sure, it's more trouble up front, but in the long run, there's fewer medical conditions, so fewer bills. Fewer surprises."

"Okay, you're a real success story. I just think a foster child would be a quicker solution."

It was sometimes difficult for Slate to tell when Hayden was joking. Slate dreaded an angry scene, but needed to express his dissatisfaction and frustration as clearly as possible.

He said, "Look, I need to be honest—I'm not comfortable with the way the story keeps changing. It's like you're moving the goalposts. You wanted me to quit my job and move here—and that was a much better job than what you found for me at HQ, frankly. But I did it. And you were right, the move made sense, things are easier. But you also said we'd have Greta bred and I don't know if you've even contacted the breeder yet—,"

From across the room, where she lounged on her large pillow, the dog's ears pricked up at the mention of her name.

"Actually," interrupted Hayden, "The vet's in charge of advising us when it's time to go for that."

"Okay, right. I know puppies might not happen right away, but still—we never discussed adopting a *foster* child. We always talked about a surrogate—

we were happy with you being the sperm donor." He hesitated a fraction before adding, "Is there something about that that you're not telling me?"

Hayden exhaled and leaned back against the sofa, throwing his arms wide. "No, everything's fine. It's just I think an infant who's a few months old, with just a bit more of a track record—about personality and so forth—might be something worth looking into."

Folding his arms in a gestural pout, Slate moved farther down the couch. His growing anger made him careless. "So, you're making excuses and breaking your promises, is that it?"

Hayden glared at him. "I never made an actual promise. We discussed things in a general way, but never had a contract. In fact," his lip curled and his words dripped with venom, "I'd never be so stupid as to make a promise to somebody as immature as you. You're a spoiled brat—you hear what you want to hear, and when you don't get your own way, you make a big stink and throw a temper tantrum."

"*I'm* throwing a tantrum? That's absolute fucking bullshit— you're the one yelling at me."

"I'm not yelling!"

Slate's gaze slid to the empty bourbon glass. Face flushed, Hayden followed his eyes and, without warning, kicked the table, almost flipping it over. The glass slid off and clunked to the floor. Greta jumped to a sitting position and watched both men intently.

Slate muttered, "Who's immature?"

"Don't you ever use that goddamn snarky tone with me again," snapped Hayden. He sat bolt upright and leaned closer to the younger man. "It's my house, my table, my glass! I don't need a little fucking prick like you acting so superior!"

Slate blinked and pressed back into the cushions. His brief surge of anger drained, replaced by fear, and a desperate desire to avert the other's rapidly flaring rage. "Okay, I'm sorry it sounded like that! I didn't mean anything—,"

The apology enflamed Hayden. "The hell you didn't mean anything—you're calling me a liar!"

"I'm sorry it sounded like that," protested Slate, his heart hammering, mouth dry. "I didn't mean it! So just…so, it's okay. Calm down!"

The moment the words left his mouth, he knew they were the wrong thing to say. Hayden jumped up and towered over him, grabbing the younger man's shoulders and shaking him with sudden, terrifying violence.

Greta stood nearby, whining in distress at the sound of her master's angry voice.

"Calm down? Calm *down*? I am calm! After you called me a liar! And don't ever complain about any mess I make in my own house! You're so damn entitled, you had every single, damn stone moved out of your path when you were a kid, didn't you?"

Slate cringed, his belly seethed with a knot of sickened terror. He flailed desperately for something, anything, he could say to derail the other's mounting rage. He could not bring himself to meet Hayden's puffy, bloodshot glare. He knew from experience it was safer to not make eye contact when things were this far out of hand.

Instead, he dipped his head vigorously. "Yeah, yeah, you're right—!"

Hayden didn't hear him. He screamed hotly in his face, flecking him with drops of spit: "Your dads were so damn perfect, they never made any fucking mistakes, did they? They never raised their voices, never laid a hand on your precious, genetically perfect body—!"

Hayden lifted his right hand and belted Slate across the face, then dropped him. Then he drew away, took an unsteady step, and flung himself back down in his place at the end of the sofa. Breathing heavily, his face was hard and set as he resumed the movie, switching his sullen gaze to the unfolding scenes of destruction and bloodshed.

Without speaking, Slate collected the fallen glass and wandered numbly into the kitchen. With robotic motions, he began preparing dinner. It did not hurt that Singer hadn't offered an apology; Slate had long ago given up expecting them.

This was a terrible way to live, but he felt powerless to fix it. He had never witnessed anything but mutual respect and patience between his fathers, and didn't know where to begin to try and heal things between himself and Hayden. Thinking over his dads' relationship, he felt a sharp pang of resentment towards his father Alan, who, after much soul-searching, had chosen to depart with his spouse Noah after the latter's terminal cancer diagnosis.

The couple's State-authorized Passing had been a beautiful, moving ceremony, the perfect finishing touch to a shared life that had a few ups and downs, but was overall happy and well-ordered. But afterwards, Slate was left alone, with no one in his life to advise him on important decisions.

When he'd met Hayden, it seemed a huge hole in his life was about to be healed.

I guess I should be grateful they aren't around to see how this is turning out, he thought.

His eyes strayed to the wall, where a framed wedding photo hung. The gossamer-thin slice of time it represented had once been real enough; Hayden had been trustworthy and protective, Slate carefree. The laughing men in the picture, so sure of their shared future, now existed only in an imaginary dimension.

CHAPTER
TWENTY-SEVEN

STANDING at the rear of Underhill's cavern-like church, Enrique Rodriguez hoped no one would notice him, or speak to him if they did. The chamber, with its throng of worshippers, seemed more crowded than it actually was. The congregation accepted his presence without question, but they also, perhaps in a spirit of understanding, kept their distance. He appreciated their respect; he longed to disappear into the shadows forever, just as he longed to escape from his own memories.

He had slipped out of the guest quarters to come to this early ceremony without waking Connie, but he sensed it was only a matter of time before she figured out where he was.

This was the third time since his arrival at the hidden village that he had attended Mass. He usually left right afterward; never feeling ready to talk with anybody, certainly not with the cleric. His head buzzed with confusion, he was tortured by his thoughts, by his emotions.

As he attempted to follow the actions of the priest at the front of the building, he was assailed by more and more conflicting emotions. The ritual of the Mass was just something he had attended once in awhile with his grandparents, years earlier. He never asked questions; never thought about it deeply enough to have any questions. Now he felt pulled in several directions at once, and was unequal to the strain.

Because there was no mosque close to Underhill, he and Connie hadn't been to Friday night prayers for many weeks, but kept up the routine of praying as a family in their quarters.

Enrique keenly felt the absence of an imam to whom he could unburden himself, but still wasn't ready to speak with the village priest. He sensed the entire community here knew he and Connie were not Christian, but they didn't seem to care. He felt they were more concerned about the family being a security risk, although there was no intel whatsoever that his captors had trailed him this far to the northeast.

There had been talk of visiting D.C. in order to give his testimony in person, but he had not been updated lately about that possibility. Maybe it was pointless, as his recorded interviews weren't generating much action. He was bitterly disappointed by the lack of national interest in the alarm he was trying to sound. He was also exhausted by trying to stay informed of the latest twists and turns, ins and outs, of the ongoing saga of how to deal with Pacifica.

'*Containment, Covert-op or Confrontation?*' The phrase was one used so often in the updates he received from Park, that he wanted to spit when he thought of the words.

Something, anything has to be done to those brutal motherfuckers, he thought with an inward shiver of frustrated rage. *They can't be allowed to get away with what they're doing.*

Yet even as he thought that, his anger flamed out. He was too exhausted, empty and forlorn to know what to do next or where to go. Even though he was under the care of the physicians at Underhill's state-of-the-art clinic, and had access to therapists, he didn't feel he was healing. He was sick to death of politics and uncertainty, he craved a quiet, normal life somewhere he would not have to think about any of these problems.

The last of the worshippers trickled out of the church. Most of the lights were switched off and the dim space became even darker. It also seemed colder, and the lingering scent of incense mingled with the rich, deep, earthen air of the cavern. Alone on his rough-hewn wooden pew, Enrique became further lost in his own thoughts.

The few lights gleamed on a series of paintings lining the walls; Enrique found himself wondering what they represented. They were similar to images he'd seen in other churches when he was young, but no one ever explained what they meant.

He rose from his seat and began walking slowly along the wall, contemplating each image. Up close, he realized they told the story of Jesus, as he was taken by the Romans and forced to carry his cross. The paintings documented the events of that fateful morning almost step by step, with bold colors and unflinching brush strokes.

The painted shadows of the cross reminded him of the shadows streaking the camp's exercise yard every morning; the crown of thorns brought back memories of the coils of razor wire. As his attention lingered more thoughtfully over each image, his hands grew sweaty, his stomach flipped when he recognized the central, suffering face in each panel. He'd seen it in real life, with his own eyes.

Vision blurred, Enrique stumbled back to his seat at the rear of the church. Lowering his head to his hands, he fought the oncoming tears. After several moments of solitary struggle, he became aware of a presence as body slid onto the bench beside him.

His kept his eyes closed, moisture leaking from his lids. He caught his breath, waiting for the newcomer to speak. Then he felt his wife's fingers caressing his shoulder, her voice whispering, "Hey, honey? When are you going to tell me what's on your mind?"

He shook his head and squeezed his eyes shut tighter. If he tried to speak, he'd lose what little control he had of his emotions. It was agony for him to have her witness this, but he was trapped, helpless and broken before her.

Wordlessly, she continued to rub his shoulder. Normally, her touch would be comforting, but now he was too agitated to appreciate it. He lifted his head and sat back in the pew, spine against the hard wooden upright.

He choked, "Why did we join the Franklin Street Mosque? What were our reasons? It's like I don't remember anything."

It was several moments before Connie answered. She sounded puzzled. "I had friends who went there. We both like the community. I know we had lots of talks about our decision."

Enrique rubbed his palms on the knees of his faded jeans. He asked, "What else?"

Connie shook her head.

Enrique tilted his head back and his wavering glance locked on the crucifix at the far wall. With broken words, he explained, "We thought it was...easier to believe what they taught, than what the Christians were preaching. Like about the Trinity...and the...*becoming man* part, what's it called? In-something."

"I don't remember."

"But didn't we think it would be simpler, more direct? Isn't that what we told ourselves?"

"Maybe," she admitted, still sounding at a loss to follow his conversation. "And yeah, about sacrifice or atonement and all that."

"Yeah," he said remotely. "And I didn't want anyone between me and Allah. And I liked the strict prayer routine."

"Sure, I remember you said that."

He felt her dark eyes, heavy with concern, fastened on his face.

Eyes still on the cross, Enrique mumbled, "I never got the point of God being one of us, of having to suffer. It seemed so…bloodthirsty, weird and tacked-on. But…but…then I saw…," His voice came in ragged gasps, his fingers gripped his knees tightly.

"What did you see?" prompted Connie. Her voice shook with dread, but her hand still rested on his shoulder.

"When they killed him, right up there in front of us all, it wasn't Nicholl's face anymore…it was *His*, dying right there with him."

Jerkily, he thrust his hand towards the crucifix as he struggled through his tears. "No one saw it but me. Am I crazy? What could it mean?"

Connie exhaled. "You were under a lot of stress, maybe your perceptions were distorted. Or maybe your memory."

"No!" Adamant, he shook his head. "I saw it as it happened! I felt…I *felt* it happen."

They were both silent. Then with a groan, Enrique slumped forward again, fingers digging into his skull, elbows on knees. "What am I supposed to do now?"

Connie said, "Honey, you just keep healing, keep up with your prayer routine. Take it one day at a time."

"What are we going to do? How will we live? Where will we live?"

"Has Greg spoken to you about what we should do now?"

Enrique thought this over. He was waiting on Park to advise him on another safe location for them. And he was desperate for a clearer idea of how he was going to make a living going forward. He wasn't relying on the Restoration to support him, but he fully expected they'd open some doors for him.

"He says he's working on it." He lifted her hand from his shoulder and held it in both of his. He turned his head, to study her face from the corner of his eye. "I think it's time we moved on, don't you?"

She didn't reply. He said, "I'm thinking I'd like to spend more time with those Nightcrawlers. Looked like there were some nice families in the group. It looked like a nice kind of life, could be a good experience for us and the kids. Away from everything."

She said, "Yeah, I guess. I'm grateful for these folks letting us stay here, but you're right…we need to start over, someplace else."

Her peaceful, practical words lifted a gray cloud of doubt from his mind. His fingers clamped about her hands. "A new start. That's what we need."

"You've earned it," she said, resting her head on his shoulder. It was heavier than he remembered, but for the moment, he was content to sit and enjoy the weight of her trust and love.

After a few quiet moments, Connie lifted her head. "Come on—let's get breakfast before the kids wake up. Just you and me."

CHAPTER
TWENTY-EIGHT

SLATE WOKE GRADUALLY and continued to lie for several minutes, listening to the hushed quiet that filled the house. His mind was locked in a haze of misery that threatened to keep him in bed longer than was healthy.

Hayden had left hours earlier for work, and now, in the cold light of day, Slate groaned under his breath at the uncomfortable memories of the previous night, at the embarrassing physical failure the men had experienced, at his own gnawing sense of dissatisfaction. As receptive and accommodating as he tried to be, their planned intimacy hadn't gone well.

Neither mentioned it aloud, but this happened often enough to add to the pall of frustration overshadowing their relationship. Even as he reminded himself that Hayden wasn't as young as he once was, and was currently enduring a lot of stress, Slate felt guilty for the jokes he'd made, half to lighten the mood, half to veil his own discontent.

After several more minutes of wallowing in the warm blankets and in his own sense of self-pity blended with remorse, he forced himself from the welcoming expanse of the bed. He yawned, stretched and staggered into the bathroom.

Surely there was a mistake, the face staring back from the mirror looked too old and weary to be his. Too disappointed and chronically worried. Roughly running his fingers through his tousled hair, he reassured himself he'd look better after drinking water and exercising.

After a solid forty-minute workout in the small home gym, Slate decided it was time to do some work in his Internal Security Agency account. Approaching his computer, he saw a note stuck on the screen: *At 11 a.m, go outside and wait in the drive.*

Slate's brow furrowed; what on Earth was this supposed to mean? Hayden had been acting a little odd since their fight a couple weeks earlier. Several times, Slate had felt the older man's gaze lingering on him with a slightly anxious expression, as if on the point of apologizing. Yet he always seemed to talk himself out of it, to change his mind and move on. It was now 10:56. Setting aside his fruitless speculation, Slate left the house and stepped into an overcast yet warm morning. He waited on the front step, feeling a mounting excitement.

Soon a low hum sounded at the end of the street; a large delivery truck approached and backed into the driveway. The driver shut off the motor and exited the cabin, waving a work tablet.

"Hey, good morning! You Slate Singer?"

Slate nodded.

Extending the tablet, the man said, "Had to jump through a lot of hoops to get into this place, should have made you come meet me at the gate. Anyways, got a special delivery for you. Sign here."

Slate scribbled his signature on the screen and handed it back. The delivery man hit a button on his key ring and opened the back of the van.

"Hey—want me to ride it out for you, or you wanna get it yourself?" He stepped back, gesturing to the rear of the truck.

"Holy *shit*," breathed Slate, gazing at the quad hovercycle resting in the cargo compartment. Its gleaming, iridescent finish of cherry-red seemed to glow in the truck's dim interior. His videoskin buzzed in his pocket, and took it out to read another message from Hayden: *I can't express in words how much you mean to me, so this will have to do it for me.*

Re-reading the text, Slate's mouth twisted in bewilderment. Was this an overblown compensation for last night's debacle? Or an apology for that vicious slap during their argument?

If the latter, Slate was flooded with a wave of annoyance that threatened to swell to anger. Part of him was repelled by the showiness of the gesture, when Hayden should know by now he'd have been grateful for a simple, heartfelt, *"I'm sorry"*.

Yet he knew that since the latter was impossible for Hayden to manage, this was the best to be hoped for. Whatever the impetus, he was relieved the older man hadn't seemed to hear last night's withering remarks, or at least didn't resent them.

Slate continued to gaze into the truck, mesmerized by the cycle's enticing, fluid lines. He broke into a huge grin. "I'll ride it out," he said, climbing up the ramp into the back of the truck.

"Here, let me show you how to start it," the man said. "Here's the key slip."

"Thanks. And I can figure it out," laughed Slate as he straddled the seat and examined the controls. They were straightforward, and while he had never owned one of these vehicles, he had some experience riding similar models. He hadn't thought he'd mentioned this more than once or twice, but it was clear that Hayden remembered. He had been listening, part of him still cared.

Pressing the slip in the correct slot, he listened with pleasure to the answering smooth hum, felt the gentle but powerful vibration travel through the chassis and up his body, as the craft lifted several inches. With care, he guided it from the back of the truck, to the side of the driveway, and then lowered it to the ground.

"Hey, you handle her pretty well," said the driver. "Looks like you're gonna really enjoy it. And don't forget the gear that goes with it."

He picked up a heavy case from the cargo compartment and deposited it near the cycle, before climbing into the cab and driving away down the street.

With giddy delight, Slate guided the hovercycle into the garage and then returned outside to collect the case, which contained a set of leather riding gear and a helmet that matched the cycle's exquisite finish. After changing into these, he returned to the garage and mounted the cycle.

He realized that, in addition to an apology, this amazing gift represented tacit permission for Slate to roam about as much as he liked. Which he was going to do right now.

After taking a few turns up and down the street, he left the housing development. Soon the secluded neighborhood was far behind him, as he joined the road leading to the main highway and traveled westward.

When music began playing in his helmet, it was clear Hayden had made sure the cycle's sound system was programmed with Slate's favorite pop songs, despite the fact he usually ridiculed these when catching the younger man listening at home. Slate broke into a happy grin as the soundtrack accompanied him down the highway.

Up ahead, against the gathering gray clouds incoming from the south, the skeletal orange form of a defunct tower crane gleamed in the morning light.

During the months he'd lived here, Slate had not seen any progress on whatever project the equipment was allegedly working on. To subdue his homesickness, he had dug into the history of the region and was fascinated to learn how the geography had been significantly altered. After the waters of the Cascadia-triggered tsunami receded, it was discovered that uplift had drained portions of the local wetlands, increasing areas of buildable land.

He found it interesting that during reconstruction, New Astoria had absorbed previous neighboring communities. The names Jeffers Garden, Sunset Beach and Warrenton now only existed in history books or on street signs, their boundaries overtaken by the enthusiastic vision of both native survivors and carpetbagging urban planners alike.

Yet, however tall the new buildings had been envisioned, the reality was that many of them had sputtered and stalled before completion. The construction boom had not been big enough to support all the companies rushing in to take advantage of the situation.

"Yeah, the city should probably look into tracking down the owners and fining them. Then having it dismantled," Hayden had remarked with a vague air when Slate commented on the abandoned construction tower. "Unless we can think of another use for it. Any suggestions?"

"An extreme-sport bungee tower?" Slate had joked. "An exclusive high-rise nightclub and hotel?"

Encouraged by Hayden's indulgent laughter, he'd proposed several increasingly ludicrous uses, but nothing struck either of them as being realistic.

Now, as he passed under the structure's lofty, skeletal arm, pitted and rusty from years of exposure to the salt air, he wondered if it was possible to do anything with it other than sell it for scrap. Nonetheless, while his craft nimbly followed the road, his mind engaged in fanciful images of what sort of apartment pods or exclusive dining experiences could be arranged in such a unique edifice.

He veered south, enjoying the unusual warmth of the overcast day. As he rode, he made note of how the machine handled, drinking in every detail. Far south of the main city, he stopped on a public beach and took a selfie. His videoskin didn't have enough roaming phone data to send it, but he planned on showing it to Hayden that evening.

Reluctantly, he decided it was time to return home and get back to work, so he reseated himself and glided northward. With the brisk breeze pushing against him, and the view of the coastline sliding past on his left, it was easy to get lost in the moment. To forget there had ever been strife between himself and Hayden. Perhaps better times were ahead for them both.

Before returning to the heart of the city, Slate rebelled against ending his joyride and took a brief detour, skirting Youngs Bay. This neighborhood marked the beginning of an extensive squatter's camp, a ramshackle village clinging to the river's edge. Today, many of the rusted trailers and crude shacks were missing, as if they had disappeared overnight.

Several busses, sporting bright government logos, were parked along the road, and there was a trickle of people waiting to board the transports. As he whipped past, Slate got a blurred impression of unkempt, ragged families, of bewildered and sullen expressions.

About time the authorities did something about that disgusting trash heap, he thought. *It will be better for everyone in the long run, especially the people who had to live there.*

It occurred to him the activity to clean up the camps might also be related to the recent terror plot the ISA was rumored to have thwarted. He felt a surge of pride in Hayden for all the work he was doing to keep the community safe. It was an incredibly stressful job, and Slate knew he should be more grateful and patient.

Piloting the cycle back to the city, he took another few minutes' detour along the far northern perimeter, close to the shore of the Columbia.

As he neared the abandoned construction tower, he noticed considerable foot traffic and a few law enforcement vehicles clogging the streets. A crowd was coalescing near the base of the crane; the area directly below was fenced off, and police cruisers, their lights flashing, kept the crowd away from the actual base.

Wondering if there had been an accident, Slate brought the cycle to a stop near the edge of the crowd and looked around. There was no smoke, there were no crumpled vehicles. An ambulance, however, waited off to one side of the scene.

Opposite the ambulance, carnival music hooted and trilled from a large van, which also offered free snacks. Bright flashing lights and exciting images waltzed across the van's portable screens, adding to the confusion of the overall scene. A short, stocky woman, dressed in an ISA uniform, stood nearby with a bullhorn clutched in her hand. The strained expression on her small, pinched face made her look lost and overwhelmed.

"May I have your attention please, everyone! Please, step over here!" she announced through the horn.

Most people ignored her, but a few drifted closer to the van. The woman lowered the bullhorn and forced a smile across her face as she welcomed them. One or two parents gingerly selected pastries and passed them to their kids.

The obnoxious music contrasted with the apprehensive looks on the faces of the people in the crowd. All around him, Slate saw expressions ranging from curiosity, to anxiety, to anger. A heavy sense of sick, impending dread began congealing over the scene, echoing the dark, foreboding clouds overhead.

Slate caught snatches of conversation, but didn't quite understand what he was hearing. Despite the distraction of the van, most attention was focused upwards, towards the jib of the crane.

Following the majority gaze, Slate squinted upward and saw the crane's elevator was rising up the looming mast to the operator's cabin.

Turning to a gray-faced, older man standing nearby, Slate asked, "What's happening?"

Before the man could reply, an official-sounding voice barked sharply from one of the cruisers: "Keep back! Stay fifteen feet back from the barricades!"

Standing as tall as he could and looking through the crowd, Slate saw some heavy orange plastic traffic barriers arranged in a loose perimeter around the base of the tower. There were also heavily armed, helmeted officers ringing the barrier.

Eyes traveling back up to the tower, Slate could just make out that the elevator had stopped, and there were several forms standing in the open door. It was difficult to tell from that distance, but some seemed armed with rifles. These prodded and pushed the others through the opening; their arms were bound and they could not stop themselves from falling.

Stifled screams came from a few throats in the crowd near him; Slate's heart almost stopped as he watched the shapes tumble downwards. Their fall took surprisingly long, ending abruptly in the soft finality of the *thuds* of their abrupt contact with the concrete pad. Slate felt a drop of moisture touch his cheek and one hand; tensing with dread, he looked down at his skin. It was only rain.

The old man beside him muttered, "They were a terror cell, planning an attack on the high school."

Slate stammered, "When…when was the trial? I didn't hear anything about a trial."

"'Wasn't one," the man rumbled. His mouth snapped shut and Slate knew to ask no more questions. The man was already walking away; the officers issued more orders through bullhorns and the dazed crowd broke up and dispersed.

I'm sure there was plenty of evidence, Slate consoled himself.

So much evidence the trial was open and shut. *The high school, for God's sake —what did they think would happen to them if they were caught? And anyway, a strong signal had to be sent, so others won't try this again.*

Shaking, Slate switched the cycle back on and waveringly made his way through the city, up the hill to the serene, elegant neighborhood. But before he reached the security gates, he swerved off the road and vomited into the tidily manicured shrubs lining the serene street.

CHAPTER
TWENTY-NINE

ABOVE THE DENSE, fertile green hills just to the east of the hacienda, a storm had been building throughout the day. By evening, the skies over the entire region were a vast, angry bruise, threatening to burst with rain. There was no escape from the oppressive humidity, the pervasive sense of brooding unease.

Recalling the deluge he'd endured during the previous month's outing with Tomás Chen, Owen MacIntyre was grateful to be indoors this evening. Yet he had no regrets about accepting Tomás' invitation; that pleasant break, damp as it had been, was long overdue. Exploring the vast and varied beauty of the *Parque natural Las Hermosas* in the company of his friend had been an experience both relaxing and bittersweet.

Yet when Owen returned home and resumed his work, the burden of managing his commitment to both Paloma and the Restoration felt as heavy as ever. He was increasingly resentful of those demands, as he grew more eager to focus on his own private project. That challenge was becoming more exciting as it increasingly consumed his thoughts.

Moving forward with this idea required wealthy connections in the tech industry, and he was thankful he had one. Although Andrei Volkov, Sofia's elder brother, was now legally his 'family', Owen hadn't had many direct interactions with the man, and still found it difficult to think of him as a brother.

Volkov was brash, opinionated and always ready to remind people of his scientific and financial successes.

However, Andrei's personality flaws were easy to overlook in light of the fact that, like all the Volkovs, he was sympathetic to *novus ignis* goals and thus was very trustworthy. Perhaps most importantly, he'd recently sold his latest start-up chemical engineering company to billionaire Jaxtyn Morse, head of the InNova Corporation. The more Owen learned about Morse, the more hopeful he was the man was a good fit for developing this unique concept.

To that end, Andrei had recently managed to secure Owen an introduction to Morse via video. Now, as Owen reviewed the footage of that meeting, he scanned the man's body language and listened to his intonations. He sensed the other's interest was genuine, the suggestion of a personal visit within two weeks had been made with a suppressed eagerness beneath a superficial, casual cordiality.

The hook was well-baited, Owen thought with satisfaction. Consequently, he'd already booked the travel arrangements to the United States.

Without warning, the room brightened as a flash of lightning exploded outside. Seconds later, a roar of thunder shouted over the sprawling old house. The lights flickered. Owen held his breath, listening for the inevitable rain. When it came, it plunged in gushing, hissing buckets. The main lights flickered again and died, then soft emergency illumination took their place.

Sighing, he admitted this might be a sign he needed to pack it in for the evening. He checked the hacienda's central control panel displayed on his computer screen, and saw there was enough power in the back-up batteries to run the freezer, refrigerator and a few lights for several hours. If there were utility lines down in the neighborhood, it was anyone's guess when they'd be repaired. Although there was also enough power to spare for him to continue working at his computer, he was ready to call it quits.

He locked his notes in the desk, shut off some apps, killed his visor's message feature for all but emergency comms, then de-cluttered his internal field of vision so that it was again within normal parameters. This process was a liberating ritual, one he knew he should follow more closely, because the most recent biometric data recorded by his vision implant indicated elevated levels of stress damage.

He had decided against forwarding this info to his physician, instead promising himself he'd 'just try harder to do better'. If next month's readings were still this troubling, then maybe he'd look into a medical remedy. But he didn't want to think about that now.

Nor did he want to recall Sofia's reaction when he'd announced he would soon be going on yet another business-related trip. Despite assurances this jaunt would be quick and risk-free, she'd seemed unusually unhappy about it.

For several moments, he stood lost in the sound of the rain drumming outside the study window. It surged with a joyful urgency, and the atmosphere inside the home was starting to lighten. He felt refreshed and energetic.

Upstairs, a bar of golden light spilled from beneath the door of the master bedroom. Sofia was running a music playlist, a woman's voice was singing, low and fruity. There was something about the music that resonated with him, evoking memories of a long-dead era, memories that weren't his own, but were still somehow a part of him.

He stood a moment in the doorway, watching Sofia. She sat upright in their bed, eyes closed while she listened to the song, long legs stretched before her on the sheets. The rain-washed air wafting through the open windows made space for the rich, slow jazz melody and the words.

Like a lightning flash, the singer's name came to him: *Ella Fitzgerald*. He listened for a moment to the moody, bittersweet lyrics, about a lost lamb without a shepherd.

As Owen entered the room, Sofia's lids unclosed and she shot him a shy look, then without speaking, turned and touched the bedside controls. A hush reclaimed the room.

He asked, "Why'd you turn it off?"

She waved a listless hand. "I guess I want to listen to the rain now."

"Are you feeling all right? You went to bed kind of early."

Lowering her eyes, she said, "The storm build-up made me feel weird."

"Okay, sure. The rain might help with that."

"I hope so."

He entered the bathroom to shower, again wondering why she'd been acting preoccupied lately. Maybe it wasn't just because he was leaving again. Maybe it was related to the pregnancy, something to do with hormones. When the sweat of the day was rinsed off, he returned and slid into bed beside her.

"Hey, how do you feel now? Are you okay?"

"Yeah, sure, I'm better. I'm fine, actually."

Light from a small, candle-like emergency lamp painted her in soft, warm tones. One lock of hair was artlessly tucked behind her ear; the remainder fell in a dark cascade, through which glimpses of her face were revealed in tantalizing fragments. She seemed unaware of how lovely she looked that night, of how his attention was savoring her.

Clearing her throat, she asked in a voice both tired and skeptical, "So, this next trip, is it for Paloma, or for Greg? More cloak-and-dagger stuff to get you into more trouble?"

His answer skimmed past her suspicions. "It's nothing to do with Greg or his people. It's a new venture altogether. I'm meeting with a business contact Andrei set me up with."

The firmness of this declaration brought her face swiveling to meet his. She looked impressed, but also exasperated. "Do you have time to take on another major project?"

"It's just an idea I want to bounce off some experts. But it might evolve into something bigger."

Relaxation softened the lines of her body, and she reclined; resting on her side, elbow bent, head cradled on her palm. "How long will you be gone this time?"

His attention strayed to the silken folds of her nightshirt, resting in the dip of her waist where it curved up to meet her hipbone. "Two or three days."

"Isn't that what you said last time?"

The disillusionment in her tone disturbed him. Moving closer, he said, "Hey, don't pout! I'm here now, so let's make the best of it."

"Really?"

"Yes, really."

Biting her lip, she again lowered her eyes. "I have a stupid question, but please, be honest…,"

He braced himself for a question about his feelings regarding his fatherhood, about the future. A question that required him to reveal something he couldn't plainly identify within himself, let alone express.

He asked, "Hey, are you worried about what sort of parents we'll be? Because I am." He hadn't been planning to share that now; the words just came out.

She started to laugh, then stopped. "For real? You seem so sure of yourself. At least on this subject."

He slid nearer. "You should know by now that's an act. Where the hell would I have learned how a healthy family operates? How to be a good dad?"

She smiled fondly. "Your folks couldn't have screwed up that badly, look how well you turned out."

"Maybe I'm just a fluke. Seriously, I have no idea what to do."

"You'll pick it up." She fell silent; it was clear her mind was focused on something else.

He asked, "Okay, what else is bothering you?"

Her awkward laugh was half a sigh. "It's silly of me, I know, but…I've tried to stay in shape and I don't think I've gained much weight…but sometimes I'm worried about…getting so big."

" 'Big'? You barely look pregnant."

"But I'm worried about how you see me now. You don't regret that I didn't get a surrogate?"

"Hon, you know I think that's a creepy practice. You're not having second thoughts, are you?"

"No, not at all. I just wonder about you."

"Trust me, seeing you now, like this…well…," Voice low, a wry grin tugging one corner of his mouth, he nestled ever closer, a hand caressing her ankle before moving leisurely up her leg. "Sofie, honestly—you can't imagine how crazy your shape is making me. It scares me sometimes, I'm almost afraid to come near you—,"

"Sometimes you seem so…well, moody." Giggling with relief, her eyes shone as they locked on his visor. She was suffused with a delectable blush, he could see her pulse racing at the curves of her throat.

"Moody? That's rich, coming from the queen of mixed emotions." His hand traveled further along her leg. Encountering the hem of her thin, silky nightshirt, he pushed it up. "So I've had some stuff on my mind, but I can't believe you really thought I was…*avoiding* you." He paused as one breast was bared to the lamplight.

Swallowing hard, she whispered, "Okay, but keep convincing me."

"Mmmm…you got it, angel." Lips brushing her warm, soft skin, he relished how her heartbeat quickened in response.

He breathed into her, "I see the prettiest woman I've ever known, who grows prettier every day—," Lowering his body, he began unhurriedly pressing his mouth along the gentle swell of her abdomen. "And who puts up with all my mistakes, and who will be the best mother to this little guy, and who's completely safe and secure, right here with me—,"

Excited by his visceral pride in having created this monumental change within her, he continued to explore her with increasing fervor, murmuring, "Never forget, this was all you and me. No white coats, no labs, no *rented* wombs…,"

"Oh, yes," she whispered. "I didn't forget…,"

She responded to his touch in ways tantalizingly coy, yet also bold and sultry. It was a heady, intoxicating blend of mixed signals, and he loved it. Enraptured in each other, moved beyond speech, time slowed as they became lost in the paradise of their white bedding.

Outside, the rain lessened to a gentle whisper in the dark; the night wind freshened and billowed the curtains into the room with a silken flourish.

CHAPTER THIRTY

"*PUMPING BLOOD, raging flame, shooting through the blackness, ripping through the pain.*"

The dark, growling lyrics, throbbing with a heavy beat, filled the small rental car.

Owen kept time, drumming contentedly on the wheel, while outside, for miles in all directions, tips of dead brown grass barely pierced the blanket of snow which gleamed in the bright sun of the November afternoon. His VIA unit allowed him to study the dazzling field of brilliant white without snow-blindness or any discomfort. He hadn't seen this much snow since the last time he'd gone skiing on Mt. Hood back in Oregon, and didn't like to think how long ago that had been.

A satisfied smile ambled over his face as he also recalled the belated honeymoon he and Sofia had spent at a mountain lodge, months after their actual wedding. As fun as that had been, the memory paled beside their most recent exploits. Now that her self-doubts were swept away, the last few nights before this trip had been more exciting than he'd thought was possible.

As the song raged, "*They don't know me, they can't touch me, I will make them stop,*" he felt unusually optimistic, the rhythms filling the cabin now perfectly intersected with his undaunted mood.

The music stirred echoes of intense emotions from his youth, when popular music had provided him, if not a refuge, at least a buffer against some of the turmoil in his life. Against the lingering trauma of his sister's death, and his mother's emotional withdrawal from the family. It provided an outlet for his rage over Evan's Passing. It shone some light in the abyss that had yawned between himself and his father.

"*Raise my voice, shatter stones, spin their bones, break the chains of pain.*"

Guiding the car swiftly along a tight curve on the narrow private road, he remembered his sense of hope and excitement, as his skills and power had emerged from that difficult period. The melodies of his favorite songs, their driving beats, had formed a backdrop to the elation he felt when he realized how popular he could be with the girls at school. Maybe at the time, he hadn't paid too much attention to the lyrics, but nonetheless the songs formed a soundtrack to his blossoming as a sarcastic semi-intellectual, to his unexpected reputation as one of the cooler kids in the community.

In his more self-reflective moments, he knew that reputation was overblown, and he was grateful Sofia hadn't known him then, that she hadn't witnessed him alternately swagger and fumble his way through those painful years. It was hard to imagine her putting up with that raw, half-formed version of himself, despite her natural patience.

Still, he had to admit he had come a long way. He had developed some formidable skills and generally felt he was putting them to good use. Even though he worked in the shadows, he was making a positive impact on the world.

"*They'll never stop me, never drag me back to dark and shame,*" he hummed along imperfectly, "*They won't forget my name.*"

Turning his attention back to the vista sprawling beyond the car windows, the landscape reminded him that a couple hundred miles to the south, inhabitants of the hidden village of Underhill were going about their daily routine. Owen wanted to visit, but knew it was unwise to attract more attention to the settlement; and besides, he didn't really have a good reason. Enrique was no longer there. Owen wasn't sure joining the Nightcrawlers was a good idea, but respected his friend's belief that that move was best for his family.

Coming around another bend, he brought the vehicle sharply to a stop. The road was blocked by a herd of cattle, his car was soon engulfed by a sea of glossy, muscular hides, as the shambling Black Angus took their sweet time crossing the road.

Except the creatures weren't crossing; instead they milled aimlessly, exhibiting a lethargic curiosity about the car and its occupant. Despite their bulk, each creature moved with eloquence, picking its steps with a delicacy that rivaled any horse for grace.

If I sound the horn, will they stampede? he wondered. *Or will they attack me?* If he inched the car forward, would they move out of the way? How would they respond to vocal commands?

Owen lowered the driver's side window and was struck by a wave of cold, crisp air. His breath steamed as he shouted, "Hey! Get moving, why don't you?" He tapped the horn.

Some of the steers ambled further away. One turned and came nearer, pausing to examine him with its large, liquid eyes. It shoved its wide muzzle into the compartment and snorted in his face, loudly and wetly, its warm breath reeking of prairie.

"Knock it off—!" Laughing, Owen pushed the animal's huge head back out the window and raised the glass. A few yards distant, a handful of buffalo were meandering about; they seemed uninterested in the proceedings. With a sigh, he muted the music, activated the screen on the dash, and attempted to call his host.

A hearty voice answered his signal.

"Hey—sorry about that! I can see where you're stuck and I'm sending help out right now. Just stay inside your vehicle."

"Not a problem."

Owen enhanced and magnified his field of vision, scanning the horizon, where a faint row of pine trees rose from a modest bluff. Soon, dark specks appeared and swiftly drew nearer. A pair of drones arrived, emitting loud signals, to which the cattle responded by sauntering off the highway, down into a meadow several hundred yards away.

As the insect-like shapes of the drones continued to gently buzz the herd, MacIntyre muttered, "Ah, the romance of the Old West dies hard."

His host heard him, and the vehicle's comms system vibrated with laughter.

The small car resumed its trek along the ribbon of asphalt. Soon Owen left the main road and turned north onto a smaller paved driveway. This wound gently up into the sparse pines that Owen had noticed earlier. He came to a heavy stone wall and waited for the black iron gate barring his way to part majestically. The drive ended before an extensive lodge-style residence. It was constructed of whole timbers on a foundation faced with fieldstone, in mellow tones of gray and brown.

Waiting patiently at the ornate, carved wood entrance, Owen reminded himself to not appear overwhelmed by the opulent surroundings. After several moments, the door was opened by a stiff-faced figure who resembled a female humanoid. The mechanism's unusual configuration incorporated life-like facial features with segments of sleek, contemporary design. Owen thought it looked like a tech-saturated teen boy's dream of the ideal romantic companion.

The apparition spoke in a soothing feminine voice, "Welcome. One moment, please. Wait for security scan."

With awkward, puppet-like motions, the android took a few steps around him, waving one hand near his body. It paused when it came to MacIntyre's implant and spent several more seconds processing this extra input before making its final pronouncement.

"Clear," it announced in a neutral tone. "Please—follow me."

The less-than-convincing humanoid led him through a foyer overseen by vaulted ceilings and an imposing chandelier, whose many amber-hued mica shades imparted a reassuring, golden glow to the space. They passed through this and entered a living room that boasted even higher cathedral ceilings. Two sides boasted massive, wall-sized windows that framed stunning views of the prairie as it stretched to the unbounded horizon. Rendered in stainless steel, small models of various rocket ship designs were placed about the room on bookshelves or occasional tables of rustic wood.

Silhouetted against the fading daylight, a man stood at the windows.

"Sir, Mr. Owen MacIntyre has arrived," announced the machine, before retiring to one side.

Jaxtyn Morse turned from the window and approached Owen with his hand extended in welcome. He was a sandy-haired, fit man in his early fifties, tall, with little, smiling eyes. His wide, good-humored mouth broke into a cheerful grin; he seemed at ease and open-mannered for someone labeled a recluse.

"Mr. MacIntyre—welcome! It's a pleasure to meet you in person!"

"You, too, Mr. Morse." Owen was relieved that the man's handshake felt firm and sincere within his own grip.

Morse said, "I apologize for the traffic jam down on the road—hope my boys didn't startle you."

Owen waved his hand dismissively. "Not at all. It's as good as a safari for an urban dweller."

He gestured towards the nearest rocket model. "These are remarkable—really detailed. Are they historically accurate?"

"Oh, sure." Morse pointed out three other models throughout the room. "Those are miniatures of the most successful test rockets that my father designed." Stepping over to one located on a display stand closer to the window, he beckoned MacIntyre closer. "But this one is a prototype for the future."

Owen read the small plaque at the base of the sculpture. "'*Novus Cygnus*'— an unusual name."

"Yes, it means 'New Swan'."

But also sounds like 'novis ignis', Owen thought with satisfaction. His visor allowed him to make in-depth study of other details about the room, without it being obvious what he was doing. He made particular note of the book titles on the shelves, noticing many familiar names. He knew some were printed from the files he had shared with Andrei, after the latter had helped him conceal some data within Sofia's VR game account before they escaped Oregon. After learning that Morse had a keen interest in forgotten or suppressed titles, Owen had insisted that Andrei discreetly share some to help pave the way to today's meeting.

But the battered copy of *'Epicyclic Theories of History'* was an original, not an illicit re-print. Judging by the cover, it seemed to be the same edition MacIntyre's grandfather had owned.

Running a finger over the smooth, gleaming surface of the rocket model, the tycoon continued, "This was to be the flagship of my father's fleet, but it was never built. It's doubtful if circumstances will ever allow me to restore the family's original enterprise."

In the strong afternoon light, Morse's ruddy, weathered face grew solemn, lost in thought, likely thinking over the rise and fall of his father's tech empire.

Many details of the history of Morse's family companies were suppressed, but Owen had scrounged some crucial nuggets in preparation for this visit. The late Kian Morse had been an entrepreneur whose many interests included alternative energy, ocean farming, and artificial islands. His groundbreaking advances in the aerospace industry had led to important contracts with the U.S. government's space program. For a time, his company was on track to dominate the private sector interests in the permanent Lunar and Martian enterprises.

But as the U.S. continued to decay and steadily cede extraterrestrial ground to China, the senior Morse's star had faded. As he grew weaker, political enemies had entangled many of his businesses in red tape or else drained him with frivolous lawsuits. Foreign companies, such as China's mammoth Gold Flower, had captured more and bigger contracts. Over time, Morse was forced to sell many of his inventions to these interests, while refocusing on entertainment tech. At least that had been exceedingly lucrative.

Breaking the heavy silence, MacIntyre said, "Maybe you won't be building spaceships again, but there may be other opportunities."

Jaxtyn Morse answered with a bitter laugh, "Well, we do furnish most of the Mars mission simulators used to train astronauts and colonists. But it's ironic that the 'Empires of Ancient Mars' entertainment franchise is far and away InNova corp's most successful property—most of our revenue now depends on a fantasy version of something we wanted to achieve in real life." He threw Owen a sharper glance. "Have you played it?"

"No, sorry. Games aren't something I have time for. And even if I did—this isn't compatible with most headset designs," Owen elaborated, touching the edge of his visor.

Morse looked disconcerted, then laughed. "Oh, yeah—sorry. Well, maybe my techs can customize something for you someday."

He waved his guest towards the leather furniture arranged before the windows. "So, hey, before we get down to business—make yourself comfortable. What can she get you to drink? Coffee, tea? I've got some great local beer."

He pointed to the android; Owen said hesitantly, "Oh, whatever you're having. Thanks."

"Two beers," Morse instructed the machine.

The construct bowed its head, then walked away. Its slow, cautious steps took it past the far wall, dominated by a large oil painting. The artwork was a full-length portrait of a beautiful, middle-aged woman arrayed in traditional Lakota dress. The natural, graceful bearing of the portrait's subject provided a gentle rebuke to the android's ungainly form.

The men seated themselves. Owen loosened his jacket, trying to get comfortable among the plethora of decorative pillows on the slick leather couch.

The artificial servant returned, bearing a tray with two bottles. Owen recognized the logo of the Underhill brewery, a woodcut of a bison standing on an open plain.

Morse didn't make eye contact with the artificial servant's optical receptors as he murmured, "Thanks, Zoe."

The machine departed. As he regarded its retreating form, MacIntyre decided the faint hissing of the robot's joints, and the smacking sound of its stabilizing suction feet, was even more disconcerting than its corpse-like appearance.

Despite past generations' popular belief that such creations would become a common part of daily life, that hadn't happened. While at the Agency, MacIntyre's division occasionally seized some illicit, life-like sex androids, but the functions of those devices were limited. Even the world-wide demographic bust had not led to wide-spread use of robots, as the imploding global economy wasn't in a position to support that level of innovation or manufacture. The fact was that, there weren't enough average customers to warrant their existence. Thus versatile mechanical servants such as the one now delivering their beers remained expensive toys for the upper castes.

Shaking off his discomfort in the device's presence, Owen remarked, "Sorry, I don't see many of those in person."

Morse uttered a booming laugh. "Yeah, she's not much of a substitute for a real servant. My wife never allowed androids in the house." His glance darted to the oil portrait. "But now she's…gone—well, what the heck, they're useful. And they don't bother me."

His laugh could not conceal the unmistakable depth of sorrow behind his words; he was obviously thinking more of his wife than the robot. Owen felt his respect for the man growing by the moment.

With a beer in one hand, Morse rested his elbows on his knees as he leaned forward to address MacIntyre. "So, Owen—that looks like an old three-thousand series VIA unit you've got there. Do you mind telling me why you had it installed? Did you suffer an accident?"

Owen smiled tightly. "An accident…yes, we can leave it at that."

"Other than gaming incompatibility issues, how's it working out for you?"

"Oh, it's fine."

"Have you ever considered upgrading to actual custom bio eyes or at least a newer model visor?"

Having no desire to discuss the technical challenges in his particular case, Owen shook his head.

"Have you customized it?"

MacIntyre smiled. "Maybe."

Morse grinned. "So, obviously, you have some experience with neuroenhancement devices. Which brings us to the reason for this meeting. Now, I've read the proposal you forwarded me after our initial video meeting, and I have to warn you I'm still skeptical. And I've got a hell of a lot of questions. So I'd like to hear the pitch in your own words."

"Yes, of course." Setting his bottle aside, Owen fished a transparent casket from his inner breast pocket and extended it to Morse.

As the billionaire twisted the casket in his fingers and squinted at the contents, MacIntyre said, "About fifteen years ago, a scientist working at Gold Flower Corporation developed an implant that sends thoughts via directly-linked consciousnesses. Those are pieces of his prototype."

Morse's eyes remained locked on the container. Voice heavy with regret, he said, "My father was not the first engineer to pour tons of resources into advanced thought-transferring devices, too—not just rocket ships and video games. These types of inventions always promised big, but delivered problematic results."

Owen nodded, keeping to himself what he knew about the ethical challenges of developing such devices in the past.

Morse continued. "For one thing, to transmit data of any significance, they need to be in proximity to an external internet connection, because there's no way we can get that much hardware in the human skull without it being housed in something larger—like that." He gestured directly toward Owen's visor.

"Exactly. Which is why this new tech is so revolutionary."

"You're absolutely certain the proof of concept was genuine, not a trick? Maybe it was a microscopic transmitting and receiving unit sending simple messages through an internet relay?"

"I am one-hundred percent certain it was absolutely genuine."

"Is it possible for me to interview the inventor?"

Owen had no reason to mention Francisco Chen's fall from grace and choice to self-exile on a deserted island in the North Pacific. He said simply, "He's no longer with us. But he left all his research behind."

"Sounds pretty mysterious." Morse squinted more intently at the fragments. "You're not hiding the fact he died from a side-effect, I hope?"

The public story was that Francisco had committed suicide, but Owen didn't want to answer too many uncomfortable questions.

He said, "Not at all, it was unrelated to this. But other than his personal experimentation, nothing's been done with his research. I'm confident I can use my own influence at Gold Flower to license this tech to InNova corp for further development. And Doctor Jakob Huber, from the Max Planck institute, is eager to follow up on this work."

Sliding back a bit in his seat, Morse pursed his lips for a moment. He seemed a shade more dubious. "Explain: what would be the advantage of a device like this over existing implantable communications tech?"

Owen answered readily, "I believe the developer wanted an undetectable form of communication—with this technology, there is no discernible signal. And it's impervious to hacking."

"Un-hackable? You're sure?" Morse's pragmatism battled his excitement. "Because I'm not aware of any useful quantum tech that's small enough to be implanted while remaining undetectable."

"It's not exactly quantum-based. As I said, it's consciousness-based. It works according to a different set of rules, in an entirely new field. As if it's in a…a different dimension, you could say."

The atmosphere in the room thickened with a monumental stillness. Voice trembling, Morse at last broke it. "You mean—he actually solved the technical mystery of how matter interacts with consciousness?"

"Yes."

Owen was surprised to see a sheen of tears in Morse's eyes as the billionaire murmured, "All those experiments with the cloud, all those minds they tried to save on chips, but were lost in the void…,"

When the other's shock subsided a little, Owen added quietly, "And aside from improved security, I'm certain there's many uses for something that can transfer information instantaneously over infinite distances, without requiring a power source or any traditional type of signal."

Morse relaxed a little as he uttered a shaky laugh. "Well, yeah—when you put it like that! I can think of quite a few—especially relating to space travel."

"Exactly."

The businessman fell thoughtful for several moments, then shook his head with a sudden, emphatic frown. "I'm not interested in funding R&D for something Gold Flower is likely to take back and exploit once they see the potential. My family suffered through similar experiences with our rocket program."

With subdued excitement, he leaned forward again. "If, on the other hand, you could induce Gold Flower to *sell* everything to me outright—," he allowed the unfinished thought to hang between them as he raised his bottle in one hand. The small casket was still hidden in his other fist.

Owen thought of all the backdoors in Gold Flower's networks through which he could move at will; arranging a private sale of assets the company didn't know they owned would not be difficult.

He saluted Morse with his own bottle. "That's a very real possibility."

Morse asked, "So what's your interest in this? Do you just want to broker the deal, or do you want to be involved in the actual development, or do you want a share in the profits?"

"My immediate interest is in development, but I'm curious about the security applications of such a device." With a slight, meaningful smile, Owen extended his hand.

Morse regarded him for a moment before dropping the casket into MacIntyre's palm. "Yes, there could be some interesting applications in that field."

Neither man spoke again for a bit. Morse toyed absently with his bottle before commenting, "I suppose it's not too early to start looking for test candidates?"

MacIntyre said, "What about yourself? Do you have personal experience with neural implants?"

Morse looked taken aback. Owen added, "Sorry—I just wondered if there's any truth to the rumor you have one of your company's old intelligence-enhancing chips."

"Well—," Morse didn't look inclined to answer, but he explained anyway: "The IQ implants my father developed weren't commercially successful. I have to admit, the tech was over-hyped. Also, there was a lot of bad publicity following a few...well, I guess you could call them *unfortunate* customer reactions. So—no, I wouldn't bother with one." He forestalled further comment by pointedly taking another drink.

Owen said, 'Then I'll contribute at least one name, and I'm sure you can find some interested parties among your own techs. If this device works as well as I believe it will, I think it's a very real possibility you'll soon be back in the space exploration game."

Morse chuckled. "You read my mind—even without an implant. That's exactly where I'd like to be again, and it might happen sooner than I thought possible."

As the tall windows flooded the room with the rich gold of the lowering sun, Morse pulled a videoskin from his jacket and activated it. "Look—this is a city in the 'Martian Empires' game, based on the designs for the original, real colony."

A diminutive, colorful 3D projection sprang to life, hovering over the slick surface. The miniature city of glittering spires and domes trembled in his hand like a child's dream of the ultimate amusement park, a magical fairytale kingdom.

"No more games," he murmured in a low voice, almost to himself. "No more living in a fantasy while others reap what my father sowed."

Abruptly, he gave a shiver and folded the device. He regarded MacIntyre with a solemn expression. "Future generations of space colonists may be very grateful for your contribution."

With smug complacence, Owen settled back against the cushions. "Future generations won't have a clue about my involvement, because I want it kept strictly confidential."

Morse gave a sober nod and raised his bottle in a toast. "Understood."

CHAPTER
THIRTY-ONE

"TODAY, as we pay tribute to the surviving pioneers whom we are honored to have living among us, let us never forget the sacrifices they have made."

The shrill, grating timbre of the teen girl's voice reverberated against the exterior concrete wall of the Internal Security Agency Headquarters. Rows of folding chairs were neatly arranged in the parking lot before the speaker, chairs occupied by a varied assortment of decrepit individuals. Some ISA personnel stood at the back of the small assembly, fidgeting in an unobtrusive, vaguely respectful manner. Two tour buses were parked nearby. It was a private event, unfolding away from the eyes of any journalists or public passers-by.

Adjusting her short-range microphone, the young woman resumed her tribute. "We can never repay the debt we owe for the risks you took, the horizons you opened up for all of us. Trailblazers, like Spence here, have been inspirational for decades…,"

Tuning out the girl's voice, and the sporadic, desultory applause that interrupted her remarks, Hayden Singer stood to one side, scrolling on his videoskin. He was unusually relaxed that afternoon, still coasting on the reports coming in from his ISA lieutenants in Seattle, San Francisco and Los Angeles, regarding the success of their latest sweeps in the Haven Shelter Network.

The master plan was to clear out these shelters and move able-bodied candidates to camps or temporary holding facilities far from the urban centers;

the empty shelters would then be filled with the lowest-caste addicts forcibly removed from the streets. These people would then undergo the same process of sorting and culling, all conducted as far as possible from the public eye. So far, it was working well, with no pushback to speak of.

Closer to home, the public action against members of the Franklin Street Mosque had dovetailed perfectly with the Comms Secretary's propaganda campaign, and Singer's spy network reported a measurable drop in potential insurgent chatter. Still, it was disappointing that the young girl who he'd caught with a Scorpio pistol hadn't revealed who the supplier was. If she'd ever possessed that knowledge, it had died with her, since she had not survived her first week at the camp.

When the speaker's remarks wound down and the ceremony ended, Singer tugged at his gloves, enjoying the sensation of the pressure of the smooth, supple leather against his muscular fingers. Soon the audience would be guided aboard the buses, and Singer would join them on the promised excursion to a dilapidated but beloved casino, located a couple hours south of New Astoria.

Hayden crossed the space to the lead bus and climbed up the steep, narrow stairs. Positioning himself near the front, he watched as the crowd shuffled towards the conveyance. Eric Marino, a potential recruit for Singer's Elite Operations Squad project, stood to one side. He was a tall, heavyset man, whose sharp, sly look glinted from beneath heavy lids in a face that looked slovenly despite being freshly shaved.

In a low tone, Singer said to him, "Mr. Marino, are you ready to enjoy plenty of fresh air and hard work as you do your part to help build up Pacifica?"

"Yes, sir. Sure am."

"And do you think you have what it takes to become a vital asset to this Elite Squad initiative?"

"Yes, sir. But that depends on what you think you need."

Singer's brows rose in pleased surprise at the boldness of this answer. "It does. Wise of you to acknowledge that." The chief resumed his inspection of the line of passengers straggling up the aisle and taking far too long to choose their seats.

Soon the vehicle was at capacity; Singer remained standing near the top of the front steps. The sound system was already playing a selection of songs that had been popular decades earlier; hopefully the nostalgia these evoked would keep the honorees comfortable. But Singer had forbidden the use of any subliminal mindtones or the smoking of drugs in such close quarters, as he didn't want himself or Marino influenced by these methods of control.

As the autodriver engaged and the bus powered up, Hayden again regarded Marino with an evaluating, critical eye. The man's temporary uniform did not sit well on his bulky, poorly-conditioned form, but his swaggering air of confidence more than made up for what the black denim jacket and pants could not accomplish. The handgun he wore blatantly on his hip also contributed to his brashness.

Singer said, "I need you to ride at the back and keep an eye on everybody."

"Yes, sir." Marino tossed his long, greasy hair out of his hooded eyes and tromped down the aisle. Singer made a mental note to hammer some basic precepts of personal hygiene and pride of appearance into the man should he join the Squad.

In general, the candidates Singer was vetting for the Squad weren't promising. Basic requirements were simple—they had to be male and under forty years of age. Physical soundness would be an added benefit, but that seemed too much to hope for. Singer was downright repelled by what he had to work with. It was going to take an intense training course to get the pathetic specimens into shape.

When he had first reviewed the candidate profiles, Eric Marino's name had jumped out at him. He recognized the man from the fornication report filed with the Public Virtue Division against Sofia Volkova, before her marriage to MacIntyre. When Singer had studied the details of that case, he detected a strong sense of personal animosity behind Marino's accusations. Further perusing Marino's official ID pod, he found the breakdown of the man's utility credits, the number of hours he'd logged on various State-sponsored VR games, and which games he preferred, what his typical score was in those games.

The files also contained an official note from the Information Technology Oversight Division linking him to the purchase of an illegal "Lolita" class silicone sex robot. Singer wondered why this item hadn't been seized at the time, but could theorize: the old Agency had always been rife with corruption, its officers ready to blackmail citizens. Now, Marino was free to keep the item, as sex dolls had been quietly dropped from the list of illegal tech. Hayden had never understood why such items were banned in the first place; but then, he was often puzzled by the inconsistent eddies and threads of morality that wound through the culture.

On a practical level, having an insight into Marino's proclivities was helpful for Singer's evaluation. Today, he'd have the opportunity to observe the man in person and determine for certain if he was Elite material.

As the bus lumbered down the highway, Singer found the driving rock music and the chatter of voices oddly stimulating. To witness the real-life implementation of his carefully-crafted plans was exciting.

Turning in his seat to look back into the compartment, he studied these 'honored citizens' enjoying a rare day of recognition, tribute and recreation. Today's outing was sure to provide a distraction from the discomfort they undoubtedly felt, trapped in such poorly maintained yet pampered bodies, bodies that appeared far older than their true years.

In the weeks following Singer's private meeting with President Gray, he had begun to enact the latter's subtle mandate by reviewing numerous private TotalityCare health accounts. He became intimately familiar with the details of numerous medical histories. Consequently, he had a pretty good idea of just how much money today's excursion would ultimately save the regime. As he had signed off on each case, he reminded himself that resources across all industries needed to be managed frugally, and that such a commitment required sacrifices.

Studying the motley assembly, he saw that lifetimes of excessive legal drug use had contributed to their reduced mental acuity, while making them compliant, yet restless, irritable and unfocused. While most of them were at least ten years older than himself, a few were nearer his parents' ages. In fact, one older man in an antique black motorcycle jacket and dyed, closely trimmed beard, reminded him of his father. Or at least, of the man he theorized was his father.

Morrigan Singer had always implied that Cade was Hayden's father. Some of Hayden's earliest memories were of trying to guess which man was his real sire, based on which one he feared or despised the least. It had been a shock when it dawned on him that the fact that Cade had similar eyes as himself meant nothing, that it was in fact Layton who held the honor of being his real father.

Singer's expression remained impassive as his revolted gaze passed from the man in the motorcycle jacket to rove the other stooped, wrinkled forms, noting that on some of them, their saggy skin must have been stretched over hundreds of excess pounds during their youth. Formerly impressive tattoos had long since faded to indecipherable smears on baggy arms and tortoise-like necks.

Over the decades, hundreds of thousands of private and public dollars had been spent on their initial transformation surgeries, and on lifetimes of follow-up treatment, more surgeries, ever more medications. He thought scornfully of the seemingly endless series of surgical procedures that had refashioned their original genitalia into either ever more bizarre and useless appendages, or else suppurating caverns of flesh. Medical tech companies had been eager to develop implants that promised these glorified guinea pigs eventual sexual satisfaction and a sense of wholeness.

Looking over the rows of passengers, Hayden could see these treatments hadn't delivered; he saw emptiness and endless longing. Their haggard faces told him they'd never attained the fantasies they'd chased when they were young, and easily preyed upon while caught up in a wave of cultural hysteria. However, they were undeniably tough; this was the die-hard remnant that hadn't opted for suicide. Maybe they held on through a sense of entitlement and sheer bitterness. Perhaps today's excursion was more of a mercy to them than he had first thought.

After a drive of almost two hours, the van left the main highway and entered a smaller road leading through a former state forest that was now, by default, a national park. They soon left this road and embarked on an unimproved logging track leading even farther into the woods. They bounced and rattled along this for perhaps twenty more minutes, before emerging into a small meadow.

Murmurs of confusion and a thin thread of complaint greeted this sight, which was different than the expansive parking lot and sprawling facilities of the casino the passengers were expecting.

Singer stood up, swaying a little as the vehicle came to a stop on the bumpy field. His commanding voice cut across the rising tide of displeasure. "There seems to be a slight change of plans—please be patient while we gather more information."

After making a show of consulting his videoskin, he announced, "Looks like we may be stuck here for awhile. I need everyone to leave the vehicle in an orderly manner."

He opened the doors, then looked down the aisle and caught Marino's eye. He gave a meaningful jerk of his head towards the exit.

Jumping to his feet, Marino announced, "Okay—everyone follow me. And hey—no talking." He lumbered down the back steps and stood to one side, hand resting on his weapon, as the passengers struggled to their feet and exited the bus.

The crowd stood blinking and muttering in bewildered, querulous resentment. Overhead, the benign, cloudless blue sky shone over the occasional weathered stumps lurking among the rustling dead grasses and weeds of midwinter. A song bird uttered a few lilting, bittersweet notes before lifting from a stump and fluttering into the taller trees ringing the open space.

The passengers moved with care over deep ruts made by heavy equipment tracks. An excavator stood nearby, its digging arm arching with unthinking grace, like the neck of a prehistoric creature rising over its ponderous yet nimble body. Its operator was an anonymous silhouette in the cab; its track treads were crusted with drying soil and a long, deep gash gaped widely in the ground before it.

More fresh, dark-red earth was mounded along the edges of this trench.

Singer moved several paces away from the bus and regarded the meadow with satisfaction, noting how pleasant it was to be walking in the fresh air after two hours in the stifling atmosphere of the bus.

An old woman approached him. "Hey, you—," she clutched at his elbow, her manner quavery yet demanding, her watery eyes wide with angry befuddlement. The faint breeze tugged her sparse hair, dyed a bright lime green.

Her voice, damaged by hormone therapy from an early age, wheezed and thundered at him. "What the fuck's going on? There's a mistake…this in't the casino. They said I was a hero, was goin' to have a day full of fun, all 'spenses paid…,"

Even in old age, she had the attitude of a midcaste who had just enough education and a high enough CitizenTrust rank to entitle her to a somewhat secure existence at the State's expense. As he studied the old woman's face, it was clear she was incapable of understanding her way of life was gone forever, that complex historical and societal forces had led to this prosaic, unremarkable meadow, to the menacing arm of the excavator that rose above them against the insipid blue sky.

"No mistake. All your expenses have been paid, trust me. This is how we express our appreciation for your sacrifice."

Hayden took her weak, brittle fingers firmly into his gloved hand and with gentle, patient motions guided her closer to the trench. Looking over his shoulder, he called, "All of you—come away from the bus and please step over here!"

They made no move to obey, continuing to stand about in irresolute confusion. Singer fixed his gaze on Marino, whose puffy face grew flushed.

Yet the new Elite Squad candidate sounded experienced and in control as he shouted, "People, you heard Chief Security Enforcer Singer! We need you all to get over here—let's get this over with!"

Slowly, horrified understanding spread over some of their faces. Defeated, most of the passengers began to creep forward, moving with unsteady, resigned steps over the peaceful meadow. The man in the motorcycle jacket paused to help his companion over a particularly treacherous patch of ruts. When at last the thirty or so people stood in a ragged line along the rim of the large furrow in the waiting earth, the wind picked up for a moment and carried the sound of whimpering and muttering across the field.

Hayden drew his videoskin from his jacket and selected a function. Then he nodded again towards Marino.

The man unholstered his weapon. With the pistol now unlocked, he took a stance and trained the weapon on the woman closest to him. Singer remained to one side, scanning Marino's body language and expression. The wind dropped, the meadow grew deathly still.

Marino fired.

The recruit's actions had the methodical but quick movements of someone who had logged many thousands of hours in VR shooter scenarios. A little awkward for real-world situations, but today, his targets were not shooting back, and were hardly fleet of foot.

Undaunted by the screams, Marino's face hardened into a mask of concentration as he picked off any forms that attempted to pull back or flee. The air became thick with the stench of burnt bone, protein and smoldering cloth. When a portion of the trench was filled with sprawling shapes, some still faintly groaning, the excavator powered up and swung over the scene, gathering up a shovelful of soil and dropping it over the remains.

When the machine halted, half the trench, still empty, yawned greedily. The deadly calm that overhung the meadow was soon ruffled by the sound of the second autodriven bus approaching over the gravel track.

Soon a financial burden on the citizens of Pacifica would cease to exist. Evidence of these 'heroes', the embarrassing survivors of an earlier era, the results of clumsy pioneering attempts to reshape humanity, would be gone.

And a new era, one that looked only forward, never back, would continue to unfold.

CHAPTER
THIRTY-TWO

A BLEAK WIND whispered like a ghost through the parking lot of the Gold Flower Corporation Laboratory. The lot was two-thirds empty that late November evening. MacIntyre guided his small rental car through the aisles, hoping to snag a spot far enough from the front of the facility that he wasn't in anyone's face, but not so far as to arouse suspicion.

He hadn't expected to be in Jinzhou, China, this soon, but Morse was hyped about his proposal and insisted that they follow up immediately. Thus events were falling quickly into place following their in-person meeting.

MacIntyre slid the car into a suitable space and cut the engine. He spent a few minutes evaluating the official-looking physical documents he had prepared, as well as the copies he had on his videoskin, and his updated ID disc.

His false identity as 'Evan Lazarus', an official Gold Flower corporate courier, had been created to aid in his pursuit of Francisco Chen's clone across Asia following the disruption of the Thorn smuggling operation.

After that crisis was resolved, Owen had kept the ID pod current, since access to the corporation's records and various departments was vital for him to supervise the supply deliveries to the genuine Francisco. That supply process was largely automated, but when discussing the details of the man's self-imposed exile, they both agreed that having a living mind involved was a prudent fail-safe.

Thus far, the arrangement had worked well; footage from drones and satellites confirmed the hermit was still alive on his frigid prison. MacIntyre didn't often think about what his former adversary's daily existence on a barren island might be like. Chen had chosen his harsh, solitary path and was paying the price; he might as well have been on another planet.

Glancing at his reflection in the car's rearview mirror, Owen confirmed that the dark glasses he'd placed over his visor looked like an average, unremarkable AR unit. As long as he didn't remove them, it was unlikely anyone would guess he was neuroenhanced. He felt surprisingly relaxed, and was thankful he had slept rather well on the long flight from Calí.

He was sanguine he could get into the building, achieve his objective, and exit without inciting too much notice. Dragging a rolling suitcase from the rear seat, he started across the lot while mentally reviewing the script he had prepared for this venture. It had been awhile since he'd exercised his Mandarin, but he was prepared to supplement with an app inside his VIA unit if needed.

His mission could only be conducted in person; he didn't trust Gold Flower employees to crate up the relevant materials and ship them to Morse without too many questions being raised. Plus, he wanted to confirm for himself that not one scrap of data remained behind.

Across the lot, the grotesque post-modern structure of cast concrete dominated the vicinity, looking like a gargantuan, alien paper-wasp hive. He gambled that entering boldly through the front would forestall too many questions. He was gratified when the security panel at the main doors accepted his disc without a hitch.

The lobby was adorned with a display of fanciful creatures, chimeras and amalgams that threw strange, distorted shadows along the floor. These may or may not have been purely artistic fictions, interpretations of what the company had once hoped to achieve, years before the world-wide crack down on human-animal experiments.

Owen did not pay these much attention as he crossed the lobby to the reception desk. The receptionist scarcely glanced at his credentials, and he then made his way to the basement level. As he'd anticipated, the building seemed almost deserted at that hour, and he traveled many minutes through the labyrinthine corridors without seeing more than one or two other people.

When he found the appropriate door, he swept the keycard over the lock pad and entered.

The lab was small and had obviously been disused for years, waiting silently in an oppressive air of abandonment, tinged with a sour malevolence. Telling himself the latter was his imagination, MacIntyre quickly secured the door and went to the multi-limbed, arachnid-like automated surgical unit lurking across the chamber.

Following the instructions Dr. Huber had sent him, he unlatched and removed the main control unit, which was presumed to contain all the data from the last time it had been used. He carefully placed the module in the suitcase. Then he began collecting all the dusty notebooks and boxes of flash drives scattered on various shelves.

Flipping through several of the books, he noted with satisfaction they were all written in Spanish and seemed to consist solely of Francisco's work. There was a locked cabinet at one end of the small chamber; he produced a signet ring, the one that previously belonged to Francisco when the latter still held his influential positions at both Gold Flower and Vibora industries.

He pressed the ring to the cabinet's unusual-shaped lock and was rewarded with a satisfying click as the mechanism responded to Francisco's old security codes. Inside were even more data storage devices and notebooks; MacIntyre noticed the books contained a few references to the illicit Thorn formula, and he wondered if these might prove useful at some point. Maybe someday he'd follow up on possible long-term side effects of the substance that had nearly killed him.

Am I overlooking anything else? he wondered, making a more leisurely pass around the room. Based on the incomplete company records he had already accessed, and a few conversations he had with Dr. Huber, it seemed likely that everything Morse needed to recreate the original device was available in that chamber.

Hearing footsteps outside the door, he froze and listened. The steps approached slowly, then stopped. The door's lock chimed, and a man entered, radiating a sense of managerial efficiency. MacIntyre and the newcomer regarded each other a moment in awkward silence.

The man's face clouded. "Security reported a light in this room—who are you?"

"Evan Lazarus, courier for the IT department," MacIntyre replied, politely bowing from the waist. He extended his videoskin, with his corporate bio prominently displayed.

In response, the man's puzzled frown deepened. "What is your business here in this lab?"

Owen swiped to new screenful of data. "I've been sent to collect some assets that were recently sold to InNova Corp. Here's all the documentation."

The man accepted the device and scrutinized the data. MacIntyre continued, "I'll be taking charge of these items and delivering them. The documentation is all there."

"Yes, I see." The man's forbidding expression hardened as his gaze scanned the chamber, then lingered on the notebooks piled in the case. MacIntyre kept his respiration as normal and calm as possible, preparing his response should things take a turn for the worse.

Then with the shadow of a smile, the man relaxed and handed the videoskin back. "Very well, carry on. I suppose it's about time all this mess was cleared up."

Rolling the videoskin and replacing it in his jacket pocket, Owen nodded. He said haltingly, "I can't imagine what they'll do with all this junk, but at least Gold Flower will finally get a little something back."

"Yes, it seems so. Do you need any assistance?"

Owen bowed again. "No, but thank you. I have everything under control."

When the manager left, MacIntyre sealed up the case and exited the room. Feeling lingering concern about the man's manner, he decided it was a good idea to leave the building and head directly back to the airport as soon as possible.

It wasn't until he'd put about five miles between himself and the lab that he fully relaxed, a pleased grin slowly suffusing his thin features. Whether or not anything ever came of this invention, he had to admit these kinds of missions were kind of fun.

A bright dawn broke sedately beyond the sprawling Calí skyline, gilding the tips of the green mountains encircling the dense cityscape. The view was veiled by the reflections of the office lights behind Owen as he stood at the large window a few moments. He'd arrived early to take advantage of the privacy of the office.

After reviewing a few Paloma-related files, he signed off on some paperwork that the executive assistant, Raul Peréz, had left for him. Then he switched mental gears to study some detailed reports from Gregory Park.

Greg's updates on Restoration efforts to discredit Pacifica were favorable; Enrique's testimony was at last gaining traction among the right sorts on various committees. There was also increased support for the current sanctions, even at the risk of further souring relations with Canada and China. Yet if there was any growing support for smuggling aid to resistance movements, Greg could not say.

Settling further into the welcoming recesses of the black leather office chair, Owen sifted through some of the notes on the desk. He pored over his hand-sketched charts of hexagonal communications cells, proposed protocols for managing the experimental comms device among more than two users. It was all very hypothetical at this point, but not too early to think about how such relations could best be structured.

The non-disclosure agreement he had signed with Morse restrained him from dropping hints to Park about work on the device, which they had dubbed an 'intravox', but even if he wasn't bound by secrecy, he doubted he would've mentioned it. Since MacIntyre typically kept his cards as close to his vest as possible, compartmentalizing this venture was second nature.

He wasn't sure what the blow-back would be when—or if—Park and the other Restoration players learned he'd gone so far out on a limb without authorization. But maybe they'd never find out.

This whole venture could crash and burn, he warned himself. *I don't want to have gotten the Restoration excited for nothing. Best to see how it plays out—act first, get permission later.*

An incoming message on the screen reminded him it was almost time to meet with Morse's technical team. He had connected the office computer to a private Quasar satellite link. This, plus the use of a VPN, made the virtual meeting quite secure. In addition to wanting to keep this project a secret from Sofia for the time being, Owen knew it was safer to work from the Calí office using this system, where he would not run the risk of any signals being traced back to the hacienda.

When the meeting started, Owen kept his camera off and added a distortion filter to his mic. The team members onscreen exchanged greetings and quickly got on to the business of analyzing data. Dr. Jakob Huber was just as skinny, white-haired and energetic as Owen remembered from before. The renowned cybernetics expert was deferred to and invited to speak first.

"Mr. Morse, I can't thank you enough for bringing me aboard this fascinating project! For several years, I have been eager to learn more about this hypertransmission device, and the material I've reviewed so far is astounding. Are either of you gentlemen familiar with the theories of Hameroff and Penrose? They developed their 'Orchestrated Objective Reduction' theory of human consciousness in the nineteen-nineties and two-thousands."

"I am," answered Morse, suddenly sounding skeptical. "I grew up hearing a lot about it from my dad. Their predictions were largely discredited."

"Perhaps. But the inventor, Don Francisco Chen, revisited their ideas concerning the action of microtubules in brain cells. With his brilliant insights into molecular biology, he discovered a way to artificially stimulate an action similar to what Hameroff had proposed, but which doesn't exist in nature."

Placated for the moment by this explanation, Morse waited expectantly for Huber to continue.

Adjusting his eyeglasses, the doctor went on. "However, I have identified several key points where changes can be made to Don Francisco's interface, which will render the device much smaller. So there will be no need for an external plate to access the implant, once it's secured in the subject's brain. As you can see from the proposal I've shared with you all, I'm recommending making the connection with preprogrammed filaments, that will attach themselves to the right frontal lobe."

"I'm looking at your proposal now," interrupted Morse. "I like what I see, but we don't have the luxury of using very many test subjects. How sure are you this will work on the first try?"

Silently, Owen waited for Huber's response.

The doctor said, "I've modeled this very meticulously, but since the model is based only on Chen's records, there is no guarantee it will behave like this once it's implanted in someone else. So I will require a complete scan of the candidates' brains before I can do further modeling. But yes—I'm confident it will work."

"How confident?" interrupted Morse. "Confident enough to try it on yourself?"

Huber's heavy white brows shot up. "Yes, of course! If you have any need for me to do that, I will be available."

Morse laughed. "I was teasing, Doc! Actually, I can reveal that our first subject is with us, and he's very eager about the whole thing."

"And yet still hiding behind a black screen," commented Huber dryly, but with a warm smile. "Well, sir, whatever your reasons for maintaining your privacy, I respect that."

Owen grinned to himself and cleared his throat. "Thank you, Doctor Huber. I do have a question, however: do you have reason to believe that a subject that already has a neural implant might encounter difficulties with this device?"

Huber's mouth drew into a tight line as he thought. "That's such a vague question, I can't answer it without more information. If you have such a device, please include the data with your brain scans."

"Yes, of course. Are you ready to take a look at those now?"

"Certainly."

"Okay, stand by."

MacIntyre forwarded the material he had downloaded from his visor. He watched Huber's face as the doctor's eyes focused on reading the incoming data: the man's expression went from puzzled to enlightened.

After several more moments, Huber addressed the camera. "Ah—a vintage Via unit, three-thousand series. I've only encountered one of those before, Mr...*MacIntyre*."

"Yes, hello!" Owen shut off the voice modulator and flicked on his camera, joining Huber in a laugh, as the old man's eyes gleamed in triumphant recognition.

MacIntyre grew serious. "Please be candid—do you think there's a chance this visor will interfere with a hypertransmitter like what we're proposing?"

Huber said, "No, no! Not at all! The connections will be in different locations in the brain. But tell me—," he paused for a moment. "I am wondering if perhaps you are ready to have even more technology wired into your brain. I recall meeting a young woman who raised some valid points about the side-effects of too much hardware being lodged in one's head."

MacIntyre smiled at this reference to the concerns Sofia had raised during Huber's exam of Owen's visor.

"Yes, Doctor, and I share her concerns. But I believe this opportunity is too important to miss. I've reviewed the plans, and also believe that it's so different from my VIA unit, that any side-effects would manifest in completely different ways."

"That's an excellent point," Morse chimed in. "I think you're right about that."

"And besides," Owen added, "I want to be a part of the initial test, even if it's risky. I don't expect others to take a chance I wouldn't take myself."

Huber nodded. "Very noble." His lean hand pushed his glasses up a little further on his nose and his pleased grin spread. "Well, gentlemen—what's the next step on this journey?"

Morse leaned in closer to his own camera; his excitement was palpable, even through the screen. "Great question, Doc. I need you to take the data you got from Owen here and model a customized plan for his device. Get it to my tech team ASAP, and they'll fabricate an actual unit."

Huber frowned. "What about the second subject? I haven't yet seen their biodata. These are communications devices, after all."

Morse's grin widened. "We are in the process of selecting the second subject—you should get their scans in a day or so."

To prevent subconscious contamination and bias prior to testing the intravoxes, it had been agreed that details about the candidates were to be kept from each test subject as long as possible. Thus, Owen would not know who'd be sharing his mind until much later in the process.

"Very well," said the doctor. "I think it's reasonable to assume I'll have the customized plans ready within a couple of weeks. How long do you estimate it will take to fabricate the prototypes?"

Morse said, "I'd say within a month of receiving your models. Then they'll be implanted and the fun will begin. So—sometime in February? That sound good, Owen?"

Owen offered a self-satisfied smile. "I'll be ready. But will you be? Will the world? Because it looks like I'm going to be gaining some mighty interesting powers."

When the meeting ended and he was alone in the quiet office, he felt an unpleasant lurch in his spirit. The fact that he was about to integrate yet another powerful device into his body stared him in the face. How would this invention change him?

This wasn't a matter of having artificial sight, or scanners or instant access to the internet. This was a linkage of his thoughts directly with others'. Potentially, he'd be receiving their impressions, their personalities. Eavesdropping on their emotions. As they would on his.

None of this was to be undertaken lightly.

Yet, if it provided even the slightest advantage over Pacifica, it was worth it. If it could contribute in any way to Hayden Singer's demise, there was no question he would try it.

CHAPTER
THIRTY-THREE

DECEMBER'S icy rain tapped rhythmically on the top of the marquee. It drummed on the microphone perched near the edge of the stage; an attendant, crouching low and moving swiftly, brought the microphone stand further in beneath the shelter of the tent. The dignitaries shuffled with a restive air.

Chief Enforcer Singer surveyed the cold-pinched faces of the attendees waiting placidly in the rain to witness the official grand opening of a ground station that would link with a recently-acquired, third-generation Mozi-class quantum satellite.

Singer thought over the update at the most recent Committee meeting. With the power grid still too unreliable to mount any significant mindshaping campaign, the Comms Department continued to make do with tried and true methods of influencing public opinion and behavior. The most recent propaganda push made a point of stating that the new satellite would improve internet access for the average citizen, not just state services.

Of course, that wasn't going to happen. But the story was sufficiently credible to keep people placated for awhile. If their own experience differed from the official narrative, they were well-trained enough to doubt the evidence of their own eyes before they'd openly question the happy fiction unfolding on the posters and placards throughout the cities.

By the time they began comparing notes with their neighbors and forming genuine questions, they'd be distracted by some other issue. The 'Liberating

Joys of Rationing' was the title of the next campaign due to roll out, now the first wave of Power Cult positivity was waning.

But for today, the narrative was all about comms tech and progress, and how strong and independent Pacifica was becoming—with a little help from friends. The satellite was a gift from the Chinese government, laundered through a series of private aerospace companies. Fortunately, the only foreign official present was Army Captain Li Jianguo, and he was clad in an understated civilian suit and a benign expression.

At the Committee meeting, Hayden witnessed much debate about the risks of the populace seeing President Gray sharing the stage with this man. The new regime continued to walk a political tightrope between projecting a sense of independence, and admitting to a reliance on China.

After that nation's release of a series of bioweapons, and a slow, de-facto economic annexation of Hawaii and large swathes of the West Coast, there had been something of a cultural backlash against all things Chinese. Even their offer of aid after the devastating Cascadia earthquake had been seen as an effort to gain an actual, physical, military foothold on the continent. Thus the offers of help had not done much to lessen distrust.

The tension between the countries had continued into space, involving 'accidental' killing of respective satellites and the undermining of the U.S. space program, which had helped China, allied with Russia, to establish dominance on both the Moon and Mars. At the highest crest of the popular backlash, cell-phone towers had been destroyed by angry mobs and many Federal and State agencies had scrambled to prove their comms tech was exclusively American in origin.

Yet that might as well have been ancient history, since so few people recalled the details. Today's ceremony was unfolding smoothly, as planned. Perhaps the Comms Department's lavish promises of free drinks and hot food had been the biggest draw for the dispirited Portlanders. In any case, it was a good-sized, well-behaved crowd.

Now the event manager cued the music, and the attendees shuffled to attention as the strains of the new Pacifica anthem competed with the gusts of wind coming off the Willamette river. When the brief opening ceremony concluded, President Gray stepped forward and began a series of perfunctory remarks, striking the expected range of tones: thankfulness, encouragement. Confidence for the future, no matter how many obstacles fate, or their enemies in the United States, might raise against them.

As Gray concluded and invited the next speaker to the microphone, Singer's attention switched to the various uniformed or plainclothes security men stationed about the venue. Directly before the stage was the VIP section, where press and other guests were safely corralled.

Slate stood in the packed group, looking a touch bewildered at being included in such rarified company. He also looked cold and uncomfortable, with a rosy flush on his pale, high cheekbones. Hayden was pleased he'd agreed to come; it seemed to him Slate had at last accepted how important it was to be a part of this milieu, and was beginning to enjoy the perks of being in such an influential club. Catching Slate's eye, Hayden gave him a self-assured smile, which the other returned.

When the speakers finished, there was another burst of upbeat music over the sound system, and the elites moved to their vehicles. Slate joined Hayden in his car.

Dashing the rain from his hair and then blowing on his cold fingers, Slate muttered, "I'm glad that's over. This fucking rain is bone-chilling."

"We need all we can get," said Hayden. "We're actually facing serious drought conditions."

"I find that hard to believe. Sure that's not part of another propaganda campaign?" Slate's tone was flippant, he flashed a tight smile as he settled in his seat.

"Don't knock them, they're remarkably effective," warned Hayden.

The private reception venue was not far; soon they parked near the landmark party ship anchored on the east side of the Willamette. The two men entered an understated but classy dining area with a large, wood-paneled bar to one side, gleaming with sparkling glassware and bottles. The ship was revered locally for the part it had played in providing emergency transportation when the city's bridges had been damaged or outright destroyed during the Cascadia event.

The vessel had recently been refitted and upgraded. Much care had been taken to re-create many accurate details, such as the 1990's-style lighting fixtures and carpet pattern. Tonight, a live pianist sat at the keys of a baby grand piano, providing an elegant musical backdrop to the scene.

When the ship was filled with her contingent of guests, the captain gently maneuvered the craft away from the dock to begin a leisurely trek southwards along the river. As Singer watched President Gray, Captain Li, and the others take drinks and mingle in the salon, he was rattled by an uncharacteristic wave of unease.

Although he was making great strides to cement his professional relationship with most of these people, he suddenly felt alienated, like an outsider, a worthless pretender. For several distressing minutes, he felt in over his head, unprepared to be a part of this cadre of elegant and influential players.

Despising his own weakness, he recalled the various intimate details he was collecting about many members of this group. As he thought of their secret vices, frailties and instances of poor judgement, a sense of occult power grew within him. In contrast, his opinion of himself suddenly improved. His discomfort ebbed, and he was soon engaged in effortless pleasantries with the acting Vice President, Irma Serrano-Ochoa.

As they conversed, he set aside his personal loathing of the woman. He didn't have much choice, since talk of special elections was becoming rarer week after week; there was a real chance both Gray and Serrano would be in power for a very long time.

Thus it was vital to maintain his true feelings behind a mask of deference and polite attention. The more he practiced this, the easier it became, he even achieved a genuine interest in her comments about the responsibilities of homeownership, and the challenges of finding reputable lawn care technicians.

Later, seated with Slate at a table by a window, Hayden was aware of the illusion that it was the cityscape on either bank that seemed to be in motion, while the craft itself stood still. Despite feeling the faint thrumming of the engine through the floor, it seemed the ship was merely treading water. The window at his elbow tossed back his and Slate's reflections, the men were superimposed over the dazzling, otherworldly lights of the city's newest and most cosmopolitan buildings. Yet there were still significant patches of darkness throughout the city.

Under his breath, Slate murmured, "A lot of neighborhoods still don't have power. How long is that going to continue?"

Hayden caught Slate's eye and mouthed silently, "Lower your voice. Everything is fine."

With a chastened expression, Slate removed his gaze from the window and focused on his own drink. Before their meal arrived, he excused himself and went to the restroom. While he was gone, Hayden continued to be mesmerized by the passing view. His own impressive reflection dominated a city that, at the moment, looked tantalizingly seductive and perfect. It was an illusion, but even seeing the mirage of perfection was somehow inspiring.

As his gaze lingered on the view, he noticed a flash of green light flare in the blackest part of the streets, in one of the districts with no electricity. It was also one of the neighborhoods that contained a few scattered street-dwelling addicts, those who had thus far evaded the sweeps.

The light lasted a split-second, but he could have sworn it was the searing white-green hue of a beam-weapon's discharge. Growing tense, he kept his eyes on the location, waiting to see if any more would appear. After a minute, two more followed in rapid succession. Frowning, he started to rise from the table, when Slate returned to his seat and sat down across from him with a troubled expression.

He leaned towards Hayden, whispering, "That group of kids over at the corner table by the piano—who are they?"

Hayden glanced toward the table in question. It was packed with sleek, well-dressed teens and young adults. He recognized most of them from his extensive files.

He answered in a low tone, "Kids of some of the high-ranking government officials and industry leaders."

Slate frowned. "What are they doing? They're acting strange."

Hayden observed them more closely, noting they were in unusually high spirits for such a subdued, refined venue. Were they drunk or using legal chemical compounds? Or did their privileged status as pampered upcastes mean they didn't know how to behave in public? He suspected the latter, and was on guard as to how to best handle a situation potentially hazardous to his own standing with the regime.

One of the youths had his open videoskin spread in the center of the table. As he and his companions leaned in to see the screen, their faces periodically lit up with green flashes. Each time there was a flash, the kids would squeal and snort with laughter. Hayden watched closely, soon confirming the flashes coincided precisely with the flashes along the river.

He rose and crossed the dining salon as unobtrusively as possible. He stopped at the crowded table and stood over the group, who were all so absorbed in the scene on the videoskin that they did not seem to notice him.

The teen in the center of the crowd jabbed his finger at the device. He chortled, "Now—look at this fucker! Look at him run like a fucking rat—!"

As the youth's finger touched the screen, another green flash blossomed. The ring of youthful, leering faces again exploded with mirth.

In a calm, even tone, Singer remarked, "You all seem to be having a wonderful time this evening. Mind sharing the joke with me?"

The group regarded him with uncertainty, but the youth handed the videoskin over. Addressing the screen, Hayden skimmed the contents. The device served as the control panel of a small drone; a customized offensive beam generator was listed as one of the drone's assets.

Hayden said, "Did I hear correctly—you've been using this to hunt and shoot rats?"

"Yeah, exactly. Can I have it back now?" The boy extended his hand in an entitled, insolent gesture. "I built it myself."

"Ingenious," said Singer, not surrendering the unit. "Does it record? Can I go back a few minutes and see your kill rate?"

Now the youth betrayed a glimmer of anxiety. Singer recognized him as the son of the owner of a large insect-protein processing plant in California, and it was pleasurable to see him squirm like a dying beetle on a pin.

But it was also dangerous; Singer needed to tread with caution. He swiped the screen settings back to the recording of the most recent events. Night vision footage, from an overhead perspective, shimmered on the screen, and he watched as several streetdwellers were flushed from their spider holes and chased down a darkened alley, falling and writhing as the bursts of blinding light enveloped them. They seemed to have survived the attack, but it was clear they were terrified and injured.

Mouth clamped in a line, Hayden stood thinking over his next course of action, while the group at the table fidgeted. They resembled fashion androids, encased in their lavish suits and gowns, hair impeccably styled and ornamented.

The owner of the videoskin slouched back in his seat with an affected air of insouciance, his dark eyes narrowly observing Singer.

The chief met this gaze with a ready smile. Knowing the answer, he asked anyway, "What's your name?"

"Mason Patel."

With an abrupt smile, Singer handed the device back. "Mr. Patel, that's an impressive bit of hacking. And I'm pleased to see you're entering into the spirit of contributing to the clean-up and rebuilding of our streets. But perhaps this particular approach comes a shade too close to vigilantism."

Placing his hands on the table, he leaned close to the young man and continued in a friendly undertone, "If you have any other suggestions for ways to bolster urban security, you're more than welcome to stop by ISA Headquarters and discuss them with me and my colleagues. Like I said, your hacking skills are impressive."

With a shrug and slight, pleased pout, the youth rolled the skin up and slipped it in his pocket. "Thanks, but no. I don't really have time for that. This was just for fun."

It was clear the offer had in fact, tickled his ego. Hayden was certain the boy wouldn't be running to his father to complain about the Chief Enforcer's meddling with that night's entertainment.

Straightening, Hayden continued to smile blandly at the group. "Ah, I understand. Well, please enjoy your meal." The youths relaxed and resumed tittering among themselves as Singer walked away.

At his table, he found the server had brought his plate of synthesized salmon compote and asparagus tips, arranged in a mathematically severe yet artistic presentation. As he reseated himself, he was pleased that Slate was studying him with a look of admiration.

Slate whispered, "I knew they were up to no good—thanks for stopping them."

"We have our own methods and timeline for cleaning up the cities. It isn't a game." Hayden reached for his glass of wine. "This country won't survive if thuggery—even at the highest levels—is allowed to run rampant. People need to see us enacting and adhering to our own routine of self-discipline."

Slate's happy look faded and he lowered his eyes, murmuring under his breath, "That includes dropping people off construction towers, doesn't it?"

Hayden froze, then hissed through his teeth, "That's not something we discuss. Not here, not ever. It did not happen."

"It happened—lots of us saw it." Growing paler, Slate set down his utensils and continued to keep his gaze locked on his plate.

In a low growl, Hayden said, "Yes, they saw it, they internalized the message, and now no one dares mention it. And they won't talk about it when another message is sent to a selected community, either. Maybe next time, it will be the Christians."

Slate's face reddened. "Damn it, what's happened to you? You sound so heartless. What happened to the you that was so…that I…,"

As Slate's words stumbled, Hayden studied him, wondering how much of a fuss he was prepared to make, how much attention he'd attract. His own pulse upticked and his hands grew sweaty. With a twitch of his head, he slid his eyes about to see if anyone nearby was listening. He was relieved to see President Gray, Serrano, and Li Jianguo were well out of earshot. Then he focused again on Slate.

"Look at me."

With a soothing yet commanding tone, he dragged Slate's troubled gaze up to meet his with his own force of will. "Don't worry, nothing's changed between the two of us. But this job requires I get, well…pretty severe when dealing with security matters. Unfortunately, that's unavoidable."

Eyes still holding Slate's, he picked up his fork and sliced off a portion of the quivering pink entree. "But still, inside—it makes me sick to see kids like that being fucking heartless animals. You believe me, don't you?"

Slate at last answered with a smile. "Yeah, of course. I believe you."

The smile was tepid and forced, but Hayden was relieved to get it. "Good, then. You see, we're on the same page."

As the luxurious ship slipped through the night, Hayden continued to relax and focus his attention on the meal, relishing the exquisite balance of each flavor, texture and color.

For one moment, at least, disaster was averted and all was as it should be.

CHAPTER
THIRTY-FOUR

A SET of keys jingled deep in the pocket of Eric Marino's black hooded jacket, but he didn't need them at the moment. He knew a more satisfying method of entering the building, which was sealed with a few perfunctory strands of ISA security tape. Hefting a crowbar in his gloved hands, he assaulted the lock on the side door, prying around it, grunting a little as the metal frame deformed enough for him to slip the bar in further.

After a series of judicious, violent shoves, he weakened the frame enough for the door to swing freely. The process hadn't made much noise, but that hardly mattered. Even though the building was fairly close to a residential neighborhood, there was no one nearby on that overcast, wet winter night in New Astoria to observe the break-in.

Picking up his large, black duffle bag from the small side porch, Marino stepped inside and entered a short corridor, moving with an arrogant stealth to the heart of the abandoned structure. It was cold, damp and dark, but knowing there was no electricity here, he didn't bother to flip on any switches. He took a small flashlight from his pocket and flicked it about, eyes widening with greed at the hints of gold and jewels that glinted back at him from the darkness.

Sniffing the air, he noted faded but distinct smells of candle wax, smoke, and something unfamiliar. Rich, spicy and exotic.

He set his bag on a side table, then caught up some of the gleaming vessels.

Some were plates that looked like they were made of gold, and there was a large, fancy drinking cup with enamel and jewels around the base.

These he stuffed into the bag, then continued to shine the light around the forsaken church. His steps following the flashlight beam, he made a leisurely circuit of the space, feeling no curiosity about anything other than easy-to-reach plunder.

At the wooden screen that divided the main part of the chamber from the small inner sanctum, he paused.

In the fragmented light, President Gray's stern but kindly visage regarded him from a poster fastened to the screen. Raising the crowbar and emitting a low, grunting chuckle, Marino approached the poster.

Idly, he scratched out the eyes and jabbed holes in the flimsy board. Then he pried off the sheet and examined the old painting beneath. His flashlight picked out scenes of stiff, stylized people with severe expressions, engaged in mysterious interactions. None of it meant any more to him than would the random splotches of mildew staining a bathroom wall.

Yet traces of gold gleamed in these scenes, so he carefully scraped some away with the tip of the bar. The gold was applied in such thin layers, he soon realized it was not worth collecting. Yet he continued to drive the metal tip across the painting, scoring out some of the faces; with a juvenile satisfaction, he jeered as ribbons of paint curled ahead of the bar's sharp end.

Soon tiring of this, he raised the metal tool and bashed out some of the supports of the wooden screen and kicked aside the artwork. Behind this was the altar. He set the bar and flashlight down, stepped over the wreckage and, sniggering, unzipped his pants in order to freely urinate around the base of the ceremonial table.

Then his eyes caught the outline of a box, crafted of wood and stone, ornately decorated and resting behind the altar. Fastening his trousers, he approached eagerly, wondering how much more valuable the contents of this box might be, if the gold cup had been left unguarded.

Marino fished the key ring out of his pocket and selected one that fit the small lock. Then he snatched at the handle and jerked the door open, retrieving the flashlight and shining it inside. The little chamber was empty.

Disappointed but not especially surprised, he lost interest in the receptacle and returned to his duffle bag. He pulled out a can of fuel and unscrewed the top. He retraced his earlier route through the church, sloshing gasoline up and down the aisles, over the wooden pews, over the screen and its paintings. He soaked the altar coverings and poured the remaining liquid over the ornate box.

The structure now reeked of the harsh chemical scent. Fighting a feeling of light-headedness from the strong fumes, he found more white cloths in the room where the gold cup had been, twisted one into a large wick and returned to the main chamber. Grinning, he touched the fabric to the flame from a cigarette lighter, and tossed it into the trail of gas soaked into the carpet.

As the flames exploded upward and devoured the trail of fuel, Marino was struck by a wave of heat and illuminated by the warm, rich glow. Eyes following the light as the fire devoured the wood, his excitement swelled and he was consumed by an urge to celebrate the destruction in an intensely personal manner. His hand strayed downward and again unzipped his trousers, but he had no time to indulge. The heat was soon unbearable, and the fire forced him back.

Catching up his bag, he went back down the corridor and out the broken side door. He strode with lumbering but cocksure movements down the street, then halted under the shadows of some tall trees, to continue watching the bright flames as they licked against the windows from the inside.

Soon plumes of smoke billowed out from the eaves, and more orange tongues escaped into the winter chill. Marino's own breath steamed in answer as he grinned. Chief Enforcer Singer hadn't explained how tonight's act fit into the greater picture for Pacifica's future, and Marino didn't care. He was enjoying himself on a very primal level.

What was important was that he had been instructed to destroy St. Columban's, and that he should at least make an attempt to have it appear the work of opportunistic vandals. Whenever he carried out Singer's orders, Marino felt good and useful. He relished the praise and rewards that inevitably ensued.

Shouts sounded from the neighboring houses as someone spotted the fire and raised the alarm. When he heard the wail of approaching firetrucks, Marino turned and disappeared into the night's darkness.

CHAPTER
THIRTY-FIVE

"OOH, SEÑORA—THIS ONE! *QUE LINDO*!"

Isabella Garcia, Teresa Ortega's granddaughter, tugged a small outfit off the clothing rack and presented it to Sofia MacIntyre. Sofia studied the infant onesie, emblazoned with a cartoonish print of spaceships and the planet Mars.

"I'm not sure," she said at last. "It's rather…bright."

Isabella waved it tantalizingly before the heavily pregnant woman. "But señora…*spaceships*. He'll love it!"

The fanciful space theme reminded Sofia of her older brother, and how his advances in chemical engineering were expected to improve the lives of colonists on the Moon and Mars. The baby wouldn't care any time soon, but she was proud of her brother's achievements.

Awash in sentimentality, she relented. "Okay, add it to the pile."

With a squeak of happiness, the young teen added the garment to the growing collection of baby clothes draped over her slim arm. It seemed Sofia had no resistance to buying very small items designed for tiny male humans, and Isabella was also enjoying the shopping trip. She was a naturally happy, thoughtful girl whose coltish demeanor showed signs of soon growing into an unusual, serene beauty.

Isabella took the garment to Diego Rojas to ask his opinion. The long-suffering guard looked taken aback and mumbled, "*Muy bonito*."

As they continued to browse the racks, Sofia thought she heard the faintest possible sigh from the man, who was always within two or three paces of the women throughout their tour of the high-end boutiques of Medellín's Poblado district.

Earlier that day, Isabella had accompanied Señora 'Lazarus' to her monthly meeting with the children of Nido de Paloma. After the music classes, Sofia had purchased a few items in the facility's shops, created by the women living in the program, the mothers of her young students.

But those garments, as nice as they were, hadn't been enough. Despite feeling uncomfortably heavy, and battling an increasing nausea and sense of disquiet, Sofia was determined to continue shopping. She sensed this was the last chance to do so before the baby came, and had the urge to stock up on clothing.

Plus, since Owen was out of town again, she was struggling against a sense of annoyance and abandonment.

He does what he has to, she reminded herself, as the three of them left the boutique and walked along the central corridor of the sprawling *parque comercial*. The controlled climate of the indoor shopping center was a relief from the general humidity of the city, and she was content to draw out the visit as long as possible.

With a pang of guilt, she thought, *Whether he's doing Foundation work, or a project with Andrei, or something super-secret with Park, he needs me to be more supportive. I just wish he'd think ahead when scheduling these trips.*

But she had to admit that, in Owen's defense, her most recent medical check-up had confirmed she'd probably go past her due date, so he had assumed there was still plenty of time.

As they immersed themselves in all things baby, Sofia was grateful for Isabella's company. Sofia still hadn't made any close friends here, her circumstances made that difficult. And she missed her own mother, but today Señorita Garcia's lively company helped blunt her general feeling of isolation.

They stopped at a café, and Sofia treated Isabella to some fruit sorbet. As she watched the girl enjoy the confection, Sofia grew clammy and jittery. A spasm of sharp discomfort passed through her body, like a giant hand gripping her belly and squeezing it with slow, deliberately cruel motions.

No, it can't be happening now! It's a false alarm, she told herself in frantic disbelief. *He's coming too early, I'm not ready. Maybe if I just relax, the contractions will stop.*

Powering through her growing discomfort, she led Isabella further along the concourse. There was a toy shop at the far end that had caught her eye when they first entered, and she focused on making it back there to browse some more.

The sensation of tightness grew. She halted, catching her breath in a startled gasp. A shopping bag slipped from her hand as she placed her palm on her stomach; the color drained from her face and a wild look came into her eyes. Diego was instantly at her side.

"Señora, are you well?"

"Yes, I'm fine." Her shaky, nervous laugh didn't even convince herself. "But I think…I think it would be a good idea if we started for home now."

Isabella stared at her. The guard nodded, took her elbow and gently guided her to a bench by the nearest exit. "Señora, stay here and I'll bring the car around."

After he'd left, Isabella gripped her arm. "Señora, is it really happening now? You'll soon be holding him!"

Sofia was touched by the excited, but partially frightened gleam in the girl's eyes.

Her own voice quavered as she tried to answer with confidence, "Oh, no, not for a few hours yet. Maybe even a day or two. But I have to call the nurse. And my husband—I have to contact him. He needs to come back—," she caught her breath again, then hissed in pain, "—*soon*."

The inexorable reality of what was coming dawned on her, and she felt a surge of sheer terror. How could she face this trial without Owen at her side? Her terror built to a wave of panicked desolation.

Then, along with the pain, this passed. For a few moments, she was filled with serenity and a calm assurance; she knew she'd soon be seeing her son face to face. But she hoped against hope his father would make it home in time to witness his arrival.

CHAPTER
THIRTY-SIX

"OKAY, CAN YOU HEAR ME?"

The tech's voice shimmered down the end of a vast aural tunnel. MacIntyre was too disconnected from his own tongue to answer. His incapacitated state soon faded and he became aware of the supporting seat beneath his reclining body, and the menacing arms of the surgical unit looming above his face.

"Yeah...I hear you."

Disoriented, fighting a wave of vertigo, he struggled to sit upright, to identify and anchor himself within his location. The arms of the surgery robot hissed faintly as they retracted and folded themselves up. There was a small smear of blood on one of the blades.

Owen grew more aware of his surroundings. The long, curving sweep of the far end of the lab was composed of floor-to-ceiling windows, framing a bleak view of snow-sprinkled hills and a few groves of leafless trees. Jaxtyn Morse's classified research facility was located a few miles from his primary residence, and was staffed by a specialized cadre of loyal employees who understood the value of discretion even more deeply than his usual workers did.

As the mild anesthesia continued to dissipate from MacIntyre's system, he was harshly struck by the reality that he had willingly had an invention, created by his former enemy, implanted directly into his own living brain. A strong sense of regret quivered on the edge of his awareness. Had he made a grave error, or merely a stupid mistake? Despite Dr. Huber's enthusiasm and assurances the theories were sound, Owen struggled to conceal his sudden doubt and trepidation. He scarcely noticed when Morse addressed him.

"Hey, tell me—what do you feel?"

Stopping himself from touching the small incision site on his right temple, Owen reported, "Outside—sore. Inside—nothing. But without at least one more person connected, I wouldn't expect to, would I?"

Jaxtyn shook his head as he lowered himself into a wheeled office chair; the heels of his cowboy boots made solid clumping sounds on the floor's tiles as he walked the chair closer to Owen. "Well, that's what the first official test will determine. You have no idea where your target is, and you've never met them in person. Try and connect now."

Despite being put on the spot as everyone in the lab focused on him, Owen tuned out his immediate environment, casting his mind into a formless void. It was easier to do than he'd thought it would be. In this non-place, his attention meandered about, questing for any sense of a separate and distinct mind. He sensed nothing, no matter how much he relaxed.

After several moments, he announced, "Sorry—not picking up anything."

Jaxtyn raised his shoulder. "Well, okay. It seems clear from Chen-Diaz's notes he believed it would work best if there was an initial, in-person contact between sender and receiver. He didn't seem interested in developing this for commercial use, it was just some sort of private project."

Owen made a noncommittal sound. It was not his place to break the trust Tomás had placed in him by revealing the shameful Chen family secrets regarding Francisco's self-cloning experiment, which had led to the development of this psionic device.

He remarked mildly, "I get the impression he had too many irons in the fire to follow up on everything."

"Sure," said Jaxtyn distractedly, looking at his videoskin. "Okay, I just texted for your test partner to join us."

An air of suspense mounted. After a few minutes, the lab's doors swung inward to admit a young woman, perhaps eighteen or so years of age. She was short and plump, her white teeth dazzled in her tawny skin as she asked the room at large, "You didn't start the party without me, did you?"

Jaxtyn grinned. "'Course not, honey. Ellie, meet Mr. Owen MacIntyre."

Turning to MacIntyre, Jaxtyn said, "Owen, this is my daughter, Ellie. She's your partner for this phase of testing."

Ms. Morse's smiling dark eyes exuded high spirits as she snagged a free chair and wheeled it close to the group. She looked at Owen with a happy grin. "Hi, Mr. MacIntyre, nice to meet you! We are the only two members in this top-secret club, isn't that cool?" She pushed aside a wave of hair and indicated a tiny bandage on her upper right temple.

Owen struggled to contain his surprise—and disapproval—that the billionaire was risking his own child in this experiment. "Ah…yeah, it sure looks like it. Nice to meet you, too."

The senior Morse picked up on the awkwardness of the moment. With a hearty laugh, he explained, "Believe it or not, Ellie scored the highest of all the candidates we screened. And I'm proud of her for insisting on being involved. She's a part of history now."

Owen said, "Yes, definitely." Turning from the girl, he addressed her father. "I need a word with you in private."

Morse's brow ruffled with a faint frown. "What's the problem? She's perfect, and eager to help out."

"I don't doubt it. That's not my issue." Owen walked pointedly to the far corner of the lab. He was well aware of the curious, puzzled glances from the tech and Ellie, but was determined to register his misgivings with Jaxtyn. The imposing billionaire joined him and stood squarely before him, with a good-humored but expectant expression.

Owen said in an undertone, "Your own daughter? After what we know of the historical risks of similar devices?"

Morse lifted a large hand. "Hey, I trust Huber's analysis of the risk. I confide in Ellie about lots of my projects, and she was really excited about this one."

Folding his arms across his chest, Owen turned his attention back to Ellie. She was just a kid, how could she possibly realize what she was getting into? However, he was far more disconcerted at the thought of Sofia's attitude should she learn he now had a direct mental connection with a vivacious teen girl. He'd fully intended to tell her about the device after a few tests, but now he'd have to think long and hard about how much information he was willing to share.

Morse's low voice broke in on his conflicted musings. "Hey, Owen, if you aren't ready for this, I understand—we can move on to the next candidate on the list. It's just that, you've already had the procedure." His persistent grin broadened, then grew hardened, mask-like. "And we've well...we've already invested a hell of a lot of time and quite a bit of money."

"I understand that."

The smile in Morse's eyes continued to fade. "If you really can't handle it, that's okay. There's other men who can, plus one teen girl."

For a moment, Owen was tempted to tell him where to stick his time and money. Then he calmed himself, seeing perhaps Morse's points were valid, that he was overthinking this and making a big deal over nothing.

Uncrossing his arms, he returned to the tech. "Okay, let's get on with it."

Ellie exclaimed, "This is so historic!"

Nico Avery, the short, stout lab tech, regarded both candidates over his work tablet with a businesslike glint in his dark eyes. "Ms. Morse, regardless of how historic this moment is, any partying will have to take place after we get some quality data."

"Sure thing," said Ellie, jiggling in place with excitement.

Avery continued, "Now, I presume the both of you have already been doing the preliminary relaxation and concentration exercises you were assigned during the virtual meetings?"

When Owen and Ellie both nodded, the tech continued. "Okay, today you're going to start by spending a few minutes talking with each other."

Ellie asked, "What about? The project?"

"No, anything else you like. The original data isn't clear on whether an initial personal connection is required for these devices to work. We'll run some experiments later with other subjects who haven't met in person, but not today."

Ms. Morse swiveled her chair back towards Owen. "I'll go first. What's your favorite meal?"

"Steak and beer."

"What's your favorite color?"

"I don't have one."

She shook her waves of nearly-black hair. "Not true, it's probably red, like most men's. Now ask me something."

MacIntyre's mind raced quickly through a list of neutral subjects. "Hmm... do you have a pet?"

"Yes, but I won't tell you what kind."

"Fair enough. Are you in college?"

"No, I'm in a customized mentor program with Prof. Alvarez from the Aeon institute."

Avery cleared his throat. "Okay, excellent. That's probably enough to establish a basic connection. Now, next step: Ellie, put this on." He extended a thin white circlet, which she settled over her thick, glossy hair. He said, "We'll be monitoring key parts of your brain with that. Now we need you to leave here again for a few minutes—return to the room you were waiting in. I'll text you more instructions when you get there."

"Great." She slipped out of the chair and left the chamber.

Avery pushed his own chair up to the work deck beside MacIntyre while handing him a large work tablet and a stylus. "You'll need these. Did you study the materials we sent you about the remote-viewing trials pioneered by the old Soviet regimes, and the defunct American agency, the CIA?"

"Yes, of course."

With excitement, Jaxtyn interjected, "The exercises are quite simple. Just relax, clear your mind and start sketching any images that come to you."

Avery did an admirable job restraining his irritation at Morse's interruption. He said in a firm, even manner, "Yes, but first, I need you to activate the app in your visor that monitors your brain activity, and stream the readings to my tablet. It's pretty convenient you have that unit."

"Great—makes it worth all the trouble I went through to get it," quipped Owen tightly.

Behind his hand, Jaxtyn's guffaw morphed to a cough. When the connection was established between the VIA unit and the work tablet, the screen soon displayed a readout of Owen's brainwaves.

The tech asked, "Does your device have settings for inducing relaxation frequencies?"

"You mean, like Theta waves? Yes, it does."

"Good—activate those and you'll get into a receptive state even faster."

As he followed each step outlined to him by the young man, Owen found himself slipping into a comfortable, dim haze, unaware of his immediate surroundings. Vague impressions drifted out of the darkness filling his head, soon growing sharper.

"Don't forget to draw what you see," urged Morse.

Owen moved the stylus rapidly over the tablet's screen. He recorded a series of circles, squares and triangles, but the images soon became more complex.

"This is a horse, a white Arabian," he laughed, swirling his stylus over a loaf-shaped blob with four sticks implanted in it. The scenes came faster and faster, he could only make a few scrawls as he reported, "This is Mt.Fuji. Eiffel Tower, Mt. Rushmore—,"

"Okay, you can stop drawing," Avery said. "But keep telling us what you're seeing. We'll record that and compare it with what she has on the tablet at her end."

The random images ceased, and for several moments, Owen again worked to tune out the intrusive awareness of the lab, the intense expressions on the faces of Morse and the tech as they observed him.

He refocused on the darkness, and began to get gradual impressions of an entirely different room.

"Gray walls," he related tersely. "A sofa with orange cushions. Bookshelf full of texts, one titled, 'Collected Dissertations on Cybernetics.' And—," he halted, overcome by a strong tingly feeling, composed of restlessness, anticipation and apprehension.

Not only was he observing the room, he might as well have been *in* it, could smell the residue of industrial cleaning solution on the floor, heard the faint rattle of the ventilation system in the overhead vent.

His head swarmed with unfamiliar thoughts; random snatches of detritus concerning whether or not it was worthwhile to purchase a new coat this late in the season, or how badly an extended academic project was going, and whether her mentor had caught on yet. And many impressions of a jumpy little dog with eager eyes and neat, red-brown, folded-over ears.

He announced, "Her dog's a Jack Russell terrier named Freddie."

The tech and Morse stared at each other, grins of sheer delight shooting across their faces. Jaxtyn slapped Owen's shoulder as he said excitedly, "Okay, okay—now you send her some stuff."

Avery called up some slides on his own tablet and Owen studied the random selection of geometric shapes and nature photos. When these were finished, he looked around the lab and focused on the equipment, before thinking of some vivid impressions of the unusual flowers that grew around the hacienda, and a large spider he'd seen there in summer.

He was rewarded with a strong sense of understanding and appreciation, followed by amused disgust. The sensation of concurrently having two sets of very clear thoughts, but only being able to control one, caused a sharp and distressing sensation throughout his whole being.

Had Francisco experienced something like this when he linked his consciousness to Alejandro, his own biocopy? How intently had Chen been watching through Alejandro's eyes, that night the clone and Tomás had visited Owen in his apartment?

Don't go back there, he warned himself. When the connection ended, he was engulfed by a harsh wave of nausea. His head reeled and he was forced to steady himself by clutching the edge of the work deck.

"Whoa, that's a hell of a weird feeling," he said with a weak laugh, as the others regarded him with concern. "Is that something you want to record?"

Avery frowned at the readings being sent from the VIA unit to his tablet. "Heart rate and temp are fine, but looks like there was a spike in a few hormones. Let's see how long that lasts."

It was a minute or so before Owen's stomach settled, and the clammy sweat stopped pouring off him. As he relaxed, he turned to Jaxtyn with an uneasy smile. "Don't mind me. It still counts as a success."

Ellie returned, reporting she had not suffered the same reaction as MacIntyre. While beaming with excitement, she threw him a serious glance when the others weren't looking.

"Wait 'til Huber sees this data," said Morse in an exuberant near-shout. He threw his arms wide in an expansive, triumphant gesture, then grabbed his daughter's hands and swung her around in a half-circle. "This is absolutely amazing! The potential is light-years ahead of anything on the market, or anything rumored to be under development elsewhere."

He released her and strode to the refrigerator, drawing out a case of beer; soon a stampede of Underhill Buffalo labels passed through the room. He winked as he handed one to Owen. "I'll order in some steak later."

Ellie crossed the room and brushed past Owen, whispering, "And your favorite sweets are vanilla ice cream and black licorice...but not together."

Startled, he answered with a reserved grin.

She said, "I'm sorry about what happened, how you got that device. It was such a terrifying experience."

Her intensely compassionate look produced in him a sensation of profound discomfort. Only Sofia had a right to know about those buried memories and emotions. Managing a smile, he said, "Yes, I suppose so," and turned away.

The group then spent another half-hour comparing notes and discussing the results of the tests. Then Owen's phone signaled; he stared at the message in stunned disbelief.

No, this can't be happening, he protested internally. *Not now. I thought we had two more weeks, at least—!*

Climbing to his feet, he announced with subdued excitement, "Something's come up—I need to get back to the airport right away."

Jaxtyn looked concerned. "Are you sure?"

Ms. Morse turned to MacIntyre with a happy laugh. "Your wife's in labor! Congratulations!"

He nodded, fighting a sudden annoyance. "Yes, you're right—thanks." MacIntyre collected his jacket from the hooks by the door. "And congratulations to everyone on the success of the project. I'll get back to you all when I can."

"I'll see you to your car," said Jaxtyn.

The men walked through the corridors to the front entrance.

Morse commented in a sober tone, "I didn't realize she was still reading your mind. I guess developing basic privacy protocols should be put to the top of our agenda."

"Yes, most definitely," MacIntyre laughed shortly. "For example—was I supposed to know her full name isn't Eleanor, but 'L.E', for 'Lovelace Effect'? But her mom called her Little Ehawee?"

The billionaire's easy laugh rattled down the corridor. "Don't worry—that's hardly a horrific family skeleton."

"No, I didn't think so."

MacIntyre didn't reveal the other impressions he'd picked up while Ellie was in the hidden room, including her burden of anxiety over her research project. He was pretty sure she hadn't meant for him to know about that, but he couldn't help being aware of her feelings below her chattering surface thoughts. *She still mourns her mom,* he realized, *but she's finally moving on. But she's worried about her dad.*

The inappropriateness of Ellie being involved in this project deeply troubled him, but now was not the time to bring that up again with Morse. He'd hoped this device would communicate limited surface information, nothing more, but that was clearly wrong. He recalled what Francisco had told him, about the latter's reasons for never developing the device: *"I did not relish the picture of the world's population communicating the collective insipidity of its useless thoughts and experiences even more swiftly than it already does."*

At the time, Owen hadn't thought much about the implications of Francisco's contempt-filled comments, but now it seemed they were worth revisiting.

Owen said, "Yeah, well, this is new territory and it's going to take us all awhile to figure out what we're doing."

"Yep, we're pioneers! Think what we can do for folks who can't use regular thought-directed communications tech—heck, we could speak with babies, maybe animals. Or even—," Abashed, Morse stopped himself.

For several moments, the man sent his gaze to roam nervously about the unadorned hallway. With a sigh, he concluded, "Never mind, just a stupid idea that occurred to me."

With a diffident grin, he resumed walking and pushed open the heavy security doors. They stepped into the winter dusk and headed to the parking area. He concluded, "But still—mankind's future just got a hell of a lot brighter."

"Maybe. I sure hope so."

At MacIntyre's rental car, Jaxtyn extended his hand. "Best of luck to you and your wife."

Owen shook it as he grinned with a self-assurance he didn't feel at the moment. "Thanks. I'm not sure I'm ready for this, but here goes."

"You'll do fine."

In the rearview mirror, MacIntyre saw Morse give him a final wave before his tall, broad-shouldered form returned to the warmth of the well-lit lab.

Communicate with babies and animals, Owen thought with a mounting sense of displeasure. *This is supposed to be a serious, classified communications device, not an Edwardian parlor trick.*

He drove to the highway, then turned north, toward a horizon oppressed by a dull, heavy gray sky. Struggling with doubt, he reassured himself he wasn't responsible for whatever harebrained schemes Morse wanted to pursue on the side.

All I want is for the Restoration to have an advantage over Pacifica, something their security forces will never see coming. But what kind of repercussions might follow from this thing? What kind of world am I helping build for my son?

Abruptly, he laughed aloud at himself, fruitlessly pondering future unproven negatives, when what was important was that the technology worked, that he hadn't wasted Morse's and Huber's time or resources. He was warmed by a glow of triumph at the thought he had helped produce a powerful tool for the actual covert agents working to undermine Pacifica. He had mixed feelings about the fact his part was done, he wouldn't personally be a part of the effort on the ground, but reminded himself he had new obligations to shoulder.

As the evening advanced, a few dry snowflakes drifted past the headlights of his car, thin snakes of wind-driven white slithered across the asphalt. With a thrill of delight at the beauty of the view, he was also grateful the weather was not worse, no actual storm interfered with his flight home.

He focused on the reality unfolding before him; in a few more hours, he'd be welcoming his son into a world that, for all its flaws and hazards, still had a lot going for it.

CHAPTER
THIRTY-SEVEN

THE NURSE MIDWIFE was a formidable tank of a woman, with short, gray-peppered hair and a brusque, experienced manner that bordered on arrogance. She blocked the doorway, her eyes narrowing as she doubled-down on her refusal to grant Owen entry to his own bedroom.

"You're kidding, right?" he demanded, instantly becoming more anxious. "What do you mean, I can't go in? Is something wrong?"

"Señor, everything is going well, nothing to worry about. Only, I would prefer if you waited elsewhere." Face brightening, she suggested, "Perhaps it would be more comfortable for everyone if you go into town, relax at a tavern and brag about your accomplishment with your *amigos*."

After a ten-plus hour flight, Owen was in no mood for her dismissive tone. Biting back his irritation, he answered with a thin veneer of calm, "Thanks, but that's not necessary. Perhaps it would be best if *you*—,"

Sofia's voice called out from behind the nurse, sounding weary but alert. "Señora Rosa, is something wrong? Is my husband out there? Let him in!"

The woman glanced over her shoulder, then back at Owen. Defeated, she offered a tight but chastened smile as she stepped aside to let him pass.

"I came as quick as I could," he murmured, drawing a chair near to the bed. Pushing back some tendrils of Sofia's loose hair, he planted a quick kiss on her flushed cheek. She answered with a look of relieved gratitude.

He said, "What'd I miss?"

"Nothing." She gave a short laugh that ended in a tired sigh. "It's taking longer than we thought."

Resting a hand on her belly, he joked, "Maybe he's got second thoughts about meeting us." He surveyed the room and saw how the familiar refuge had been invaded, not only by Señora Rosa, but also her collection of medical equipment and supplies. He lowered his voice. "What do you need me to do? Do you want me here or not?"

While he was pretty sure none of his skills were of use in the proceedings, the idea of being anywhere else was stressful. But he'd abide by her wishes.

She squeezed his hand. "Please, just be here—*oh*—!" Her fingers tightened on his hand, painfully digging into his flesh, as a nearby monitor registered a contraction.

"You got it. Squeeze, pinch, yell—whatever you need."

Breathless, she nodded.

Yet as the hours crept along, he wasn't sure Sofia had even needed him there. She became preoccupied, to the point where it seemed she was no longer aware of him, or of anything outside her own body; she was not frightened, but the disconcerting, remote expression in her eyes told him she had entered a dimension where he could not follow.

As the process continued, time quickened and shifted into a different gear, his own perceptions grew disjointed and unreliable. Sofia became disheveled, more sections of her sweaty hair pulled free from her pony tail and obscured her strained face. He wanted to brush it back and secure it for her, but she shook him off, almost without noticing him. Helpless before her increasing pain, all he could ultimately do was offer an arm for her to clutch. His encouraging voice, seconding the midwife's orders for her to *push*, masked his own bewildered anxiety.

Eventually, it was over. The small form, slick with patches of creamy vernix, was immediately placed on his mother's breast, her wild hair cascaded over him as she wept with joy.

The following day or two were a blur. Once the midwife departed, a sense of privacy slowly returned. As MacIntyre's mild shock over the event continued to fade, his natural mode of responsible protector began to reassert itself. Now, as Sofia slept beside him, he relished the rapturous, silent moments as the warm bundle of his tiny son rested on his chest.

Although Teresa Ortega was somewhere on site, at the moment, the house seemed almost deserted. For a few hours, at least, the outer world and its demands no longer existed. Owen's time and attention was entirely at the service of the two other people in the room.

He was grateful Sofia had not noticed—or at least, had not mentioned—the small healing cut on his scalp, near his hairline. At the moment, the idea of the intravox was far from his concerns, and he was glad Ellie Morse was honoring the privacy protocols sketched out for use of the device. She had responded to his updates, but otherwise hadn't intruded on his privacy. Those brief exchanges had been more in the nature of traditional texts, and thankfully, hadn't contained the depth of shared perceptions he'd experienced in the lab.

The display inside his visor told him it was sunset, but he might as well have existed in a place outside the normal flow of time. Sofia continued to sleep lightly. The bedroom curtains moved in the breeze, revealing a sliver of turquoise sky, streaked with violet. There was subtle alteration in the light, and he realized it was because the world itself was a little bit different than it had been before Dylan's birth.

As the baby slept, Owen studied him, marveling at every little detail, from the gentle pulses of the soft spot on the top of his skull, to the minute hairs on the backs of his wrinkled, red fingers.

What will you become as you grow? Owen's heart asked. *Are you going to be shy, or be into everything? Loud or quiet? Where will you go? What will you do with your life?*

Feeling the baby's rapid, birdlike heartbeat against his own, Owen was thankful they had opted for the prenatal treatment to correct genetic anomalies. His own parents claimed they had not been able to afford such therapy for him, and it was a great feeling to know Dylan wouldn't have the same shadow of a faulty heart cast over his own life. It was certain he'd face plenty of other trials.

A vivid memory of a past vision came to Owen: the sensation of a stream of sand and gold passing through his hands and down into another's. Months before, he had interpreted this as being related to his responsibilities at Paloma being some day passed onto his son, but also knew the mysterious, Thorn-induced visions he'd experienced after Francisco's attempt to kill him, were almost impossible to decipher.

He also thought of the dreamlike encounter with Evan a few months before.

Was it a warning about becoming too attached to a specific idea of what life was supposed to be like? Of striving too hard for an unattainable goal, while missing what was right in front of him?

With a gentle rustling sound, Sofia awoke and sat up, her bleary smile surfeited with sleep and contentment. Eyes locking on Dylan, she murmured, "Can you believe he's real?"

Admiring the baby's fingers as they curled around his, Owen said, "Nope. But here he is. And everything's different, isn't it? I knew it would be, but I didn't expect to feel it so strongly."

"No, me neither." She nestled closer and rested her head on Owen's shoulder. It seemed like all the birthdays and Christmas mornings she'd ever lived were reflected in her expression of disbelieving possession.

He asked, "Are you hungry? Do you want me to call Teresa?"

"I suppose so. Maybe in a few minutes."

At the sound of their voices, the baby stirred. Soon he was awake and rooting against Owen's shirt.

"Well, you can't help him there—." With a glowing, smug expression, Sofia took Dylan in her arms.

Owen adjusted some pillows around them both, then moved to help as she fumbled her shirt open, offering, "Let me—,"

For a split-second, he hesitated. Would his touch there now be unwelcome or somehow inappropriate? Her thankful, intimate smile told him otherwise and he pulled the fabric aside, clumsily helping settle the baby's mouth over her nipple. The sight of her breasts, enlarged with milk, triggered complex feelings; it didn't seem possible he could have more admiration for her breasts, but now their fullness and utility, their shape became even more beautiful.

He also fought a twinge of regret that he was somehow dethroned from a privileged place. Just as the breathtaking sight of Dylan's head emerging from between her legs had stunned him and provoked emotions that would likely take days or longer to resolve, he now had a deeper appreciation for her body that resonated in ways he had not anticipated, something that approached wisdom.

Sofia said softly, "You should go get some fresh air or something to eat. Go on."

"Yeah, sure."

After enjoying a soft, lingering kiss, he left and went downstairs and walked about the patio, reveling in his feelings of accomplishment, of excitement for the future. Overwhelmed with happiness and not at all tired or hungry, he stripped off his pants and shirt and plunged into the pool.

The sheer joy of being in the water, of feeling weightless beneath the stars, was all the nourishment he needed at the moment.

CHAPTER
THIRTY-EIGHT

RICHARD MACINTYRE WANDERED HIS MINUSCULE, tightly constrained trek from the kitchen, through the dining area, to the front room of his condo.

Here he paused in his routine to stand at the window and mindlessly regard the lights twinkling in the neighborhoods several miles distant. Those lights taunted him with the knowledge that electricity now flowed more reliably to certain parts of the city, but not to him. His own living quarters were dark and cold; he knew there was power somewhere in his building, but it was allowed to reach him.

With a sigh, he returned to the kitchen and contemplated whether or not he should eat a can of cold soup. He wasn't hungry, and knew he needed to ration what food he had left. It was a shock when he had gone out, nearly two months ago, and found that he couldn't enter a grocery store or restaurant. This was not a matter of his CitizenTrust score being downranked—because so much of the region was still without internet, few businesses could check his ID pod and find his rank. Rather, he could tell by the shifty, anxious expressions shown by anyone he interacted with, that they had been personally ordered to refuse him service.

But he did not know what he would have paid them in, considering that he couldn't access his accounts. He couldn't pay his bills. With his phone service and internet inoperable, he couldn't contact the bank. He had tried accessing the internet through the public kiosk a few blocks away, but that was useless. It had formerly been connected to the official United States network, but was now shut down by the Pacifica authorities.

Restlessly roaming the neighborhood was one of the few activities left to him. Sometimes he stopped to stare at an office building or a public park that he had helped design, but was so emotionally removed, they brought him no pleasure. His career, his former life, was ancient history. He made all his excursions on foot, as no public transport system or private taxi service would take him.

As he wandered, he had a vague, nagging sensation he was being watched and followed. This was different than the awareness of the ubiquitous survcams on all buildings and streetlights, and the bloated drones that careened low over most streets, issuing bland, encouraging slogans. But he tuned all this out and went about his aimless quests. On the margins of the city, he found some impromptu pop-up markets where he was able to barter, with a few items he'd scrounged from his condo, for a handful of fresh vegetables.

The last of that food was long gone, so he had nothing to accompany his can of soup that March evening. He downed the concoction in a dull, dispirited manner. He was dazed and detached from the whole situation. It seemed his mind could not come up with a viable solution, just the same half-hearted and clearly unworkable plans. It was beginning to dawn on him that he had been formed for a very predictable and secure existence, and was incapable of navigating this new life in Pacifica.

He realized he couldn't blame his father for this—Evan had tried to instill a bit more resourcefulness in him, but he had rejected his advice, preferring to embrace as easy and as conformist a life as possible.

Deep down, he knew a way out of this, but was afraid to confront it. Much of his discomfort would disappear in a flash once he gave the unpleasant 'Man with the Dog' what he wanted: information leading to Owen's whereabouts. Several times over the last months, Richard was tempted to fabricate some plausible nugget of information about his son, but talked himself out of it when he realized The Man—whom Richard had recently been shocked to learn was in fact one of the officials overseeing security for all of Pacifica—did not seem like he'd be so easily fooled.

So Richard spent most of his days pacing back and forth, sometimes distracting himself by sketching, returning to the old-fashioned tools of pencil or pen on paper, since his computer had died long ago. He was hoarding the last few bars of power on his videoskin, only checking it once a day for messages, although he knew he wasn't likely to receive any.

As he finished the soup straight from the can, he was startled by a loud knock at the front door. His heart jumped; had the two officers returned to escort him back to a private conference with The Man? Would he in fact be able to save himself by offering some of the fake intel he'd dreamed up?

When he edged the door open, he was surprised to behold a lean, wiry, older woman, with a freckled face and pouches under her close-set eyes. She was dressed in the leather traveling uniform of a hovercycle operator and had the impatient air of someone who made deliveries for a living.

Since he hadn't ordered anything for months, he wondered if she had the wrong address.

"Hey—you Richard MacIntyre?"

"Yes, how may I help you?"

"This is for you." She jerked a small plastic packet from her vest and waved it before him.

Brow contracting in puzzlement, he reached for it, then paused. "Do I owe you anything?"

"It's prepaid. But I wouldn't say no to a token of appreciation for all the trouble it took me to pick this up at the border." She lowered her voice conspiratorially. "The authorities makin' it even harder than usual to move deliveries around the region."

"I'm sorry to hear that. But I don't have anything to spare today." He grasped the envelope and avoided meeting her disappointed expression.

She said, "Well, do I wait for a response or not?"

"No—it's pointless, I can't pay you."

"And you're very much welcome," she snapped as she turned and stomped down the corridor in her battered leather boots.

Richard withdrew into the condo and stared at the envelope, heart quickening. He pulled out a sheet of paper covered in his ex-wife's handwriting and read Jocelyn's message. He supposed it was good news, even if delivered with a healthy dose of complaints. But the contents stirred nothing in him, his emotions were too numbed by his own immediate concerns.

Dimly wondering if he should bother to respond, he then realized the courier was long gone. He returned to the living room and gently placed the paper on his drafting table in the corner. Was there anything in that message worth passing on to The Man? While it didn't reveal Owen's location, it was still technically a significant piece of information. But was it significant enough to satisfy the authorities, while being too vague to follow up on?

Despite the recent supper, his stomach rumbled. It sounded unpleasantly loud and forlorn in the cold, dark room, the walls of which were covered with sketches for architectural projects that no one would ever want or be able to him pay for.

I'm not going to live like this any longer, he thought with a shudder of sullen resentment. Sliding out a desk drawer, he located the private protocols for establishing contact with The Man with the Dog.

The corner office was more cluttered than Richard remembered. It was obvious that Hayden Singer, Chief Security Enforcer, rarely visited it, and thus it was now being used for storage. Lt. Easton Foster, with a cheerless, triumphant twitch about his grim mouth, had collected MacIntyre about forty minutes earlier and brought him here. The chamber was unoccupied; Foster crossed it and activated the desk computer. He motioned Richard closer and tilted the screen, which now displayed a live feed of Singer's face.

"Good evening, Mr. MacIntyre," said the chief. "Please, take a seat."

Richard pulled a chair closer to the desk and sank into it. His entire body trembled slightly.

Singer said, "It's been quite awhile since we last spoke. You look well."

"Thank you."

"I'm eager to hear any updates you have."

Richard nodded and cleared his throat. He struggled to keep his voice even and confident. "Yes, sir. I wanted to share with you that I just received a communication from my former wife."

"Communication?"

"A letter, delivered by courier."

"I assume it has valuable information?"

"Well, sir, I don't know. It's just that she wanted to let me know that my son's wife had a baby in February, a boy."

The chief frowned. "Congratulations. But why did you feel this was relevant information?"

Shrugging, MacIntyre sat up straighter and assumed something of the demeanor of a salesman. "Well, not so much in itself. But perhaps this might change their plans—she might want to visit her family. Or they might visit her. So they might be easier to…trace."

As he spoke, his voice faltered uncontrollably. "I don't know…I don't know…but I figured you might be able to do…something with the news."

"Perhaps." Singer's manner grew guarded. "Thanks for letting me know. Of course, this isn't new information, as we intercepted and read that letter earlier today."

Richard's jaw fell. "What—?"

"Yes. But I'm impressed with your loyalty in reporting this as soon as you were informed. When you return home, you'll find the power restored and several hour's worth of internet use added to your FreeVox account. To say nothing of a token of appreciation deposited in your bank."

Rather than the feelings of relief and normalcy he had craved for months, a wave of nausea writhed in MacIntyre's gut. He said dully, "Thank you, sir. That's very kind of you."

The call ended. Richard sat numbed, feeling his core shrivel into a tiny, dried speck of shamed nothingness.

Foster prodded him in the upper shoulder. "Hey, Grandpa—time for me to take you back home."

CHAPTER
THIRTY-NINE

A STRONG BREEZE came off the mouth of the Columbia, pushing through a bank of trees and down the street, sending March's chill breath over the muddy construction site. The charred remains of St. Columban's were long gone, a new foundation dug. Rebar set in the forms awaited the sloppy, wet embrace of the concrete about to be pumped from a nearby truck.

Heedless of the mess, Hayden Singer was touring the site, accompanied by Eric Marino and the construction foreman.

Hayden had lectured Marino about remaining alert and silent during such outings. Thus far, the man was shaping up to be a reliable asset whose loyalty was to Singer foremost, ISA secondly.

The construction project technically fell under the jurisdiction of the Department of Communications, but since Singer lived nearby, he enjoyed stopping by to observe the progress.

This afternoon, the foreman was eager to point out various attributes of the new building. Extending his work tablet, he showed off the designs for the emerging Power Cult Gathering Place.

"It's an amphitheater design, but almost entirely round. You can see how, with seating arranged in semi-circles, the participants have no choice but to look across the chamber at each other during the ceremonies."

Singer asked, "What's the point of that?"

"It makes them uncomfortable. Then when the ritual starts, they'll be more interested in focusing their attention where we want it to be."

"Ah, I see."

As Singer's own attention shifted from the tablet and roamed the worksite, he noticed one or two people toiling away on the margins. They looked too weak and unskilled to be part of the regular crew; in a flash, he recognized them as some of the St. Columban's parishioners he'd questioned at Headquarters.

A thin, remote smile played over his mouth as he watched the dispirited workers struggling to erect an edifice noxious to their beliefs, on the very foundations of their former temple. He was certain the symbolism of the situation would leave a lasting impression on the community at large.

He turned to the foreman. "Well, this all looks impressive. I won't take up more of your valuable time."

"Not at all, sir. A pleasure to speak with you."

Singer ambled away, back to his personal vehicle. Marino followed, but Singer stopped him, saying, "You can return to HQ. I'm going to run a private errand now."

Looking disappointed, Marino nonetheless nodded. "Yes, sir."

One hand on the open door of his sedan, Singer pointed back to the construction zone. "Looks good, doesn't it?"

"Yes, it sure does, sir," said Marino, a sly grin oozing over his heavy face. "If there's anything else you need done like that, let me know."

Singer regarded him sternly. "I'm hoping that won't be necessary. You can focus on your official training in the Squad for now."

He took his seat, engaged the motor and drove away.

The sign, warning the restrooms at the former state park were 'closed', had hung there for many years. The paint was faded to near illegibility, the building's roof was partially sunken and overgrown with weeds, the sides of the structure weathered and stained with moss.

The parking lot was criss-crossed with cracks that belched forth more straggling weeds. In the privacy of the abandoned property, Singer sat in his parked vehicle, eyes riveted to the confidential files on his videoskin.

Some photos were very familiar to him, especially those from old Agency personnel records. Others were from medical records, official ID pods, and survcam images. He studied the two faces, male and female, from all available angles. With a few effortless passes of his fingers, an AI program composited the images into something new, and he was delighted at the results. The subject's projected bone structure, eye shape, expression, intelligence ratings, were all exactly as he had hoped.

For months, he had devoted his scarce spare time to setting each stone in the foundation of this monumental endeavor, constructing an elaborate edifice which he had no assurance would ever be used. Still, he had waited and hoped, watchful for the right moment to put the scheme into action. He savored each incremental advance, enjoying a depth of delight that was entirely private, and would always remain so.

The fact that President Gray had expressly forbidden him from further involvement with MacIntyre led an extra edge of piquancy to his scheming. When the letter to Richard MacIntyre was intercepted, Hayden was that much closer to success, to handing his adversary a blow from which he would never recover.

Looking up from his device, Singer absently viewed the empty highway snaking beyond the edge of the lot, shadowed by tall trees. Lowering the car window, he was only dimly aware of the slight breeze on his face. The gentle sounds of the woods did not penetrate far into the cloud of intense rumination that gripped him. He could not spare a thought for the subtlety of color or the fresh, pungent scent of leaves and evergreen needles.

He was skilled at tuning out most of the sights and sounds of the forest, because the memories they brought were not relaxing. For him, the dark that lurked far beyond the trunks of the towering firs held more menace than the average hiker might imagine. The solitude was only useful for helping him think of the future, not for remembering the past or enjoying the present.

Soon he heard a low, electric droning from down the road. A battered hovercycle, painted a dull black, came around the bend and entered the parking lot. The operator guided it to the ground and disembarked. The short, wiry newcomer slid her helmet's visor up as she neared Singer's vehicle.

The woman's lean, freckled face had a hard, cynical look that reminded him of a coyote. As she stood near the open window and surveyed him with unspoken expectation, he reached with slow movements into his jacket's breast pocket. A small envelope of rip-proof plastic rested between his fingers. Inside was a thumb drive, rattling as he shook the envelope.

He said, "Thanks for being punctual. It's imperative this be delivered to the Texas Department of Child Protective Services in San Antonio. If possible, by the end of the week."

She nodded. "You got an updated travel permit for me?"

"Of course."

Singer drew an iridescent disc from another pocket and handed it over, along with the envelope. His face assumed a look of compassionate concern. "It's important those records get there soon. A child's life is at stake."

"Sure, mister, no problem."

Stowing the envelope and the disc in the recesses of her battered leather uniform, she quickly distanced herself from him and returned to her cycle. Its low hum faded and he was again alone.

It looks like this is going to pay off, after all, Singer thought. A shiver of pleasurable elation flitted over his body as he started his vehicle's motor, guiding it away from the rest stop, in the opposite direction from the cycle.

CHAPTER
FORTY

TOSSING THE BLANKET FROM HIMSELF, Owen jumped to his feet and raced out the bedroom door. Dylan was crying; a long sustained wail, blended of anger, possibly pain and disorientation.

Pounding with desperation down the corridor, then down the staircase, Owen found himself out of the house before he even realized how far he had traveled.

The trees towered far higher and with more menace than they should; a path glimmered in the dark at their bases, calling him. He halted; insistent, plaintive cries had drawn him this far, but now the clear calm of the night jolted him to full wakefulness.

He remained on high alert, ears straining for more sounds. Nothing. He checked the hacienda's security system through his visor; all was normal.

A door opened on the far side of the patio and he watched as Diego approached him. The bodyguard was barefoot, wearing boxer shorts, shaking off his sleep as he placed his security AR glasses on and joined Owen.

"Señor, what's wrong?"

MacIntyre made a helpless gesture with one hand. "Sorry, I guess it's nothing. Thought I heard something…must have dreamed it."

Rojas grinned. "Señor, I think you are still sleep-deprived from *el niño's* arrival. You are imagining things. Go back to bed, and I will check everything out here."

Owen ducked his sheepishly. "Yeah, you're probably right. Okay, thanks."

He went back to the house and made his way to the master bedroom. Gently moving aside the tossed blanket, he saw Dylan, sound asleep and safe. Pressed against Sofia, who was blissfully unaware Owen had left. Perhaps the crying had been a dream, after all. Or some type of aural hallucination, perhaps related to the intravox.

Crawling back into bed, he rested his arm over the both of them; Sofia stirred slightly but did not wake. Owen wondered if the illusion of sound was a random snippet of something related to Ellie Morse's current thoughts or state of mind. He was eager to dismiss this theory and reminded himself that over the last two months, a solid protocol had been developed that required he always be the one to initiate contact with Ellie. So far, she'd obeyed that, and they'd had no contact since the last scheduled test.

"Only a dream," he murmured, fighting to ignore the disconcerting, fluttering hiccup in his heartbeat, which had commenced during his few moments of terrified confusion.

Yet it hadn't *seemed* like a dream, but had instead been a perfectly loud, recognizable, and very real sound. An animal cry, perhaps; some of the monkeys in the forest nearby made pretty strange noises, shrill and almost human-like. Yet this had sounded so much like a baby, like Dylan.

Occasionally, in the years since his clinical death and return to life, Owen experienced fragments of visions, glimpses of different planes of existence, but he tended to discount these as something impossible to investigate or rely on. Because these incidents were so unpredictable and beyond his control, it was simpler to ignore them and live his life in parallel with whatever reality they represented. He dreaded, even resented, the times when they randomly appeared and intersected with his daily experience.

Too awake, too agitated to go back to sleep, he yet forced himself to relax. Sofia's hair, spread across her pillow, tickled his face. He felt he needed to remain vigilant and kept his awareness locked on the sleeping figures beside him. It was a peaceful moment, but he could not enjoy it. He couldn't handle the idea of anything bad, however theoretical and unlikely, happening to them. They were not abstract—they were *his* wife, *his* son. The very smell of them was thoroughly bound in his heart. Yet he didn't for one moment regret taking on these responsibilities.

I suppose this is what it means to be a parent, he thought with chagrin. *I'll never have another relaxing moment. I'll always be worried something bad is going to happen to them, somewhere, somehow, and I can't stop it. You'd think I'd be used to that by now—that's pretty much how I live my life all the time, anyway.*

He wondered if this was how Richard had felt about him, and his sister. It was so hard to tell what his father was thinking or feeling; Owen wanted to believe Richard had normal parental feelings, but it was clear the man was held back by some inner inhibition.

Joycelyn, however, he assumed was more conflicted. He wondered if it was in fact time to take Sofia and Dylan back home and spend time with family. Politically, things seemed to be settling down. He had not found any sign that Singer or any Pacifica agents were an active threat outside their own borders, so perhaps it was time to be less fearful.

Owen focused on willing his heart rate to fall to normal. The significance of any little blip or stumble in its beat was one he wasn't ready to face on top of everything else in his life. He had to assume it would return to normal on its own, he could not deal with adding a round of medical inquiries, or even procedures, into the mix of his currently swamped routine.

Activating the Theta waves in the visor helped calm him even further. Soon, he was comfortable and genuinely relaxed. Yet still very alert; jungle sounds outside the window reminded him it was close enough to daybreak that he might as well get up.

Easing out of bed, he dressed and then went downstairs, ready to focus on the day's work.

CHAPTER
FORTY-ONE

AS SHE SKIRTED the shade of the lush trees bordering the patio, Sofia jostled Dylan against her shoulder. He was fussy, and she grew more anxious at his increased noise and dissatisfaction.

Nothing I do works with him, she thought with an inner sob of frustration. *Why won't he stop fussing?*

As the 'honeymoon phase' of motherhood, with its sense of wonder and joy, had faded over the weeks, she was frazzled and sleep-deprived much of the time. She was lost in a landscape of bewildered helplessness, which heightened her sense of isolation. She didn't know what she was doing, and was afraid of making mistakes all the time. She didn't want to ever put him down, wanted to always be holding him or watching him or near him if at all possible.

It had been weeks since she'd had even a remote lesson with the kids at the Nido de Paloma residence. She recalled Señora Gomez' subtle skepticism when Sofia had bragged she would continue her work after the baby arrived.

What was I thinking? She was dismayed and ashamed at her lack of drive and organization. *I was a different person when I thought I could do that. Everything's changed now, this is harder than I thought.*

From the French doors behind her, Isabella came and stood near her shyly. "Señora Lazarus, let me hold him for you. I watch my cousins a lot, I know how to care for babies."

Sofia shot her a weary smile. "Of course, I know you do, dear. It's just I feel like I need to do it myself."

"But Señora, I want to hold him!" Isabella grinned, arms held out.

Sofia relented. "Okay—here, yes, take him! Thank you, I think I'll take a siesta."

"Sí, Señora! And a long bath, with candles around the tub."

"Well, I hadn't thought of that, but maybe I will. Sounds wonderful."

"Señora, take all the time you need. I will show him the flowers and birds."

The novelty of being in someone else's arms did quiet Dylan, who regarded Isabella very seriously for a moment.

While he was distracted, Sofia slipped back into the house and up to the bedroom. She lay down, but her mind would not let her sleep. She continued to toss and turn under the shadow of a list of obligations, hanging over her like an iron sword.

I need to work harder, she told herself. The sentiment came in a stern voice that seemed determined to speak over a low-level panic always at the back of her mind. *This was supposed to be fun…joyful…why do I feel so lost?*

She realized that what she wanted more than anything was to be with her mom, even if only for a few days. She pushed down her melancholy feelings and said a few prayers. She had nearly drifted off to sleep when the bedroom door opened and Owen entered.

"Oh, there you are. Where's the baby?"

She groaned and pushed her hair from her face as she muttered, "With Isabella."

"What's wrong?"

"Nothing. I'm trying to sleep."

"Okay, sorry…I'll leave you alone in a minute. But I need to tell you something."

His unusually happy manner drew her up into a seated position, regarding him with curiosity as he sat beside her.

She asked, "What's up?"

"Well, I wanted to let you know that a few weeks ago, I went ahead and told my mom about Dylan. I even sent some photos. Are you okay with that?"

"Yes, of course. I mean, we already told my folks, it doesn't make any sense to not tell yours, or at least your mom." She paused. "But what if she tells your dad?"

"I'm not sure she would even know how to contact him. And if she did, I don't know how or why he would use that information against us. There's still no way of tracing us here. And for the time being, Pacifica seems to be behaving itself and not exerting obvious influence in the United States."

A thought occurred to her. "Does that mean I can visit my folks? Soon?"

"Well, I don't know about —,"

Her mouth drew into a tight line and her mild gray eyes became hard and resolute. "Yes, I'm going. I'm tired of hiding out."

Taking her hand, she could feel his doubt and hesitation as his fingers closed protectively over hers. "You're right, you should go. I remember how hard it was when you lost your CitizenTrust rank and just stayed home all the time. I don't want you to go back to that…that dark place."

She squeezed his hand in return. "Thanks for understanding."

He grinned. "So, I guess there's no reason you can't take him for a quick visit. With false IDs, of course, and with Diego. Probably best if I stay out of the picture for a bit longer, though."

"I'd love if you could join us, but this is better than nothing." She gave a squeak of delight and tightened her grip on his hand.

"I have another business trip scheduled for next month, to South Dakota. You bring Dylan along, and Diego can accompany you both from there to Texas."

Throwing her arms about his neck, she whispered into his ear, "This is so exciting! I'm so happy things are getting back to normal."

"Yes, looks like it. I think we've both earned that, don't you?" He kissed her brow. "You've been way too stressed lately. Now, trust Isabella to take care of Dylan while you go back to sleep."

When the door closed behind him, she realized she wasn't tired enough to sleep. Collecting some of the real wax candles from the bookcase, she went to the master bath, placed them about the tub, and ran the water.

As she slid into the filling tub, and the warm depths caressed her shoulders, her burden of nebulous worry dissipated from her spirit. Evaluating her body through the water, she had to admit she had recovered her shape nicely after the pregnancy and looked almost as slim and toned as before.

She grinned to herself, embarrassed at her immature behavior. She was truly grateful to be cared for by Owen, Isabella, Teresa and Diego.

When she left the bath and again lay down, she felt wrapped in peaceful security, glowing with happiness at the thought she'd soon see her family again, imagining her parent's faces when they held their only grandchild for the first time.

CHAPTER
FORTY-TWO

LIKE A BULLET, Greta shot down the beach, dismissed by Hayden's subtle but commanding hand cues. The dog bunched and stretched, bunched and stretched, the cycle of her motion echoing the more leisurely rise and fall of the nearby ocean waves.

Much of that unseasonably warm May afternoon had been devoted to relaxing on the beach and refreshing the dog's recall training. It was exceedingly satisfying for Hayden to have such control over another living entity, to issue orders at a distance and know they would be followed. And all was achieved without tech, instead being the primal conflict of a superior intelligence and will, shaping and dominating another.

At the water's edge, gulls scattered into the sky like shreds of paper on the wind when the dog tore through their flock. Hayden whistled again; Greta wheeled about in a big loop, then trotted closer and re-joined both Hayden and Slate as they ambled along in the glorious blaze of the advancing sunset. Only a handful of other couples were scattered about; while this was not a private beach, it was difficult to access, and was known to be connected with a nearby private resort.

At the moment, Hayden felt justified in taking a few days off to unwind, and so had surprised Slate with a weekend at this secluded spot, miles to the south of New Astoria. The exclusive resort nestled on cliffs between two headlands, a few miles south of Tillamook. It was located on the grounds of a former Scout camp; the extensive property had been sold off many years before when that organization slid into disfavor and bankruptcy.

Private cabins nestled among manicured undergrowth at the feet of towering Douglas firs and Sitka spruce. The previous structures on the property had been severely damaged during the Cascadia event, and the cliffside still bore a huge scar and fall of rubble, over which the ensuing decades had draped gentle dunes and flourishes of beach grass.

"This is a nice place," murmured Slate, as he picked up a smooth driftwood twig and flung it for Greta. "I'd heard about the resort, but never thought I'd get a chance to stay here."

"Yes, funny how circumstances change," said Singer complacently.

They walked southwards down the shore. Slate glanced up toward the fringe of forest topping the cliffs to their left.

He asked with feigned carelessness, "Is there any truth to the rumor about mushroom cultists out in these woods?"

Hayden didn't answer.

Evidence of what lurked in the darkest reaches of the wilderness, beyond civilization, pointed to a wide rage of possibilities. Rumors included isolated cranks, sitting atop arsenals and cases of hoarded, rotting stocks of food, to extended clans of off-gridding recalcitrants, to the nightmare menace of alleged cultists.

The standard policy regarding all these potential enemies had been to pretend there was nothing out there, and focus attention and resources on urban areas. For the moment, ISA was continuing this policy, but Hayden knew that couldn't last forever.

However, Slate didn't need to know the truth. "Those filthy, moss-covered whack jobs?" Hayden eventually snorted. "Sure, there's a handful living under logs, way out in the old national forests, but not around here. And certainly not enough of them to be a threat if you stay alert to your surroundings."

His attention turned to Greta, who had wandered several yards away to investigate a seagull carcass. He ordered, "Greta—leave it!"

Slate insisted, "Okay, but I heard there's some around who have some super crazy beliefs and practices. I mean, don't they sacrifice to Bigfoot or something?"

Hayden's laugh was hearty and genuine. "Who knows? Doesn't sound any more crazy than most religions."

Slate didn't smile and Hayden studied the anxious look in the younger man's eyes. Growing serious, he said, "Maybe it's not a bad idea if I assign someone to look into it. But in any case, this particular property is very well protected. So don't worry."

"Hey, I'm not worried, I just wondered."

Nonetheless, it was plain Slate was relieved by Hayden's words; he visibly relaxed, and Hayden was buoyed by the other's trust.

They walked without speaking for another quarter-mile or so, until they reached the impassable headland jutting out into the waves. Then they turned and went back to the rough trail cut in the cliffside of stone, streaked yellow and cream. By now, painful twinges in his lower spine reminded Hayden that he had walked too long on the uneven, treacherous sand.

He uttered a sharp, commanding whistle and, several hundred yards up the beach, Greta turned on a dime and raced back to them. They returned to their private cabin, located in a grove of trees several yards from the main path that wound through the resort grounds.

Struggling to sound calm as a cramp gripped him in a wave of pain, Hayden said, "Wipe her paws off before she gets to the carpet."

Slate grabbed a towel and brushed the sand and pine needles off the dog's paws as Hayden entered the bathroom and grabbed his preferred painkiller.

Standing before the mirror, he waited for the dose to take effect, while fighting to not plunge into the image that stared back. He knew better than to gaze over-long into the eyes in the glass, while clenching against the threat of growing pain, a pain which jerked long-submerged memories closer to the surface with each spasm.

Soon his reflection, his ephemeral persona of a haughty and powerful man in his prime, was shattered. Replaced by a weedy child, a fearful but conniving boy who drifted through his days, hoping to avoid the notice of his elders, even while craving positive interaction.

Unable to face that picture, Hayden's eyes slid to the toothbrush resting in the glass by the sink, but that view couldn't restrain the past. Biting back a yelp of pain as his body remembered, he prayed for the pain meds to kick in soon.

Layton had been his mother's favorite of her simultaneous husbands. Hayden loathed both men, but his hatred and fear of Layton glowed most fiercely, buried in the years like embers of a fire dormant beneath the black ashes of memory.

Years after embarking on his own law enforcement career, Hayden had done some digging in hard-to-reach places. He discovered both Layton and Cade had been active in an anarchist terror cell, had even been arrested for fire-bombing a Federal courthouse, but due to a lenient political climate, had not served time.

To an outside observer, the polyamorous Singer household was unremarkable. Inside, it was slatternly and disorganized.

Bovine-like in her obtuseness, Hayden's mother, Morrigan, seemed to have no inkling about Layton's true motivation for encouraging her to fly across country to attend a week-long convention. If the trip had in fact been part of a larger plan hatched by her husbands, they had put nothing into prepping eight-year-old Hayden beforehand. There had been no bribes, no build up, no gentle seduction. Why should there have been? He had no reason to distrust them; as much as he disliked the men, they were still family. Thus he had been thoroughly shocked when he found himself helplessly plunged into the unstoppable horror of a nightmare.

He recalled the sensation of suffocating as he screamed into a pillow, Cade holding him immobile to ease Layton's access. He remembered the disbelief, the sense of betrayal. He remembered feeling he was going to die, and later wishing he had. Now, he understood that the rushed brutality of the first assault had been a key part of the kink for both men.

But at the time, his child's mind was caught in a maelstrom of confused, helpless panic. After an eternity of hell, they were satiated, and left him to recover a bit while they waited for their reserves of lust to refill. Imprisoned in his room, he wallowed alone in pain, blood and filth—none of which could compare with his sense of terrified betrayal and shame. Mercifully, once Morrigan returned, he was safe for awhile. That was the first and only time he could recall ever being glad to see her.

Yet Layton still found more reasons to be secluded with Hayden, whether at home or in remote spots in a state parks. Morrigan never objected or asked the sort of questions which would have led to her son's rescue. Instead, she sank further into an inert self-absorption, even as her academic reputation grew more august, and she acquired more accolades and requests for interviews. In the interviews, she became another person; not exactly lively, but brighter, more engaged, almost articulate.

Her brightness disappeared when the recording devices were gone. At home, she lived at her computer, presumably researching. Writing articles or papers or editing videos. Hayden's most persistent memory of her was of an unresponsive lump hunched before a screen, eyes obscured by the blank, impenetrable reflections cast onto the lenses of her glasses. She was stolidly unconcerned about his injuries, as was his pediatrician.

He learned later that injuries of that nature, in children his age, across all social castes, were not unheard-of. They were also typically handled with a discretion that bordered on blindness. No uncomfortable questions were ever raised or addressed, either beneath the pitiless florescent lights of the exam room, or in the shadowy chaos of home.

There were extended periods, often for many months, when Layton and Cade left him alone. Periodically, he'd be reminded to keep his mouth shut when meeting anyone outside the family, and a few hours spent shut in a dusty, unlit closet would drive that message deep into his psyche.

Hayden lived in a state of numbed cognitive dissonance, steeped in dread while going through the motions of a mostly normal, shared daily life. Reaching past Cade for a box of cereal in the morning, or traveling to and from his own grade school with Layton, he was forced to wall off great portions of his mind. He learned to answer Layton's innocent small-talk in a way that was equally unremarkable, but beneath the interactions of all three Singer males lurked the vast, unspoken reality of what had happened, what was likely to happen again.

It was like living in two different dimensions at once. The emotional strain was incredible, but somehow, Hayden survived. Instinct told him his personal experiences were out of the ordinary, but he had only a hazy idea of how far below others' standards they fell.

Trivial things, such as the banality of seeing his tormentors' toothbrushes resting crookedly in the holder each morning, made Hayden ill. At the time, he could not articulate why the sight filled him with a speechless dread, but he later guessed it was a subconscious realization of the mundane fact that such monsters were bound by the same rules as everyone else. Layton and Cade were subject to the normal, human routine of tooth cleaning, eating, sleeping. They could be anyone; anyone could be them.

Once, despite the threat of the closet, he conceived a plan to reach out to his teachers for aid, but soon realized Layton's connections in the system made those efforts fruitless. They even heightened his own danger, should the man suspect his victim was reporting him.

On their drives to school, Hayden often looked up at the unattainable homes high on the hills, imagining what sort of safe, beautiful lives were lived behind those aloof and genteel walls. He fantasized that someday, he'd meet with a family up there who'd somehow learn of his plight and would rescue him, take him away to live in a shining mansion. Perhaps they would look into his eyes and read his thoughts, see the whole story, without him risking Layton's wrath by saying a word.

As he matured, his growing resemblance to Layton was impossible to miss and it sickened him. Gaining more height and muscle, he grew less boyish, less desirable, and Layton and Cade violated him less frequently. Eventually, the family achieved, in private, a numbed state of equilibrium. Outside the home, Hayden drew close to one or two boys at high school and in a crude, bumbling manner, caught glimpses of what true kindness and intimacy could be like.

Yet ever at the back of his mind, deep within his entire person, writhed a seething resentment. This resentment grew bloated and twisted, seeking expression, becoming at last a concrete strategy. After a year or so of careful scrounging and conniving, Hayden worked out his plan and constructed his alibi. Through some of the less-savory connections in his neighborhood, he acquired the prize of an illegal, older-model, semi-automatic pistol and half a box of ammo.

Deep within an overgrown, rarely-visited state forest in Northern California, he had gone hiking with Layton. He could still vividly recall the exact pattern of stripes of sun and shadow cutting through the moss and lichen-speckled undergrowth, painting the bases of the immense, ancient sequoias towering above them on the trail. He could not forget the way in which the older man, after one lingering, desperate look at Hayden, had then slid his empty glance away, into the forest. That simple action had all the significance of a formal surrender.

Layton had then turned away completely and gone ahead of his son up the trail. Both hikers grew increasingly quiet during the trek from the parking lot to the trailhead, Layton stumbled over roots and stirred dust as his pace grew more broken, as they both traveled inexorably to a secluded spot deep within the heart of the brooding woods.

At the first sharp, ringing gunshot, startled ravens had exploded, cawing, into the evening air from the overhead branches. Layton had flinched convulsively, but only the slightest of inarticulate cries escaped him.

Whenever Hayden relived the scene, he again experienced the satisfaction he'd felt while kicking the dying man over onto his back, in order to stare with savage determination into his face as round after round was pumped into his chest. When the gun was empty, Hayden shoved it into his waistband and caught up a chunk of stone.

He could still feel the reassuring weight of the rock in his young but strong hand. Could savor again each blow, long after all motion ceased, the shattering of the skull as it splintered into the brain. He had put all his strength, mental and physical, into the obliteration of his tormenter.

Even now, the glimpse of pink-gray brain matter and white skull, all gleaming through a sheen of hair and blood, sometimes leered at him from the recesses of his dreams. Like a crooked, apologetic grin. Perhaps not putting up a fight had been Layton's way of apologizing; perhaps he was grateful that he'd no longer have to bear the burden of his own memories, his own crushing guilt.

Hayden later wondered what he would have done if any other hikers had happened along, but since they didn't, he was able to drag the body deep into the lush undergrowth. Then he hiked back to the road. Distance meant nothing, he had traveled as with wings.

When he returned home, the rest of the household wordlessly acknowledged his changed manner, his attitude of relief and triumph. They avoided him.

Following Layton's disappearance, Cade soon drifted out of their lives. His departure was helpful for drawing suspicion away from Hayden, but the reality was, the investigation into Layton's fate was tepid and short-lived. Morrigan never once asked Hayden point-blank if he knew what had happened. After several months, it was if her husbands had never existed.

Over the following weeks, Morrigan became even more animalistic and reclusive; Hayden moved out as soon as possible and cut off all contact with her. A year or two later, he learned that she had a government Passing kit delivered to her, but hadn't arranged for any kind of follow-up.

Her body was discovered when the neighbors complained of the stench.

When the medication kicked in and soothed the muscle spasms, Hayden's memories released him. He was again strong and in control. The past no longer mattered; what was important was what he did with every opportunity that came his way going forward. After several more minutes, he emerged from the bathroom, feeling much more at ease and ready to take Slate to the resort's restaurant.

"Do you think Greta will get up on the sofa while we're gone?" asked Slate plaintively an hour later, as he bent over his plate of scallops, risotto and steamed vegetables. "What if she gets upset and scratches the door? Will we be charged extra if she damages anything?"

Hayden lifted an indulgent brow. "She's too well behaved. You know she won't utter a peep unless there's a real threat. But if she does make a mess, I'll pay for it. Just put her out of your mind and enjoy the rest of the evening."

"Will do." Slate offered a half-hearted grin and reached for his wine glass, raising it in a salute.

The dining room was nearly full. Dishes clinked and there was a low, steady murmur of voices and light laughter against the backdrop of almost unnoticeable music seeping soothingly through hidden speakers.

The restaurant was constructed of huge beams of local fir; genuine flames crackled in the river-rock fireplace dominating the far end of the dining area. Slate nodded towards this with a tip of his chin. "Wow, it's real, not a hologram."

"Membership has its privileges," said Hayden. "They received clearance for a wood-burning fireplace when this place was rebuilt, and we've had no reason to revoke it. It helps that the managers have been especially… supportive of the new regime."

Slate acknowledged this with a faint grunt.

Hayden added in a knowing whisper, "They also burn wood in the outdoor fire pit, up in the Arena. Do you want to check that out later?"

In answer, Slate gnawed his lip and lowered his gaze, apparently fixing it on a spot on the floor. Hayden decided against pushing the matter at the moment; he'd try later, when Slate was more relaxed and compliant.

As the meal progressed, it was clear the younger man had something on his mind. Hayden asked, "Missing your hovercycle?"

"No." Slate looked up with a slight laugh. "I mean, I love it, but geez—I can go a couple of days without it, you know? But I think I'm going to have to take it to a mechanic soon. I feel a hiccup sometimes when I try to push it past sixty."

"Yeah, get that checked out. And soon—there could be supply issues if you wait too long."

"Okay, sure." Slate's face became shaded with dissatisfaction. Pushing away his unfinished risotto, he said dryly, "Speaking of supply issues, should we have Greta seen by the vet before we take her to the stud again?"

Suppressing a sigh, Hayden's fingers slowly twisted the handle of his fork. "Look, I know it's disappointing that she didn't get pregnant this time, but maybe it's just as well. Maybe we're not ready for that much work in our lives right now."

Slate pouted, "When *would* be a good time? Do you think things will ever *not* be busy? You know what? I think you're making excuses. For this and for —everything."

"Are you bringing up the surrogacy failure again?" Hayden deliberately kept his tone light.

"Yeah, maybe I am. What am I going to have to do—get a womb transplant myself?"

Slate's sarcasm was blatant, but that didn't stop a wave of revulsion from rising in Hayden at the suggestion. Memories of his mother instantly arose, tied to his disgust that he had ever existed within her putrid form. He was horror-struck at the thought of Slate's sculpted abs becoming swollen and grotesquely distended, like roadkill bloating in the sun, looking more full of death than life. Afterward, his body would be flaccid and scarred following the inevitable c-section.

He said quickly, "Don't even think about it. None of that matters, anyway. Here—," Glowing with a self-satisfied smirk, Hayden unrolled his videoskin and passed it to Slate. "Read this."

As Slate pored over the text on the screen, Hayden drew his wine glass toward himself. He swirled it, contemplating the firelight reflecting off the sides of the light gold depths.

With an impatient smile, he asked, "Well? What do you think?"

"Seriously? You found an infant! That's—," Face transformed with delight, Slate dropped the videoskin on the table. He fell back against his seat and unconsciously ran his hands through his long hair. "Damn—this is fantastic news! How soon can we get him?"

"Soon." Hayden sipped his wine then set his glass back down. "Very soon."

"Okay, sure. Man, this is so exciting! A boy—how old?"

"Less than five months."

Slate couldn't stop grinning in stunned delight. "How long were you going to wait before telling me?"

Hayden grew solemn. "I was waiting for the perfect moment this weekend, and well—I guess this is it."

Restless, Slate spent the rest of the meal throwing out disjointed but enthusiastic suggestions for items they needed to buy, changes they'd need to make about their home, plans to decorate the nursery.

"I'll leave all that to you," said Hayden generously, as they left the restaurant.

"Thanks!"

Hayden said softly, "Yes, I'm sorry it's been such a long wait, and you've been very patient. I appreciate that."

Stars gleamed through the network of branches high above. The night was mild and still. Sparkling tendrils of small, cheery accent lights lined all the walkways, snaking through the *salal* bushes and up the columns of trees. The lights led to other cabins, to the exercise rooms, the pool and sauna, and the shops.

The main path through the resort eased uphill, into the dark of the thickly wooded grounds. Outside the clubhouse, Slate hesitated. "I thought we were going back to the cabin?"

Hayden glanced up the smooth black ribbon of asphalt disappearing into the trees. "To be honest, I kind of wanted to go up and check out the Arena." He said it casually, but with an unmistakable hint of steel below the shape of the words.

For a split second, Slate's face fell. Then he hitched his mouth up into a knowing smile. "Okay, sure. Sounds fun."

But his steps lagged as Singer led the way up the path. They heard voices behind them as others began to come up the same trail. Ahead were a few other men, silhouetted against a faint glow that lit the edge of the trail's surface and the trees.

Hayden and Slate emerged into a cathedral-like clearing, ringed by towering columns of trees surrounding a small bonfire. The air trembled with curls of sound, eerie not-quite-music. Notes muttered and whisked past their ears from speakers concealed in the low-growing ferns and shrubs.

A performer occupied the center of a dais on the far side of the small amphitheater. Lit by a stage light of hypnotic, deep magenta, he hunched over a keyboard that controlled an array of cylinders and membranes stretched across a skeletal armature. He was deeply absorbed in the task of producing a series of insistently seductive cadences.

Slate seemed disgusted yet mesmerized by the implied obscenity of the musical apparatus. He was also a little concerned, asking in an urgent whisper, "This isn't…it's not a mushroom cult ceremony, is it?"

Hayden grimaced. "Of course not. It's just the…*Arena*."

More men arrived. In the uncertain firelight, eyes glinted, smiles flashed out of the dark. Low voices and snatches of guttural laughter sounded on all sides.

"Do we have to stay long?" asked Slate in an undertone. Anxious sweat glinted on his brow and cheekbones. His voice elicited a flutter of desire in Hayden that swiftly grew to a clamor.

Hayden said, "Let's just check it out. I promise we'll leave if you get too uncomfortable."

With slow, seductive movements, he took the other's arm and guided him down to the ground. Cushions were spread on all sides of the gently curving bowl of the venue.

Unfastening his waistband, Hayden then pulled from his pocket a small tube, which he wordlessly extended to his companion.

Slate avoided touching it. "I don't know…out here, with others around…,"

"I really feel like celebrating. We've accomplished so much, we're finally getting a son. Don't you feel it, how everything in our life is shifting for the better?"

Hayden's hand massaged Slate's upper arm as he drew him closer and with languid, deliberate movements, eased his shirt over and off his shoulders.

"What are you afraid of? There's nothing shameful, only beauty. We have something special together, no reason to hide it."

With a half-smile, Slate relented and accepted the cylinder. He opened it and applied a little of the contents to his mouth. Mesmerized by the faint sheen this left on the other's lips in the flickering light, Hayden's gaze was locked there as he slipped out of his own shirt.

Uncovered, he felt the scorching sensation from the nearby fire along one side of his body, contrasted with the icy, black breath of night on the other.

Slate stretched himself over the cushions. From behind, Hayden enclosed him in his arms, cupping his chin and stroking the stubble on his jaw. He twisted Slate's head back toward himself and began devouring his mouth with exquisite gentleness.

Despite the chemicals now working through Slate's system, he was still rigid and on edge. Hayden sensed he was too much aware of the other couples just beyond the reach of the firelight.

"Relax," he said in a playful growl.

Slate muttered peevishly, "I'm cold out here...Greta's been alone too long, she'll pee on the carpet...I want to go back to the cabin...,"

"Hey kid, stop making excuses." Chuckling breathily, Hayden rested his chin on the other's shoulder, putting his mouth beside his ear. "Forget anyone else is out here...they're all wrapped up in each other, anyway. It's just you and me."

And baby makes three, he thought with a thrilling stab of exultant triumph. *I'm getting everything I ever wanted. But no matter how powerful I become, I'll always look out for you...*

The flames leaped, the music became more urgent, driven by a bass so deep that it was sensed more than heard. Low, deep sound waves thrummed outward from the stage, vibrated through the air around the listeners and the ground beneath them.

It drove through Hayden's body. Pulsing into his heart, it interwove itself through his blood with each beat.

Unbidden, his resentment against MacIntyre flared in his mind, weaving inextricably with his current awareness. *You're going to pay for everything,* he taunted his absent enemy. *You'll pay for trying to disrupt the Successor's plans, for rejecting me. You'll pay for distracting me from Slate...*

"Not now, not like this—," Distressed, Slate tried to pull away, fighting against Hayden's forceful embrace.

"It's okay, it's okay…just relax." The older man's breath became heavier, hungrier, more frantic.

Within moments, Hayden's last, lingering sense of tenderness slipped into a confused delirium. Slate's whimpers of protest and sharp gasps of discomfort drove Hayden to cling all the tighter. Inside, he was torn asunder; deep in his center, the last untainted fragment of his true self sobbed for restraint, cried out for mercy, for light.

The urgent throatiness of the pipes became lost in the throbbing of the drum's thick membrane.

As the thrusting, hammering ferment engulfed them and built to an agonized crescendo, a different noise burst overhead. Hayden was only dimly aware of a surge of wind, like an outraged, inarticulate roar of both triumph and desolation, tossing through the upper reaches of the trees. Small branches cracked and snapped, a few spun down into the Arena to land near the scattered revelers, who seemed oblivious to the danger.

From far away, the sound of Greta's distraught, terrified barking stabbed through the night.

CHAPTER
FORTY-THREE

WITH SLOW, stealthy movements, Sofia placed Dylan in his playpen to sleep. Then she hovered over him a moment longer, holding her breath as she watched to make certain he was truly settled. When she was convinced he was deeply under, she moved away without making a sound.

He'd probably awaken in fifteen minutes or so, but she was determined to make the most of that time to assist her mother in tidying the kitchen of her parents' rambling, single-level ranch home.

"Does Jocelyn drink? Should I offer her sangrias?" Maggie Volkova asked, joining her daughter to clear up the leftovers from the evening meal.

They were expecting an imminent visit from Jocelyn Griffiths, Owen's mother. Jocelyn's eagerness to see her grandchild had led to a veritable campaign of polite harassment against the Volkov family, and Sofia had recently agreed to formally invite her forceful mother-in-law to the home. She had mixed feelings about the meeting; the fact Maggie and Jocelyn had never met in person only added to the mounting tension.

"Yes, I'm sure she'd love that," said Sofia.

"Well, whether she will or not, I'm making them," said Maggie.

The middle-height, stocky woman with short, no-nonsense, dyed-brown hair and snapping dark eyes added with a grin, "Liturgy today seemed longer than usual and I'm still tired. I just want to kick back and relax the rest of the evening."

"I'm not sure how long she'll stay," said Sofia. "I'm sorry for the trouble. And thanks for agreeing to let her come."

"No trouble, dear. Of course, I understand why she wants to see him. And by graciously opening my home like this, I can establish my reputation as the *good* Grandma."

"Don't worry, you'll always be the good one. I bet even Owen agrees," Sofia snickered as she collected some of the used plates and coffee cups scattered throughout the kitchen.

Maggie continued to expound on her new favorite subject. "I know I'm biased, but Dylan's such a delightful baby. A bit fussier than you or your brother were, but he'll likely outgrow that soon."

"I hope so! I sure miss a good night's sleep."

"Oh, honey—that ship has sailed and isn't coming back! Get used to feeling like a zombie for a bit longer. But he's absolutely precious—so smart and alert! And his hair—so blonde, it's almost white. Neither of you looked like that."

With a playfully sad twist of her mouth, Sofia said, "It won't last. Owen said his was that color at that age, and you know how dark it is now."

"Then I'll sneak a few more photos later, while I can," said her mother. Loading plates and cups into the dishwasher, she added with feigned carelessness, "Unless you think you can talk Owen into settling nearby. Now that he's working with Andrei's company."

Sofia placed some leftovers in the refrigerator. "Oh, he's not working with him—Andrei just got him an introduction to Jaxtyn Morse."

"Morse? Wow, that sounds important. Do you have any idea if it's related to his other work?"

"No, he doesn't share much about that sort of thing," admitted Sofia.

Sensing her tone of regret, Maggie pressed gently, "Do you have any idea how long you'll both be living in…well, in *exile*?"

Sofia's brow clouded. "Don't call it exile. I think there's a real possibility we can move back to the States sooner rather than later."

"But still—you're traveling with personal security."

Sofia gave a self-conscious but dismissive laugh. "He's more like an extra hand to help us out. It has nothing to do with Pacifica."

"Okay, so Diego's a nanny?"

"Well, no—,"

"I'm teasing, he seems like a great guy," Maggie acknowledged, as she ran some water into a dirty pan resting in the sink.

During the five-day visit, Diego had hit it off with Sofia's father, John Volkov. This evening, John didn't feel equal to meeting Jocelyn, and over Maggie's objections, had invited Diego to join him for a walk around this sprawling housing development located in a suburb of Borger, in North Texas.

Maggie shut the water off. Eyes averted from her daughter, she continued to regard the billowing suds in the pan. "Tell me—are you okay living like this?"

"Living like what? Owen just travels for business and takes a few extra precautions, that's all." Sofia focused on tipping leftover tortilla chips into an airtight container as she added, "In the meantime, I'm grateful we have a beautiful place to stay for now. And it really is a safe environment."

"Even with all the snakes and giant spiders running around in Colombia?"

"You know those never scared me."

"Fair enough," said Maggie. Hands on hips as she surveyed the tidy kitchen, her typical easy smile returned. "This is good enough for now. I think we've earned those sangrias—what do you say I get them ready before our guest arrives?"

"I say 'you bet'," laughed Sofia. "I'll take care of the trash while you mix them."

Tugging the overflowing bag from the kitchen wastebasket, she exited the backdoor and went around the side of the house. While waves of the day's intense heat still rolled up from the pavement, overhead, the evening was glorious with smears of salmon-colored clouds against a deep green-blue sky. A blessed breeze rustled through the leaves of the few trees in the yards nearby. She drank in the scene, listening to the homey sounds of children playing in their yards, dogs barking, a few vehicles passing down the old, pitted asphalt road.

It had been a remarkably rejuvenating trip thus far. Although her parents had moved here recently, simply being in their company again felt like returning to a childhood home. She felt as safe as when she was little, but was also full of optimism. All the threats plaguing her and Owen over the last two years seemed to fade to nothing in the warm, cheerful atmosphere of this unassuming subdivision with its cozy houses clad in shades of sun-bleached pastels.

She was thankful for this gift of a moment of beauty and peace. It was very different from the beauty of the Liturgy she had attended earlier that day, different from the peace she felt among friends and family. The ceremony in the church reminded her that when she returned home, she'd make an effort to attend more regularly. And it was time to have Dylan baptized.

Reentering the kitchen, she heard a murmur of feminine voices drifting from the front room. Jocelyn had arrived early and Maggie had ushered her into the home. Dredging up courage, Sofia put on a welcoming smile and stepped forward to greet her mother-in-law.

The slim, older woman had her dyed blonde hair pulled back in a severe pony tail, and wore a neat, tailored outfit redolent of upper-middlecaste comfort and security. But her wary posture emitted an air of unease.

"Joycelyn—it's so wonderful to see you again," Sofia said brightly, offering the woman a perfunctory embrace. As Jocelyn's arms encircled her, Sofia was surprised by the sincerity she sensed in the woman's return pressure. She added, "And I guess you just met my mom?"

"Yes, we exchanged all of five words," said Jocelyn with a nervous titter.

Maggie said, "I'm delighted to finally meet you! Would you care for something to drink? I was about to make sangrias."

"Oh, thank you, that sounds wonderful."

When Maggie left, Sofia and Jocelyn stepped further apart from each other; the older woman looked her over, eyes shining. "Oh, don't you look lovely! It feel like ages since we last met."

Sofia deflected this observation with a compliment of her own. "You look great as ever, too."

"Not like a grandmother?" The older woman's glance strayed to the playpen in the corner. "Is he—?"

"Yes," said Sofia. "That's him."

Ms. Griffiths crossed the room and stood observing her grandchild as he lay sprawled comfortably, stripped to his diaper, sweaty white-blond curls clinging to his brow.

Sofia pretended to not see the tears trickling down the older woman's finely-sculpted face. Jocelyn fumbled in her handbag and drew out a stuffed toy rabbit.

With a self-conscious laugh, she explained, "This belonged to Amanda. I had it cleaned and refurbished. It's like new now. May I?"

"Yes, of course. What a lovely idea."

Jocelyn placed the toy beside Dylan. Stepping away from the playpen, she then collapsed in an armchair near Sofia. With a smile, she struggled to speak. "He's beautiful."

"Thank you."

Brushing away a tear with her long, fine fingers, Ms. Griffiths lifted her head and looked about. "Where's Owen?"

Sofia said, "He's traveling on business. But I'll tell him you said hi."

Joycelyn bit her lip and looked thwarted.

Maggie re-entered the room and distributed the drink glasses.

Flustered, Jocelyn fumbled with her purse on the floor beside her chair. She pulled out a package and rose, handing it to Maggie. "I brought this for you, I hope you like it."

With a polite exclamation of pleasure, Maggie accepted a small package of handcrafted goat's milk soaps.

Jocelyn said, "I know it was a bit…forward of me to have basically invited myself over, but I couldn't keep away…," Her voice trailed and she waved a hand toward the playpen.

"Perfectly understandable. And we're delighted you're here," said Maggie firmly. "And these will look perfect in my bathroom. They smell wonderful." She set the soaps on the end table near her seat.

For several moments, the three women sipped their drinks and looked around without speaking or meeting one another's eyes. Sofia fiddled with her glass, wondering if she should wake Dylan up and formally introduce him to Jocelyn, or if it was best to let him sleep a bit longer. Abruptly, she recalled that Owen had revealed his mother had undergone numerous elective abortions before he and Amanda were born. She couldn't imagine what sort of emotions the woman was struggling with at the moment.

The tension was shattered by a loud, commanding knock reverberating down the entryway from the front door.

"I'll get it," said Maggie, setting down her glass and rising quickly.

From the entryway came sounds of raised voices. Maggie soon returned, looking shocked and upset. She was accompanied by a male police officer and a woman in a business suit.

At the sight of them, Sofia's stomach plummeted and her palms grew sweaty, but she strove to appear unconcerned.

The woman was older, with short, steely hair and a pleasant expression hovering over a deeper attitude of world-weary experience. "Good afternoon, ladies. Which of you is Sofia MacIntyre?"

"There's no one here by that name," interjected Maggie forcefully. "As I told you outside, you have the wrong house. You don't have permission to even come in here."

"I'll be the judge of that," retorted the woman. She flashed an ID card dangling from the lanyard about her thick neck. "Constance Peña, Department of Family Services. We received a credible report that a male infant at this location was being neglected or possibly abused."

Maggie bristled. "Report? From whom? You can't just barge in here and start making accusations!"

"I can't tell you who alerted us, but since a child endangerment report was made, we have to follow up on it." She turned to Sofia. "Are you Sofia MacIntyre?"

Sofia looked markedly hunted and flustered, praying Jocelyn would keep her mouth shut. Before she could answer, Maggie tilted her chin and said loudly, "There's a mistake. This is a friend of the family, Natalie Lawson. My daughter is out of the country."

The woman turned to Sofia. "Ms. Lawson—may I see your ID?"

"Oh, yes, of course—!" Sofia rose from the couch and lifted her purse from a hook near the kitchen entryway. She tried to move with confidence; after all, she had no reason to believe the fake IDs that Owen had provided wouldn't be powerful enough to withstand the scrutiny of these locals.

Her fingers stumbled over the flap of the inner security pocket; digging through the pocket, she grew frantic when she couldn't find the two sets of the ID slips. Then she remembered she'd transferred them to a different slot, and seized one with relief.

She turned to the woman with a smile of triumph. "Here you go. And my son's, too."

The official waved the disc over her small tablet and studied the results. "There must be some mistake. These photos are a possible match to what I have on file for Sofia MacIntyre."

"'Possible'?" echoed Sofia. "I don't understand, what does that prove? And did you check his ID?"

"Yes, but it's confusing." The woman thrust the discs into her pocket. "Until I sort out what's going on here, I'm taking this child into protective custody."

The two grandmothers looked stunned and confused. Sofia uttered an angry, inhuman wail of denial, and flung herself at the playpen. The armed officer intercepted her and brutally flung her aside.

As she lost her balance and fell, the air rang with screams. The man whipped out his gun and held the older women at bay, as his superior scooped up the baby. Startled out of sleep, Dylan commenced screaming.

His cries drove Sofia deeper into a frenzied panic. She climbed to her feet and grabbed for the baby, but the officer shoved her back down to the floor. Maggie also lunged forward to stop the woman, but the man instantly brought the butt of his gun down on the side of her skull. She fell beside her daughter.

The two intruders disappeared down the hall. Jocelyn dashed after them.

Hyperventilating and inarticulate, Sofia crawled to her knees, choking, "The police...call them! Hurry, *hurry!*"

"Where's my phone? Where is it?" groaned Maggie as she began searching among the clutter on the coffee table and then in the kitchen.

Gaining her feet, Sofia stumbled down the front hall and through the door. On the porch, she halted and looked up and down the street. She had no idea which way they had gone.

Turning, she went back inside and collapsed on the couch. Rocking back and forth as she sobbed and wailed, Sofia was unaware someone had joined her until she felt a hand on her shoulder. She looked up to see Jocelyn, red-faced and out of breath.

"Black, unmarked car," Jocelyn gasped. "It all happened so fast—I tried to follow, but on foot, I wasn't fast enough—," Her voice broke and she shook her head helplessly.

Maggie had found her phone and quickly dialed the police, relaying as much info as she had: a detailed physical description of the suspects and their vehicle.

When the call ended, she seated herself beside Sofia, hugging her tightly.

"They'll be here soon," she said with a shaking voice. "They're issuing a bulletin, they'll catch them. They can't possibly get away...and there's the security footage from the camera on the porch...,"

Sofia uttered a low, inarticulate moan of grief. "We shouldn't have come, it was too dangerous—,"

"Everything will be alright," Maggie murmured. "It's going to be alright. They'll catch them in a few minutes, you'll see—,"

Two more men came through the open door. John and Diego had returned and stood staring at the women in confused dismay.

"What's wrong?" demanded John.

Maggie explained as succinctly as possible, her relation of events punctuated by Sofia's sobbing. When she had finished, Rojas announced, "Señor Volkov, I need your car *now*!"

With a grim nod, John answered, "I'll go with you!" Both men dashed for the garage. The sound of squealing tires soon followed as the vehicle tore out of the driveway and sped down the street.

They can't possibly catch them, Sofia thought in numbed horror. *They have no idea where to go.*

"It's a horrible mistake," said Jocelyn dazedly, to no one in particular. "They got the wrong house. They'll bring him back when they realize…,"

Sofia responded with choking sounds. After ten more minutes of agony, two police officers arrived and came down the hall.

One called, "Ma'am?" and Maggie rose with alacrity to greet him.

She gave her statement first, allowing Sofia time to calm down a little before it was her turn to be questioned. The first officer focused his work tablet on the side of Maggie's skull, recording the bloody scrape from the pistol butt. "Ma'am—you want that seen by medics?"

"No, thanks," she said, brushing him away impatiently. "It's not important."

When they finished recording her account, they approached Sofia. Even after composing herself, she was barely comprehensible, brokenly recounting her version of events. When she finished, Maggie shared the front porch survcam records on her phone.

"Look, here they are! The man didn't give his name, but the woman said she was Constance Peña, from the Department of Family Services. She didn't clearly show us her credentials, so they must have been false," she concluded confidently.

Both officers solemnly regarded her screen for several moments. The first man checked some data on his tablet, then announced, "There *is* a Constance Peña employed at DFS. And your survcam footage matches her profile photo."

"What?" Maggie was horrified. There was a subtle but unmistakable change in both men's demeanor as they began to regard Sofia with more interest.

The first officer added, "And here's the DFS documents, too, alleging your daughter, Sofia MacIntyre, as the abuser. Father's whereabouts unknown, but might have a violent criminal record." The man stepped closer to Sofia. "Ms. Lawson—may I see your ID?"

In a daze, Sofia fished the back-up disc from her purse and handed it over.

The officer accepted the disc and ran it over his tablet's sensor. "I'm gonna confirm with a face scan, okay?" He held the tablet to her tear-stained, blotchy visage and the device soon chimed.

"Everything checks out, Ms. Lawson. Looks like there might be a legit mix-up at DFS." He handed the disc back. "I'm afraid I need to request that you remain on the premises for the next few hours, while we go back and try to get to the bottom of this. But with that alert out, your son should be found soon."

Clinging to this scrap of hope, Sofia nodded in wordless gratitude. When the officers left, Jocelyn took her arm and guided her back to the couch.

"You need to lie down," she said, her nurse's instinct seeming to kick in as her own shock subsided. "I'll bring you a drink of water."

She made her way to the kitchen and Sofia curled weakly on the cushions. This was worse than any nightmare, even worse than when Singer had held her hostage at the high school. To have Dylan gone and in peril was like the world itself being torn apart.

More male voices sounded outside, then in the hall as John and Diego returned.

"Lost them," announced Mr. Volkov with a bitter crispness. "Any word from the cops?"

"Yes," Maggie began, but was interrupted.

Diego dashed across the room, calling to Sofia: "Señora—get up, we must go at once!"

She looked up in confusion. "They said they'll get him back soon—,"

"Señora—*vamos ahora!*" Grasping her upper arms, he hoisted her upright and set her on her feet. "We must leave this place at once!"

Dazed, Sofia found herself accepting a glass of water from Jocelyn, gulping it, then taking her purse and travel bag from her mother's hands as Diego rushed her to the family car. Rojas called to John, "Señor Volkov, take us to the nearest vehicle rental place!"

As he pushed her into the back seat, Diego said with controlled urgency, "I've just contacted your husband—he wants you as far away from here as possible, as fast as we can do it! He will be meeting us, but I can't say where!"

Without even a chance to say goodbye to the others, Sofia watched the pleasant suburban houses flying past the windows, and realized her own levels of terror were fading. As she studied the grim, focused edge of her father's face as he managed the controls, she dimly wondered if Jocelyn had slipped something into that glass of water.

If that was true, some part of her was dimly grateful. She didn't see how she could face the next hours without all the help she could get.

CHAPTER
FORTY-FOUR

IN SPITE of the unbearable sense of urgency, the private Paloma jet hadn't been immediately available to take to the skies. Owen had been in South Dakota, overseeing some intravox training, when his world was shattered by Rojas' urgent call. Concocting a barely coherent pretext, he'd immediately left Morse's lab, mind reeling as he also scrambled to form a plan with so few facts.

It had had seemed to take forever to drive to the airfield. He grudged every moment it took for the Paloma craft to become airborne and then arrive at the Hutchison County airport in Texas.

Each passing moment took Dylan farther and farther away from them, into the unknown.

Still seated in the passenger cabin after the plane powered down, Owen looked through the aircraft's windows toward the entrance of the small airfield, searching for the headlights of the car that was bringing Sofia back to him.

Morse's laboratory seemed a million miles, an eternity, behind him. The work there was negligible, worthless. Owen didn't know how much of the truth Ellie could sense within his chaotic thoughts and emotions, and he was too distraught to care much.

I suppose this is a good test of how much she can pick up when I'm under profound stress, he thought distantly, attention locked on the end of the road. *At least we'll see how well the protocols work under extreme conditions.*

The problem-solving portion of his brain continued to function on a type of deadened auto-pilot. This numbness was a defense mechanism—if he paused to examine his emotions, the pain would devastate him, render him incapable of producing any response other than impotent rage.

Restless, he rose, went to the open door in the craft's fuselage, descended the metal steps. A breeze wafted over him; he paced on the tarmac, feeling caught between the warmth of the surface below him, and the cool expanse of the star-emblazoned night sky above.

The ultimate responsibility for this situation rested with him; he had been lax. He also knew there was no point in focusing on failures at the moment. Setting aside the 'how' of what had happened, he began to focus on what came next. He had impressed on Rojas the importance of not allowing himself and Sofia to be followed, and so assumed they had taken a circuitous route from her parents' home.

If they were trailed to the airport, Owen would have to ensure the pursuers didn't leave the facility. Slipping his hand under his jacket, he felt the hard, smooth handle of his deadly Scorpio pistol.

Traffic on the road leading to the airstrip was light; his heart leapt, then sank, with every set of headlights that drew near and then sped past. For security, they had agreed to use only burner phones, and those in the most dire situation; he hoped it was a good sign that he hadn't heard from Diego for an hour and a half.

Activating his videoskin, he began reviewing the facts that he had pieced together on such short notice. The implications were grim, and explaining the situation to Sofia was going to be a highly unpleasant task. He wasn't sure he could face it now.

At last, a vehicle approached and parked nearby. It matched the model Diego said they'd be arriving in, but Owen didn't move to greet it until the driver's door opened and Rojas stepped out and waved. MacIntyre quickly approached, asking, "Were you followed?"

"Señor, I'm certain I lost them when we switched rental cars. No sign of anyone following us after that."

"Good."

Rojas continued, "The only trouble was from her father—the señor wanted to come with us, because he thought we were going at once after your son, and I believe he wanted to kill the abductors with his bare hands."

A wan smile twitched over Owen's face. He did not know John Volkov well, but had no difficulty imagining the man's reaction to this crisis. Maggie's reaction was doubtless similar.

He lowered his voice and made a tight gesture towards the car, where Sofia was huddled in the rear seat, clutching a stuffed animal. "How is she?"

Diego's face fell as he glanced toward her. "Not good, señor. But quiet."

"Thanks for bringing her back so quickly."

Rojas was exceedingly uncomfortable, unable to look MacIntyre in the face. He forced himself to say, "Señor, I apologize for letting this happen. It was my fault."

Owen interrupted, "We can discuss that later. I still need your help, so you're not fired yet."

He approached the car as Sofia opened the rear door and sleepily looked out at him. He hesitated a fraction, studying her disheveled hair and drawn, mask-like expression.

Unbidden memories of his mother's numbed, empty stare following Amanda's death now flooded him. Would Sofia sink into a similar emotional wasteland, one that would require medication and therapy to navigate?

He slid into the seat beside her and, because he could think of nothing to say, remained silent.

Twisting a gray plush rabbit in her fingers, she spoke with a painful rasp, "Your mom brought this for him. It was your sister's."

"My mom?"

"Yes—,"

Sobbing, she sank into his arms, burying her face in his shoulder with an inarticulate moan. He could feel her relief at his presence, her trust that he would somehow fix this nightmare.

After several moments, she said, "Your mom was so brave...she ran after them...right out the door...even though they threatened her with a gun."

"Yeah, she's tough." As the meaning of her words sank in, he asked in a troubled voice, "How did she come to be there?"

"She kept calling *my* mom, asking if there was a chance Dylan would be in town soon, and if he was, could she see him? I said it was fine, so of course...oh, my God, it was my fault, wasn't it? I shouldn't have let her come!"

Setting aside the implications of what she'd just revealed, he managed a soothing tone as he answered, "It's much too early to know exactly what happened. We'll figure it out later."

She whimpered, "What do we do next? How do we get him back? We can prove we're his parents—legally, they'll have to give him back, won't they?"

Rubbing her shoulder, he said slowly, "Of course they will."

"Then we need to go back now and confront them. Soon, right?"

He sighed. "It's not that simple."

Drawing back, she regarded him with horror. "What do you mean? What's wrong?"

"I'll explain more on the flight home."

She shook her head wildly. "Leaving? No, we can't! I'm not leaving, I need to stay here in Texas, as close to him as possible."

He thought his way through a landmine of facts and inferences, and how best to present them. In a low, earnest voice, he said, "Look, I want to chase after him and bring him back right now, too. But that's what they want us to do. Besides, he may already be out of the state. Maybe even the country."

She sputtered, "Singer's behind this, isn't he? This can't possibly be a coincidence!"

"No, I doubt it's a coincidence," he admitted. "But I don't have a lot of evidence yet."

Her voice rose. "But you'll get what you need, right? You'll be able to explain to the authorities what happened? They'll give him back?"

"I'll do everything in my power to see they do."

Tears again streamed down her crumpled, reddened face, her voice was an anguished, broken squeak. "But why? Why is this happening? Why did God let this happen?"

"You know this isn't God," he said grimly. "It isn't a disease or an accident. It's...," his voice stopped.

"Evil? Insanity? Politics?" she whispered. "Or all of them?"

Owen shook his head wordlessly. He thought, *At this point, it doesn't really matter. That's the thing about vendettas—not much logic involved, they're driven by emotion. Or maybe he wants Dylan as bait, to exchange him for my intel on the Restoration movement.*

But it was impossible to share these thoughts with her.

Sofia's face went from red to pale green; she dived from the car and vomited onto the tarmac. Then she reseated herself with a strangely calm air.

"Done?" he asked.

She nodded. He fished out a water bottle nestled between the seats, and handed it over. She took a long, unsteady gulp, spilling drops down the front of her top.

After she replaced the bottle, she asked, "Are you *sure* Singer is involved?"

"Yes. Nothing else makes sense. I'd bet anything Dylan is on his way to the Pacifica border. He's being taken to either Seattle or New Astoria."

She said, "Can't we get the word out and stop them before he gets any farther away?"

"I've already contacted some trusted operatives, asked them to keep an eye out, but they haven't reported back."

Slightly reassured, she sniffed and wiped her eyes.

His mind shifted abruptly. *Seattle,* he realized with a jolt of icy horror. How did Singer know for certain that Dylan even existed? Could his father possibly have been the one to tip him off?

Owen thought over how he convinced himself it was safe to contact his mother, how he had phrased everything in such a vague manner so she didn't have any actionable data. Unless—.

A possibility thudded into his mind that made him both ill and angry. Had Jocelyn been *so* elated by the news of Dylan's birth, that she had ignored Owen's warnings and contacted Richard anyway?

He had no idea what his father's current circumstances were, but it was easy to conjecture that Singer was keeping an eye on him and monitoring his comms. Perhaps the news of Dylan's birth had been the catalyst for a redoubled effort to surveil both Jocelyn and Sofia's family. For the moment, he didn't want look any closer at this scenario.

Sofia began sobbing again. Owen bore the discomfort of listening to this for a little while, then said, "I promise you, I'm getting him back."

"I know you want to, but really—is it possible? Can you know for...for sure?"

It was clear her tone meant, did he have any precognitive hints about the future? She didn't often reference his intermittent visions, but still, he sometimes regretted sharing that they were a possibility.

"No," he said glumly. "You know, it's an unpredictable phenomenon. When I get any impressions, they're usually confusing and unclear. It's an almost useless ability."

She whispered, "But I don't think I can bear this, not knowing...,"

Massaging her knee fondly, he said, "I'm not going to rest until he's back with us. Nothing else matters. So trust me."

The faintest trace of a smile gleamed through her tears. "Okay. I trust you. But what's next?"

"The plane is almost ready to leave. So what's next is, we get out of the country as quickly as possible before any more of Singer's agents collect more data about us. And then when we're back at the hacienda, I'll start planning."

Pulling her close, he again held her tightly. He felt very strongly that he would succeed, that in the end, he would get Dylan back. He didn't need to be able to read the future to know that failure was not an option.

CHAPTER
FORTY-FIVE

WHEN THE DOORBELL SOUNDED, Greta positioned herself before the entrance and growled, but she was too well-trained to bark much at the visitor.

"Coming!" shouted Slate, juggling the fussy baby against his shoulder, while he shooed the dog into the nearby powder room and shut the door. He eagerly pulled open the front door and regarded the petite, almost doll-like young woman who stood placidly on the welcome mat.

"Ms. Pham, good evening. Please—come right in," he bubbled with relief as he ushered the nanny into the home.

There had been a point on the previous day when Slate had despaired of ever finding a live-in nurse who met Hayden's exacting, almost paranoid standards, but after background checks and two interviews, Hayden had grudgingly admitted that Lucy Pham appeared a competent and unobtrusive choice.

The attractive young woman entered the hallway and started to set a large bag down on the floor, but Slate stopped her. "You'll share the baby's room until we can finish the guest quarters. Here, I'll show you, follow me upstairs—,"

As they passed the powder room, they heard a sharp, dissatisfied bark. Ms. Pham said quickly, "I know you mentioned there was a dog, but I'll need to be introduced to her."

"Of course. But Hayden does most of her training, so he'll be in charge of that later."

The woman followed him upstairs and down the hall to the nursery. Her pleasant, ready smile did not indicate what she actually thought of the set up, which contributed to Slate's nervousness.

He babbled, "If you need anything changed in here, or if anything is missing—please, don't hesitate to let me know!"

"It's perfect, Mr. Singer." Setting her bag near the dresser, she held out her arms. "Let's talk about this little gentleman, shall we?"

"Well—," Slate shifted Ashtyn in his arms and passed him over. The baby stopped crying as his eyes fastened on a new face. "I guess he's colicky. That's normal at this age, right? But we don't know what to do about it."

Fingering the curls at the back of Ashtyn's neck, the woman bounced him lightly against her chest, while simultaneously swaying from her hips. "Constant motion helps. And I have some drops we can try in his formula later. What do you know about his history?"

"Oh, well, I guess he wasn't in foster care for very long before he came to us."

"He might be upset about that change, too. Do you know what type of formula he was on before?"

Slate racked his brain, then realized there had been no information about that in the documents that had accompanied Ashtyn's sudden arrival. "No, sorry. I don't know."

"Can I see the kitchen?"

"Oh, sure."

In the kitchen, Slate showed her where all the bottle equipment and formula was kept, and explained the household's basic schedule.

"Things are usually pretty quiet around here. As we said in the interview, I typically work full-time, but that's mostly from home, so I will be around. And Hayden works overtime—too frequently, in my opinion." He gave a nervous laugh.

He added, "And we like to go out on our own once or twice a month. I hate to admit it, but a new baby is a bit more work than we had anticipated, and we'd like to have a few more hours to ourselves."

She smiled indulgently. "That's why I'm here. Don't worry, I'll make sure he settles in, and you'll get some sleep." Her capable, business-like tone was at odds with her delicate appearance.

Still carrying Ashtyn, she made her way back upstairs to the nursery and began cataloging the equipment and supplies there.

Slate followed and hovered in the doorway, reluctant to walk away. He was already very protective and responsible toward Ashtyn, but also self-conscious about his inexperience. As he watched Ms. Pham settle into the glider chair and dazzle Ashtyn with her steady smile and flow of talk, he felt the strain and disorientation of the last week begin to lift.

A future where he and Hayden could actually enjoy the baby's company now seemed possible.

After a few minutes, he sensed the nurse found his presence intrusive, and so wandered back into his home office. He didn't have to do any work if he didn't choose to, and wondered if it might not be better to take Greta for a walk. Then he thought what Hayden would likely say if he found out the baby had been left in the charge of the nurse, unsupervised. Until she had proven herself and become an actual part of the household, Slate knew Hayden was going to regard her with suspicion, no matter how glowing her references.

For some reason, Hayden was even more paranoid about Ashtyn's safety than Slate was, and had ordered the child not be taken off the premises without both men and the dog being present. He had even arranged for an Elite Squad officer, Eric Marino, to do guard duty at the house several hours a week. Hayden called Slate to check up on Ashtyn once or twice a day.

It was touching, in a way. The last years of daydreams and idle planning had been shattered by unexpected opportunity, and as difficult as it was, Slate also knew it was worth it. He could not remember when he had seen Hayden so happy, almost triumphant. Of course, this came in waves and flashes, and was also accompanied by periodic outbursts of temper. Or strange episodes of absent-mindedness, when he seemed lost in profound thought.

As Slate gained a greater understanding of how Hayden's position of authority in Pacifica's government came with massive amounts of stress and responsibility, he was more determined to help out by being supportive and making their home a welcoming sanctuary.

Wide awake, Slate stared into the dark, cringing at the sound of Ashtyn's relentless, disconsolate cries drifting from the nursery down the hall. He was also aware of the various sounds Hayden was making beside him in their bed: discontented sighs, the rapid breathing of mounting anger.

After several tense minutes, Hayden's voice hissed into the dark, "Can't that little slut get him to sleep and *keep* him asleep? What are we paying her for?"

"Give it a few more minutes," groaned Slate wearily. He dreaded intervening between Hayden and Ms. Pham once more, to try and blunt the growing rancor between them. He was reluctant, but knew it would very likely come to that again.

It was becoming clear Hayden had second thoughts about their decision to adopt, and resented the money and disruption put into finishing Lucy's quarters. Slate's stomach turned to jelly at the thought Ashtyn was driving them apart rather than drawing them closer.

Furthermore, neither of them had spoken aloud of what had happened that night at the Arena, and Slate wasn't sure he trusted his own memories enough to ask Hayden about it. He only knew the older man had been acting more or less normally since then; perhaps he was uncomfortable with his own behavior and wanted to bury the event.

Yet it was also obvious he was struggling with a burden of frustration and anger, and small things could trigger him. Hayden seemed particularly unhappy about having a third party on site to help out. He resented Lucy's natural way with the child and was constantly finding fault with her, as well as subjecting her to more draconian and unrealistic house rules. But Slate knew Hayden well enough to know he also enjoyed the fact she was now trapped in her job, that she didn't dare complain about his treatment. He relished his power over her.

Five more minutes of Ashtyn's wails seemed like an hour.

Hayden snapped, "If she doesn't shut him up, I will!"

"No, wait—I'll take care of it—!"

Hastily throwing off the blankets, Slate dashed from the bedroom and padded down the corridor to the nursery. Lucy stood in the middle of the room, shifting the baby in her arms. The air of calm professionalism she'd worn when she first arrived had long since been replaced by a frazzled, harried manner.

Looking at Slate, she offered a weak smile. "I'm sorry Mr. Singer, but he's quite hard to soothe. If I could be allowed to take him out in the stroller or drive him around in the car? Sometimes they like that."

Closing the door behind him, Slate shook his head, whispering, "Don't suggest that again. You know *he* won't allow it."

"I'm running out of ideas! Look—," She picked up a bottle from a nearby table. Seating herself in the glider, she cradled Ashtyn in one arm while holding the bottle's silicone nipple to his mouth. His earlier fussiness grew to red-faced rage in an instant and he batted the bottle out of her hand, knocking it to the floor.

Helpless, she looked at Slate. "I know he's hungry, but he hates the formula. It's not what he's used to."

As she spoke, the baby reacted to the sound of her voice and grew a little calmer, rooting hopefully against her breast.

Lucy said, "Do you see that? What did his records say about the situation he was taken from? Because it looks to me like he was never even weaned. He must have been with his bio mom until quite recently."

It was some moments before Slate answered slowly, "The records weren't very detailed. But I'm sure the circumstances were dire enough to warrant his immediate removal."

"But he's so healthy—,"

"I'm sure there are many kinds of abuse, not just neglect or obvious violence," he said, picking the bottle off the floor. "Here, let me try."

Ms. Pham gladly rose and traded places. When Ashtyn was in his arms, Slate began speaking to him in low, calm tomes, finding a rhythmic, reassuring cadence that eventually mesmerized the boy to silence. Then the child succumbed to hunger and sucked the formula. As the peaceful silence grew from seconds to minutes, Lucy and Slate traded relieved smiles.

"Do you want me to take him back?" she whispered.

"Thanks, but no. You go to bed, I'll sleep here in the chair with him." When the nursery door closed behind her, Slate continued to contemplate the groggy child, reveling in the way his curls were illuminated by the gentle lamplight.

Who were you before you were Ashtyn? he wondered with a slight shiver, gently lifting and fondling the baby's fingers.

"*Other forms of abuse*," he had told Lucy. Such as having two parents who'd been reported for possessing or distributing illicit tech or censored information.

Not that the U.S. government enforced those restrictions as stridently as they had in past decades. But if the parents had powerful enemies—.

Slate began humming, and then singing, a soothing little nonsense song. With the collar of Ashtyn's pajamas, he gently blotted away the formula that was dribbling from the baby's mouth.

Slate found his thoughts reviewing the data in his own personal origins file. He knew all the details about the age and ethnicity of the surrogate who had borne him, down to the itemized payments, and a lavish tip, that his fathers had showered on her.

He had read the medical documents with an air of solemn detachment, feeling little curiosity about the woman whose very name did not appear anywhere in the files. Even if he had been more curious, it would have been difficult to contact her, as all parties had agreed to enshrine legal precautions against it in the contract. He wondered if her desire for anonymity was spurred by embarrassment at having agreed to the process.

Yet subconsciously, Slate had created an imaginary construct of what she looked like, the sound of her voice, the way she smiled or gestured with her hands. Sometimes he looked at himself and wondered what part of *her* he was seeing. He remembered reading somewhere that, during gestation, cells from the fetus migrated to the mother and lodged permanently, a process known as microchimerism.

Which meant that, wherever she was, a part of him was still with her. Once in a while, he wondered if she also knew about that biological phenomenon and ever thought of it. Ever thought of *him*; had that huge fee been enough to stifle any idle thoughts or wistful regret? He also wondered if the phenomenon was a two-way street, and did some small part of her live in him? Reluctant to make his fathers uncomfortable or sad, he'd kept these questions to himself.

Slate had only glanced at the documents that had accompanied Ashtyn. Hayden had handled all of the details, as he usually did. Slate could not help recall the box of random photos and clothing Hayden had brought home last year, and how vague and evasive the older man had been concerning their origins.

Slate didn't know much about procedures at the ISA, but even he knew that bringing home evidence and giving it to a spouse was illegal. Over the last week or so, when he noticed that whenever he happened to wear one of the hand-me-down shirts, Ashtyn would calm down for a few seconds, then grow confused and agitated. These odd occurrences had caused a gut-loosening plunge of suspicion, a plunge that Slate discounted and worked hard to ignore. He didn't dare ask any questions.

But the matter kept haunting him. Staring into the baby's blue eyes, they reminded Slate of the digital inkarn, the image of the mysterious man in the VR game Hayden had investigated months before.

The baby's eyes grew heavy and lowered, and he finally slept. The words to Slate's song changed. "Where did you come from?" he quavered in a low whisper. "And how did you end up with us?"

CHAPTER
FORTY-SIX

THE DUSTY BACK OFFICE IN the New Astoria high school had been secluded, granting privacy and ensuring sound wouldn't reach the rest of the facility. It was outfitted with a bed and little else. As much as Sofia tried to shove away memories of the hours she'd been captive there, the current crisis brought it all back. She relived her utter physical revulsion at Sergeant Bauer's leering insinuations about her impending fate, recalled the unimaginable horror of Hayden Singer having so much power over her.

She could not forget the terror she'd felt at the time for the safety of her new pregnancy, which she did not dare reveal publicly. She'd desperately prayed that Owen would somehow find her and break her free from the nightmarish place. The wild joy that exploded in her, when he finally arrived and helped her slip out the window, would always be one of her most treasured memories.

Had that entire episode marked the high point of his abilities? Was it beyond him to find a way out of their present hell? Was the child she had feared for then, now gone forever?

She was jolted out of her dark thoughts by the gentle clatter of dishes, as Teresa Ortega set a tray on a nearby table in the master bedroom.

Listlessly, Sofia forced herself to look up at the woman with a pale smile. "*Gracias*, señora."

The assortment of lovingly prepared food did not appeal to her; she could not remember the last time she'd eaten. But beneath her shirt, the discreet pumps working away at her breasts reminded her it was her duty to eat something.

Isabella hovered behind her grandmother, shyly observing Sofia with concerned eyes. Gesturing towards the apparatus barely discernible beneath Sofia's shirt, she asked, "Señora, what do those feel like?"

Sofia uttered a tired, dispirited sigh. "Uncomfortable…it's terrible. I should be in a dairy barn."

"Why are you doing it?"

"Because I don't want my milk to dry up before he comes back."

Teresa spoke gently, "That is a very wise choice, señora. When he's back, you will be glad you went through this trouble. And he'll appreciate it, too."

Sofia nodded. Tears no longer stung her eyes whenever Dylan was mentioned. The days since her and Owen's return to Palmira were a nebulous eternity of loss and pain, but as each hour passed, she grew more resigned to her circumstances, more able to endure them. After all, what choice did she have?

Teresa urged, "My dear, you have no excuse to not eat. You know that."

Sofia reached for one of the fresh *arepas* on the tray. She ate dutifully, and as the flavor registered on her tongue, a little of her appetite returned and she ate it all.

In the strained, unhappy hush, Isabella fidgeted, then crossed the room and flung herself into Sofia's arms.

"Señora, I miss him so very much! But I know he'll be back home soon! He just has to—God won't let this go on for much longer."

Her warm-hearted empathy drew a deeper smile from Sofia. She reached up and stroked Isabella's head, nestled close to her own. "Thank you, sweetheart. I believe that, too. I really do."

Drawing a chair nearer and seating herself, Teresa said, "Señora, I know the details must be kept secret, but does Señor Lazarus have a plan?"

Sofia said, "He hasn't told me. But he was shut in the study with Diego for hours yesterday. I suppose that means they were discussing something important."

"Poor Señor Rojas," murmured Isabella. "He thinks this is all his fault."

"Please let him know we don't think that," said Sofia, rallying herself enough to sound sincere. "And we need his expertise to get Dylan back."

Teresa said, "I'm sure he'll do everything in his power to help." Then she fell silent, studying her hands as they rested on the knees of her practical slacks.

Sofia said, "I apologize for all the trouble we've caused since moving here. I know we're poor substitutes for Don Tomás, that we're outsiders who don't fit in, we're—," her voice failed as she buried her face in her sleeve.

The old woman said gently, "Señora, I'm sorry you feel like an outsider here. I've done all I can to make you feel at home."

"Oh, Teresa—! I know that! You've all been wonderful. It's just that the circumstances are so awful. They were from the beginning, and now they're so much worse."

Teresa took her hand and gripped it. "I never learned the full story of how Don Tomás came to know your husband, but I trust his judgement. Isabella is right—this won't go on much longer. Señor Lazarus and Diego will see to that."

Sofia returned the pressure of the woman's strong fingers. "Yes, of course."

When Señora Ortega was satisfied Sofia had eaten enough, she gathered up the tray and departed, shooing Isabella ahead of her.

Alone once more, Sofia fell to reliving the most recent information Owen had shared with her the previous evening. He had revealed that what little evidence he could get from the Texas DFS confirmed that Dylan had been placed in foster care, and then fast-tracked to adoption. His other sources had not been able to confirm whether a child that age had been taken over the Pacifica border, but it had been a long shot to expect reliable intel there, under the circumstances.

After this stunning blow, it had taken her several minutes to calm down enough to hear what else he had to say. He was drained and grim as he said, "I'm going to explain everything I've discovered, and when I'm finished, we'll discuss our options, okay?"

Deathly pale, she nodded expectantly. He continued, "There's no point in challenging Texas DFS right now. It's obvious they had all the paperwork ready beforehand—,"

"We need a lawyer—,"

"No, you don't understand! The law won't help us."

"Why not?"

"Because Singer had your medical records altered."

Stunned, her mind struggled to accept this claim. "What...what exactly do the records say?"

Anxiously, he ran his fingers through his hair and took a deep breath. "So... I know this is uncomfortable for you, but think back to your last night at that Citizen Assurance camp. It was clear Singer had seen your private medical records, he knew you had consulted a fertility doctor. They claimed to know where you were at in your cycle, because they had no idea you were already pregnant with Dylan. Remember?"

Swallowing, she nodded. "Of course."

"Well, based on your genuine records, Singer fabricated an entire scenario: that you were fully admitted to the program, that I was the one with fertility issues and that *he* is the official sperm donor on record."

Owen delivered this report in as crisp, cut-and-dried manner as possible. Yet his tone also smoldered with anger.

Tamping down her revulsion at this news, Sofia asked, "How does this give them the right to take Dylan?"

"Remember—according to TotalityCare's terms, the first viable pregnancy from a fertility treatment belongs to them. Pacifica's new version of the medical program just re-creates that stipulation. Anyway, Singer is pressing paternity rights, while claiming you and I had no right to take Dylan out of the country. And that we're neglectful and abusive."

Outraged, she said, "He's demented."

"Yes...and it doesn't help that he and I were enemies from the moment we met. Even before he found out about my involvement in the Restoration."

"Why? What did you do?"

Owen answered with obvious distaste, "I guess it was more of what I *wouldn't* do that got him mad. If you get my drift."

Sofia stared blankly for a moment, then comprehension dawned. The end of her nose crinkled in disgust. "You're kidding."

He grimaced. "No accounting for taste. But more likely, it's a sick power thing with him."

"Demented," she repeated. After several moments, she said, "But you can change everything back, right? You do that type of thing all the time, don't you?"

He exhaled glumly. "Technically—yes, I could. But they'd still press those false charges of neglect against us, and Singer would still end up getting Dylan

—and be completely protected by the law. And he obviously has spies and allies in key positions in the system."

Brow furrowing, she said, "But he's part of a renegade regime. Why would U.S. law uphold his claims?"

"Yes, that's a complication that could drag this out for months, at least. And he's taken care that those working for him outside Pacifica are trustworthy allies."

Growing more discouraged, he continued to explain, "I'll be honest—I can't just go back into any system or records at this point. Pacifica's internet is inaccessible to us, they're data-localized. Hell, no one's entirely sure what's going on inside their borders. I do have some contacts, but it's really tough to get accurate information at the moment."

"But how is he communicating with his allies, with…with the people who took Dylan?"

"There's some spotty phone coverage, but I suspect he has his own couriers."

"You're saying there's nothing we can do? You're just going to let Singer get away with this?"

Ignoring her escalating, frantic tone, he had answered with calm assurance, "I'm not saying that. I'm working on a comprehensive plan now, and I have plenty of my own resources. Trust me, if it's the last thing I do, I will get Dylan back."

The iron-hard resolve in his tone and face reassured her to the point where she almost got a good night's sleep.

Twenty-four hours later, she still had a glimmer of hope. Nonetheless, her moment-to-moment existence was a gray, heavy slog. She missed the feel of Dylan, the scent of him, with an ache she could not bear but could not set aside.

Sighing, she detached the pumps and walked into the bathroom off the master suite. With stiff, leaden motions, she opened the valves and shook out the contents, watching the pale liquid trickle down the basin.

CHAPTER
FORTY-SEVEN

SHEATHED IN DOVE-GRAY STUCCO, the historic, 1920's Tudor-style mansion exuded a sense of complacent affluence into the gentle twilight of the mid-July evening. The structure was not imposing or ostentatious, as might befit the home of Pacifica's President. Rather, Mahonia Hall's quaint turrets and tall windows overlooked small formal gardens at both the front and back of the dwelling. The overall effect recalled the elegant charm of an illustration from an antique book of forgotten fairytales. Tonight, the windows were ablaze with sparkling lights, the rooms heavy with the scent of fresh flowers, rich foods, and the din of voices.

Staking out a position in the formal front room, Hayden Singer occasionally glanced towards the entrance, watching as the guests trickled in. Each visitor was greeted by an attendant and provided a choice of a flower crown or a simple, restrained corsage. Singer noticed that most men chose the latter, and even at that, they seemed a trifle embarrassed as each clumsily pinned the flowers to their shirt fronts. However, the women were delighted to drape the loose ropes of leaves and bright blooms about their necks or entwine them in their hair.

The formal rooms were accented with heavy beams of dark wood and appointed with classic, understated furniture and lamps. As more guests crowded in, the atmosphere became stuffy. Understandably, President Gray was the most popular person there, constantly orbited by a small, select group of businessmen or others associated with the Committee.

After exchanging a few cordial words with Gray, including a heartfelt thanks for hosting tonight's official celebration of Ashtyn's arrival, Hayden otherwise avoided the President. Sometimes, when in the man's presence, he was too keenly aware of the gulf between their respective statuses, of his lingering resentment from Gray's private rebuke. He was afraid he would over-compensate by behaving in an obsequious manner; since his self-regard wouldn't allow him to risk that, he intentionally kept their interactions as professional as possible.

Soon, Hayden worked his way through the press of exquisitely attired bodies and into the kitchen to re-fill his wine glass. All about him, as more drinks were consumed, laughter grew more frequent and boisterous. The greenery and colored petals of the women's headgear and necklaces bobbed and slowly drooped in the warmth of the crowded rooms.

Slate drifted past in the opposite direction, meeting Hayden's eye across the crowd and pulling a face that conveyed his boredom. With the least obtrusive of the corsages wilting on his breast, for the first twenty minutes or so, he'd kept to the sidelines looking a shade out of place.

The videoskin in Hayden's breast pocket vibrated and he took it out to read a message from the nurse. Ms. Pham was upstairs with Ashtyn, and wanted to know how much longer they were expected to wait for the main ceremony to begin.

Hayden moved to the doorway and glanced into the rooms off the corridor. Gray had migrated away from the green-tiled, wood-framed fireplace that was the focal point of the front room; finding a free pocket in the crowd, the President stepped closer to Singer and clapped him on the back.

"How's fatherhood? Or is it too soon to say?"

Hayden smiled readily. "It's a disruption, that's for certain. But we're adjusting."

The President saluted him with his drink. "Was it worth the trouble and the wait? And where is he? I haven't seen him yet."

Thinking of every secret detail he had planned with such care, Hayden's full lips parted further and revealed more of his fine teeth. "He's certainly worth the trouble—he's changed our lives for the better and we wouldn't have it any other way. We'll bring him down soon." He addressed his videoskin and texted Slate.

Gray turned to the crowd and cleared his throat meaningfully. Voices were stilled mid-sentence as all eyes turned to the President.

Catching the entire room in his easy, confident smile, Gray announced, "Everyone, I believe it's time we adjourned to the back lawn to begin the real reason for tonight's gathering. We don't want to keep the guest of honor up past his bedtime."

As the others followed Gray in a trickle to the French doors leading to the back terrace, Hayden went the opposite direction. He stood at the base of the twisting staircase with its bannisters of rich, dark wood and waited. Soon Slate came down, with Ashtyn in his arms.

"He's just finished his bottle," he said, as Hayden took the boy. "And was changed."

"Great. That should keep him quiet during the ceremony." Ashtyn became stiff and wary in Hayden's embrace, but didn't cry. His round blue eyes met the older man's with an open, curious expression. Hayden found himself returning the innocent gaze with an unexpected depth of interest and regard. Then Ashtyn twisted back towards Slate and started to whimper, holding out his arms to the younger man.

Tamping down a spurt of displeasure, Hayden distracted the baby by moving quickly. As he processed down the corridor with the infant displayed proudly in the crook of his arm, he was gratified to see so many faces turn to him with admiring smiles.

At the rear of the house, most of the interior lights were switched off. Hayden, Ashtyn and Slate passed through the French doors and across a darkened terrace. A few torches were lit about the lawns and walkways. Beyond the reach of the flickering light, the dark line of the hedges and low, manicured trees formed a wall of subtle, intriguing shadows.

On the smooth lawn, several feet from the base of the rear steps, stood a simple wooden table. It held a copy of the Book of Guidance, a large ceramic basin filled with water, and a wooden tray displaying an assortment of shells, colored stones, and smooth twigs. All were arranged in precise geometric patterns, with bundles of dried leaves to one side.

A short, solemn-faced older woman waited near this arrangement, a flower wreath adorning her flowing, deep-violet hair. She wore loose silken robes of subdued lavender shades; about her neck glinted chains studded with rough-cut gemstones, and hammered silver discs representing phases of the moon.

Her face was open and welcoming. Eyes gleaming, her fluttering hands beckoned Hayden, Ashtyn and Slate closer as she pointed to where she wanted them to stand before the table. President Gray stood unobtrusively nearby, and more and more of the guests crowded closer to get a better look at the proceedings.

Hayden grew self-conscious and a little uneasy, as an expectant hush fell over the assembly. Overhead, the sky was deepening to rich peacock and violet hues, while burnt orange lingered on the western horizon. One or two stars shone.

As the hush grew and the voices ceased, the primal dancing light from the tongues of flame threw an air of mystery over the gathering.

With studied movements that were still somehow graceful and sincere, the presider lifted the book and turned to a specific page. The woman's voice sounded thinly against the growing dark and the silence as she began to read aloud.

"This evening, we greet Ashtyn Singer and honor the Power his life manifests. We honor the Power manifested in the love of his parents for him and for one another. We honor the Power residing in the community that now welcomes him."

Setting the book down, she selected a bundle of leaves from the tray and set it to smolder from the nearest torch. As Hayden held the baby facing outward, the presider wafted the aromatic smoke over them, then over Slate. She signaled for them to bring the baby closer and hold him over the basin. She set the smudge aside and took up a cockle shell. Dipping this into the basin, she scooped up some water and trickled it over the infant's head. Falling drops of liquid sparkled like jewels in the firelight.

"Ashtyn, we welcome you in the names of the Powers. May you always live according to our ways of community and inclusion. May you always tread lightly upon the Earth, dance beneath the Moon, and hold the Sun in your heart."

The child squirmed. Hayden held his breath, expecting the baby to explode with shrieks, as he often did at the slightest provocation. But Ashtyn was too fascinated by his surroundings to scream at the moment.

Like a bud stirring to life below layers of soil, a marked sense of fondness grew inside him as Hayden hefted the baby. Holding him closer to his heart, he studied the way the torchlight was reflected in the child's eyes, large and filled with wonder at his surroundings.

Hayden surged with relief that his plan was successful, while feeling a burgeoning sense of protective fondness. Many months of plans and dreams had culminated in this moment, in a way he couldn't have predicted. That his own clandestine machinations added a layer of danger only made the moment more satisfying. And the fact MacIntyre was presumably suffering more than he ever had in his life, put a final glaze of inexpressible pleasure on the situation.

In twos and threes, the guests approached to offer congratulations, then departed to freshen their drinks. Hayden's glance sought Slate, and saw his face aglow with pleasure as he looked at the baby.

Slate murmured, "I still can't believe he's real, he's with us at last."

With a self-satisfied, triumphant tilt of his head, Hayden beamed at him. "I told you it would be worth the wait, didn't I?"

CHAPTER
FORTY-EIGHT

"MAC, I understand—I really do, but I can't emphasize enough that you absolutely are *not* authorized to take any personal risks—,"

"Hey, no! Greg, listen to me—this is my son we're talking about! I don't need anyone's *authorization* to get him back."

Like cold steel, MacIntyre's voice slashed through Park's objections. The videoskin on the coffee table before Owen relayed a distorted image of Greg's distressed countenance. The older man rubbed his hand over his brow, and he leaned closer to the camera.

"Listen, I know this is a terrible experience for you—,"

"You think?"

"—but we believe pursuing legal action is the best route for now. Ebersol tells me he helped you engage the best family law counsel in Texas."

"Yeah, that's a good start. But you have no idea what this is doing to Sofia. I can't watch her suffer anymore. A purely legal route takes too long. Plus, I know you guys are trying to avoid an international incident that might escalate after we accuse a Pacifica official of kidnapping."

"I know it seems like that to you, but we can actually move this along more quickly." Park's voice took on a tone between pleading and warning. "Mac, don't do anything stupid. You have no idea how much is at stake—,"

"I know exactly what's at stake," Owen snarled. "And I know what to do about it. With or without your help."

He never had kids, he doesn't understand, he realized in a flash as he saw the frustration in his mentor's face. The frustration of an administrator seeing his plans at risk was nothing at all like the agony of a distraught parent. *He's all about logic, the big picture, the greater good. But he can't possibly imagine what this is like for me.*

The conversation ended shortly afterwards. It ended abruptly, with an unprecedented amount of rancor on Owen's side. Unsettled and fighting a nagging headache, he threw himself back against the sofa cushions. The temptation to get a beer, or something stronger, was fierce, but he pushed it aside. In his current mindset, he didn't trust himself to keep it to one or two drinks.

The toy rabbit was partially hidden beneath one of the cushions beside him. He pulled it out and regarded it with a severe expression. He had no memory of his sister playing with this thing, its blank, insipid face made him ill. He was gripped by emotions that were too similar to what he recalled from years ago, when he maintained a cool façade among his high school crowd, but inside, was a terrified boy helplessly watching his family disintegrate.

Resisting the urge to drop-kick the rabbit across the room, he instead tossed it with a gentle flick to the far end of the couch.

From outside the open French doors across the large room, he heard the peaceful sounds of the advancing night, the faltering twitter of birds against the lowering curtain of insect chaos. Within his visor, he watched some recordings of Dylan. Sleeping, sucking his fingers, face lighting up with recognition as he reached for his father.

Each image, each little sound struck him like a blow, and cemented his resolve to get his son back as soon as possible.

Let Greg and the others dither and waste time with lawyers, he thought with fury. *I'm tired of all this.*

Plowing his fingers through his unkempt hair and exhaling forcefully, he reminded himself how he had taken the bold step of developing the intravox on his own initiative. How might he turn this private family crisis into an important strategic opportunity?

"Personal risks," Park had phrased it. Which meant they believed MacIntyre was too big an asset to lose behind Pacifica's borders. They had been willing to rescue Enrique, but Dylan wasn't an asset to anyone other than his parents. And Singer.

Is that bastard using him to lure me out to where he can take me? mused Owen for perhaps the one hundredth time since this ordeal began.

Sitting upright, he picked up and contemplated the report from Ebersol's operatives: no sign of Dylan being taken across the border by land. Likely, he had been taken on a private flight. But they did confirm that, several months previously, Singer and his partner had relocated from Seattle. Owen now had the address of his and Slate's new home.

Owen studied the map of the high-end, gated neighborhood, wondering how good the security was. Then he reviewed the falsified medical records. It had taken a lot of work to create those, just to take one specific child—was it, in fact, all meant to lure Owen back to New Astoria? Or was Singer unhinged at last, obsessed to the point where he was willing to invest this much effort into taking Dylan simply because he was *Owen's* child?

Maybe those reasons weren't mutually exclusive. *I won't take that bait,* he thought. *Even with back-up from resistance operatives in Pacifica, I can't risk confronting Singer and surrendering to him. But I can make him think I'm seriously considering it.*

Whatever the motivation behind Dylan's abduction, MacIntyre knew he would have to proceed with extreme caution and not allow his emotions to cloud his judgement as he built his plan. Park was right on that score—no one would benefit from an impassioned, ill-planned reaction to the crisis.

Through their lawyer, extensive progress was already made that was expected to draw Singer's attention to the impending legal battle, even as Owen concentrated his own efforts elsewhere.

He had considered the possibility of back-channel communications with the CPS agents responsible for taking Dylan, to establish contact with Singer and offer up intel on the Restoration.

But he soon rejected this option when he realized there was no real chance of drawing Singer out of Pacifica. Better to keep the man's attention focused on what was happening in the family courts, while Owen's true plan took a very different route.

As the layers of Owen's strategy developed further, he put more distance between himself and his underlying feelings of impotent terror. He also put distance between himself and the sensations of betrayal that threatened to engulf him. Jocelyn had admitted that she had informed Richard about Dylan's birth, but she was adamant she hadn't given any clues as to the family's whereabouts.

But she needn't have; it was clear that Singer's allies only required a tip to re-double surveillance of the Volkov family. While Owen had no proof, he was growing more certain Richard had provided that tip.

There was no point in worrying about that now. *Compartmentalize and focus on what you can do, not on what went wrong,* he lectured himself.

Sofia entered the room and regarded him with a look of timid concern, then seated herself beside him. The puffiness in her face, due to weeping and lack of sleep, had finally subsided. Now she looked drained and resigned, but there was a glimmer of strength in the way she placed her hand on his shoulder and squeezed it.

She asked, "How are you feeling?"

Like absolute hell, answered his heart dully. He'd let her and Dylan down; no matter how much he wanted to blame Singer or his dad, the family's safety was ultimately his responsibility, and he had failed. So he was trapped, furious, unable to weep with her, terrified of failing again; how could he add to her burden by dumping all this on her?

Taking her hand and stroking it, he said, "I'm doing okay. What about you? Get any sleep?"

"A little. Señora Gomez texted me with questions about why I've canceled all my classes with the kids…I can't face teaching right now, but I don't know what to tell her, other than the baby's sick."

"Yeah, we can't let news of what really happened get out, it could jeopardize our false IDs. Not that I really give a damn anymore," he concluded with a flare of bitterness.

With a shrug, she said brokenly, "I feel so bad…I waited so long, now it's too late…we may never have the chance…,"

Puzzled, he continued running his fingers over her hand. It was as cold as ice. "Waited too long for what?"

"To have him baptized. I kept putting it farther and farther back in my mind, made excuses for why it didn't need to be done so soon. Now, I feel… abandoned by God…,"

Her sobs were nearly silent, drained of noise by her sheer weariness.

He said, "It's okay, he's safe. They aren't going to hurt him. Then when we get him back, we'll do that."

"Okay," she sniffed. Pointing to his videoskin where it lay uncurled among the notes and documents, she said, "About the allegations the DFS brought against us… you're sure it wouldn't do any good for you to get into their records…and…and somehow change all this back? Get rid of the abuse charge that's in the Texas system?"

He jumped at a chance to lose himself in explaining the technical details of the situation.

"Oh, I intend to do that. For two reasons: we need as airtight a case for ourselves as possible, even if it never sees the light of day. Secondly, I'm pretty sure Singer expects me to do that, so I plan on keeping him distracted through cyber activity for as long as possible. I want him to believe we're only pursuing legal or diplomatic solutions. Of course, he's counting on us failing, but only after we've spent weeks or months falling down those rabbit holes."

"I know you can't tell me much about what happened with Enrique, but would any of those people who helped rescue him be able to help us?"

"Maybe," he answered evasively. "But the fewer people who are involved, the better. This needs to be a surgical strike, in and out. So, the reality is that we're more or less on our own and are going to have to take direct action, and before Singer expects it."

"Action? What do you mean?"

Owen regarded her solemnly for several moments, turning over possible ways of phrasing his answer. She'd find out soon enough, so there was no point in hiding it any longer. "Rojas and I are going to Pacifica to extract Dylan."

Her eyes brightened and she trembled with excitement. "What's the plan?"

"The details are still vague, but I'm setting up a false ID for Diego, and lining up some counterfeit Pacifica travel permits and some of their new currency. I'll go in ahead of him and do some reconnaissance. And I do have some contacts in Pacifica who might be able to help. Then Rojas will join me—just a quick, two-man operation. If they don't know we're coming, we can get in and out pretty quickly."

He had expected shocked protestations. Instead, her hand twisted in his, tightening over his fingers.

"Is that why you're growing a beard? As a disguise?"

"Every little bit helps."

"I guess taking matters into our own hands is our best option. And if anyone has a chance of success in taking matters into his own hands, it's you," she concluded with a wan smile.

A hush fell as they both became wrapped in their own serious thoughts. Then Sofia spoke again, hesitantly. "I think you need a third person on your team."

Beneath the stubble of his new mustache, his mouth twitched in annoyance. "No, we can't afford the security risk of bringing another party in."

"I didn't mean just any party. I meant me."

He snorted gently. "I know what you meant. And I forbid it."

"No, hear me out—,"

"No, listen—you'll be a huge liability. I don't need to be worrying about you on top of everything else. As well as being at risk for retribution if you get caught. You didn't see Enrique's briefings about what happens in those camps. You are absolutely not taking the risk."

"I don't care about the risk."

"You don't know what you're saying." His voice rose with exasperation. "You are not coming."

Her voice was weepy, but determined. "Have you given any thought at all to how difficult it will be to get him out of the region without me keeping him quiet? A baby traveling with his own mom is going to be less likely to stand out than a baby traveling with—well, with you two guys. No matter what sort of weird cover story you come up with."

He didn't answer immediately, reluctant to admit her point was a good one. Since most countries still had not established diplomatic ties with Pacifica, it had been difficult to set up an itinerary, but Owen had planned a route from Venezuela to British Columbia, to Portland. And back again; it was important to have a very convincing story to get in and out of the region, and having Rojas impersonate a Venezuelan oil broker was their top contender. But so far, they hadn't accounted for why said businessman and his American personal assistant would be bringing an infant back with them.

"You know I'm right," she pressed gently. "I don't think you or Diego want to pretend to be married to each other."

Shaking his head, he chuckled.

She added, "And besides, you can't stop me."

With a sigh, he threw himself back against the sofa cushions and regarded her with irritated amusement. "What do you mean, 'I can't stop you?' Just watch me."

"If you leave me behind, I'll charter my own private flight and find a way in to Pacifica, even if it means walking across the border."

"Sweetheart, forgive my bluntness, but that's bullshit. You'll mess up the entire operation."

Leaning close, she fastened her gaze on the expressionless black band of his visor. She formed each word firmly and succinctly, "You. Can't. Stop. Me."

"You're. Not. Coming."

The irrational intensity of her expression was disquieting; he was glimpsing another woman behind the mask of her familiar gentle expression. But he knew he had to push past his discomfort.

"Please—don't ask me again. It's stressful enough working out these details without having you adding to my burden."

He hated himself for speaking to her in that high-handed, heartless manner, but was at a loss as to how to make her understand: it was unthinkable for her to be a part of the rescue operation.

After several strained moments, he sensed she was relenting.

Shoulders slumped and head lowered, she nodded. "In that case, I want you to do something for me."

"Honey, if I can, you know I will. What is it?"

"I want you to contact Tomás at his seminary and ask him to pray for us. I think his prayers might be…oh, I don't know…somehow more powerful than other peoples'. At least more powerful than mine…he's been more faithful than me."

A disconcerting, sharp stab of jealousy pricked Owen at her words. But he discounted this and said with feigned eagerness, "Yes, of course I'll do that."

Overcome by emotion, she was unable to speak further. He reached for her, but she pulled away. Rising, she fled the room.

He half-rose to follow, then stopped. No matter how hurt he was by her rejection, he couldn't escalate any risk of this crisis tearing them apart. They needed each other, they needed to be closer than ever. Yet it was clear she also needed to be alone now, so he would be patient and understanding of her agony, without burdening her with his own.

He would be dependable, but most importantly, he would do whatever it took to thwart Singer's vindictive and depraved plans, and bring Dylan back safely. After several moments of fantasizing about how this might play out, Owen collected his thoughts and grimly re-focused on the business before him.

If he was ready to take control of this situation, that meant knowing where else to seek aid. The Restoration may have let him down, but he was ready to work without them. In addition to Charles Ebersol, Jaxtyn and Ellie Morse had been apprised of the crisis. All three made it clear they were more than ready to help in any capacity.

Picking up a list of notes from the chaos on the table, he reviewed the wish-list of technical items that were vital to the success of his developing plan. Then he began composing a business-like, detailed message to Ebersol.

CHAPTER
FORTY-NINE

HER RETURN to Oregon unfolded with the unreal, eerie sensation of a dream. In fact, she often had similar dreams where she found herself here again, walking familiar trails and admiring breathtaking views. Breathing the damp, cool air.

In the tense days counting down to this venture, her dreams had become darker and more frightening, but at least she had always awakened to a sense of hope. Now that she was here in person, the reality felt like a nightmare she couldn't escape.

Sofia hadn't slept well on the long flight from Venezuela, despite knowing how important it was for her to be well-rested and alert. She was too stressed, and so self-conscious, that it seemed each fellow-passenger could read her nervousness, see into her thoughts and was ready to betray her, to pounce. It seemed that no matter how much she tried to emulate Owen and compartmentalize her anxiety and focus on one step at a time, she was still almost paralyzed with fear.

Even so, she had doggedly made it through each excruciating hour, existing moment to moment. The strain of passing through customs and security had reduced the process to a jumbled blur, but it had been successful. The false ID pods had passed muster, and the counterfeit currency was accepted without question at the car rental office. She had the feeling things were still rocky and uncertain in the new country, to the point where the security officials were inexperienced in the new protocols.

In disbelief, she kept reminding herself that she was at last back in the territory once known as Oregon, where she had spent her late childhood, teen and early adult years. She had gone to college here, tried to support herself as a teacher, but had struggled in the decaying economy and culture. But then she met Owen, and at last the nebulous hopes and dreams of her early girlhood had a chance of coming true. It seemed decades since she had last been here, not less than two years.

She had averted her eyes from the large People's Democratic Republic of Pacifica flag that overhung the international airport's main concourse, tried not to stare at the regime propaganda blighting nearly every vertical surface in both the airport and the rental office. She struggled to appear as if she was used to messages blaring forth from billboards and the sides of businesses, perhaps found them comforting or even took pride in their vague and bombastic themes.

As the rented vehicle sped westward from the airport, she kept her eyes fastened on the familiar terrain and vegetation. The surroundings seemed prosaic and a little dull compared to the tropical landscape she'd been living in over the past months. The sights evoked a strong sense of bittersweet melancholia in her. Despite how strongly she had wanted to leave this region a few years earlier, she was now gripped by a sense of compassionate fondness for the place. Everything looked nearly the same as she remembered—of course it did, how could it change in only a handful of months? Yet there was an undeniable sense of it all being 'off', a tinge of unreality was cast over the buildings, the fields, the thickly wooded hills. The parched vegetation told of a harsh summer thus far; it was only late June.

When they were about five miles out of Portland, they pulled to one side and made the necessary adjustments to the automatic tracking system, as well as tampering with other aspects of the onboard computer.

It was late afternoon when they left the main highway and began the tedious climb into the Clatsop State Forest, seeking one of the many disused logging roads snaking through the densely packed trees and underbrush. Sofia's heart began to pound disconcertingly as they drew nearer to their destination; her palms were damp and she squirmed in her seat.

Calm down, she ordered herself. *Everything is going to be fine. It might be rocky for a few minutes, but then it will have to settle down.*

At last they found the turn-off and left the main road. They jolted along the abandoned track, raising dust clouds that settled on the broken fringes of rusty, dead sword ferns drooping along either side of the road. There were fresh tire tracks ahead of them, and she felt reassured they were in the right place. They drove with caution along the hazardous trail, but it seemed to her overwrought nerves that their tires were shouting their location through the surrounding quiet.

They progressed into the forest, the trees on either side becoming older, taller, clad in shaggy coats of moss. Some seemed almost imbued with a rudimentary, watchful sentience. The entire forest floor was darker and more overgrown than she remembered; a heavy air of menace was tangible, even through the car windows.

After nearly twenty minutes of laborious jouncing and rattling, a flash of dull blue and a gleam of light shown through the shrubbery up ahead; they rounded a corner and found another car parked off the shoulder of the narrow track.

As they came to a stop behind this one, the driver beside her turned with a pleasant grin. "You see, señora, how easy that all was. No need to worry."

Sofia returned Diego's confident smile with a quick, nervous twitch. "Yes, but the easy part is behind us."

Pulling courage about her like a jacket, she opened the door and stepped out. A part of her awareness relished the fresh, clear air and strong scents of trees whose upper branches had been basking in the sun all day, releasing a strong piney aroma. The driver of the blue car exited at the same moment; Owen stood, frozen and speechless, every line of his body betraying his shock at seeing her.

As the color drained from his face, his dark beard stood out against his skin. Then the blood rushed back to his cheeks; she could tell by the way his jaw worked and his nostrils flared that he was more furious than she had ever seen him before.

In a strangled voice, he asked, "Diego, what the hell were you thinking?"

Sofia stepped forward. "Don't blame him! I was the one who convinced him to let me come!"

"Yeah, I guessed! But of course I'm going to blame him! He's supposed to be helping protect us all, not bringing you into more danger!"

"Forgive me, señor, but she made a strong case for coming," said Rojas resolutely. "So I had someone I know make her an ID based on the one you gave me." Other than a mildly chagrined manner, he seemed unperturbed by his employer's justified anger.

"It doesn't matter how strong her case is," Owen growled. "She absolutely should not be here!"

She hung back, noting how his distress was barely restrained, how his hands trembled as they hung impotently at his sides.

"I'm sorry," she said quietly, hoping a suitably chastened tone would placate him. "It was just that—,"

"No, you aren't sorry," he cut her off. "I made it very clear why I didn't want you here, and you just up and defied me! This isn't a game!"

"*Game*?" she repeated, wounded outrage flaring as her eyes filled with tears. "How can you say I think this is a game?"

"Señor," Diego said diffidently, but loud enough to override the both of them, "I believe we will have more of a chance of success with her than without."

Sofia said, "You *see*—! I tried telling you before—it will be easier to get Dylan out if I'm with him!"

Owen turned towards Rojas. "You and I will have one *hell* of a long talk in private when we get out of here." But the anger was already fading from his tone.

The guard shuffled his feet. Sofia stepped closer to Owen and stood before him. Her whole demeanor was charged with a pleading determination.

"Don't be mad," she said. "Please listen! Did you ever read those old fairy tales, the ones where the heroine lost her true love and had to travel the world to find him?"

He did not answer. She proceeded, "I used to think they were symbolic, but now I know they aren't. Because I know, deep in the bottom of my heart, there's no danger I won't face to get him back. I mean it, more than you can possibly imagine—nothing frightens me as much as the thought of living the rest of my life knowing he's being raised by someone else, that he'll forget us."

Her voice started to break up, but she powered through the tears. "And if I'm left sitting back home waiting for you…and if it all goes wrong and I never knew what happened to you…that's the worst torture I can think of. Worse than being in one of those camps."

In the quiet that fell after her voice faltered, she glimpsed the situation from his viewpoint, and could feel his seething emotions. Chief among them was a burden of sheer terror for her. But it was too late, she could not leave.

Unable to endure his prolonged quietness, she added, "Diego believes in your plan, it's not hopeless."

She stepped close and Owen grabbed her in his arms. Resting her head on his chest, she sobbed, "But even if it's a disaster and we all die or get caught, here I am. And there's nothing you can do to stop me."

His arms crushed her; she felt his heart drumming against her own. He whispered, "You're right, I can't." For a moment, she remained motionless, sensing all the tears he could never shed, and her own eyes continued to overflow for them both.

As he continued to hug her, Owen said with suppressed excitement, "He's okay—I've seen him!"

"What—? When?" Emitting a disbelieving cry, she took a step back, searching his face with an eager, hungry look.

He said, "I cased Singer's housing development earlier today! There's only one gate in and out, but my remote decryption unit worked without a hitch on it, so I parked on a side street and walked around like I lived in the neighborhood. And I caught a glimpse of Dylan, in the back yard with the nurse."

Earnest expression dissolving into a wry grin, he added, "Actually, before I saw him, I could hear him yelling all the way down the street."

"Oh, thank God," sobbed Sofia in mixed joy, relief and longing. "Thank *God!*"

He squeezed her shoulders. "It took everything in me not to grab him right then. But we need a better plan than that. So come on—let's get to the motel!"

He retrieved two pieces of luggage from the small blue car, locked the vehicle and joined Sofia and Diego in their rental.

Soon a fresh curtain of dust lingered behind to mark their passage as they left the overgrown logging track and drove the back roads to the narrow, broken highway, and began their surreptitious approach to New Astoria from the southeast.

CHAPTER
FIFTY

STANDING at the window of the shabby motel room, MacIntyre absent-mindedly stroked his short beard; it still felt new and unusual beneath his fingertips.

He was surveying the parking lot and far beyond it, the view of the city. To the casual observer, the city looked much the same as ever. But he recognized an unmistakable pall of gloom; the prosaic familiarity of his childhood surroundings was soured by a feeling of oppressive dread. He noticed the parking lot was less than a quarter-full and traffic was light. And far more businesses were closed or had reduced hours. Most ominous were the enhanced patrols at major intersections.

There was a general sense of disquiet which went beyond what one might expect in such a new dictatorship. It was a feeling that the entire enterprise was weaker and far closer to collapse than a casual glance could reveal.

Maybe that's just wishcasting on my part, he thought glumly. *I want to believe the fuckers in charge here are unprepared and in over their heads. I want them to fail quickly and utterly, yet without bloodshed. But I know the odds are against that.*

When—or if—serious pushback ever threatened the fledgling regime, he guessed the authorities would be ruthless in quelling it. However, that issue was lower down on his list of concerns at the moment.

He turned from the window and watched Sofia as she slept on one of the room's twin beds. He wished he could sleep as peacefully as she did, but he had to reach a deeper level of exhaustion before that could happen. He was glad she was happier since he had reported seeing Dylan yesterday. Now she looked relaxed and trusting, although a frown intermittently whispered over her brow.

He was still flabbergasted she'd come, and devoutly wished she hadn't. Watching her, he was seized by a strong desire to insist she remain here in the hotel room, safe under Diego's watch. But he couldn't leave either of them behind; he needed at least one extra body along on his mission.

She stirred and whimpered in her sleep, reaching for a child that wasn't there. He admitted to himself she was strong enough to endure whatever they'd be up against, so it was likely she could be helpful in this endeavor.

Overall, his trust in their chance of success was boosted by the fact their false IDs, counterfeit travel permits and currency, had all been accepted without question. His experience in signature reduction techniques, and some extra help from Ebersol's contractors, were certainly paying dividends when it really mattered.

Collecting his travel pack from the corner of the room, he set it on the second bed, opened it and began re-cataloging the few vital things he had smuggled through airport security, concealed in scan-block. Using too much scan-block to transport illegal tech could backfire and trigger closer scrutiny, which was why most of the items he needed for this venture had been sent separately, by couriers working for Ebersol.

MacIntyre's flight into Portland International Airport had arrived late in the evening, the day before last. After collecting his rental car, he had driven about fifteen miles to the east, where he met a small boat on the shore of the Columbia River and made contact with Miguel Campos to collect several secure packages of important items. But these remained hidden in the blue rental car he'd left in the forest, intended for a different purpose.

Satisfied the tools he had with him now were sufficient for the rescue operation, he took two shirts out of the bag. They were formed of light-weight, reflective material; he hoped he and Diego wouldn't encounter any beam-pistol fire, but it was best to be prepared. Unbuttoning and removing his shirt, he pulled one of these form-fitting, nearly fluid armored tunics snugly down over himself, then drew the normal shirt back on.

He seated himself at the small table and thought over the plan thus far. After debating the merits and hazards of several different scenarios, Owen had to take a leap of faith and choose one. He studied a rough sketch of Singer's neighborhood and a floor plan of the target's home. The device that Owen used to gain entry to the development had worked without a hitch, but that was only the first level of security to be breached.

A new fence was under construction about the property, but was still full of gaps. The precise model of home security system was unknown, but it was presumed that regime players were given priority to the Mozi satellite, and that Singer's system was likely connected to headquarters that way. Breaching an unknown armed system without triggering a remote alert would likely be the biggest hurdle of the operation, and Owen hoped his newer-model decryption device could handle the job.

It was unknown how large a private security detail Singer had—if any—but Owen was prepared to encounter at least one armed man. Did they still own the dog, Greta? Owen hadn't seen her when he cased the home the day before, but recalled Singer bringing her to the Agency at least once. He had the impression she could be a formidable threat.

With all this intel, Owen was ready to piece together a rudimentary plan. Still, he couldn't get too far without a clearer picture of the household's schedule, and Diego was out at the moment working on that angle.

"How long was I asleep?"

Sofia was sitting up and looking about herself; disoriented, with her hair tumbling appealingly around her face.

He grinned. "An hour or so. It's almost four. How do you feel?"

"Much better." She pushed back her hair and her face grew thoughtful. "Did you remember to contact Tomás?"

"Yes, of course."

"What did you tell him about the situation?"

"Nothing specific. Just that we were asking for prayers. He probably thinks it's a medical emergency."

"Well…God will still listen to him." Yawning, she slid off the bed, picked up her travel bag, and entered the bathroom. Soon the quiet of the small room was broken by the sound of water thundering in the shower stall.

Owen stared for a moment at the blank bathroom door, still wrestling with the mindset behind her comment. He concluded that if her faith helped keep her at peace during this ordeal, then it was a good thing. He knew his mother had slipped her a sedative in the minutes following Dylan's abduction, but was grateful that she hadn't needed any more since then.

Diego's voice sounded within Owen's visor, announcing he was almost back to the motel. The visor had a two-way comms capability, which they had tested beforehand to determine the range between the VIA unit and the bodyguard's AR glasses. It wasn't a significant range, and it was awkward to subvocalize, counting on the built-in mic to pick up noiseless signals traveling through jawbone and cheek muscles. It was better than nothing, but could never match the intuitive flow of the intravox.

Owen still had not revealed the existence of that implant to either Sofia or Rojas. He wasn't even certain it would be useful on this venture, but was glad to have the option available.

Rojas soon arrived, carrying shopping bags heavy with several white cardboard take-out containers.

"Señor, here is supper," he announced, placing the food on the table.

"Great, thanks." MacIntyre added in a low voice, "Okay, what did you learn?"

Face animated, Diego said, "Señor, I visited every restaurant that was a good candidate, especially ones that seem to have reliable electricity service and fuel for their generators—ones that might be getting favors from the big men around town. I spoke with every host and even some kitchen staff. Everyone was somewhat fearful to speak with me at first, everyone looked over their shoulder before they whispered to me."

Spreading his hands, Rojas added, "But when I tell them I am businessman from Venezuela looking for best place to have a private meal with some members of this new government, they got more interested. So I learned for sure which places are most exclusive."

Containing his impatience, Owen asked encouragingly, "What else?"

With a triumphant flourish, Diego announced, "Señor Singer has reservations for dinner tonight at seven o'clock, at the Sunset Grill and Brew Pub."

MacIntyre stiffened in disbelief. "Tonight? Are you sure?"

Rojas grinned. "Señor, the little hostess seemed very eager to oblige and prove how exclusive the establishment is."

"Just the two of them?"

"Sí, señor—no infant tonight. She said they brought *el niño* the week before last, and he cried too much. She thinks the men want a night out in peace."

"Good going, Dylan," Owen murmured with pride.

Then he restlessly combed his fingers through his hair as he began to pace. "Okay, okay—so much for the luxury of coming up with a set of back-up plans. Damn, we have less than three hours to prepare for our strike! Let's look at that diagram again."

As he scanned the sketch, MacIntyre unthinkingly opened one of the food cartons and took a bite. He paused and furrowed his brow at the contents. "What the hell *is* this?"

Rojas lifted an apologetic hand. "*Lo siento*, it was the best available."

"Thanks, no problem. You did great." Owen scooped more of the dismal-looking concoction onto a compostable paper plate. Although he was too keyed-up to feel hungry, he knew it was a good idea to eat when food was available; the next few hours were uncertain.

From the bathroom, sounds of showering ceased, replaced by the high-pitched whine of a hairdryer.

Thoughtfully chewing a mouthful of what might have been deep-fried, battered tofu—or just deep-fried batter—MacIntyre soon followed this with a long drink of tap water, hoping it would wash the taste of the meal out of his mouth.

Returning to the table, he jabbed a finger toward the diagram. "Okay, park the car here, near this clump of trees. I'll get as close to the house as I can and scan it. Of course, we have no way of knowing if Singer is going to the restaurant straight from his office, or if both of them are traveling together from the house, in one vehicle. I don't know how punctual they are, either—I expect Singer can be as late as he likes and they'll still hold his table."

Munching on a nearly-burnt spring roll, Diego nodded.

Owen said, "But let's assume that even if they're running late, they'll be out of the house by seven-thirty. I want to be in, secure Dylan and be back in the car by seven forty-five."

Behind them, the sound of the hairdryer cut out, as the electricity monitor apparently decided that Sofia had used enough power. The bathroom door opened, and she re-entered the room. Owen stared at her, pausing with his own spring roll half-way to his mouth.

"Well—what do you think?" she asked shyly.

She had changed out of her preferred clothing of dark-blue slacks and flowing blouse, and now wore a bulky jacket, jeans and heavy boots. Her brown hair was hacked short, just below her ears, and dyed nearly black. Still wet, it stuck out at right angles all over her head.

Into the stunned silence, she protested, "I figured since we'll have to dye Dylan's hair, I might as well change my appearance, too. I thought it would help if I looked like a boy. From a distance."

She seemed oblivious to the fact her thighs had grown more curvy after the pregnancy, and that since she hadn't brought the pumps with her, her breasts looked uncomfortably full.

Owen shot her an indulgent, lop-sided grin. "Sorry, honey—you don't look like a boy." He stoically resisted the urged to say she reminded him of a punk hedgehog.

"No, señora, not at all." Diego dipped his head as he stifled a chortle.

A blush mantled her wide cheekbones as she focused on scraping some of the food onto a plate, then seated herself on a bed.

She said defiantly, "In any case, I don't think it hurts to look as different as possible."

Joining her, Owen put a placating arm over her shoulders. "I thought you wanted to travel back as his mom? Now you don't match your ID."

"That won't matter up close, women change their hairstyles all the time and don't update their IDs." She tilted her chin. "I only need to look different for casual witnesses."

"Okay, that makes sense. You have a good mind for this kind of operation. You think of important details, and I appreciate that."

Pressing his lips gently against her forehead, he then released her. "We're getting him back this evening, after seven."

With a gasp, she lowered her utensil. "That soon? What's the plan?"

"Pretty basic, which means there are fewer elements to go wrong. We watch to make sure they are gone, we drive in. Diego stays at the wheel, you stay hidden in the back seat and wait while I breach Singer's home security system. I take care of anyone else in the house, grab Dylan and get out. Then we leave slowly, to not attract attention. Then we drive into the forest and switch cars."

Sofia's countenance grew gray. "What do you mean by 'take care of' anyone in the house'?"

"Exactly what it sounds like."

She nodded and closed her eyes.

Owen added, "And I hope they didn't give him a tracker. I have a removal tool, but it will leave a little wound. Sofie, are you prepared for that?"

"Of course."

Pausing, he considered how to word his next set of misgivings. He said with gentleness, "And when you're waiting in the car for me, can you stay quiet and focused and not panic if you think something's gone wrong? It's going to be extremely difficult."

Voice steady, she said, "I'll do whatever I have to under the circumstances. I won't screw it up, if that's what you're afraid of."

"Of course I don't think you'll screw it up—,"

"I'll stay calm, I promise. It's like a medical procedure, I guess, and I have to trust the experts, no matter how horrific it looks. I'll be praying."

"Yes, pray harder than you've ever done before." Owen flashed her a grin before turning to Diego. "I brought a beam-repelling tunic for you, it's in my bag." His face fell, and he turned back to Sofia. "I didn't bring one for you. You'll have to wear mine—,"

Diego laughed. "Señor, I brought my own. She can have the other one."

Owen hugged Sofia again. "Fantastic! You'll look like Joan of Arc!"

"I hope I'm as successful."

He rose and went to the notes on the table. "Now, Let's go over each step a few more times while we can. Seven o'clock will be here before we know it."

CHAPTER
FIFTY-ONE

ATTENTION FOCUSED on the front of the palatial Singer residence, MacIntyre strained the limits of his VIA unit's scanning capabilities. Even with digital enhancement, he could barely decipher the wavering shapes of the nurse as she walked Dylan about in the upstairs nursery. He knew both Singers were gone, but from his location, it was impossible to tell for certain if there was a guard onsite.

Under strict orders to remain with Sofia unless summoned, Diego waited at the controls of their car, parked at the end of the block. Along one side of the residence, construction of a new fence was underway, but was easily penetrable. Fencing supplies were stacked to one side, muddy tire tracks marked where the construction crew had left for the day.

Through his visor, Owen now murmured to Rojas: "Nurse has Dylan upstairs in the front room. I'm going in now. Alert me if anything happens out here."

"Sí, señor."

Taking a deep, steadying breath and uttering a heartfelt prayer for success, Owen stepped from beneath the trees and went up the sidewalk. His expanded field of vision confirmed there was no one in the immediate vicinity to witness him as he slipped through the rhododendrons. Pausing at the edge of the house, he listened for any noise from the dog. Nothing.

At the rear, a large, beautifully proportioned wooden deck hovered between the house and the manicured lawn. MacIntyre halted and held his breath: scarcely two yards away, on the deck, a man lounged in a chair. A guest, and perhaps the couple wasn't out at dinner after all? Yet if this man was a guard, he was plain-clothes and sloppy, his attention fixated on his videoskin.

Should the mission be scrubbed? With a split-second to decide, Owen consulted his gut. He couldn't afford to keep lurking in the shadows, planning for the perfect moment to act. Perfect moments didn't exist, he must work with what he had.

Without a sound, he drew his weapon and stole forward.

The man did not hear Owen approach from behind. After one pulse from the pistol, held just behind the skull, the man emitted a heavy groan and slumped further into his seat.

"Hey—hands up!"

Even with his enhanced field of vision, the fact Owen's attention was focused on the first guard meant he wasn't aware of the motion of a second man advancing through the sliding glass doors onto the deck. The newcomer was also plainclothes, holding his pistol with an experienced stance. And the edge of a comms implant gleamed just above his left ear.

Keeping his back to the man, Owen said nothing. The guard took one step closer.

"I said 'hands up'!"

Owen whirled toward him; a tight flash seared into his midsection as the guard fired. Beneath his shirt, the reflective tunic stopped the energy beam; he ignored the burning wave that quickly passed over his skin. Jerking his hand up, Owen fired his pistol alongside the man's face. The beam melted the man's skull-implanted comms relay, fusing noxious, dripping plastic into skin and hair.

With an agonized cry, the guard staggered, doubling over in shock and pain. Owen kicked up, catching the man under the chin and snapping his head backward with a sickening crunch. Neutralized, the guard sprawled on the deck.

Assuming that Singer had already been alerted, Owen urgently messaged Diego, "Be ready for company!"

"Sí!"

MacIntyre regarded the wide open kitchen door with disbelief; the guards had been circulating at will through the residence, the alarm was shut off. There was no need for him to breach the system.

Grateful for this unexpected advantage, he entered the home and passed through the kitchen. He registered fleeting impressions of a large chamber redolent of aloof luxury, lit with delicate lighting fixtures that gleamed on expansive marble countertops and new appliances.

Passing through this and then the dining area, he moved without noise to the corridor leading to the stairs. He was caught short by an alert from Diego vibrating in his visor: "Señor, a man is coming to the front door, maybe just a visitor, I will intercept him—,"

Perhaps it was a coincidental visitor, or perhaps it was a third guard. Even a casual, unsuspecting witness could be worse than an inconvenience; he could be a dangerous liability.

Owen thought swiftly and hissed back, "Hold your position, but be ready to get Sofia out of here on my signal."

Desperate to stop a knock or bell that would alert the nurse, Owen crossed the foyer in two strides and pulled open the front door. A man stood on the doorstep; a hulking, unfriendly figure who regarded him with a look of shock that instantly morphed into recognition.

They stared at each other for a raw, electric moment.

Even with combed hair, shaved skin and reeking of cologne, MacIntyre recognized Eric Marino, his former neighbor and Sofia's assailant. The man who had, after she'd escaped his advances, reported her to the Public Virtue Division and had her CitizenTrust illicitly downranked through an inside contact. The man Owen had later beaten within an inch of his life for those actions.

The last thing Owen needed was to get caught in a brawl with this hulking animal. Faster than Marino could react, Owen grabbed the front of the man's jacket and heaved him across the threshold, into the home. Throwing him to the floor, he kicked him in the gut, distantly noting that Marino had lost much of the fat that cushioned MacIntyre's blows during their previous fight.

The thug reacted with a bewildered groan as he scrambled to his knees, hand reaching for an inner jacket pocket. He was not fast enough to evade a pulse from Owen's gun, and a moment later, sprawled senseless on the flagstones. Or maybe he was dead; Owen was in too much of a hurry to notice.

With adrenalin surging and distorting his sense of time, the clock in Owen's visor seemed useless. His awareness screamed at him that he must keep moving as fast as possible. Breath coming in quick jerks as he grew more anxious, Owen fumbled through Marino's jacket to collect his weapon and phone, then raced up the stairs, and along the hallway to the front of the house. He subvocalized a reminder for Diego to remain where he was.

The visor's scanner revealed a dog-shaped form shut in the master bedroom, standing in the center of the room with her head cocked quizzically toward the door. Owen thought he heard her utter a confused, high-pitched whine. Panther-like, he moved to the nursery, holding his pistol safely aside as he gently tried the handle. It was locked.

A woman's voice, scared and tremulous, called out, "Mr. Marino, is that you? What's happening down there? I told you, I don't need your help with the baby! So please, stay away from me! I'll call Mr. Singer if you try to come in here again!"

The door was no obstacle to Owen's scanning abilities. He saw the young woman standing near the crib, her posture signaling indecision. A deeper scan for tech indicated there was a phone on the dresser. How quickly would she reach for it if he burst the door open?

In desperation, he took two steps back, then rushed forward and delivered a savage kick to one side of the doorknob. The follow-through carried him crazily into the room and across the floor to the young woman. He grabbed her before she could touch the phone.

She shrieked, "Who are you…? What do you want? Get away!"

"Be quiet," he commanded, spinning her around so she faced away. "On your knees. Don't say a word, don't make a move and you'll be fine."

"Don't hurt me!" she wailed in a frantic chirp. "I'll call the police—!"

"I'm not going to hurt you, but be quiet!" His grip tightened on her shoulder and he forced her down. "I said, on your knees!"

At the sound of his voice, the infant stirred and whimpered.

She complied, but protested, "You won't get away with this! Mr. Singer will be here any moment!"

"He'll regret that," grunted Owen. "Hold still!"

Pulling zip ties from his pocket, he fastened her hands behind her back and secured her ankles. He didn't pull the strips too tight; she'd be incapacitated and uncomfortable, but not harmed. She was sobbing in terror and he fought to numb himself against her distress.

"Lady, I'm sorry about this, but please be quiet—," Removing a long strip of cloth from another pocket, he threaded it loosely through her mouth, pulling the ends to the back of the head. His gloved hands were clumsy and shaking; the girl's slippery dark hair became entangled in the knot of the cloth as he jerked it, but he had no sympathy to spare.

Rising, he said, "When you see Mr. Singer, tell him he's damn lucky I'm not sticking around to execute him for kidnapping!"

Striding to the crib, he caught the baby up with a sense of triumph. Dylan looked bewildered for a split second, then his eyes widened and he cooed happily.

Owen grinned, "Hey, buddy, let's go!"

Spotting the au pair's phone on the dresser, he knocked it to the floor and crushed it under his boot.

His son grasped tightly against his shoulder and the gun in his right hand, he then fumbled open the other bedroom door. With a growl, the dog rushed him and sank her teeth into his upper right thigh. He pulsed the gun against the top of her head; her grip loosened, she fell to the floor with a short whine, twitched, then lay silent.

He surveyed the room; it was expansive but cluttered with storage containers. A home gym took up much of the space, and an office was tucked in a nearby nook.

Ignoring the strange thrill that gripped him as he invaded Singer's inner sanctum, Owen approached the desk and computer. The paperwork on the desk indicated this was Hayden's workspace; sweeping his glance across the surface, MacIntyre's visor instantly recorded all the documents he could easily access. Setting his gun down for a moment, he collected all memory sticks from the drawers.

Grabbing his weapon, he rammed it into the computer screen, destroying the blank surface. Holding the pistol's muzzle against the vent on the CPU housing, he then pulsed several shots into the unit. He muttered a command for Diego to now drive slowly toward the residence, then, accompanied by the acrid stench of melted plastic, wiring and dog hair, he charged back downstairs.

Dylan began to make agitated murmurs, but quieted at the sound of Owen's voice. "Hey, hey—we're going home. Mom's in the car."

Passing through the lingering scent of Marino's burnt flesh, MacIntyre opened the front door. Maintaining an even, brisk pace, he crossed the street to the waiting car, then slid into the rear seat.

Seconds seemed like hours as, amidst Sofia's inarticulate sobs of delight, the vehicle moved down the lane at a restrained rate.

"Congratulations, señor," said Rojas with a tight grin as he steered the car to the end of the block, turned the corner and began the journey through the meandering streets toward the front gates.

"Don't pop open the champagne," Owen shot back. "We aren't out of the woods yet."

"Woods?" echoed Diego. "We are still in the city—,"

"Never mind," said Owen with a tense, slight laugh that died almost at once. "Just get us out of here and onto route two oh two. And don't anyone stop praying."

CHAPTER
FIFTY-TWO

THE MASSIVE PICTURE windows of the Sunset Grill offered an expansive view of the city and the indistinct boundary beyond, where sky, river and ocean all met. As the window glass automatically shaded itself in response to the lowering sun, the dining and bar area became bathed in a digitally enhanced yellow light that gilded the lily of the genuine evening.

Hayden sat at the bar, awaiting Slate's arrival. Despite the decreasing amount of deep-gold liquor in his small glass, he felt alert and in control. His videoskin was open on the table before him; the screen was filled with updates from his contact in Texas Child Protective Services.

As he had anticipated, MacIntyre's appeal process was advancing glacially, but still—it advanced. It was too early to tell how tight a case they were building, but even if the court ruled in their favor, what recourse did they have? It was doubtful the U.S. authorities would have the stomach for escalating an international family dispute. The fact that MacIntyre was focusing on the courts indicated he was virtually powerless to take direct action, that no one in his circle of subversive compatriots was willing to step up and help take the child back.

An initial hearing was expected to be scheduled soon; if the couple showed up in person, Hayden wondered how easily they could be targeted. Realistically, he doubted he'd be able to pull off an attack under the circumstances, but he was at least laying a breadcrumb trail to a scenario where he could force his adversary to negotiate with him.

Of course, no matter how much the latter capitulated, Hayden would never give Ashtyn back. But it was infinitely satisfying to imagine that no-talent, arrogant prick forced to beg—with every atom of his being—to no avail.

Hayden's fingers tightened about the shot glass and he tilted a few drops onto his tongue. Savoring their fire, he contemplated his victory. Whether or not that particular vision, of a direct confrontation, ever became reality, nothing would alter the fact that Hayden had orchestrated a decisive blow against the other man. To have struck with impunity into the heart of MacIntyre's family, while still remaining untouchable at home, was indeed a satisfying outcome.

On the videoskin, he dismissed the legal updates and called up several graphics provided by the fencing company. It had taken longer than he liked to get the design finalized, as it had been difficult to strong-arm the HOA into allowing him to construct an obvious security fence in that neighborhood. In theory, he could do whatever he liked, but he wanted to maintain a good relationship with the neighbors, at least publicly. Thus the process required more behind-the-scenes negotiations and veiled threats than he was used to.

In the end, he'd gotten what he wanted. He was becoming very skilled at that. It was taking longer than he preferred, as the contractors could not conjure supplies out of thin air, but after a week or two, there would be yet another layer of security about the home.

Continuing to scroll through the 3D graphic of the finished project, he paused at one particular image. In addition to the fencing diagrams, the company had provided him with several options for custom play structures. Each was shown integrated into the existing yard with varying degrees of success. He had never thought he'd want his property disfigured with such an edifice, but these were nice. One resembled a castle, others pirate ships, or space exploration capsules.

A spaceship theme might look the best with the home's style. He thought he had made a good choice in that house. It was a comfortable fortress on a hill, overlooking the prosaic squalor of the average dwellings that crowded against each other down the narrow, winding streets into the city. One of the things he liked most about his home was how much newer and up-to-date it was than the deteriorated mansions that had overseen his childhood.

"Hey—sorry I'm late." With a wind-blown and decidedly moody

demeanor, Slate slid onto the neighboring seat. Hayden instantly put his guard up for possible trouble.

Slate added, "The cycle wasn't ready to be picked up when the mechanic promised."

"It's okay. I ordered for you." Hayden twitched a finger toward the cocktail resting beside his own shot glass.

A shadow of annoyance passed over Slate's face. "Oh—thanks."

"Trust me, I know what you want." Hayden's knowing smile contained an edge of possessiveness. "Did you go on a joyride afterwards? How's it handling now?"

"It's handling great, especially the acceleration. Just wish it hadn't taken so damn long to get the parts."

"That's the new reality for the foreseeable future. How was the rest of your day?"

Slate frowned. "Took me a lot longer to find formula and diapers than I expected. But Lucy thinks she has a lead to a supplier who'll set some aside for us."

"Okay. How's Ashtyn? I haven't seen him since early this morning, and I didn't want to wake him then."

"He was less fussy today. And he actually laughed at Greta this afternoon. Look—," With an eager grin, Slate pulled out his videoskin and shared footage of the baby. "He think's she's hilarious. He tries to pull her fur when she gets close."

Hayden regarded the scene with a faint smile hovering over his lips. "It's good she has a laid-back temperament, and she's accepted him as one of the pack."

Slate's face clouded. "What's with the new guys you sent over tonight?" He put his device away. "What about Marino?"

"It's his night off."

"Why do you need him, anyway? Why not replace him with these guys permanently?"

"He has his uses. His uses," Hayden repeated with a distant air.

"Well, I don't like him. He gives off bad vibes, and I can tell Lucy isn't comfortable around him."

"She's too sensitive, she imagines things."

It was clear to Hayden that Slate was too tense, that he wasn't enjoying this first evening out, just the two of them, since Ashtyn had come into their lives. He understood this, as he himself had forgotten what it was like to have a few carefree hours away from the crush of daily obligations, the looming burden of his duties to the regime.

He asked, "Are you happy?"

Slate didn't look up. "What do you mean, exactly?"

"About Ashtyn. You kept asking for a kid, and I got him for you. Doesn't that make you happy?"

Slate finally met his eyes with a slightly puzzled, thoughtful look. "He's both of ours, right? And sure, of course I'm happy. Just kind of tired."

"Relax," Hayden said warmly. "I don't want you to waste this evening worrying. We need to enjoy ourselves once in a while. Oh, that reminds me—look at these and tell me what you think." He passed his videoskin over and studied Slate's face as the younger man regarded the play structure designs.

Slate said, "They're great."

Hayden took the device back, folded it, then set it with exaggerated precision to the right of his empty glass. "You don't sound very enthusiastic. I remember you told me you had a treehouse as a kid, that you really enjoyed it."

With a wistful smile, Slate commented, "We all designed and built it together. It was clumsy and messy, but it wasn't prefab. It could be anything I wanted it to be...you know, a basic clubhouse to hide out in and read, or the crow's nest on a pirate ship."

Hayden closed his eyes as he listened to Slate's memories. He thought, *you hammered nails in scraps of wood with your dads at that age...when I was eight, my dad was hammering me. I never told you that.*

Beads of sickly sweat trickled down his spine, but he ignored them. Why had he never confided to Slate about the realities of his family life? Hints had been dropped in unguarded moments, and he was afraid he sometimes cried out in his sleep when he relived some scenes. But he had never willingly drawn back the curtain to reveal the pain of his past.

Did some part of him want to shield the younger man from the misery? Did he also fear to see the revulsion he often felt for himself, mirrored in the other's reaction? Which did he fear more: disgust or pity? Memories of the Arena intruded, and he felt a wave of confused guilt over his behavior that night. Yet he hadn't apologized or even mentioned it. He hated apologizing.

He wondered why he couldn't move past these agonized doubts, once and for all. Why was he so dissatisfied, so fearful, much of the time? Now that he was achieving so much of what he'd always longed for, why wasn't he happier?

Eyes flickering open, he refocused on Slate. "Building it ourselves...you know, that's a great idea. No reason we can't do it ourselves. If the homeowner's association gives us trouble...I'll see they get some trouble of their own."

"Okay, sure." Slate still looked uneasy and glum.

A server set down their plates, but neither man made a move to eat.

"What's wrong?" asked Hayden. "We knew he'd be a huge disruption and responsibility, but I can tell you're more stressed than you want to admit. Am I right?"

Slate snapped, "You don't need to talk to me like I'm some kind of hormonal new mom."

Hayden bit back his own irritation at the other's lack of gratitude. He wrestled with an urge to savage and belittle him, but ultimately tamped this down. "Well...okay. I'm sorry that's how it sounded. But do you want to tell me what else is on your mind?"

Slate sighed. "Not really."

Hayden regarded his plate as he slowly forked up a mouthful of seasoned quinoa. "This is excellent. Try a bite—,"

Slate bristled at the offer, then relented. Swallowing, he returned the fork with a mumble. "Yes, it's fine."

Hayden added, "If you're not going to share what's bugging you, let's drop it. I want to enjoy the rest of our night out—,"

He was interrupted by an alert on his videoskin. Picking the unit up, he frowned at the screen. A guard had initiated a message, but it was incomplete.

Stomach clenching in fear, Hayden dialed Lucy's number. It went straight to voice mail. He rose from his seat.

"What's wrong?" asked Slate.

"I don't know, maybe nothing, just a glitch in the comms systems. But I need to get back and check in person. Stay here, I'll be back soon."

"No." Slate pushed his chair back. "I'm coming, too."

Even as Singer approached the front of the house and slid his hand in his jacket to retrieve his pistol, he told himself nothing had happened, that there was a simple explanation for the interrupted comms.

He stopped telling himself this when he entered and saw Marino's body sprawled in the entryway. Pistol drawn, Singer warily ascended the steps and made his way to the nursery, to see Ms. Pham, bound and struggling on her knees by the window. The crib was empty.

Replacing the pistol, he kneeled, drew a small knife from the clip on his belt, cut her hands loose and then pulled down her gag. Instantly, he was assailed by her hysterical voice, spewing a wall of incomprehensible distress. Helping her to the chair, he then stood over her and tried to make sense of her garbled account of events.

"How long ago?" he demanded, face becoming a mask of barely controlled fury.

She shook her head and waved her hands. "Maybe ten minutes ago."

"What did he look like? Did you see more than one accomplice? Was there a car nearby?"

"He was a man with a dark beard, and sunglasses. I looked out the window and saw him get into a little gray car, someone else was at the controls." She gasped and struggled to catch her breath. "I just caught a glimpse, but I think it was another bearded man."

That was moderately helpful, but he'd have to access the recordings from the front door security camera in order to get a better description. And he'd have to upload that data to ISA manually when he called in his report. Which he should be doing now.

"Go downstairs and get a drink or something," he ordered Lucy. "But stick around in case I need to ask you anything more."

As he turned to leave the nursery, he halted. Slate, face deathly pale, blocked the doorway. Even with improved acceleration on his cycle, he'd only just arrived from the restaurant.

"What the fuck happened?!" Slate choked.

"He took Ashtyn."

Eyes averted, Singer pushed past him and headed for the bedroom.

"Are you fucking kidding?" Slate followed him down the corridor. "Who? Who took him?"

With dread, Hayden was aware the scents of singed fur and flesh were growing stronger. As he swung the bedroom door open, he felt a pang, but no shock, at the sight of Greta's corpse.

"Oh, God—*no!*" wailed Slate, still close behind. "Why? What happened to the guards—,"

"Shut up!" Hayden crossed the room and surveyed the destruction of the computer system and open desk drawers.

"Aren't you going to call for help?" gasped Slate. "Time is running out—,"

"Will you shut the fuck up?" Hayden rounded on him. "It's not that simple! I have no clear description or security footage. Just a little gray car, and a man with a beard."

The idea of standing before President Gray, attempting to explain what had happened, made his blood run cold. Was mounting a manhunt worth the risk of exposing his grave security miscalculations? Fury rose in him at the idea that his prey was so close, but still out of reach. His mind was caught in an agonizing vapor lock of indecision.

"Well, what do we do?" Slate's nagging voice sawed through Hayden's thoughts.

Pressing his fingers to his temples, Hayden thundered, "Let me think, damn you! I have to *think!*"

Slate threw him a long look of mingled hurt and confusion. He shouted as he ran for the stairs, "We're running out of time! *I'll* try to find them!"

Singer moved to the street-facing window and watched Slate pull on his helmet, straddle the hovercycle and then glide out of the driveway.

He has no clue where to begin looking, thought Hayden, astounded at the latter's boldness. *But at least he's doing something.*

For several minutes, his gut continued to roil as he considered his options. To have the trap sprung under his nose was unbearable, to risk exposure as an incompetent was unthinkable. The entire situation had to be handled with utmost discretion. He was loathe to even call in back-up officers, suddenly seeing his most loyal men as potential snitches.

But he had to do *something.* Abruptly, he sprang to life. Maybe Slate was right, maybe if they somehow, miraculously, caught up with the kidnappers, this situation could be handled privately. Perhaps he could gain a little time in which to concoct the perfect cover story for the event.

CHAPTER
FIFTY-THREE

"CAN'T WE GO ANY FASTER?" pleaded Sofia, breathless and trembling.

Dylan was red-faced and fussy, ready to burst with screams as he arched his back and writhed in her arms.

"They'll spot us if we're racing out of town," snapped Owen, tugging off his sweaty leather gloves and stowing them with his other gear. "The idea is to *not* attract attention."

"Sí, señora," concurred Rojas from the front seat. "Don't worry, I'll get us away safely."

With the vehicle hovering near the speed limit and obeying all traffic directions, it was unlikely they would be noticed. *But how long can that last?* Owen wondered grimly, given how many extra patrols of both ISA troopers and Pacifica Guard he'd already seen in this sector.

Remembering to scan Dylan, he checked the infant's limbs and announced, "There's no tracker!"

"Oh, thank God! Look at him, *look* at him—he's grown so much in just a few weeks!" Sofia continued to study the restless child in her lap. His eyes met hers and he looked away, crying even louder. "He doesn't recognize me!" she wailed in horror. "Owen—he's forgotten us!"

"No, no—he's just confused! Keep him still while I rub the dye in his hair!"

From the bag, he grabbed a canister, and haphazardly applied the contents to Dylan's white-gold curls. As his own hands turned brown, he realized he should have left his gloves on. "Oh, shit—!'

Sofia uttered a slight, nervous laugh, then cut herself short as she pulled the baby closer, whispering, "It's mommy, sweetie! Mommy's here, hush, it's okay, mommy's here—!"

Dylan reacted to her voice and quieted somewhat. Then he began clinging to her clothing and grew agitated again. She choked, "Oh, thank God—he *does* remember! He's *hungry!*"

Owen helped her unfasten her jacket, then watched as the baby found her nipple and began to nurse furiously. It was a relief to see how reassured Sofia was by this, it was a relief to be able to keep an emergency sedative injector concealed in the bag for the time being. He turned his attention to the view out the back window.

At the moment, there was no sign they were being followed. In less than ten minutes, they would be out of the city proper and onto the highway, heading southeast. The thin traffic made him uneasy, as he would have preferred to be able to mingle with, and become lost among, a bigger crowd of vehicles.

Yet he also regarded each car and truck in their vicinity as a potential enemy, containing people who might remember and report them later, even though he knew that was unlikely. A rusty, antique blue pickup chugged ahead of them, while a black delivery van was passing them on the left. Directly behind them cruised a sleek, silvery sedan.

"We should be back where we left the other rental car in about forty-five minutes," remarked Diego gruffly. "If all goes well."

"Yeah," said Owen. "If."

Allowing himself a few moments to relax and breathe normally, he reflected that thus far, the extraction was faster and more simple than they could have dared hope. He had no regret over Marino or the other guards.

Now he gently took Dylan's foot in his stained fingers and emitted a long, unsteady exhale. He could hardly bring himself to believe in the solidity of his son's warm, pudgy flesh. "My God, he's really back, he's here with us," he whispered.

Sofia turned to him; the tears welling in her eyes told him more than anything she could have expressed in words. Tears of ecstasy, mingled with disbelief and continued terror that something could yet go wrong with their plan.

He said, "It's all going to work out. Trust me. It will be over in a few more hours."

Soon they turned left and began route 202 along the swampy environs bordering Youngs Bay. The water was low and the scattered, forlorn spears of dead tree-trunks stood sentinel over an expanse of mud, where an occasional heron picked a slow, fastidious path.

Behind their vehicle, only the silver sedan and a red hovercycle continued to cruise. Soon the sedan turned onto an even smaller side-road, and the cycle continued to trail their own vehicle.

MacIntyre leaned toward the front seat, saying to Rojas in a low, urgent voice, "There's a series of old logging roads coming up ahead—take the third one on the left."

Rojas gave a curt nod.

As Owen had feared, Sofia picked up on his concern. "What's wrong? Why are we turning off the road?"

"I need to check something, that's all."

Diego asked, "Señor—is it the cycle? Do you want me to lose him?"

"Yeah, let's try that."

"You got it."

They left the highway and traveled a relatively deserted backroad, dappled with dying sunlight and heavy patches of shadow. "Don't look back," Owen urged Sofia, as her head swiveled to glance out the rear window.

She asked, "Do you recognize him?"

"No."

Their car followed the road through several gentle, snaking turns, and then from behind the last curve, the cycle hovered into view, keeping its distance and making no effort to pass them.

Owen ordered curtly, "We're almost to the logging road. Once we're around that bend up ahead, pick up the pace and take the next left turn into the woods."

"Yes, señor—!"

They nearly overshot the entrance to the correct road, which was obscured by overgrown trees and underbrush. At the last moment, Rojas jerked the wheel to the left and the car departed the main road to shoot up the bumpy, pot-holed gravel trail, into the concealing shadows of the thick woods.

"Pull over and shut it off," instructed Owen.

Rojas complied. The anxious silence was broken only by their breathing and an occasional grunt from the determinedly nursing Dylan. MacIntyre monitored the road they had just left, hoping desperately to see the red cycle sail on past.

One minute ticked by, then the cycle did in fact whip along, bypassing the bottom of the gravel track.

Sofia said, "So he just happened to be going the same way as us—,"

"Maybe," said Owen. "Give it another minute or two—,"

His voice died as the cycle now returned and approached from the opposite direction, coming to a controlled hover at the entrance of their hiding place. The driver looked up in their direction, then urged his craft up the road.

Sofia whispered, "Is it Singer or the other one…?"

"Slate? I don't know…let's see what he does."

Owen watched as the cycle operator slowed to a hover, then landed with a puff of dust. With cautious movements, the man removed his helmet. His face was taut, his high cheekbones stained with the red flush of agitation. He looked up the hill where the car was parked, and seemed racked with indecision. Then he climbed off his craft and stomped up the road toward them.

"Get down!" Owen hissed to Sofia. They both crouched low, he prayed the windows were tinted dark enough to obscure them. He also prayed Dylan, already squirming and agitated, would remain silent. Owen stroked the baby's cheek, willing him to go to sleep.

Holding his breath, he listened as Diego lowered the driver's side window and said, "Hello, sir—I noticed you were following me. Is there anything I can help you with?"

The cycle operator's voice sounded confused, almost embarrassed. "I got a description of some folks who may have grabbed my kid. Similar vehicle."

"Well, is this not a common-looking kind? Sorry for your loss, but maybe you should be back in town working with the police, instead of chasing folks into the woods on your own."

The operator, presumably Slate Singer, did not reply for several seconds. Then he said, "Yeah, okay. Sorry for the mix-up."

Without warning, Dylan lifted his head clear from Sofia's chest and uttered a squeal of displeasure.

Slate's voice cried, "That's him! You won't get away with this! The authorities are on their way! If you've harmed him, you're dead!"

Instantly, Diego leaped from the vehicle, opening the door into Slate, knocking him off balance.

Owen lurched from the backseat and joined Rojas. Both men had their weapons out, MacIntyre's arms were braced statue-stiff as he kept his pistol trained on Slate.

Owen thundered, "If you take one step nearer to my wife and son, I'll drop you!"

Slate looked angry and appalled. "*Your* son? What the fuck are you talking about?"

"You know damn well what I'm talking about! Singer stalked me and my family, then sent his agents in the Texas CPS to take him! I have copies of all the documents, I know every trick he pulled!"

Slate grew even paler, his jaw worked. He stuttered, "That's…that's crazy! You're crazy!"

"You know it's not crazy! You live with him, don't tell me you have no idea what that fucked-up bastard is capable of!"

The look of betrayed horror dawning on the man's face was all MacIntyre needed to make his next move. He nodded to Diego, who stepped forward, pistol leveled towards Slate. The guard produced a heavy zip tie from his jacket.

"Hey—!" Slate's protests were half-hearted and weak. Rojas pulled him like a beaten dog to the side of the road and forced him to stand with his back to a nearby sapling, fastening his arms behind him around the trunk.

MacIntyre collected a large rock and advanced on the hovercycle. As he pounded the stone into the craft's controls, he heard Slate shrieking behind him, "What the fuck are you doing? I just got that back from the mechanic! Stop it—!"

Dropping the stone, MacIntyre switched his weapon back to his right hand and approached the captive with an intentionally menacing pose. White with terror, Slate babbled, "Keep away! I mean it—whoever you are, keep away!"

"Be quiet! You're lucky you're only a stupid chump, getting off with just a few minutes' discomfort. When Singer shows up, tell him that if he follows us, he'll regret it."

"Tell him yourself! I'm not kidding, I called him as I was following you! He'll be here any moment—with back-up!"

"We'll be gone by then—," Owen began, but his boast was shattered by the sound of tires crunching on gravel. A dark-gray car with a solitary occupant rapidly drove up the track towards them and came to a stop.

MacIntyre pressed his pistol into Slate's temple and murmured to Diego, "*The man in the car—be ready to stop him.*"

Rojas replied with an almost imperceptible nod and they watched as Hayden Singer, with controlled, predatory movements, exited the car. With a pistol in his hand, he wordlessly faced the fugitives. For a long moment, the air between them was acrid with tension.

An icy smile crept across Singer's face as he finally addressed MacIntyre. "Welcome back. You can't possibly escape, so put that gun down and let's wrap this up without anyone getting hurt."

He moved as if to step further from the car, halting as MacIntyre commanded, "Not one step nearer! I'll sear his head off!"

"No, you won't."

Singer's gaze suddenly flicked away from MacIntyre. Sofia had opened the vehicle door and revealed herself, with Dylan on her lap. Her face was frozen in a mask of both fear and detestation, nostrils flared, furious eyes boring into the silver-haired man.

"Don't let leave the car," Owen warned her. "Don't say anything, for God's sake, don't leave the car—!"

Singer said, "My poor little boy! He must be terrified. Please—give him back and we'll pretend this never happened." His voice seemed unnaturally loud, and an unnerving, feverish intensity glinted in his eyes.

Owen spat through his teeth, "You despicable, lying piece of shit—!"

He swung his pistol from Slate's temple. Two energy bolts flashed, one each from Owen's and Diego's weapons. A horrific, agonized shriek rang through the air and Singer crumpled beside his vehicle; a sickening *thunk* sounded as his skull impacted against a large, rough stone on the edge of the road.

Against the backdrop of Slate's hysterical profanity, Owen urged Diego, "Quick—destroy the vehicle control panel, get his phone, keys and gun!"

To Slate, he snapped, "Hey, pal—shut the fuck up, will you? Just sit tight, and someone will be along to find you."

As Slate clamped his trembling mouth closed, MacIntyre searched through the man's pockets, collecting his personal items.

"Nice shirt," he growled, snatching a videoskin from the breast pocket of a deep blue-gray, silken garment that looked familiar to him from his own closet.

Following the sounds of destruction, he saw Rojas emerge from Singer's vehicle and cast aside a large chunk of basalt. After slamming the car door shut, he ran to Owen, handed him the spoils and they returned to their own car. Sofia regarded them with a face that was all the more deathly pale in contrast to her uneven halo of unnaturally black hair.

Hurling himself into the seat beside her, Owen pulled a cable from his pack. Fingers shaking, he plugged one end into his own videoskin, the other into Singer's device, praying the phone was still unlocked from the last time it was used. With a gratified thrill, he watched as the contents of the phone began transferring to his device. When he had all the data, he then sent a signal that killed the device's tracking app.

Meanwhile, Rojas engaged the controls, spun the car around in a tight u-turn and drove down the track.

As they passed Singer's body sprawled on the side of the road, Sofia whispered to Owen, "Is he dead?"

"That's the general idea."

"Shouldn't you go back and make sure? If he survives—,"

"Then at least he's badly wounded," he said, agitated and breathless. His heart hammered painfully in his chest, his body ran with nervous sweat. "We don't have time to check, there's others on the way!"

They peeled onto the main road and continued racing eastward, Diego pushing the car well over the speed limit.

"I just want him dead," she moaned as she huddled Dylan closer to her breast. Her voice rose and there was a wild look in her eye. "I don't want him following us. Or thinking about us. I can't stand the idea of us being in his mind."

"Me, neither." Owen squeezed her arm as he forced his voice to take on a semblance of confidence. "But for now, let's worry about getting as far away from here, as fast as possible."

CHAPTER
FIFTY-FOUR

THE WORLD LURCHED VIOLENTLY for a moment, a moment both fleeting and eternal. A split second later, the shudder from the heavy impact dissipated. Disoriented, Owen gasped, "Everyone okay?"

Beside him, Sofia groaned in the affirmative; she'd struck the side of her head against the back of the driver's seat as her body curved protectively over Dylan, where he was now secured against her in a soft fabric infant carrier.

Diego's inarticulate grunt was muffled by the cushion of the deployed airbag.

Rojas had tackled the narrow, winding road with far too much aggression, abruptly losing control when he swerved to avoid a patch of small fallen rocks spilling across the poorly maintained road.

Springing to action, MacIntyre urged, "Everyone out—!"

They struggled to extricate themselves from the damaged shell of the small rental car, kicking and shoving at the crooked doors until these popped open. They then huddled on the road's narrow shoulder, evaluating the situation. The vehicle was perched on the edge of a ravine, the left fender and a portion of the engine block crumpled against the immobile trunk of a majestic cedar.

"Damn, that was close!" Owen leaned back in through the rear door and began retrieving their travel packs. "Diego, I don't think we had anything in the trunk, but check it anyway!"

When their scant belongings were secured, MacIntyre turned to Rojas, ordering, "We have to hide this quickly—help me push it off the edge!"

Still trembling from the effects of the collision, the guard nodded. Both men heaved and strained against the car, shoving it away from the tree and closer to the edge of the ravine. It soon hit another obstacle and refused to budge.

"Tire is blocked…by a rock," wheezed Owen after several tense moments.

Searching among the bracken, Rojas caught up a sturdy fallen branch and crouched to one side of the tire, calling, "Señor, find a big stone—!"

"Got it!" MacIntyre located a promising rock and quickly dug away the soil at its base. When it was free, he rolled it beneath the car.

Angling the branch into position below the axle and beside the obstruction, Diego used the new stone as a fulcrum. Owen returned to the rear of the car, and continued trying to rock it free.

Sofia stood anxiously on the margin of the road. She hadn't uttered a word, and the part of Owen's mind that could be spared, wondered if she was in shock. He dismissed this concern when he saw, from the way she repeatedly glanced down the road, that she was terrified someone would be along any second. Which was their most immediate concern, so he was glad she was alert.

Growing desperate, MacIntyre redoubled his efforts, but the job was further complicated by the fact he was in danger of losing his footing should the car shift suddenly.

"It's loosening…," gasped Diego after a few tense moments. He stood up, breaths coming in huge, ragged chunks. Joining Owen at the rear, the men stood shoulder to shoulder and braced their hands against the chassis.

Rojas said, "*Uno, dos, tres*…!"

There was a loud rustling sound as, after their final coordinated, monumental heave, the car tipped closer to the edge. It hung a moment, then plunged down through the bracken. Small shrubs cracked and rustled beneath as it lurched downward. About ten yards from the top, it landed with a momentous *thud* against another tree.

As the men struggled to catch their breath, Sofia gripped Owen's arm. "I hear a car coming!"

"Get down!" MacIntyre motioned everyone off the side of the road, where they scrambled a few feet into the undergrowth and crouched among the rusty shafts of sword ferns, the glossy-leaved *salal* shrubs and prickly Oregon grape.

He was thankful the light was failing fast; perhaps whoever was approaching wouldn't notice the fresh impact damage on the big tree. If they were just passersby, they'd be unlikely to investigate. But if it was Singer's men, they'd be on alert for exactly that kind of sign.

As the vehicle droned steadily nearer, Owen relaxed somewhat when he decided it was an old truck, not a newer police cruiser. It slowed to maneuver around the rockfall, then swished and rattled past them. The woods again grew silent.

MacIntyre rubbed Sofia's arm. "Thanks for being on guard. We don't want to be seen by anyone now, not even the average citizen."

She nodded weakly. The side of her face was still red from the impact of the seat, but there were no cuts.

He asked, "You okay?"

All three climbed to their feet. Sofia busied herself adjusting the straps on the baby's carrier.

Hands and voice shaking, she said, "Not sure, but I guess I'm fine. What's next?"

Owen turned to Rojas. "First, we shave and change out of these shirts. In case we do run into anyone, we need to look as different as possible from the nurse's description."

"Sí, señor."

When they'd done what they could to alter their appearances, MacIntyre stepped away from the others and tried to place a call via satellite phone. He was disappointed but not surprised that he couldn't establish a connection. Despite the advantages of his visor, without a clear comms line, he felt blind and helpless.

Maybe it's time to nudge Ellie, he thought with reluctance. *This is a good place to test her 'guardian angel' capabilities.*

Walking a little further along the shoulder of the road, he calmed his inner turmoil and formed a concise question, aimed solely at the girl's awareness. He imposed his view of their current location on a bare-bones, imaginary map. He had not practiced this skill much, so he was gratified when, after a moment, he sensed the girl's response touching his own mind.

He was answered with the distinct impression that the few remaining U.S. Quasar satellites over Pacifica had just been deactivated according to President

Chakrabarti's orders, but not destroyed. Ellie had no estimate for when service might be restored.

He returned a sense of anger and disappointment, and the questions: *why don't they shoot down the Mozi? What's the point of disrupting comms for the citizens?*

Ellie sent back an apologetic sense of having no further intel.

He asked, *Have you or your dad found anyone who can patch in my phone to the U.S. military comms satellite?*

No, sorry.

MacIntyre asked, *Okay—I gave you contact info for a man named Reed—can you raise him for me on his burner?*

He stood tensely, awaiting her update and listening for sounds of approaching traffic. The forest was ominously quiet, and the light was failing fast.

After a minute, she replied, *I'm sorry, I can't reach him. I guess his phone is out of range.*

Okay, I'll try later. Stay around, will you?

She replied with an eager affirmation.

Ending the communication, he withdrew the burner phone from his pack, confirming with disappointment the 'no signal' icon. *I'll try again at the top of the next ridge,* he thought.

He turned his attention back to Sofia as she stood nearby with her arms wrapped around Dylan. She still looked anxious, but also alert and ready for the next phase of their journey. For a moment, the responsibility he bore of somehow guiding them all through this treacherous woodland and back home, struck him like a blow.

Don't think about what's at stake, he told himself sternly. *Just keep moving.*

He consulted his pre-loaded internal map, considering the implications of the data before rejoining the others. He announced, "Looks like our other car is less than five miles away—as the crow flies."

Rojas's brow wrinkled in puzzlement at this expression.

Sofia snorted, "Okay, Icarus—I forgot to pack my wings. So what does that mean for us?"

"It means a hike over broken terrain through thick woods, and climbing up and down two steep ridges." Owen heaved the straps of his travel bag over his shoulders. "In the pitch dark," he concluded with a grim smile.

Sofia's face fell, but she kept her tone calm as she asked, "What about staying on the road?"

He sighed with a shake of his head. "If we follow this road, it's a walk of over eight miles. Sure, it's much easier going, but there's a huge risk we'd be seen by anyone coming along. And it's where the authorities will start looking. Diego, what do you think?"

He kept his tone light and easy: this was not the time to express his profound disappointment with Rojas' screw-ups, and besides, he sincerely wanted the man's opinion.

The guard's dazed, hang-dog look melted as he considered MacIntyre's question. He looked back down the ribbon of pot-holed asphalt curving away into the murk.

"Walking through the forest will be hard, but I agree, señor—it is best to not be seen." He concluded with a shrug. "This way, we disappear into the trees and cannot be followed."

"Exactly."

Hanging back, Sofia's face looked markedly thin and drawn in the advancing dusk. "But no matter which way we take, aren't we going to miss our flight back?"

Owen grinned. "That's the plan. If they have any sense, they'll check at the airport right away, and converge there to wait for us. By the time they realize we aren't coming, we'll be over the eastern border."

She looked a bit overwhelmed at this information. "Isn't there any way at all for you to monitor communications to find every place their troopers are searching?"

Owen shook his head. "No, sorry."

Extending his hand to Sofia to help her down the slope, he then began to cautiously forge a path a few steps ahead of her through the vegetation. He added, "But even though I hope they concentrate on the airport, we have to assume they're everywhere else, too."

Beneath the heavy canopy of trees, the last shafts of sunset disappeared and twilight threw its blanket of gloom over the travelers faster than expected. Without a trail, progress was exceedingly slow and treacherous. It took perhaps ten minutes to reach the bottom of the ravine; the ascent up the opposite side was far slower.

For nearly thirty minutes, the only sounds were of thrashing branches being pushed aside, clumsy footsteps slipping on the steep slope, and anxious, labored breathing. The latter was intermittently seasoned with mild expletives.

When they reached the top and rested for some moments, Owen held his hand up for silence, scanning the woods behind and around them, alert for the slightest motion, or shadowy heat impression. He saw nothing.

He signaled for them to continue. "Sorry, I thought there was something behind us. Guess it was my imagination."

"Señor, what about snakes?" asked Rojas, as they resumed stumbling through nearly waist-deep bracken and grasping ivy. Soon they found themselves on an extensive portion of almost level ground, a relief following the recent scramble up the hillside.

With an effort at an easy laugh, Sofia answered the guard before Owen could. "Don't worry, there's no dangerous snakes around here. In fact, there's not many creatures at all in these woods."

Even in the weak light, Rojas' look of misgiving was palpable. He and Owen trained their powerful flashlights low to the ground just before their feet, revealing fragmented glimpses of tangled underbrush, fallen logs and lumpy ground beneath a thick layer of briars, needles and leaf-litter.

Dylan now slept in trusting oblivion, held against Sofia's heart by the sturdy infant carrier.

After another half-hour of frustratingly slow progress, they took another break. As Sofia sank with gratitude onto a fallen log cushioned with springy moss, Owen consulted his internal map. Without internet or satellite connection, there was no way to determine how far off their route they were inevitably drifting.

He thought glumly, *Maybe just keeping track of the number of ravines we pass through will be enough to guide us.*

Wondering if they were at a high enough point for his burner phone to get a signal, he opened and read the screen. At the moment, there was a faint signal. Quickly placing a call, he waited anxiously for it to be picked up. There was no answer, so he instead composed a detailed text describing their situation, hoping against hope it would be read soon. He had to trust that the contact on the other end was expecting to hear updates from either him or Ellie, and would thus check his messages frequently.

"Who are you calling?" asked Sofia, her weariness falling away in a rush of hope.

"Just a long shot," said Owen briefly. He put the phone away and took out his water bottle, holding it toward her. "Need any?"

She took a few swallows and handed it back. He turned to Diego, who shook his head and drew his own bottle out of his pack.

Replacing his own, MacIntyre said to Sofia. "Ready to go? Let me carry Dylan for a while. I can see my footing better than you can, and you'll be able to move faster."

She looked reluctant for only a moment, then slid out from the carrier and helped Owen into the contraption. Dylan slept blissfully through the exchange.

As soon as she was free, Sofia said apologetically, "Give me a flashlight and wait for me." The beam shifted and shook as she made her way unsteadily into some denser brush several yards away, seeking a place to relieve herself.

Owen turned to Rojas. "We need to get to the next side road in an hour or less. Communications are spotty, and I might not be able to contact him again about any more changes in our timeline."

Rojas nodded.

Sofia crashed her way back to them, muttering, "That was a lot harder than I remembered from camping. And I don't want to hear you guys bragging about how easy it is for you to pee against a tree trunk."

Owen grinned. "I'm sure you did great."

Rojas looked startled. "Camping? Señor, you were happy to sleep out here in this cold, this wetness?"

MacIntyre laughed. "This is actually quite mild and dry. You should be here in November."

"No, thanks, señor."

Owen turned to Sofia. "Everything should be smooth sailing from now on. Except for the river."

Dismay shot across her face. "River?"

"More of a tiny creek, actually. One of the forks feeding into the Klatskanine."

"I don't suppose there's a bridge?"

"Only where the road crosses."

She sighed. "Of course. But how far?"

"Other side of this ridge, and it marks the half-way point to the road."

She rubbed her temples. "Okay, sure."

Noting the quaver in her voice, Owen was concerned about how exhausted and grim she seemed. But there was nothing he could do about it. They had no choice now but to forge ahead without over-thinking everything.

He announced briskly, "Well, it's time to get going."

Diego said, "Excuse me a moment, señor," and went back through the underbrush to seek a more private stand of trees.

Once he was out of earshot, Sofia asked softly, "Are you still mad at me?"

Owen lifted a shoulder. "There's no point, what's done is done. But when we get home, I'm having a serious talk with Rojas—about who calls the shots in our business relationship."

"Don't be so hard on him. He feels terrible about this whole thing." She smiled wanly. "But I'm glad to hear you talk like we're really going to get home."

He drew closer and stroked her head, pulling a small twig from her tangled hair, still unsure how he felt about its new look. He admitted it was pleasingly silky. "Actually, let's not even think that far ahead. Just take it one minute at a time—,"

The watchful dark of the forest was shattered by the sound of a man screaming in terror and pain, underlain by the deep vibrations of a powerful, inhuman growl.

"My God—Rojas!"

Without thinking, Owen leaped away from Sofia and charged toward the hideous noises. Cradling Dylan closer to himself, he fumbled his pistol out of his pocket. Twisting his body to turn the infant away from the danger, he aimed at the massive, heavily muscled feline shape that had latched onto the guard, its huge teeth sunk into the side of his skull, partially embedded in his AR glasses. Like an unstoppable machine, the puma's powerful forelimbs tightly engulfed the man's torso.

Focused on the action before him, Owen was less aware of Sofia's distraught screams from behind. At the sudden burst of noise and confusion, Dylan awoke and added his noise to the mix. Owen tuned him out.

With the huge cat's head so close to Rojas' own, and with both figures locked together in a thrashing, chaotic dance, MacIntyre hesitated to fire. But the hunter was intent on rending its prey; MacIntyre realized he could step right up and fire point-blank.

He did so; the creature responded with a strangled yelp, followed by a determined, vibrating growl as the beast redoubled its grip.

Firing again, this time Owen aimed straight into its ribcage; the cougar's hold at last weakened, then its tawny body slumped and fell away into the thick bracken at the men's feet.

Replacing his pistol, Owen caught Diego clumsily under one arm and guided him to the ground, then he fumbled his backpack out from under the straps of the infant carrier. He extracted his first aid kit and then surveyed the guard's face. His glasses were broken in two, held together by a damaged tendon of exposed wiring.

"*Que diablo puma,*" whispered Rojas tremblingly.

"Sí, they're all devils when they're hunting," said Owen, raising his voice over the baby's howls. He eased the broken security glasses off the man's blood-sheeted face and saw the dented housing. "But damn, these saved your eye! Lucky you won't end up like me!"

Diego's shaky laugh ended in a groan and he sank back further against a fallen log. Sofia hovered nearby, her eyes fastened on the prone cougar. "Are you sure it's dead? Give me Dylan!"

"In a moment—,"

MacIntyre glanced at the char marks and the small open wound leading directly into the cat's viscera. It wasn't breathing; the air was foul with the scent of burned flesh and fur.

"Yeah, it's dead, we're perfectly safe now," said Owen, unfastening the carrier and surrendering Dylan, who promptly stopped crying.

He resumed examining Diego's wounds, mopping away the blood, scanning the damage with his visor. On the left side were deep, ragged punctures in the man's temple, upper cheek and above his ear, with corresponding smaller wounds on the side of his neck. The creature had not had time to tear away too much of the flesh.

Sofia waited anxiously to one side, trying to keep a steady beam of light on the men as MacIntyre shoved aside Diego's torn jacket and armor tunic to evaluate the savage claw marks on his front and back.

"These aren't too deep," Owen pronounced with relief. "Your head, though —scalp wounds bleed like hell, so it's hard to evaluate...but these need stitches."

Diego struggled to rise. "Not possible, señor...we must get moving soon!"

Owen gently pushed him back. "I know stitches aren't possible, but I'll do what I can. And you need to rest for a few minutes before we get going."

After applying bleed-stop, he continued to clean the ragged flaps of torn skin, then treated them with antibac spray and applied adhesive dressings. The bandages were strong enough to grasp and hold the edges of the wounds, although they weren't a long-term solution. There was no point in bringing up the possibility of whether the animal was rabid; for the time being, they'd have to assume its behavior was perfectly normal.

Clearing her throat, Sofia asked in a low voice, "Do you think there are any others nearby?"

Owen answered with a curt shake of his head. "They're solitary, each one usually has its own huge territory."

Her voice sank lower. "What about bears?"

"Don't think they hunt much after dark."

"What about—,"

Anticipating her question, he murmured, "I checked. There's been no credible reports of cultist activity in this part of the forest for a couple of years."

"Okay." She relaxed somewhat, but her fingers protectively encircled Dylan's fists as her anxious, hunted gaze continually raked the menacing shadows among the underbrush.

CHAPTER
FIFTY-FIVE

A WHITE SLASH of exposed skull leered shamefacedly out of the darkness; echoes of Layton Singer's dead gaze stared into Hayden's mind through a curtain of dark, sticky blood. Raucous, derisive laughter also jarred his aching head as he struggled through a crushing sense of dread, forcing himself to open his eyes.

The vision of death softened and disappeared, taking with it the mingled horror and triumph. The strange laughter faded into a soft rustle of wings, as the dim outline of a crow launched itself from a nearby branch and sailed past his disoriented sight, disappearing into the gloom.

With a deep, shuddering groan, Hayden rolled to one side and endured a wave of excruciating pain slamming through his body. Two, then three more black-feathered silhouettes passed over him, as the birds headed home for the evening. Hayden's finger's explored his temple and felt crusted blood. The pain from that wound competed with the hot, searing agony relentlessly drumming through his neck and upper chest.

Despite the heat in his flesh from the energy-beam wounds, the rest of his body was clammy and shivering. The pain triggered an unstoppable wave of nausea, but he beat down the urge to vomit. Staggering to his feet, he focused his foggy gaze on the car, recalling there was a first aid kit in there; after checking his pockets and looking around himself, he was furious to discover his keys were gone. The vehicle was locked; peering inside, he saw the control panel was smashed.

"Oh, my God! You're alive!"

From several yards up the road, Slate's wearied voice cracked the quiet of the forest with gratitude and relief.

Slate had slid down the tree trunk and now rested in an awkward sitting position. He looked uncomfortable, but Hayden made no move to free him. Nor did he answer and explain that he survived because he was wearing a lightweight, beam-diffusing armor plate, and his assailants were rushed.

Stupefied in his world of pain, Hayden fumbled his shirt open and glanced down towards his left shoulder. The agony spurred by the motion nearly caused him to faint again; gingerly touching the left side of his neck below his jaw, he felt a patch of oozing, open skin.

The other burn damage was localized at the top of his left pectoral, just above the top of the armor. Despite the raw, peeling red, he was pretty certain it was not serious. Yet the agony throbbed in time to his heartbeat, taunting him with the humiliation of having passed out in front of so many witnesses.

His face darkened as another wave of torment gripped him. Through his pain-clouded mind, thoughts raged: *He's going to regret he didn't finish me off. I don't care what the President said. I'm going to make him pay for this, the goddamn bastard—.*

But as the jumbled facts of what had happened fell back into place, his rage turned to confused distress.

"Are you okay?" Slate's hoarse calls finally penetrated Hayden's internal haze of disoriented wrath.

"Yes—,"

Fumbling for his videoskin, Hayden swore under his breath when he realized that was also missing. As his pulsating head cleared somewhat, he remembered that, as he had rushed after Slate, he had called in an Amber abduction alert based on the nurse's description of MacIntyre and the driver, but he hadn't known the make of the vehicle.

He also didn't know if Marino and the other guards were alive or dead, and had no idea how to deal with either scenario.

He stumbled to Slate's side, drew his knife and slit the zip tie. He demanded, "Quick—give me your phone!"

Slate fell to one side into the ferns and grass, sobbing, "Oh, God—my arms! They're totally dead—!" He shook uncontrollably. "They took my phone, too!"

"Fucking hell," gasped Hayden. He removed his own jacket, gritting his teeth against the pain of tugging the sleeve over his scorched flesh; he draped the garment over Slate as he then clumsily seated himself beside the other man. Pulling Slate upright, he began massaging his arms. "Here, let me help."

Slate hissed in discomfort as the feeling returned to his arms. Hayden gently stroked the side of the other's face, brushing away dirt and pine needles. "Did he do anything else to you?"

"No—," Slate gasped through chattering teeth.

"You're in shock. Try to calm down and think clearly."

"What…what…do we…we do now?"

"We get up and walk until we find a patrol. We'll be home before too long."

"You told him back-up would be here soon…!"

"That's not true, I was trying to rattle him."

"Then they'll be gone by the time you get help! They'll escape!"

"We'll see about that. Sooner or later, they'll regret this."

"They will, or we will?"

Hayden's eyes narrowed. "What do you mean by that?"

Words tumbled slowly from Slate's pale lips. "Ashtyn fussed so much because he wasn't used to formula. Because he hadn't been weaned…and he missed his mom…," Gaze lowered, he finished in a mumble, "The adoption papers you showed me…were they…accurate?"

Hayden thought a moment before answering, "Whatever that man told you, he was lying. He's a dangerous, deranged, sick individual. I had to let him go from the old Agency, and he hasn't gotten over the humiliation. But more than that, he's an enemy of Pacifica."

"Pacifica's enemy or *your* enemy? Maybe your…obsession? He's the same guy as in those pics, right?"

Hayden stiffened. "What do you mean? Which pics?"

Slate's eyes lifted, but roved about the scene, aimlessly touching the nearby vegetation. "The ones with his clothes, in the boxes you brought home. And in the game…you think he looks like me, right?" His voice trembled with hurt disappointment. "Or is it more important to you now that *I* look like *him*?"

Hayden prodded his mind for a convincing response. "No…no, that's… ridiculous. He's a criminal, I've been collecting evidence against him, he's been harassing me for months, making wild allegations. This kidnapping accusation is the most serious. He's crossed a line, and it's clear he has no problem with using violence to get what he wants."

It was a long time before Slate replied. "Really? Why did you confront him on your own? Why didn't you wait for back-up? Was it because you didn't want witnesses?"

Nostrils flared and face ashen, Hayden didn't answer. He struggled to focus on the unassailable data in Sofia's medical records. The data that eloquently and inarguably proved Ashtyn belonged to him, was as much his as any child who'd been ordered in a lab and implanted in a willing surrogate.

His voice stuttered, "It's in black and white...black and white...right there in all the documentation...the fucking documents say Ashtyn is one-hundred percent my property. Legally, morally. Emotionally."

Slate's ghostly face stared at him in the failing light. "Your...*property*?"

Feeling wretched, Hayden gasped, "No, no, no...I didn't mean that!" Grimacing as another wave of pain washed over him, he tightened his grip on Slate's arm. "Our son...he's our son!"

With his swollen, purplish hand, Slate rubbed his nose and then brushed his hair back from his face. He gazed down the gravel track to his damaged hovercycle.

"No, he's not."

"Well...what the hell are we supposed to do about all this?"

"Why not...why don't we just let them go, while we get on with our lives?"

Hayden's head sunk and his eyes closed as his thoughts reeled. Getting on with their lives and covering up the event was the easiest way out, but it meant he'd lost.

At last, his eyes flew open; he climbed to his feet and extended his hand to Slate with a shade of his former dominance. "Come on. We'll flag down a ride, then call in an updated description."

Slate refused to move. Raising his shaking voice, Singer pleaded, "Will you get up...!?"

Heaving a deep sigh, Slate grasped his partner's hand and was hauled to an unsteady standing position.

Hayden's wound was too hot and raw for him to take much notice of the advancing cold. His thoughts spun uselessly, as he saw in his mind's eye the destroyed computer back home, the ransacked desk drawers.

How could he collect the shattered remnants of his life, how could he rebuild without anyone in authority getting wind of this debacle? What was to be done about Lucy Pham, Marino and the others? Stifling any rumor of this serious security breach was paramount, but was it even possible?

Of course, he'd issue an updated description of the suspects, but it would be perfunctory. There would be no massive, country-wide manhunt to incite comment and inquiries. He couldn't afford it.

The men shambled unsteadily down the gravel track to the main road. As Hayden's soul writhed in the face of his failure, he stifled a frightened whimper. Hardly aware of Slate's distant presence, he became trapped in the growing darkness, as night's punishing shadows enclosed him like a locked closet door.

CHAPTER
FIFTY-SIX

AFTER NEARLY TEN minutes of rest and a few bites of an energy bar, Diego insisted he was ready to continue. MacIntyre helped him to his feet and the three resumed their frustratingly slow, irregular rhythm, picking their cautious yet rushed way through the hazardous gloom.

In the full dark of night, Owen's enhanced vision helped somewhat as he attempted to guide the others; with Rojas' AR unit damaged, the guard was reduced to using a mere flashlight, as was Sofia. They soon crossed the top of the ridge and began their painstaking descent down the far side. Even with the flashlight, Sofia continued to become entangled in vines and to trip over roots.

"I'd ask if we were lost," she grumbled, "But we'd have to know the way in order to lose it, wouldn't we?"

"Good call," snorted Owen. "But you'll take those words back before dawn."

"What are the chances we'll still be crashing around out here then?"

Owen said, "I don't know if you've noticed, but we're going downhill—which means we'll find the river any minute now."

Clearing his throat, Rojas said with effort, "Please, señora, don't worry. We aren't lost. Everything…everything will be fine."

The grateful smile she shot him was absorbed by the darkness. Soon her face fell again. "I'm just terrified we're going to come out on the road and find a bunch of officers waiting for us."

"Won't happen," said Owen with a lightness that belied his doubts. The task of keeping Sofia's spirits up was becoming more important by the mile. "They have no idea where we are."

"And another thing," she added. "I don't know if I can walk all the way back to the other car. I mean, I'll do my best. But I'm no Sacagawea."

Owen said earnestly, "You're doing great. Trust me."

"Honestly, I have no idea how she managed that," Sofia continued to mutter, exasperated. "Carrying a baby, all the way from North Dakota...,"

"When you have no option, you put one foot in front of the other and just keep going. She wasn't any braver than you. But do you want me to take him back for awhile?"

"No, thanks, I'm fine." Her gaze focused on him for a moment, he sensed her thankfulness and trust reaching toward him in the heavy dusk.

After perhaps a quarter of a mile, the gloom lightened somewhat where the trees were less crowded. They heard the gentle murmuring chatter of swift, shallow water gurgling over stones. They stumbled down the remainder of the ravine and emerged onto a narrow shore formed largely of treacherous tree roots and large, smooth rocks. The ambient light from the sky above the water seemed bright compared to the forest behind them.

They removed their boots and Diego volunteered to go first, testing for sudden drop-offs in the river bed. Sofia gripped Owen's arm but didn't utter more than a slight, suppressed gasp at the coldness of the water or the occasional sharpness of a stone beneath her bare feet.

"Be thankful it's not winter," said Owen. "And this summer's been dry, so the water's pretty low."

They soon reached the opposite bank, replaced their boots and plunged back into the darkness to climb up the next ridge.

Their progress up the slope over the next forty minutes was slow but sure. Above them, the stygian murk lightened once more as the vegetation thinned; an even line of dark, horizontal gray could be seen gleaming faintly behind the guardian shapes of the trees.

"Is that the road?" asked Sofia.

"Yes," replied Owen. "But it's not the one where we left the car."

"So which road is it?"

He ignored this question. "Don't rush out yet. Stay under the trees while I check it out."

Owen went ahead through the remaining few yards of underbrush. When he stepped out onto the asphalt, he scanned from side to side and saw no sign of non-vegetal life.

Pulling his phone out again, he re-dialed the last number and waited tensely. After two tones, it picked up and a voice demanded, "Hey—do you know where you are?"

Checking the map on his internal display, Owen replied, "I'm guessing we're about three quarters of a miles north, along California Barrel Road."

"Good, I'm real close. Stay there, I'll see you in about a minute."

Replacing the phone, MacIntyre trained his attention down the road, listening alertly; soon he heard a faint hum. Then headlights swept around the bend as a vehicle approached him. The driver pulled to a stop a few feet away; the craft was a large, late-model pickup with tinted windows and a camper shell. Silencing the engine, the driver exited and approached MacIntyre.

"That you, Mr. Lewis?"

"Hey, Mr. Reed! Delighted to see you again."

They shook hands; in the gloom, the illicit gunsmith's white grin shone brightly within his lean, black face. "You sure picked a lousy time to visit our shiny new nation of Pacifica."

"Yeah, the tourist brochures oversold it."

"Ain't that the truth! So—I understand you have some valuable packages for me?"

"Yes, but not here with me. We need a ride to where they were left."

"'We'?"

Turning, MacIntyre made a broad overhead wave towards the figures waiting under the eaves of the forest. As they stepped nearer, Owen caught Sofia's arm and drew her to his side, then ran his free hand over Dylan's head.

"My son. Singer took him. So I got him back." He gestured to Rojas and then tightened his grip on Sofia's hand. "*We* got him back."

Reed stared as he uttered a low whistle. "Damn—the Chief Enforcer's not going to be happy about that."

"Not sure he's in a position to care anymore. So he can suck—," abruptly, Owen altered his phraseology on a dime. "He can suck it up."

Reed grinned. Then catching sight of Rojas' damaged face, he stepped closer. "Hey, man—that's some serious shit! What happened?"

"Puma," mumbled the bodyguard.

"For real? That needs some serious medical attention—,"

"Yes, but we've got to keep moving now," Owen interrupted. "Listen, I'm not asking you to put your life on the line for my family for the heck of it. In addition to the shipment of phones I mentioned before, I've got some Agency-issue firearms, videoskins, IDs and keycards. Including Singer's."

Reed's sketchy brows shot skyward. "Quite the treasure-trove of data. Okay—show me where you need to go."

Owen accompanied Reed back to the truck and consulted a worn and dirty paper map the man spread on the passenger seat.

"Right here," said MacIntyre confidently, placing his finger square on a faded bit of green print.

Reed scanned the route. "I heard an Amber alert on the radio with a general description of you, so we might run into heightened patrols, even out here. You prepared for some discomfort?"

"What do you mean?"

"Check this out—," Reed led him to the rear of the truck, then flipped up the hatch of the camper shell. Reaching into the space, he pushed aside some bins of odds and ends and some blankets. He hooked his fingers into a hidden latch and tugged. The entire floor of the camper lifted to reveal the actual truck bed beneath.

He said, "It'll be snug, but I think you'll all fit. And it's lined with scan-block."

Sofia and Diego had now joined them and were looking into the truck.

With a fretful tone, Sofia asked, "How long do you think we'll have to be in there?"

"Probably less than half an hour," said Reed. "But it might seem longer from your perspective."

"You're going to be fine," Owen said to her soothingly. "Just don't think too far ahead. Remember—one minute at a time."

The blankets were quickly spread in the bottom of the compartment for a little extra comfort, then they removed their packs and Sofia lifted Dylan out of the front carrier.

"He's waking up," she announced. "He might make noise."

"We'll just have to see that he doesn't," said Owen, holding the baby for her as she clambered over the end of the truck and lay down. Owen handed Dylan in, then climbed in beside her, followed by Rojas and their packs. It was tight and suffocatingly uncomfortable. And when the false bottom was replaced above them, they were sealed in a tomb-like pitch blackness.

Then came the noises of a door closing and a motor starting, sounding louder than expected through the uninsulated metal walls of the small space. On Owen's left, he was aware of waves of stoically silent displeasure coming off Rojas' unseen but very present form, wedged against him.

Turning to his right, Owen engaged his night vision, and saw that Dylan was wide awake and staring into the blackness—bright-eyed but obviously confused. And about to start crying again.

"You'd better nurse him," he advised Sofia.

"Okay, sure."

After several moments of rustling in the claustrophobia-inducing dark, the baby grew content. Soon there was nothing but the sounds of tense breathing and the hum of tires over the asphalt. The space quickly grew warm and stuffy with their body heat and nervous sweat. It was also clear Dylan's diaper needed to be changed. Counting the minutes since Reed had given them an estimate, MacIntyre grew more anxious as they came nearer their destination.

"About ten more minutes," he whispered. He felt for and took Sofia's hand. He was aware of her racing pulse. On his left, Rojas seemed to be holding his breath while sinking into a silent trance.

As the truck picked up speed, the fugitives began to breathe more easily.

Owen whispered into the dark, "We're almost there."

Sofia squeezed his hand; he was gratified to feel it was the pressure of confidence, not the terror-stiffened death grip she'd employed earlier.

Smiling at her through the dark, he whispered, "You're doing wonderfully."

"Thanks," she whispered back.

CHAPTER
FIFTY-SEVEN

THE GENTLE, reassuring thrumming of the motor, vibrating through the body of the truck, was almost comforting. But in Sofia's tense state, she was aware of any slight imperfection in the surface beneath the tires. When they hit yet another pothole and were jarred roughly to one side, she remembered how bad the roads were here; highway maintenance was clearly not any more of a priority for the new regime than it had been for the old.

Her heartbeat clamored less stridently in her ears as they sped ever further into the night. In the dark, she ran her fingers through Dylan's sticky hair and over his cheek muscles. Businesslike, he continued to nurse, even as he was falling asleep.

She whispered to Owen, "Now how much longer?"

"I don't know…maybe five minutes."

She trusted him, believed they would soon be back to where the other car was hidden, deep in the forest. She could not think past that point, to the next hazardous leg of their journey, could only focus on the solidity of the vehicle waiting for them in the dark beneath the trees. Whenever the truck took a sharp turn, she jostled either against the unforgiving metal wall of the compartment, or else into the comforting mass of Owen's body.

After several tense minutes, they felt the truck turn to the right and leave the pavement. Soon they were bumping over an uneven, gravelly surface for several hundred yards.

"Is this it?" she whispered.

"Don't know—hope so," answered Owen tersely. "Feels too soon, but he's driving fast—,"

The vehicle slammed to a stop with an abrupt urgency that sent her heart back into her throat.

Something was wrong.

They heard voices shouting, drawing closer from all sides in the blackness. There were thumps and cries; she heard a door slam and realized that Reed had left the controls. She thought he was yelling; he sounded upset, but she couldn't make out his words. What was clear was that the authorities had caught them.

On each side of her, she sensed Owen and Diego tense up.

"Oh, *shit*," hissed Owen through his teeth. He shifted and awkwardly tugged his pistol from his jacket.

Without warning, they heard the back hatch of the vehicle thrust open, quickly followed by sounds of violent ransacking just above their heads. Then the false bottom was lifted up and a wave of fresh night air assaulted the fugitives. Rough hands prodded and poked them, as distorted, nightmarish shapes loomed out of the blackness.

Sofia's ankle was roughly grasped; she savagely kicked herself free. Instantly, both Owen and Diego jumped upright, firing shots at their attackers.

For a moment, the two men formed a shield between her, the baby and the crowd. She heard an angry scream and realized someone was hit by an energy pulse; there followed a disorienting thrashing of bodies, and more shrieks.

There were too many assailants to keep at bay. Owen, Diego and Reed were instantly swarmed and overwhelmed by hulking figures that seemed to no longer fear being shot. The strange forms did not resemble Agency troopers. The guns were successfully wrested from the mens' hands. Sofia saw Rojas aim a hefty punch at the jaw of the attacker nearest him, then the guard disappeared behind a seething wall of bodies.

"No—stop! Please—*stop!*" Sofia's shrill, terrified cries echoed through the woods, but were met with inhuman grunts and jeers. She was dragged without ceremony over the back end of the pickup; she fought to keep Dylan tight in her arms and stood crouching over him, shielding him from the chaos. By now, he was awake and screaming; she bounced him and spoke in a calm tone, soothing him with a weak façade of serenity.

Between the shifting bodies of their attackers, she caught horrifying glimpses of the three men, sprawled face-down on the ground nearby, their arms jerked behind them while being secured tightly with rough strips of cloth or leather. Their captors then resumed pawing through the vehicle, snatching up anything of value.

Beneath the weak starlight, the dim, confusing shapes pressing all around her seemed confusedly furry, almost animalistic. The beings communicated among themselves in low grunts or sharp barks and yips. After a moment's confusion, she recognized they were not wearing much actual fur, but were instead clad mainly in torn fabric, which was covered with layers and layers of moss and crude, fluttering leaves cut from various materials. It was an extremely effective, viscerally disconcerting camouflage.

With a plunge of sheer horror, Sofia realized she was living in one of her worst nightmares; these people were probably adherents to one of the more advanced mushroom cults rumored to hold sway over large swaths of the forest. She struggled to keep calm. Panicking now wouldn't help.

Their attackers had seized the flashlights; Sofia shrank away as hands clutched and held her; bright, searching beams played over her face, blinding her. Her legs felt like water, but she remained upright. Her assigned captor shoved her forward and she wailed, "Owen—they're taking me with them—what do I *do?*"

His disjointed voice straggled through the crowd of grunting, shoving forms: "It's alright—stay calm! I'm…coming… too…!"

Flashlight beams swept brokenly over the group and she caught sight of Owen, Reed and Diego corralled between the threatening, shaggy figures.

The three men were now standing upright and were also being herded forward into the blackness, deep into the forest. She felt a glimmer of relief; at least it seemed they would all be kept together for a while.

They commenced stumbling over tree trunks and fallen branches, as menacing forms marched on all sides. Sofia moved gracelessly, her arms determinedly enclosing Dylan.

The trip seemed to take an eternity. She expected at any moment to fall headlong or at least twist her ankle. Whenever she stumbled, her guard grabbed her arm and dragged her forward in a harsh, relentless grip.

The mysterious people continued to occasionally vocalize and mutter to each other. Sofia sensed they were excited and happy to have captives. Her spirits rose a little as she thought perhaps they were not an immediate threat, but she could still not let her guard down. She knew nothing about the customs and practices of these local cults; she had no idea if they regarded their captives as potential recruits or sacrifices. Or sustenance.

Or perhaps as hostages to be exchanged for rewards from the authorities. Her blood ran cold; she could not decide which was worse—being sacrificed to a demonic drug god, or being delivered into the State's hands. Surely Owen and Diego—and that man Reed—could think of a way out of this? Even if they hadn't planned for this particular contingency, they were resourceful, weren't they?

It was reassuring to know that Owen could at least see clearly through the black of their surroundings, and despite the communications difficulties, she trusted he had some other skills associated with the visor that she was unaware of. She prayed frantically for miraculous aid, her incoherent, terrified thoughts stumbling through her mind even as her feet tripped over unseen roots and stones.

After another twenty hellish minutes or so, she saw lights up ahead. The captives were shoved out from between the trees into a space overseen by the deep bowl of the summer sky, containing a few twinkling stars. Smaller than a meadow, the clearing was still large and dotted with rude hut-like structures, some built of cinder block or logs. Others were haphazard lean-tos loosely formed of scavenged beams and plywood, with a crazy-quilt of multi-colored tarps stretched over them.

The small village radiated a strangely cheerful, childlike energy, aided by the numerous lights. Lamps glowed in the windows, strings of colorful party bulbs decorated a few of the structures. The cultists presumably had access to batteries or good quality solar. Sofia did not hear a generator, and supposed that, even if they had one, it would be nearly impossible to get it refueled.

Their captors pulled off Owen's and Diego's jackets, exclaiming delightedly at the sight of the men's beam-repelling undershirts. The captives bond's were briefly freed as these garments were also stripped off and passed around the crowd with a wave of murmured awe.

Several men approached Sofia and began examining her more closely; when her own shiny tunic flashed in the torchlight, another chorus of delighted hoots echoed through the circle and hands clutched at her from all sides. In the disorienting chaos, she complied, offering one arm at a time to be stripped free of jacket and shirt, not resisting as the tunic was pulled over her head, only caring that she could somehow keep Dylan safely clutched in at least one arm during the frenzy.

Afterwards, she was dimly aware that her plain cloth shirt was draped back over her shoulders. She dazedly wrestled it on but forgot to fasten it when she was shoved to a sitting position near the center of the clearing. The ground here was nearly bare dirt, strewn with pine needles and many roots. Sitting cross-legged, Sofia struggled to give her aching arms a break by maneuvering Dylan into her lap. He started fussing again and she worked to shush him.

Rojas was on her left, Owen to her right, Reed on his far side. She kept glancing at Owen, trying to get his attention. After a moment, he shot her a tight but reassuring smile. This slight action was enough to send a bolt of confidence through her. Her trembling lessened and she grew more alert to her surroundings.

The guards loomed behind them, exuding an air of growing anticipation. In twos and threes, people emerged from the shabby dwellings. A few carried lanterns or flaming torches, and stood on the margins of the clearing. In the wavering light, Sofia studied the faces of these newcomers—men, women and even children—all clad in either normal but well-worn styles or else imaginative handmade creations, pieced together from ragged scraps she guessed were salvaged from garbage bins, or the refuse piles that bordered the city's open-air markets. Most of the garments were the color of dirt or rock, or shades of green that blended well with the shadows of the forest.

From the largest hut, a small man wearing a battered leather motorcycle jacket and sporting a headdress crafted of antlers from a yearling Black tailed deer, emerged. Accompanied by a torch-bearer, he advanced with menace towards the prisoners. Stopping before the captives, he tossed the trailing leather thongs of his headpiece over his shoulder in a dramatically careless gesture. At his signal, a shaggy guard stepped forward, handing him the seized weapons, the phones and ID discs.

Antler Man studied these a moment, then handed the guns back to the guard. Squatting down before the group, he stared into their faces, one at a time. He seemed in his late thirties, with bright gray eyes peering from his seamed brown skin. Sofia returned his gaze with an expression she hoped was neither craven or antagonistic.

The torchlight flickered over his slowly spreading grin and revealed the dark gaps of some missing teeth.

He said, "So, tell me—what y'all are doing here this far out in the woods on this fine evening?"

Reed cleared his throat and said evenly, "I was giving my friends a lift back to their car."

Beneath the leather strap that kept his antler crown in place, the man's brows twitched upward. "You often stuff your friends down in a hidey-hole with a bunch of junk atop of them when you taxi them around Mr.—?"

He glanced down at the ID discs in his hand, which had abbreviated bios stamped on the surfaces. Without an official security tablet, and without reliable internet, there was no way he could access their full identity pods. But he didn't seem to care.

"—Mr. Kurtis, I think that's you? That right?"

Reed nodded as he added, "Okay, look—you know things are a bit…challenging at the moment when it comes to traveling safely around the region. Cut us some slack."

Antler Man chuckled. "I only 'cut slack' when I'm sure it ain't gonna come whipping back to hit me on the ass, know what I mean?"

Reed smiled weakly. "Great plan."

The man turned to Owen. "And you, Mr. Lewis? You enjoying your visit to Pacifica?"

"Sure am, the natives are so friendly. And they say travel broadens the mind."

Sofia held her breath, hoping her husband's sardonic drawl wouldn't anger the man.

The interrogator's chuckle morphed into a hearty laugh. "You got that right, man. And some ways of traveling are more mind-broadening than others. Mind-blowing, in fact."

He looked down at the confiscated devices and zeroed in on the most impressive videoskin. He picked it up. "This one belongs to which of you?"

No one spoke. He insisted, "Who can unlock this? Nobody?"

Owen said, "That one's not going to work under current conditions…no satellite access, no reliable carriers."

The man grunted, then called over his shoulder to one of the boys crouched nearby. "Fetch Ezra."

The young boy dashed across the clearing and soon returned with a wiry, gnome-like individual who wore a crowded tool belt and a bursting pack over his shoulder.

Antler Man handed him the videoskin. "Can you unlock this?"

The newcomer snatched the device with his nimble, claw-like hands and powered it up. After the screen flicked to life, he rooted through his pack and took out a small black box with a small screen. He activated this and entered some codes. After a moment of staring intently at the videoskin, his dirty gray mustache lifted above his triumphant grin.

"I'm in—and *holy shit*—this belongs to Hayden Singer!"

With a low whistle, the man with the headdress snatched the device back as he shot a startled look at Owen. "Okay—how'd you 'acquire' this?"

Owen rolled a shoulder carelessly. "He wasn't using it, so I borrowed it off him."

The man's eyes narrowed as he considered this less than helpful answer. "Okay, mebbe we'll revisit that later." His leather jacket creaked as he turned and shuffled closer to Sofia. "And you, little lady. Brave of you to bring Baby all the way out here, even with the protection of your man and these other fine gentlemen." His sharp eyes flicked from Dylan to Rojas; it was clear he had doubts concerning the narratives told by the false IDs.

She swallowed and fought to speak. "Yes, well…I had no choice."

Frowning, the man thrust his face uncomfortably close. His eyes slowly raked the path of exposed skin between the unclosed edges of her shirt, focusing on her breasts where they nearly spilled from her bra. She pulled Dylan up over her chest and hugged him.

The man asked in a low tone, "You goin' with them willingly? Everything okay between y'all?"

"Yes, yes, it's fine," she stammered, "We're all together!"

"You want to tell me how y'all got that videoskin? Who's after you?"

She bit her lip and shook her head.

The man snorted and turned to Reed. "You say you're takin' 'em back to their car…would that be the dark blue Comet rental that was left a couple mile further up the road where my people found you?"

None of them answered. Then MacIntyre said boldly, "Yes, that's our car."

"Parked without permission, in our terry-*tory*," the man said. "But we ain't trashed it yet. Waitin' to see who came back for it. Waitin' to see if it was worth it. Will it be worth it?"

In the silence that followed this question, the torchbearers shifted about slightly. Sofia closed her eyes and prayed as she awaited some sort of response from the others.

She opened her eyes when she heard Reed say, "Guess that depends on your expectations, doesn't it?"

"Yeah—," Antlers straightened and stood upright. He put his hands on his hips as he continued to glare down at the captives. "But that ain't up to me. It's up to *them*."

That growled final pronoun sent a frisson of dread up Sofia's spine.

The man's grin faded and his tone grew solemn."So—pay attention. Y'all are in for the treat of a lifetime. You are about to have an audience with Foxy Turner *themselves*."

Glancing back at the people ringing the clearing, he uttered a sharp, animal-like cry of command and twitched his antlers towards the trees encompassing the village.

Sofia thought Owen grew even more tense and jerked his head up at the name 'Foxy Turner'; this caused a new lump of fear to rise in her throat. It was impossible for her to ask what he thought would happen next, if he had any information or insights about this particular cult.

She stared into the blackness, following the leader's gaze. After several tense moments, she saw a faint gleam of light wavering there, then glimpsed the outline of another, larger structure. It seemed a door was opened or a curtain drawn aside. More lights came toward them, and she noticed they were accompanied by a low, almost musical humming. Multi-colored lights, like racing fairies or whooshing comets, swirled about the advancing shape, a form with an unusual yet somehow familiar silhouette. As it grew more distinct, the lights resolved into a dancing halo of simple holiday bulbs.

The humming grew louder. Inches above the ground, the apparition floated ever closer. Ponderously, it entered the clearing, where the wavering torchlight at last allowed Sofia a clear look at what was looming before her.

Her mind could not quite process what her eyes saw; her stomach lurched, her lip ran with blood where she bit it to keep from screaming in uncontrolled horror.

CHAPTER
FIFTY-EIGHT

SOFIA BARELY REGISTERED that Owen tensely gasped, "*Chimera*," under his breath at the sight of the apparition. He added another word that sounded to her like "*Ardhanarishvara.*"

The being before them seemed melded onto a makeshift throne, which was in turn mounted on a small hover vehicle. Whether the craft was operated remotely by someone nearby or by the rider itself, was impossible to say. The floating platform came to rest near Antler Man, who knelt before it and bowed low, antlers pressing into the dirt.

Sofia could not tear her eyes away from the nightmare before her. From a basic human torso sprang an extra set of arms, while a third eye, an obvious electronic implant, glowed within its forehead. A zone bisected the person's center, from the middle of the skull down to its groin, dividing one half into a beige flesh-tone, which displayed a flabby, pendulous, female breast. The other half of the body, presenting a broader, more masculine appearance, was an uneven, speckled gray-blue. A loincloth of deep red, embellished with cheap, faintly gleaming spangles, hid the secret of the figure's ultimate gender.

A necklace of rubber snakes loosely encircled its neck and shoulders, which were grotesquely distorted where the extra arms burst forth from the tortured skeleton.

Sofia gazed with fascinated revulsion as both the dancing fairy lights and warm torchlight licked over the grotesque, twisted form. What frightened her most was the relatable expression in the normal eyes, the calm intelligence and serene curiosity shining through what was likely a prison of physical discomfort, if not outright agony.

Nauseated by the sight of the monstrosity floating before them, Sofia at last lowered her head and screwed her eyes shut.

From Owen's far side, she heard Reed mutter: "I think I know where this is going. Do you want me to volunteer—?"

Sofia's eyes flew open and she stared, disbelieving, at her husband as he replied under his breath, "No, let me. I know what to do."

She hissed at him, "What are you—?"

"*Shhh*," he cut her off, as the living idol made a labored, awkward movement with one of its extra limbs. It was gesturing towards the captives.

The guards prodded them and they scooted nearer and kneeled obediently. An ominous hush fell, and this seemed to draw Dylan's attention; he writhed and twisted, attracted by the colorful flashing lights and the ring of faces. For a moment, Sofia feared he'd scream when he saw the chimera. Instead, he gazed at the scene with mild curiosity, eyes growing round. Irrelevantly, she made note of how matted the dye was in his hair; she protectively clutched a few strands in her fingers.

When the apparition spoke, its voice was not deep or impressive. The import of the words came from their slowness, the way they trickled forth after much consideration.

"*You.*" The being's skeletal hand sought out and twitched towards Reed. "You are the one known as the slim rod that grows on the water's edge and bends in the wind. But you are also the 'shadow that spits fire', is this true?"

Sounding confused, almost fearful, Reed answered, "Yeah…yeah, that's me. I guess."

The creature acknowledged this with an inclination of its head. Despite the chintzy garishness of its adornments, it radiated a smoldering sense of majesty.

"Yes, we know you as well as you know us. Through whispers, through rumors among roots traveling through the earth. We know you are the one that crafts the weapons, the sharp scorpions that sting with light."

Sofia heard a grin in Reed's voice. "Oh, yeah, that's me for sure. Is that a good thing? Can I interest you in a volume discount?"

Antler Man stifled a snort but kept his eyes on the ground. The living idol made no reaction to this offer. Its gaze left Reed and traveled to Diego. It strained to lift another weak, trembling arm and singled out the bodyguard.

"You," it rumbled. "You are the wall that puts itself between harm and injury, between life and death, are you not?"

Rojas' broad face was a mask of bewilderment. He said doubtfully, "Sí, señor."

"You will not return the way you came," stated 'Foxy Turner' ominously. It gave a slow and deliberate blink. When its eyes reopened, they fell on Sofia. She held her breath.

"You are a doe flying through the woods with her fawn, pursued by... by...," The shadow of a frown ruffled the chimera's brow. "By *the dog*," it concluded harshly.

Sofia remembered once petting Greta at an Agency event. Now she had a mental picture of the German Shepherd's spirit entering into her Master as he continued to scent blindly through the darkness for the fugitives. But of course that couldn't happen—Singer was dead. But she replied with an almost imperceptible, terrified nod.

Then the idol turned its attention to Owen. "You are not the machine that sits in the shape of your skull. You are the wolf, the enemy of the dog. The wolf that killed the screaming cat that killed two of our family. Although you do not wish to do so, you have the power to walk on paths above these others', nearer my own realm. You will join me in the other place."

At these words, the being made a gesture and Antler Man climbed to his feet to step nearer and confer briefly with it. Then the intermediary signaled one of the people standing at attention in the shadows. This young man turned and disappeared obediently into a hut, to return a few moments later with a small clay vessel, which he offered to Antler Man.

Antlers stepped forward, removed the lid and showed the contents to Owen. Owen remained outwardly impassive as he studied what looked to Sofia to be a strong-smelling, goopy brown liquid.

"*Mushrooms?*" she whispered through her teeth with distaste. "Are they going to make you eat that? Don't! You could lose your mind—or—even *die!*"

"Been there, done that," he murmured, throwing her a crooked smile. "So don't worry."

The lab-created deity nodded towards the vessel. "That is the doorway to the place where we will go and speak further."

"I don't need it," announced Owen loudly. With his hands still strapped behind him, he lurched haphazardly to his feet and planted himself before the monster.

"Listen, I'm happy to meet you 'beyond', or wherever you want to go and have a private tête à tête, but I don't need to eat that stuff. I can get there a different way. My own way."

A mutter of confused disbelief passed throughout the assembly. The chimera studied him with a serene, inscrutable manner, then nodded and gestured for the intermediary to bring the vessel to it. It reached for this with its more functional arms, then lifted it to its mouth and drank.

After a few moments, its eyes blinked, then shut. It slumped forward, but was saved from falling by the straps connecting it to its throne. It began to tremble, trickles of sweat gleamed on its body.

Antler Man approached Owen and freed his arms. Wordlessly, he again offered the clay vessel, but Owen waved it away.

Sofia's gaze remained captivated by her husband where he stood upright and still, appearing even taller and stronger in the ever-shifting torchlight. His attention was locked on the bland countenance of the lump of distorted humanity sitting before him.

She could not tell if Owen had been bluffing when he said he didn't need any drugs to meet this creature in an alternate dimension. She knew he believed some of his past experiences had perhaps stimulated some intermittent psionic powers, but she was disturbed to think he would gamble their safety on the off-chance he might be able to do something now.

Or perhaps this was part of a delaying tactic, and somehow he, Diego and Reed had thrown together a rough plan without her noticing. She herself could not think of anything other than surviving each moment as it came, while perhaps ingratiating herself with these people. Unless their demands became too horrific.

Bit by bit, Owen's head bowed and he sank, resting his knees on the ground. Sitting back on his heels, with his elbows out, hands resting on his thighs, his attitude echoed a Samurai warrior. It was clear he was attempting to relax as much as possible under the circumstances, but other than that, she had no idea what was happening inside his mind.

The chimera's shaved skull lifted and its eyes flew open. A glassy, faraway look gleamed in its dark irises. It seemed unaware of its surroundings, it appeared to be looking and listening deep within.

The encircling crowd began to chant, "*Foxy Turner, Naranari,* walk the dark, walk the stars. *Foxy Turner, Naranari,* bring us truth."

The voices were joined by gentle drumming and musical tones, as a few villagers started tapping out tunes on overturned plastic buckets or else blowing notes on simple flutes. Scratchy but more sophisticated, pre-recorded melodies came from a speaker system in the largest hut.

Dylan was distracted by the music but was also growing tired. He began to push against Sofia while grunting. He repeatedly twisted towards Owen while holding out his arms. Sofia caught his hands and brought her lips to his ear, whispering with a forced smile, "Daddy's busy—look at this!"

She snatched up a twig from the ground beside her and held it just before him; he made an excited cooing sound and began gnawing on it.

She looked back at Owen; he was shivering and his bare torso glistened with perspiration. Each line and plane of his face and body were now strangely alert, yet also somehow softened by an inner submission. Whatever was transpiring between him and the surreal figure dominating the clearing, she couldn't begin to guess at.

The music grew more insistent, the chimera gave a little twitch; then its perverted body convulsed and writhed. The expression in its eyes grew more aware of its surroundings. The villagers stopped the music.

In a resonating croak, the being said, "Through water, blood and fire...I see fire... I see you passing through water, through blood, through black smoke of death into the dawn of life...," The voice trailed and jerked to a halt.

Owen remained motionless. The shifting lights reflected in his visor and on his sweaty brow were the only sign of life about him. His head sank even lower and with an abrupt convulsion, he collapsed and fell in the dirt.

Sofia shrieked; as the sound faded, there followed a moment of strained, watchful silence. Then Diego dove towards his employer's side, but with his arms still bound, could do nothing but glare at Antler Man.

The latter approached and put his fingers on Owen's neck, feeling for a pulse. He grunted, "It's okay—he's alive."

Groaning, Owen dragged himself to his hands and knees, retching. His last meal long since digested, only saliva and bile were available to trail from his gasping mouth into the dust.

His reaction elicited a murmur of approval from the watchers ringing the clearing. Antler Man helped him to his feet and clapped him approvingly on the back.

Shuddering, Owen turned to Sofia with a wan grin, sweat pouring off his brow and cheekbones. He choked, "I'm back...what happened while I was gone?"

" 'Gone'?" she echoed. "Nothing—it's only been a few minutes!"

He shook his head in confusion. The enthroned personage spoke again, this time stretching all its arms to both Owen and Sofia, pulling its twenty digits inward with fan-like, folding motions.

"Come before me."

Holding Dylan in one arm, Sofia reached for Owen; his hand engulfed hers. The prisoners took a few anxious steps closer and halted before the throne. Up close, the person was unimaginably more repulsive and tragically pathetic. It smelled appalling.

It looked from one to the other, without blinking, then said to Sofia, "You are not with the big man, the wall." It made a flicking motion towards Owen. "You are with *this* one, and each of you makes up the other's missing half. And he—," One of its long-nailed, spidery fingers pointed at Dylan, still contentedly gnawing on the twig. "—is the expression of the whole you have created with your bodies. Give him to me."

For a terrifying moment, Sofia wondered if they meant only to examine him more closely, or if they wanted him permanently.

Her voice scrambled in her dry throat, but she answered boldly, "He'll cry."

"What of that?"

"It's okay," came Owen's whisper. "Do what they say."

Trembling, Sofia lowered her child into the monstrosity's limbs and stood watching, holding her breath. Dylan was fascinated, and played with the mottled gray fingers for a moment before looking up. He and the chimera gazed at each other solemnly.

The idol inclined its head in a sedate, gracious arc as it then handed the baby back. They intoned, "A dead world awaits him. A graveyard of dreams, but dreams that many will not give up lightly."

Sofia could think of nothing to say to this, but held Dylan close and bowed with a respect she was surprised to feel for the figure.

Then she and Owen stepped back to wait as Antler Man moved in to once more consult with 'Foxy Turner'. After several tense minutes, he also bowed, then issued orders to a few villagers before returning to the captives. Behind him, attendants swarmed up to the idol and obligingly held a bucket, as it vomited up the hallucinogenic compound.

Antlers directed the guards to unbind Rojas and Reed.

With a look of subdued awe directed to Owen, the intermediary announced, "Gentlemen, seems we're 'bout to have a hot and heavy discussion about the terms of your release."

At this point, there was an unspoken shift in the overall mood, and in their status; they were no longer 'captives', but something closer to 'guests'. Overturned plastic crates and log sections were dragged or rolled forward and offered as seats. A few children passed among them with trays of food, mostly strips of dried elk, cups of cold nettle tea and a few plastic-wrapped, pre-made pastries, obvious delicacies.

The small girl presenting food to Sofia had a halo of unruly light hair and dark, beady eyes. She stood staring hungrily at Dylan, who stared back and then crowed with delight and hopped in his mother's arms. The girl gingerly reached out a short, dirty finger towards his head. Sofia smiled and nodded; the girl stroked his curls before scampering back to the older villagers.

Addressing Owen, Antlers said, "*They* wants you to give us directions to the cat's body. They wants the pelt."

"Sure—," Owen kneeled, smoothed out the dirt before him and began scratching out a diagram of the general location of where he had shot the cougar.

Behind him, the guards set down the previously inspected phones, discs and weapons. Then they tossed the contents of the traveler's bags, and of Reed's truck, onto the ground in a pile. Squatting, Antler Man began sorting the items into different categories. There was an excited chatter of voices among the crowd when they saw the tools, the personal grooming items and clothing.

Antler Man shooed them away. "Not for you," he said. "We ain't robbin' our guests. We's *nego-shee-atin'*."

He handed some clothing and the ID discs back to the guests, but was most interested in the pistols and the phones.

'Foxy Turner', surrounded by ministering acolytes, seemed to have lost interest in the proceedings. The hovering throne was soon accompanied back to the hut in the trees.

Sofia squirmed closer to Owen; when he finished fastening his shirt, he gripped her hand while they watched as their other belongings were catalogued.

After several minutes, Antler Man sat back and surveyed the piles. He picked up one of the phones and thoughtfully twisted it back and forth in the firelight. "Satellite?"

"Yeah, that one is," Owen answered.

"Good. Might be able to use that."

"Satellite coverage is out at the moment."

The man squinted at him shrewdly. "Got any inside dope on when it'll be back?"

"Afraid not. You'll have to keep checking."

"Okay, sure. And I won't say 'no' to these burner phones, neither," he added, scooping up the other devices and stowing them away in various pockets.

He then leaned over the piles and pulled the pistols closer to himself. There were five: Reed's, Owen's, Diego's, Marino's and Singer's.

With obvious disappointment, he jabbed at the last two. "Agency-issue. Won't fire with the safety chips enabled."

Owen spoke up. "Might be unlocked. Test it."

Antlers picked it up and ambled to the far side of the clearing. He aimed into the forest and squeezed the trigger. Nothing happened. He returned to the group with a look of disappointment.

Reed piped up. "The safety sometimes re-engages after a set period. But I'd probably need Singer's phone to unlock it." He pointed to the videoskin in the pile. "I'd guess he has the master codes for most authorized sidearms throughout the region."

The man regarded him skeptically. "Okay," he said with misgiving. "Mebbe we can talk 'bout that later."

He set Singer's weapon aside and picked up Owen's Scorpio pistol.

Owen said, "I'd really appreciate it if I got that back soon. You know we're being hunted—in fact, for your own safety, it would be best if we were away from here in case the authorities track us to this place. Just give us one pistol and one burner phone and let us go."

As the others waited tensely, Antler Man's expression grew more mocking. "You make a good case for offing y'all and burying your bodies in the bushes, understand?"

"Yes," said Owen. "But I'm pretty sure *Ardhanarishvara* ordered you to let us go on our way."

Sofia stiffened as she watched Antler Man's reaction. If it was understood the Agency was searching for them, would they be regarded as useful hostages, or did these people wish to have as little contact with the authorities as possible? Whose side were they on? And if they had no side but their own, did that make them more dangerous?

The lull became uncomfortably protracted. Owen said, "*Naranari* showed me the meadow where there was a massacre, the bodies of the old ones who had been refashioned into things they weren't meant to be. I saw their spirits are still trapped. Do you think that won't happen here?"

The man waved his hand carelessly. "Forget it. We don't fear them—anyone they send out here won't ever make it back to the Agency."

Reaching for a strip of dried meat from a nearby tray, he took a bite and chewed it in a pointed, almost threatening manner.

Reed cleared his throat. "They sure as hell wouldn't make it back if I brought a shipment of more weapons for the use of your comrades here."

Antler Man's chewing slowed, ever so slightly.

In a low voice, Reed continued: "Y'all may be telling yourselves you got a scary enough reputation that Singer's men'll steer clear of you, or that they don't care about you, or they won't find you way out here, or else you can take care of them if they do, but let's go worst-case scenario." Reed took a breath, spreading his hands in a matter-of-fact gesture. "They're not going to tolerate a set-up like this out here for very long. Once they get things sorted out in the cities and countryside, they're going to turn their attention to the woods."

The intermediary looked unconvinced as he stroked his chin. He grunted, "Could be any of those might happen, could be none. Or maybe somethin' no one thought of."

"Maybe," said Reed. "But you know my workshop is pretty far south of here. I'll give you directions to a neutral meeting spot where I can deliver a crate of my pistols." Reed stood up and held out his hand. "Do we have a deal? And can we get a guide back to where your people picked us up?"

The intermediary also stood tall, but said nothing. Beneath the patterns of light and shadow cast by his branching headdress, Antler's lined face grew grave and thoughtful. Then he beamed and took Reed's hand in a brief but decisive grip.

"Deal."

CHAPTER
FIFTY-NINE

LIT BY WEAK STARLIGHT, the outline of Reed's truck was difficult to see against the dark backdrop of the forest. The second rental car, the small blue Comet, stood a few yards further up the logging track, all its doors open and interior ransacked.

After accepting several satellite phones that had been retrieved from packs attached to the bottom of the car, and returning a Scorpio each to Owen and Reed, their guides had melted back into the blackness of the brooding, primordial forest.

When they were safely alone, MacIntyre crawled once more beneath the rental and retrieved two additional smuggling packs.

Dropping the packs to the ground before Reed, he shook his head. "Can't believe they didn't find these."

"It's miraculous," said Sofia in a tremulous, half-joking tone as she watched him place his thumb against the biolocks and pop the lids open.

Reed drew his breath in sharply. "Quasar units—you got to be kidding me!"

With ill-concealed excitement, the man selected one of the six sleek units, each the size of a large book. "Singer's thugs did door-to-door sweeps for these right after the coup. Not sure how many he got, but these are sure gonna come in handy."

"Provided the U.S. authorities agree to bring the functional satellites back online," grumbled MacIntyre. "When they do, you'll have these, too." He passed over one of the satellite phones that had been packed with the Quasar units.

He added, "When I get back to the U.S., job one is convincing them to do that. As well as getting more supplies to you through some new channels. "

Pausing, he mopped some sweat from his temple; he was struggling to tamp down his nausea and ongoing sense of disorientation. These reactions were far more violent than anything he'd experienced with the intravox thus far. Maybe it had nothing to do with that device. It reminded him more of when Francisco Chen had attempted to kill him with a dose of Thorn.

Reed chuckled. "Excellent plan. And speaking of plans—," He set down the phone and dug into a hidden slot in the trim of his jacket, squeezing out a thumb drive and passing it to Owen. "Get this to the folks who need to know. Comprehensive list of all the communication cache sites in Pacifica."

MacIntyre accepted it with a tight smile. "A dropbox network? Sometimes the old ways are the best."

"Yeah, but that's not all that's on there." Reed leaned closer. "We've got some informants on the inside, they passed us some classified docs about the long-term plans at those detainment facilities. Chakrabarti might have use for that intel."

"Damn, that's awesome," breathed Owen, as he hid the tiny device securely in his jacket. "Anything else you can tell me about conditions on the ground?"

Setting back on his heels, Reed said, "Well, you told those 'shroom heads you saw a mass grave, so I figure you know about the massacre."

Owen nodded. "It was just an impression, so I wasn't sure it was real."

Reed continued grimly, "Yeah, it was real enough. They tried to keep it secret, but the guy running the excavator leaked the details. Plus in the city, they're using a construction crane for public executions. All places of worship have been shut down or converted to Power Cult centers. Shelter Haven Networks closed down, street-dwellers and campers rounded up, disappearing."

One shoulder hitched up as his voice grew more disheartened. "Lots of stores empty or closed, and blackouts are unannounced, and last for a few days instead of hours. Looks like there'll be even less fuel and electricity this winter. And less food. Hoarders are being reported to the authorities and publicly shamed. Snitches are rewarded."

MacIntyre asked, "Any pushback, or are most folks just going along with it?"

"It's still early, there's a lot of uncertainty." Reed's teeth gleamed as he grinned, "But I can tell you all those Scorpio units you ordered from me way back when, are greatly appreciated by the locals. There's even some spots right on the edge of the city that Singer's men don't dare go."

"Excellent, just as I'd hoped—," Owen was interrupted by a gasp from Sofia.

"Gunrunning? Don't tell me you were *gunrunning?*"

Impatient, he waved a dismissive hand. "It was more of a leisurely ramble."

"When did you do this?"

"Almost two years ago—,"

"Was this for Greg?"

"No, it was my own idea."

"With your own money—?"

"Hey, can we discuss this later?"

Owen pointedly turned back to Reed. "But that's just here on the coast—what else can you tell me about the whole…damn I hate to call it a 'country', but you know what I mean."

"Not much intel from up north, but we are making our own diplomatic ties with some groups in the Mexican territory. I'd say we actually have the beginnings of an armed resistance forming. There's more details on that drive."

"Fantastic." MacIntyre punched him lightly on the arm. "Looks like I left the place in good hands, Mr. 'Kurtis'."

Reed shrugged demurely. "Just living my life and doing what needs to be done."

Both he and MacIntyre rose. Owen added lightly, "Then I'd say you've got everything under control here and don't need any outside help."

"Man, I wish that was true. But don't leave us high and dry."

MacIntyre grew deadly serious. "I won't."

Reed said, "Now, about your trip home… I can tell you the route to the southeast is less likely to be monitored. But you probably knew that."

"Yeah, I'm still weighing the options. I laid a crumb trail back to the airport, so I'm banking on them assuming we'll take the quickest way out. The southeast is a much longer route, which presents another problem." Owen went to

Diego. "How are you feeling? I guess not even working for the Chen family could prepare you for an adventure like this."

Rojas forced a smile. "I'm well, señor." But his haggard, unsteady appearance told another story; he was exhausted from stress and weakened by blood loss.

Reed joined them and helped MacIntyre evaluate the wounds. The dressings had loosened during the struggles with the cultists; streams of fresh blood seeped down the side of his face and neck.

The gunsmith shook his head. "No, my man, you are not well. You need to be seen by a professional, like *immediately*. Stitches, antibiotics and a rabies series. There's a doc at my place, with an emergency clinic for our operatives."

For a moment, Diego was agitated and undecided. Then his shoulders relaxed and he smiled apologetically at MacIntyre. "In that case, señor, I think you must go on without me."

Sofia stared and uttered a faint, dismayed cry.

Looking abashed, Rojas admitted, "Señora, I do feel very badly, and don't think I can travel much further."

"You can't stay here," said Owen. "It's too dangerous."

Diego flinched in pain as he shook his head. He looked deadly serious. "Señor, it's my fault he was taken in the first place. I have made so many mistakes on this mission…if I can help you all get out by doing this one little thing…," his voice trailed.

Silently, they regarded each other in grim realization.

"We'll take good care of him and see he gets back home," interrupted Reed. "So don't worry—I can see he is one tough hombre, he's going to be fine."

"Oh, Diego—!" voice quavering, Sofia embraced him. "Thank you for this! Thank you for all your help, you've been so wonderful!"

"*Vaya con Dios*," said Owen, gripping Rojas' hand.

"*Gracias*," the man murmured as he turned away from the couple to move closer to the darkness at the edge of the road.

Owen took Sofia's elbow and led her to the car. She fought tears as she fastened Dylan into the awaiting infant seat. The vehicle's quiet motor came to life and they jolted down the trail.

"We'll see him again soon," said Owen.

"Oh, I dearly hope so! But the next leg of our trip…how long is it?"

"Give me a few minutes to calculate that."

He decided to nudge Ellie again, asking, *Have you had any luck contacting Campos? Any word of increased patrols on Highway Thirty, between the coast and the airport?*

It took her longer to reply than he would have liked. After several moments, she reported a total blackout in that sector, concluding, *I'm afraid you know as much as we do about conditions on the ground.*

Hoping his feelings of disappointment and anxiety weren't too obvious, he projected a sense of bravado as he thanked her, then ended the communication. He consulted his gut, wondering which was the safest route to take. He could not shake the feeling that Singer would concentrate his efforts on Highway 30.

There were numerous gaps along the border fence, but it seemed likely those would also be places with enhanced patrols. Owen was inclined to head for a place that was restricted, but with fewer guards.

He switched his attention to the map inside his implant, plotting a passage that bypassed the bigger cities.

"Over four hundred and ninety miles," he announced after a minute or so.

"As the crow flies?"

"No, as the rental car skulks on back roads. And at speeds that don't attract too much attention. With as few stops as possible, and really pushing it. Maybe we can make it in eight hours. Fortunately, this model has a pretty good range, so we may only need to charge it once or twice."

Assuming we can even find reliable charging stations, he thought grimly.

She sighed and settled in beside Dylan. "Okay. I doubt I'll get any sleep, but I'll try anyway."

"Go for it."

As they drove, the ceaseless panorama of trees whipping past the headlights took on something of an unreal, mesmerizing theatrical backdrop.

After fifteen minutes or so, Sofia remarked, "Your friend said that places of worship have been shut down...do you think that includes St. Columban's?"

"I'd be surprised if it didn't. But we don't have time to investigate."

"No, of course not. I didn't mean that." She thought a moment. "Eight hours...I'll be counting the seconds. This place isn't home anymore, that's for sure."

"I know, honey. It stopped being home a long time ago. But who knows—maybe someday, it can be again."

Her voice dripped with weary skepticism. "Do you really think passing a few phones and guns out to these guys will make a difference?"

"It's a start. Realistically, I'm sure things will get worse here before they get better. A lot worse. But once people can freely communicate, they have a lot more options. They have hope."

She heaved a melancholy sigh. "I pray you're right."

Mouth drawing into a grim line, he had no more to say; at the moment, he wasn't interested in mulling the distant future. The people in the car, and the narrow road directly before him, were now his entire world.

Mile after mile passed beneath their tires; as the overgrown state forest grew thinner, they passed a few more scattered small towns and settlements. They descended the eastern slope of the Coastal Range and skirted the far southern edge of the Willamette Valley.

MacIntyre had intentionally chosen a time-consuming and twisted route along back-roads and older, poorly maintained highways, hoping to make up time later on the straight-aways cutting through the empty desert.

They didn't have much food with them, and what little there was, Owen insisted Sofia have. She was too nervous to eat, and so the energy bars, nuts and jerky remained untouched. As the first hour crept tensely by, Owen began to feel a little more confident. The knowledge that both Sofia and the baby were now sound asleep, cast a safe, peaceful atmosphere throughout the car.

Once, they passed an electronic notice board that proclaimed the Amber child abduction alert was still in effect. He was pleased to see it listed three suspects and the wrong make of car. They had not yet encountered any checkpoints or even seen any patrol cruisers.

He wondered if this was a sign resources were scarce, or if in fact the search was concentrated elsewhere. *Whatever's happening, this luck can't possibly last*, he thought. Yet he prayed it would. He prayed their pursuers had checked with all the airlines and fallen for the false itinerary he'd planted. Given how few flights were in and out, it should not be difficult to locate the one he had fabricated.

When Sofia woke, she passed him an energy bar and insisted he eat. They spoke very little, mutually absorbed in their cocoons of worry. Yet as the uneventful hours passed, and the miles lengthened behind them, tension continued to release Owen from its grasp. He began to believe he had, after all, chosen the best route.

They ascended into the wooded foothills of the Western Cascades and traveled through another dense forest for hours. After a time, they descended again and entered the southeastern part of the state. The pervading damp green was now a distant memory. Forests were intermittent, sparse and dry. Their route took them along the shores of remote lakes, gleaming placidly in the starlight.

At last, even the thin forests were gone. On all sides, a vast quiet nothingness of scrub and low, rocky hills lurked in the blackness. He knew there were occasional towns along the way, but these flew by almost unseen, mere rumors in the dark, with only one or two lights shining in a window, or a handful of streetlights illuminating a glimpse of a deserted side street. It seemed not much electricity was diverted to the smallest and least important enclaves east of the Cascades.

The continuous unwinding of the nebulous, ill-defined landscape had a soporific effect on Owen and his concentration started to slip. He was already relying on extra stimulation from Beta waves generated in his visor to help keep him alert, but now those effects were failing.

While he could have re-engaged the car's autodrive and taken a rest, he'd always distrusted autonomous driving and preferred a human mind be on call, even one as groggy as his. Yet he wasn't ready to ask Sofia to take over.

As the adrenalin in his system ebbed, his debilitating weariness worsened. He hadn't slept much since he began planning this op; and the experience with the chimera had dealt him an unexpected blow. He knew he had no choice but to push through until they were safe, but part of him began to admit this might not be possible.

When the car's battery was dangerously low, they paused at a rest stop to add some charge. He was disappointed to see a severe restriction on how much juice they could draw, but hoped it would be enough for the last leg of their journey. If nothing went wrong.

They walked about, shaking the kinks out of their muscles; the sky above was cloudless, the stars were sharp and immediate. While Sofia used the restroom, Owen stood outside the car, where the fresh air revived him a little. There was an unspoken promise of encroaching dawn in the chill breeze.

When Sofia rejoined him, she was drying her hands on her shirt as she remarked, "Thank goodness that one was unlocked. No towels, though. And I'm glad I packed enough diapers."

He laughed. "You could have improvised with dried grass and leaves."

"Yuck." With a tired grin, she drew near and he put his arm around her. Tenderly stroking his face, she commented, "I'm glad you shaved."

"Me, too. And your hair looks great."

"Yeah, sure."

They stood together, basking in the vast serenity for several moments before she whispered, "It's another world out here. There's no one else for miles. There's nothing between us and this big, beautiful, peaceful silence."

He sighed. Voice raspy with exhaustion, he said, "Too bad it's an illusion, there's still people out here."

He again wondered if living in a place like Underhill would ever be an option for them, or if there weren't too many people, even there. He also wondered if his craving for solitude was a passing reaction to his recent experience. He was beginning to realize it would be impossible to ever be truly comfortable with the intravox's presence.

Sofia said, "Don't become a cranky old recluse. That's selfish. Everyone has to learn to live with others."

"I'm willing to try, but there's quite a few people on this planet that make it…challenging."

"Like Singer?" Her smile faded. "Why didn't you double-check that he was dead?"

Caught off-guard by her question, he asked himself the same thing. Why *hadn't* he done that when he had the chance? Because he was in such a hurry to leave before reinforcements arrived? Or because he was weak, and had faltered at a critical moment?

"Believe me…believe me, I wanted to. It took everything in me to not… go back and break Singer's neck with my bare hands…to grind him to a pulp."

His words slurred and stumbled. "Would it have made you…*happy* to see me do that?"

Her expression was unreadable. Was she sympathetic to his failure in a moment of rushed confusion? Or was she disappointed in his reticence, after his earlier tough talk?

A frown came and went over her brow, like the faint breeze now playing over them both. She said, "It would have made me happy. But only for a moment. And it would have been the wrong sort of happiness, I guess."

The relief that filled him at these words soothed his inner doubts and regret regarding his missed chance.

Sofia asked, "And what was that horrible...*thing* in the forest? I know it's human, I feel so sorry for it, but it's hard to think of it as anything but a monstrosity. What did they call it? Foxy Turner?"

Happy to change the subject, Owen chuckled blearily. "I think they were trying to say *'Vox Aeterna'*. They're crafting their own religion out of random bits, so I guess they've thrown in some Latin to label their personal copy of *Ardhanarishvara*."

"Who is that, anyway? He looked sort of familiar, but I don't know if it's from a nightmare or a history book."

He waved his hand. "The manifestation of Shiva, the one that's a mash-up of male and female characteristics."

"Oh."

Owen added reluctantly, "There was a lot of experimentation, years ago, and before the practice was banned, some of the...results made their way into private menageries or even isolated villages, where some wound up worshipped as gods."

"Yes, I remember my Dad mentioning things like that happened, but I was little and it was too scary. I didn't want to know, I tried to forget."

"I had no idea one was living all this time so close to home. Guess the woodlands guard their secrets well."

Eyes fixed on him, she asked, "What happened between the two of you? Were you faking it? Or were you actually communicating?"

Before he could reply, the quiet was cracked by a startled yelp from far out in the grasslands. The coyote's bark was answered by a wave of yips and mournful, unearthly wails, seeming to come from all around the couple.

Ignoring the animals, he answered, "It was real...at least, I guess as real as something like that can be."

"What was it like?"

Because it was impossible to explain aloud, he didn't. Instead, his exhausted mind reluctantly flicked over the intense yet obscure sensations, of how he had concentrated on opening a path between his immediate awareness, and where he wished to join the chimera. And how the path had appeared, a narrow passage between his surroundings, and a dim sense of Ellie's presence. By some instinct, he had avoided the latter and aimed his mind at the indistinct plane far beyond both the others. Once there, an exchange of genuine knowledge was frustratingly veiled by disturbing, enigmatic visions.

"Hard to describe," he said with a dismissive shrug. "And I'm still... processing it. Try me some other time."

"But he was making a prophecy about Dylan, wasn't he? Could it possibly be real?"

"I don't think so. Best to forget it."

Yet even as he said that, he couldn't help wonder if he and the chimera had genuine abilities that were triggered or enhanced by exposure to hallucinogens, whether natural fungi or the lab-created Thorn compound.

Stiffening, he listened to the sound of an approaching vehicle. They both watched as a battered semi-truck lumbered off the road, pulled into the parking lot, then wheezed to a stop.

"Should we leave now?" asked Sofia.

"No, our car needs to charge a bit more. Just act natural."

They continued to converse with exaggerated unconcern as the truck driver exited his cab, hitched up his sagging jeans and made for the facilities without a glance in their direction.

Owen checked the power gauge on the rental's dashboard, commenting in a strained undertone, "Still a few more minutes before we can leave."

When the driver emerged from the restroom, he paused and regarded the couple a moment before ambling nearer with an ingratiating smile.

"Nice evening, inn't?"

Owen nodded. "Yeah, nice and quiet."

The man tipped his dirty cap back and scratched his scalp. "Yeah, it's usually pretty quiet out here. Never was much traffic, but now there's a day or two when I don't see any other cars on this road. They even cut the numbers of guards at the crossing."

Owen did his best to sound bored. "For real? That seems careless."

The man slowly wagged his head. "After word of a few shootings got round, most folks got the message. So what the hell kinda trouble could be out here?"

"Guess you're right."

Pulling a pack of gum from the pocket of his stained and torn shirt, the driver took his time selecting a piece while adding, "Course, there's a report of some fugitives what stole a little kid and left the coast."

"Got a description?"

"One man in dark glasses, little boy with light blond hair. Driving a gray four-door. Probably heading north."

"Okay, we'll be on the lookout for that."

The man's stubbly jaw shifted as he worked away at the gum. "Course, they may not be heading north at all. And if they're desperate, they could be dangerous. So watch out."

"Thanks. We will."

Tugging his cap forward, the man gave a tight nod, headed back to his truck and soon departed.

Sofia exhaled noisily. "He suspects us. Did you see the way he looked at you when he said 'dark glasses'?"

"Everyone suspects everyone else under these conditions," Owen said wearily. "But yes, let's leave as soon as possible."

She studied his face in the starlight and reached up, running her fingers gently down his temple and along his cheekbone, saying, "You're really tired. Let me drive."

Admitting defeat, he grinned sheepishly but also with relief. While they waited for the charge to finish, he drew her a rough map of the rest of the route. "According to the data I collected, the best place to cross should be somewhere southeast of Drewesy."

When they were ready to leave, Sofia took her place in the front as Owen seated himself beside the baby. He added, "Stay alert for patrols or anything else that strikes you as 'off'."

Sofia flashed a grin at him over her shoulder as she switched on the motor. "If you fall too deeply asleep, nothing will wake you."

Making himself comfortable in the corner of the rear seat, he retorted, "With you at the wheel? I'll be too stressed out for anything but a light doze."

"Jerk," she muttered fondly.

Outside, the blackness streamed by unheeded. As he regarded the baby's, soft flushed cheeks and tendrils of hair plastered to his sweaty brow, Owen grew more relaxed and sleepy. Soon the quiet overtook him completely and he was conscious of nothing more.

CHAPTER
SIXTY

"OWEN, wake up! Damn it—*wake up!* They're behind us—what do we do now?!"

MacIntyre fought blearily through a black void of fathomless sleep. He sat up to see flashing lights of red and blue quickly overtaking them. *Only one cruiser, thank God—!* he thought. *No sign of others—for now.*

He said, "It might be a routine traffic stop! Did you do anything wrong?"

"No, of course not! Maybe—I have no idea—!"

"That bastard trucker," he muttered angrily. "Where are we?"

"We passed through Drewsey a few minutes ago!"

"Why didn't you wake me up then?"

"I tried, but you just kept snoring! Now what?"

About three miles ahead, the night was pricked by intense points of illumination; security fixtures at a fortified, official, international border crossing, where no one was allowed to cross. Their vehicle was about to be overtaken and pinned there between their pursuers, and any guards on duty up ahead.

Thrusting himself between the front seats, he tapped the control screen, quelling all the lights on their vehicle.

"Quick—turn off here to the right, and head to the southeast as fast as you can!"

"Are you sure? There's no road—!"

"Do it!"

She wrenched the wheel sharply and they shot off the asphalt, jouncing into the dark, lurching over hollows hidden by dead grass and clumps of sagebrush.

"Push the accelerator all the way to the floor," he urged, exasperated at the way she fumbled the controls.

"I can't see where we're going!" she wailed.

"Here—let me take over!"

He lunged forward and caught the wheel as, beneath his arms, she ducked down and slid over to the passenger side, while he forced himself between both seats and fell heavily into the driver's place. Part of his mind passively regarded the maneuver with admiration, recognizing that if they had practiced for hours, they couldn't have pulled it off more smoothly. Then, with his night vision engaged, he urged the car ahead.

"There's a chance we might be able to lose them," he said, feeling the cheap, underpowered vehicle struggling to respond to the unusual conditions. The limited charge they had been allowed to take at the rest stop was now draining at a terrifying rate, and he didn't think he could get much more out of the machine.

"But don't they have their own scanners and things?"

"Yep."

"And their car can handle this terrain better—they're gaining on us!"

"I can see that!"

"They're going to shoot us!" she gasped.

He answered in a clipped tone, "Very likely. And drones are patrolling up ahead. Do you want to shoot back while I drive?"

"Are you kidding?"

"No—but we only have one firearm—."

"Oh—!"

Blue and red strobed insistently behind them, while ahead, thin beams of illumination swept over the ground, stabbing downward from a passing drone. That mechanism was almost two miles away, but still too close for comfort.

"What do we do? What do we *do?*" Responding to her distressed voice, Dylan awoke and commenced howling.

Owen's mind raced through their rapidly dwindling options. Then he shouted without warning, "Get back there with him! And hold on—!"

As she climbed back between the seats and flopped down beside the baby,

Owen spun the wheel violently to the left, while also slamming on the brakes. Jabbing at the control screen, he cut the last of the safety features and switched the car to full manual mode.

Enveloped in a thick cloud of slowly settling dust, they watched as the patrol cruiser advanced inexorably straight for their position. About twenty yards before them, the law enforcement vehicle skewed to an abrupt stop. The siren was silenced but the red and blue lights continued to pulsate into the amorphous, pre-dawn gray. There was no sign of motion from the occupants.

"What do we *do?*" whispered Sofia.

He shushed her. There was still no movement from the troopers. If they were calling for back-up, there wasn't much choice left, he had to act now.

Lowering the window beside him, he drew his pistol from his jacket. He commanded, "Brace the baby and hold on—!"

Slamming his foot full-force on the accelerator, he sent the car careening over the desert, straight for the cruiser.

The other driver reacted by backing up, but Owen increased speed. With his hand out the window, he squeezed off several shots as the distance between both vehicles shrunk almost instantly. The cruiser's wind shield sent back dazzling flashes as the beams were deflected, but he counted on the occupants being disoriented by a sudden frontal attack.

In an instant, the rental collided with the front left fender of the cruiser. The impact was jarring, but not hard enough to deploy his airbag.

Not as bad as I expected, he realized with dim surprise, as he leaped from the car and raced around the hood of the cruiser to the passenger side.

The door was ajar, voices shouted at him in angry confusion. He slammed the door full force against the body of the emerging officer, then jerked it open wide enough to aim his weapon into the compartment. A bright bolt streaked past him and he returned fire, repeatedly and wildly.

Ignoring the agonized cries, he then aimed several more bursts at the cruiser's front tires. Without pausing to look at the aftermath, he instantly reentered the driver's seat of the rental and threw the car into reverse.

The distant security lights marked the line of the border wall; they traveled almost parallel to this, as fast as possible over the broken ground, through clumps of sagebrush. It was a bone-jarring, chaotic ordeal, ending with a whimper when the last of the power ebbed and the little car died on the edge of a fissure snaking across the desert floor.

Owen wrenched open the door, commanding, "Out, quickly!"

Accompanied by the sound of Dylan's startled cries, he caught up both their travel packs in one hand, then helped Sofia fasten Dylan into the front carrier. Then he grabbed her shoulder and pulled her away from the car and towards the concrete barrier, now about a quarter mile ahead.

He said, "I don't know if reinforcements are coming, but we have to keep moving!"

Sofia's breath came in shallow, ragged gulps as she stumbled alongside him.

"It's about three miles along here to where the wall ends, and then it might be easier to cross," he explained. "Do you think you can jog that distance?"

"I'll try. But won't we be spotted on the way?"

"That's a possibility."

Studying her taught, drawn face and watching her stumble, he realized she could not walk that far, even if he carried Dylan for her. The concrete wall, a low gray smear to the east, now seemed fifty miles ahead instead of two or three.

He pointed to the barrier. "Then we'll have to go over it, as soon as possible."

Dispiritedly, she nodded her resignation to this sudden change of plan. "I'll do my best."

Urgently, his mind reached for Ellie's, explaining they were almost to the border, and needed her to alert Idaho authorities and have someone sent to meet them.

Her response was instant and delighted, but she needed their exact location.

Agreeing, he halted his steps. He stood perfectly still and turned to look up to the heavens.

Overhead, the sky was an infinite dome of faint, almost colorless yellow-gray, with a handful of lingering stars gleaming cheerily to the west. He adjusted his visor to gather and amplify enough light that many of the hidden stars became visible.

He 'thought' this view to Ellie, urging, *Check the image I'm seeing, calculate our location from the stars! I'm looking to the northwest!*

Holding his breath, he waited anxiously for her response.

After several moments, she replied: *Yes, I've calculated your position, and am now contacting the Idaho border patrol. They'll send a team to meet you!*

But Ellie, I'm going to need a lot of help once we're over the first barrier...you know why. I want all the data I can get.

Understood. Don't worry!

Thanks, Ellie, you've been amazing!

Feeling more reassured but still tense, he resumed walking, aware that Sofia was regarding him with a questioning expression.

She said, "What were you looking at?"

"The stars," he said with an encouraging laugh. "Don't they look awesome?"

"Yeah, sure. What were you really doing?"

"Saying a quick prayer to our Guardian Angel."

She rolled her eyes. "Are you feeling okay?"

"Feeling pretty good, actually."

Scanning behind them as they trudged, he saw no sign of other vehicles approaching. But low in the sky before them, red pinpoints marked where two drones patrolled.

Before he could speak, Sofia made it clear she'd also seen them.

Her voice shook. "Still feeling good? How...how can we get past those without them spotting us? Without them shooting us?"

Slowing his steps, Owen answered, "Maybe like this."

Re-drawing his pistol and calming himself, he fired. A dazzling beam lashed at the device; the drone lurched to one side. He fired again and it flipped, shooting sparks like a Catherine wheel as it spun randomly away into the desert. The second drone reacted by changing course and heading for them, taking an erratic, evasive path through the sky.

It moved so quickly, it took him three shots to take this one out. As the dark bits of wreckage drifted to earth, he turned to Sofia with a shaky grin. "They never had a chance."

She answered with a gulp. They continued forward, steadily covering the remaining yards to the barricade. When they reached it, Owen quickly searched for hand-holds on the surface of the wall, which was about fifteen feet high.

"Look at this shitty job," he said with delighted contempt. "Look at the size of those air pockets! As good as a ladder!"

Taking a pair of wire cutters from his pack, he placed them in his back pocket. Then he re-settled the pack and pulled himself up the wall via the holes and imperfections. Near the top, he grasped the wall with his left hand and took out the cutters. He trapped a wide, loose curl of razor wire in the blades of the cutters.

"Not sure these are sharp enough," he puffed in disgust. "Hard to get the right leverage at this angle—oh, fuck!"

The wire abruptly separated and one sharp, springy end rebounded and whipped past his face, leaving a slit along his jaw.

Sofia gasped, "Are you okay?"

"Yeah, it's nothing." He pulled himself up further and flung one leg over the top of the barrier before stretching down towards Sofia.

"Come on up! But watch out—some of those hand-holds are crumbly."

With a speechless nod, she started to scramble up. It was a challenge to manage the climb with the baby in front, but after several tense moments she was seated, panting, beside Owen.

Spreading below them was a strip of earth about a hundred yards across. It looked as if it had been plowed, then loosely covered over again. On the far side was a much lower barricade, topped with more vicious loops of razor wire.

"We're almost there," she whispered with incredulous relief. "We made it—!'"

"Not exactly. Stay here."

With great caution, he let himself down the far side of the wall. Standing as close to the barricade as he could, he guided her down to join him. When she was on the ground, he grabbed her arm, restraining her from stepping forward.

He said, "*Landmines.*"

She inhaled with a hiss of terror. Owen squeezed her hand. "It's okay, there aren't very many."

"It only takes one!"

"I have an internal map of this section, plus an external guide reading satellite data, and my own scanners. It'll be as safe as walking across the kitchen to get a cup of coffee."

"How stupid do you think I am?"

"Okay, you're right. Not exactly a kitchen. But we can do this, no problem."

"You…you knew this was here and didn't *tell* me?"

He answered evasively, "I was prepared for anything. And besides, you were supposed to stay home, remember? But here we are."

Placing his hands on either side of her face, he regarded her huge, frightened eyes. If these were their final moments together, he didn't want to see her so consumed with fear.

He planted a slow, warm kiss on her brow. "If we go, we go together. But trust me, we'll make it—I promise."

It seemed like an eternity before she exhaled. "Okay, I trust you."

Engaging the scanners and the map he'd preloaded, he then sought Ellie's mind and sent her an image of exactly where they were standing in relation to the mines.

Got it, she replied.

He then became aware of what she was seeing on her own computer; the very latest imagery from U.S. military satellites.

When Owen combined the old and new maps, he saw they aligned perfectly with what his scanners reported, which considerably boosted his confidence. At his feet, a grainy, otherworldly landscape was revealed. Unmistakably artificial forms lurked just below the surface, distributed randomly.

"I see the way, clear as crystal," he announced. "But we'll have to move very, very slowly, and you need to walk right behind me—put your hand in my belt and put your feet exactly where I step."

"Yes."

"Then let's go."

They proceeded to pick their way cautiously forward, rarely speaking, and then only in whispers. As if the devices hiding below their feet were actively listening for them, might burst up and out upon them if they made too much noise. Owen was also alert for the sound of approaching sirens or drones, but heard nothing. All about them, the last remnants of night died as the morning advanced.

"I need to stop," said Sofia suddenly, a disquieting catch in her voice. "I...I can't take another step. I feel...I feel paralyzed."

"That's fine," he said reassuringly, turning toward her. "Take a little break. Take a deep breath, don't think about what's happening."

She nodded, but her face was pale and hard, and he didn't like the distance growing in her eyes. Fear was devouring her sense of trust.

"You have to do this," he ordered her gently. He scanned the next few yards. "We're almost there."

They resumed stepping from clear spot to clear spot. Sofia's face was chalky, her ashen lips twitching in soundless prayer. In this nerve-wracking, tedious manner, they crossed the expanse of treacherous earth and reached the second barrier. He cut the wire, they crawled over the low concrete, and stepped onto the inert soil of Idaho.

He choked, "We made it."

Sobbing, Sofia collapsed against his shoulder.

Owen said, "That wasn't so bad, was it?"

"It was *hell!*" She struck him lightly on the arm, laughing through her tears. Dylan, growing restive in his carrier and feeling crowded between them, fussed and kicked.

Sofia stiffened in fear. "There's a truck coming straight for us—who are they?"

"Our ride home," said Owen, scarcely regarding the border patrol vehicle drawing nearer over the rough terrain. A dust plume rose behind it into the pure morning air.

Ignoring his son's displeasure, he pulled Sofia back toward himself and caught her in a possessive embrace. With inexpressible relief, he buried his face in the short, silken waves of her unkempt hair. He whispered, "Good job, Saint Joan."

The long shadows of their three forms merged into one, stretching across the tawny earth, as the rising edge of the sun poured the molten gold of its light over the barren hills.

EPILOGUE

THE HACIENDA'S study was cool, dim and welcoming that afternoon. On the desk's computer screen, the live image of Greg Park's face looked weary yet animated. Hopeful, even.

He said, "The data you brought back, the classified docs, the stuff you pulled off Singer's phone—I can't believe it! It's all extremely high-value. We're still processing it, and we've been working around the clock the last three days to draft notes for a classified presentation to President Chakrabarti's security advisors. It's looking quite good."

Owen offered a vague nod. Despite being physically recovered from the recent ordeal, it was a strain to focus on Greg's discussion. He felt removed and wanted to forget, at least for the time being, much of what he'd read on the files Reed slipped him about the regime's activities in Pacifica—especially concerning true purpose of the detainment camps. He needed a break from the bad news, was fiercely guarding a personal space where he could catch his breath before seriously considering where to go from here.

Yet he forced himself to ask, "What about the contacts in the resistance? Are they going to get any help?"

Park said, "Yes, of course! My colleagues are preparing to push for a sustained, multi-pronged approach to dealing with Pacifica. Not just sanctions—we need a plan to support the insurgents, and perhaps even mount some limited special military actions."

"Convince them to bring as many satellites back online, as soon as possible. That would be a big help," said Owen with undisguised irritation.

"Yes, that should happen in a few days. But about the big-picture plan—,"

In his excitement, Greg began circling back to territory they'd already discussed, following Owen's detailed report on what he had observed during his hours in the region. Owen was growing weary of the subject. In addition to bad tidings, he'd also had enough of reports and plans in general for the time being.

Repeatedly, his attention strayed to the view outside the study window, where the rest of the household was gathered on the patio. Teresa carried a tray of food to Diego, as the latter reclined in a chaise lounge. Rojas had arrived home late the previous day, and after being checked out by a doctor, was taking a week or two off to do nothing but relax and heal.

As the housekeeper fussed over the wounded man, Owen watched Sofia take Dylan from Isabella, and laughing, nestle him against her shoulder. Her body swayed in a slight dance, and the baby beamed in delight. Sunlight outlined the spikes of her crazy short hair, which she had reassured Owen would grow out soon.

Not that he cared much; she was beautiful no matter what she did with her hair or what she wore. What was most important was that Dylan was back in her arms, and that each day brought her closer to her typical light-hearted self. He was proud of how they had worked together through such a hellish ordeal, and had emerged victorious. He was also grateful for Reed's assistance, and even admitted that on some level, he was aware Tomás Chen's prayers had helped sustain them.

Closer to home, Owen was gratified to learn the lawyer working on their behalf was clearing their record with the Texas Child Protective Services. Furthermore, Constance Peña was on leave pending an investigation into how closely she'd worked with Singer's agents.

Distractedly, Owen finally answered Park: "All that sounds great, keep me updated. But that wasn't why I went. It was for my son."

After a pause, Greg said awkwardly, "Of course. I still can't believe you pulled this off. Basically single-handed—waltzed right into Pacifica and took Dylan out from under Singer's nose. I really don't know what to say. Thank God you all made it out."

Owen nodded, answering in his head, *I can't believe you're surprised.* He remembered being lectured by this man under similar circumstances, after he returned from his successful hunt of Tomás and the clone, Alejandro.

Absently smoothing his hair behind his ear, Owen said in a low, firm tone, "It wasn't single-handed. I had support, remember? When it counted. And why wouldn't you think I'd take matters into my own hands, now that I have even more skills and connections?"

Greg looked away from the camera. He said, "You're right. It's just that...," Pausing, he wrestled with what to say next. Owen watched the man's affection battle with his burden of professional obligations.

With an uncomfortable smile, Greg continued, "It's not that I'm not proud of you, and everything you've accomplished so far. It's just...I need more assurance about where and how those skills are going to be utilized. I guess I want to know if you're still on our team."

It was clear Greg still had no clue about the existence of the intravoxes, and at the moment, Owen saw no reason to enlighten him. He thought of how delighted Morse was with how well the devices had performed, but they had both agreed it needed further testing, and should continue to be kept top-secret. Ellie was scrupulously abiding by the comms protocols; Owen had not picked up the slightest whiff of her current emotional state or concerns.

He said, "It's a big league, there's plenty of room for more than one team. Or even lone agents. I'm sure you understand why I might be more comfortable on my own."

Greg's brow wrinkled. "I'm not certain I do. I suppose you have a good reason for that choice, and I'd like to hear more."

Nervously rubbing the tight muscles in his temple, Owen took a deep breath. "Okay, it's just that I have serious questions about how you and your colleagues intend to prosecute this...well, I don't want to call it war, but you know what I mean. This action against Pacifica."

"That's not all, is it? Come on Mac, I sense this is personal. Tell me what's wrong, what I've done."

The last thing Owen wanted was to open the scars of their problematic past. Studying the serious face on the screen, he recalled the times he'd been at ease in the older man's company; the fishing trips, the hikes, the intense personal conversations. He balanced those memories against when he believed Greg had placed Restoration interests over what was best for Owen: sending him into danger without fully explaining his motives or the risks, choosing the installation of an inferior neuroprosthetic because it had qualities peculiar to the Restoration's needs.

None of it really mattered now, he felt no bitterness, only frustration that Greg needed this spelled out.

He said, "Greg, I'm never going to forget the good times we had, and everything you've done for me. You know you mean more to me than I can express—you always will. So I'm not going to re-hash the times when I felt you didn't make the best calls, that somehow, I was being sacrificed to the greater good."

The older man's face clouded. "You may not believe it, but some of those choices were harder for me to make than for you to experience."

Side-stepping an argument, Owen agreed. "Okay, I'm sure that's how you feel. And anyway, I knew a lot of those risks came with the territory. But it might be a while before I can forget you didn't support me when I wanted to get Dylan back—," His breath caught as he struggled to express himself. "My dad had already betrayed me to Singer. Do you realize how that felt? I needed you to have my back, and you let me down."

The room was filled with a strained hush, eventually broken by sounds of faint laughter from the patio.

Heaving a long, trembling sigh, Greg removed his glasses and blinked, as he raised his hand in a random, helpless gesture. "Mac, I...I deserved that. And I can't imagine what you've been through. I'm sorry I let you down. More sorry than I can say."

Eager to move on, Owen exhaled and offered a tight smile. "Okay...sure. Apology accepted."

"Thank you." Clearing his throat, Greg said, "Oh, hey, I have a question about Singer—is he alive or dead? You weren't clear."

"Because I wasn't sure."

Without warning, Owen was engulfed by the vivid yet chaotic sensations he'd experienced during his communication with the chimera. He'd seen a dog, left for dead, springing to life and lunging for the throat of a bloodied wolf, a wolf caught in a trap. The wolf tore its leg free as it met its opponent. The creatures had grown vast but indistinct, two forms locked in a desperate battle as the world about them dissolved in a curtain of fire and ash.

'Be wary of false visions,' his grandfather had warned him. Or perhaps he

hadn't; how could Owen know for certain that dreamlike encounter with Evan was true?

Maybe he needed to trust his instincts more. At the moment, they told him Singer was still alive, that there was a remote chance they might meet again.

He spurned the idea, shaking off a sense of oppression. *I can reject that future any time I please, I can take any path I wish, no one is controlling me any more.*

Shrugging, he said aloud, "If he survived, he's suffered a bit of a career setback. Whether he's going to retain his high position in internal security, or be demoted, punished…who knows?"

At the moment, Singer's fate was the least important thing in the world, and he didn't want to waste time speculating on it. He moved away from the computer, announcing casually, "Say, Greg, thanks for the update, but I've got some important things to work on now. We'll connect again soon, okay?"

Greg hesitated; then when he spoke, he sounded at peace. "Sure, I'll update you about the plans. Take care."

"You, too."

The computer screen behind him fading to black, Owen crossed the cool, tiled floor and walked from the darkened study. His lean face was brightened by a smile as he headed to join the people awaiting him on the sun-drenched patio.

IF YOU ENJOYED THIS STORY...

...PLEASE LEAVE a review at either Amazon or Goodreads! I read them all and am always delighted to engage with my readers!

Don't forget to follow me on Amazon:
https://www.amazon.com/S-Kirk-Pierzchala/e/B086FY7BFG/ref=aufs_dp_fta_dsk

and Goodreads:
https://www.goodreads.com/author/show/20304945.S_Kirk_Pierzchala

You are also welcome to contact me via my website, where you can sign up for updates on the entire Beyond Cascadia series, and enjoy a variety of other fiction and non-fiction offerings:

www.skirkpierzchala.com

S. Kirk Pierzchala lives in the damp and mossy corridors of the Pacific Northwest, and has decades of experience crafting fine art, weaving tales and creating children. Her short stories and non-fiction essays have appeared in Silence and Starsong magazine, Fellowship and Fairydust, The Northwest Connection and Catholic World Report.

STARE AT THE SUN: BEYOND CASCADIA FIVE
2024

When the rogue nation of Pacifica arises on the West Coast, the new leaders rapidly forge international alliances and intensify their reign of terror, creating a nightmare existence for those trapped within their borders.

The beleaguered United States scrambles to form their own coalitions, in a desperate bid to hold back the threat.

Cyber defender Owen MacIntyre has his hands full secretly working to oversee assistance to a growing network of insurgents and mercenaries. But as the chaotic clouds of war grow ever darker, it's clear not all missions can be accomplished behind a computer screen.

As he's forced ever nearer to a showdown with Pacifica's Chief Security Enforcer, the ruthless Hayden Singer, MacIntyre faces a stark realization: if victory is to have a fighting chance, he'll have to put his own life on the line.

THANKS TO...

...family and friends who assisted on this project, especially: Mike Freiling, whose relentless insights encouraged me to pull no punches when dealing with the darker themes of this tale; my eagle-eyed son, Jonathan; and the peerless beta readers of the Laureate group. The meticulous feedback offered by all was crucial in making this tale as focused and exciting as possible.

ALSO BY S.KIRK PIERZCHALA

Echoes Through Distant Glass

Eclipse Rising

Solitude Of Light

Made in the USA
Columbia, SC
11 April 2023

029e2fd2-c5de-4ebf-8d0c-bf7bb87162c5R01